Rebecca

By
Tamalyn E Scott

Edited:

Christine Luckett Brown

Cover design:

Daun Daubenmeyer

Acknowledgements

I would like to dedicate this first to, God, who gave me the gift of imagination and vision to write this book.

To my wonderful husband, Luther Randall Whitehead Jr., thank you for putting up with me during this long journey. I know you're an absolute precious gift from God Himself and I love you with all that I am. Thank you for being my Knight!

To the many contributing editors and proof readers, Lisa Midkiff, Faith Oakman, Beth Livingston, Patricia Perry, Sally Chambers and Sandi Thompson, my dear friend, that never stopped believing in me. I adore and love you all for your work and encouragement.

To my fans who patiently waited for Rebecca. I pray you all enjoy her let me know what you think! Your reviews are the reasons I keep writing and help others interested in taking a chance on Rebecca! Thank you each one for your support and love. Enjoy the journey…

Author, Elicia Clegg:

"If you are looking for a way to break up the monotony of everyday life, Gracey is the book for you. This romantic period piece gives you a sense of being Gracey, you will experience her ups and downs, you will feel what her heart feels, and you will find that Ms. Scott is a fabulous author who puts her heart and soul into her writing. Though I normally steer clear of so-called romance novels...this book delivers something more, and I eagerly await the arrival of her next book." Author, Elicia Clegg:

Novels by Elicia,
Stygian,
Vexation
Castigate My Sins
Running With Chaos
Soul Distortion

Special Editor's note:
A special message for Tamalyn's readers!

Be SURE to take your sneak peak of Tamalyn's next book, Bethany, at the end of this book!

Table of Contents

~ Prologue ~

After the Great War, a new government was formed and a new way of life was born. However, rumors of the old ways were still whispered through the years and passed down from generation to generation. The schools taught vaguely about the past and The Great War, only to say that the entire world was almost annihilated by man's hand and the obsessive struggle for power.

Over several hundred years, people congregated and started over from various places. A new military was created to preserve the peace and to prevent another atrocity from ever happening again.

There were also rumors whispered of knights in our lands who protected the secrets of the past, as in the ancient Templar Knights, from hundreds of years ago, but no one has ever confirmed that they exist and they remain a legend.

Robert and I moved toward the North West Territory in the year of our Lord, 2564, to start a new life, after we were married. However, the area was sparse of people and the wildlife was very abundant and dangerous. The general population sought to reside in the more populated areas, as in major cities, but not Robert. Robert wanted his own land and wanted to raise his own food. There he promised children and a wonderful life without the influence of the city in our future children's lives.

God has his own plan, no matter what 'we' try to achieve. Robert always said that 'we' get in God's way, and if 'we' stayed out of God's way our lives would be much simpler. He believed that God had reasons for everything and, in time, we would know the answers to why things happen. Most people believe that everything happens in God's own time, not ours. Little did I know how those words Robert spoke would affect my life in ways I have never dreamed...

~ Rebecca ~

My eyes watered as the wind blew and bit at my face. Numb...I feel so numb...but I promised Robert I would go and I had so far to go, so far. I took the reins and clicked my tongue. Don't look back! My thoughts screamed as my heart ached deeply with an unforgiving pain. I was never going to see this place again, and in my heart, I knew I would never return, never.

I let out a ragged breath, giving in to tears I could no longer hold back. This was it, I thought, feeling my heart breaking all over again. I was leaving everything Robert ever dreamed about. My thoughts cried out knowing how he loved this place and how he had worked so hard to make this our home.

Closing my eyes, I was in disbelief knowing that the house was falling down and the roof was damaged beyond repair after the storm. Taking a deep breath for composure and strength, I pulled my hood around my face and snapped the reins. Fella dug into the hard dirt and yanked the wagon forward with a heavy labored jerk. My heart sank as I felt the wagon moving away from what Robert and I called home.

I tried to clear my thoughts, needing to think clearly now more than ever. I looked down in the seat next to me,

"Well, Jack, we have a long way to go." I patted my three year old Australian Shepherd as I wiped my cheeks, trying to calm myself down. Jack has been my best friend and faithful companion ever since Robert passed, never leaving my side. I also had Fella, my horse, and I was grateful to have their company.

The wagon passed the gate of the graveyard and without realizing, I pulled Fella to a stop. I just couldn't help myself... needing one last goodbye. I slid off the wagon seat and walked toward the small rickety fence to the lone marker. My fingers touched the crude cold wooden cross as tears fell. One last goodbye and I would go...

"Well, Robert, I'm leaving as I promised." The pain of leaving him behind out in the middle of nowhere alone was almost too much.

"Oh, Robert! Why did you have to die?" I looked at his name, feeling as if I touched his name on the cross, it would be as if I was touching him in a way. I traced his name with my fingers...

Loving Husband Robert James Grayson
6-15-2528   to   4-18-2563

"How am I going to do this?" Tears flowed as fear swept over me. I numbly laid my forehead against the cold cross as I wept.

"Why did you insist we move out in the middle of nowhere? If only there was a town nearby, I could have gotten you a doctor to save you!"

I blamed myself for allowing him to talk me into moving to the west. The weather was so unpredictable and, even now, snow was coming, and soon. Feeling a bitter chill in the air, I knew we had to leave now or we, too, would surely perish. I had nothing to stay here for, now that Robert was gone. All I had was Jack, Fella, and a wagon with everything I could salvage from the house and that didn't amount to much.

I pressed my lips against his name, promising I would always love him and would always keep him in my heart, always.

As I stood, a gust of wind blew the dust all around me, reminding me it was time and I had to leave. I looked down at the cross, wiped the tears from my eyes and went to the wagon.

"One last check on the wagon and the reins and we'll go, Jack." I glanced at Jack and felt that somehow, he too, was sad this day.

I made sure everything was securely tied down and pulled myself up, settling on the cold hard seat. With a click of my tongue and another labored jerk, the wagon lunged forward.

Feeling the cold wind bite, I nuzzled down into the collar of my coat as my mind uncontrollably flashed back to the night of the storm. I could see Robert running from the barn yelling, but I could not hear him.

The wind blew and howled like I've never seen or heard before. Rain was coming down in sheets, blinding me from all directions. I couldn't hear Robert...

"No! I can't think about this now! I need to keep focused!" I cried out, as I shook the thoughts from my head and closed my eyes tightly. Uncontrollably, I flashed back again. I saw myself standing at the back door watching in frozen horror as I heard a deafening crack and saw a bolt of lightning struck the huge oak tree...it started to fall...I screamed, trying to warn Robert but he could not hear me...and the tree fell...

Fighting the wind and rain, slipping through the mud, I ran to him, finding him so still! The oak tree was not on top of him and I hoped he was just unconscious. I took his head in my hands and called to him.

"Robert, wake up...please wake up!" He was so still! I gently laid his head back down and saw my hands covered in blood! Along with the wind, the mud and rain soaking us to the bone, I knew I had to do something! I struggled to get him into the house, dragging his heavy body across the yard. In the light I saw the deep gash on his forehead, and by all the blood on the floor, I knew there was another wound on the back of his head. Tears streamed down my cheeks, remembering his words

"I love you...Go to your mothers....I'm...sorry." His voice whispered weakly as he fought to keep his eyes open. I tried to help him, but I was powerless. A strange darkness slowly shrouded his eyes, as instant fear engulfed me. It was then I knew in my heart, he was dying. Slowly, he opened his eyes again, whispering in a weak voice,

"I'm not...going...to make it." He grabbed his chest.

"Robert, no...don't say..." I tried to tell him, but he stopped me.

"Rebecca! Listen to me..." His hand clutched my blood soaked dress as his eyes widened in a way that frightened me like nothing before! His hand let loose of my dress, flopping down on his stomach.

"Just...listen..." He took a deep, ragged breath and winced, closing his eyes tightly in pain.

"Rebecca....you can't stay... money...under the stone...by the well... dig....a box.....take it...go. I love...you...so...mu..." His eyes widened and again, he grabbed his chest harder and gasped out. His eyes never left mine and then...the life in them, became empty! He was gone! My world was gone!

Deep shock enveloped me as I found myself outside screaming. I had not remembered even going outside, but the sound of thunder finally brought me to my senses. I cried out, "Ohhh, why...God...why?" I cursed the storm and myself, feeling so empty and lost. All I could do was cry.

I don't recall how long I sat in the rain, but I remembered trying to think. I had to think! What was I going to do? The box! By the well! Robert said to dig!

I stood up shivering, drenched and so cold. Suddenly, the wind had stopped and so had the rain. An eerie silence surrounded me as I looked at the huge ominous haunting tree, now lying by the well and on the house. I looked down and saw the rock. Falling to my knees, I heard Robert say, 'dig'. I plunged my frozen fingers into the cold wet mud digging, as small stones cut into my fingers like razors.

"It has to be here! Robert said it would be here!" My fingers bled and stung as I frantically plunged into the mud, finally hitting something hard. The box! It was there as Robert promised!

I dug the mud away from around the box and finally pulled it out. I held it to my chest and ran back into the house. My frozen hands were bleeding and shaking as I tried to open the box with every ounce of strength I had left. It finally opened! I saw a jar and carefully opened it seeing what looked like a note and money inside. I had taken the note out and unfolded it.

Dearest Rebecca,

If you are reading this something went terribly wrong and I am no longer with you. God only knows how I wish you were not reading this now. I know I promised to take care of you and love you for the rest of my life, but there has been some unforeseen accident and I'm sorry with all my heart.

Rebecca, you must listen to me carefully now. I know you want none of this, but you must do as I ask. I want you to take a deep breath and read this slowly. God will give you the strength.

In this jar is money I was saving to build a bedroom for our first child, but now it's to be used for a very important purpose...your survival.

God has a reason for everything he does but you must realize that I never intended to put you through what you are going through now. Please try to understand this and do not mourn for me. You are still very young and have so much to offer. You need to be strong now more than ever and my last request is...that you go on living, Rebecca.

I pray you will find someone who will love you and give you everything I could not. I wanted to be the one to make you happy and give you children but this was not in God's plan and the work God had for me here on this Earth is now done.

Rebecca, honor me with your strength and courage by doing as I ask. There is enough to last for a while if you are careful.

Rebecca, lastly, please don't be angry with me...After all, I did keep my promise. I did love you for the rest of my life...

Forever, Robert

I remembered holding the letter to my heart and wept. Robert was the love of my life! Yes, I would go on living but this pain was something I would not bear again. I wiped my tears and took a deep breath, recalling that somehow, I had taken care of Robert, burying him and making a cross. I don't remember much of that and it's mostly a blur, which is a blessing, but I do remember the cross and using Robert's knife to carve his name. I thought sometimes God has a way of protecting you by not allowing you to recall every detail, and for that I was very grateful.

Days turned into weeks as I sat numbly, trying to get my thoughts straight. I felt so lost and cried so much that I couldn't cry anymore. I would often find myself at Robert's grave talking to him as if he was still here. Perhaps I was trying to find answers, perhaps secretly hoping to hear from Robert.

Mr. Lang, from the nearest town, rode in as he had from time to time on his way back to his home, but I couldn't remember the last time he was here. How long had it been since Robert passed? What day was it? Numbly, I glanced toward Mr. Lang as I stood next to Robert's grave. He looked at the house then back. I stared at Robert's grave, feeling Mr. Lang, now at my side. He said nothing as he turned me toward him. Silently, he held me in his arms, allowing me to cry. He offered to take me back with him to his home, but I refused. Of course he asked how Robert passed away and I told him all I could remember and what Robert wanted me to do. I told him my plan to do as Robert requested and that Robert had provided me the means to support myself for a while.

Mr. Lang assessed the damage that the storm had caused, insisting on patching the roof with old boards to prevent the weather getting in while I gathered what I was taking. I recalled Mr. Lang saying it would take at least a week to get to mothers, and that was if the weather was good. Even though I tried to refuse, Mr. Lang left me some supplies to survive on. I offered to pay him but he flatly refused.

Much of the days and weeks after Robert died were like a long dream. No matter how much time had passed, it was as if time stood still. Then one day, like waking up from a long dream, I found myself loading the wagon.

I looked down at Jack with his head on my lap and tried to keep focused on the road and my surroundings, but my thoughts were elsewhere. I really didn't pay much attention to how far or how long we traveled though I knew the farther east and south we went the warmer it got. That…was a good thing.

The air started to feel cooler and the sun was setting, making me realize it was time to stop for the night. Fella was tired and needed a well-deserved rest. I unhitched him from the wagon and led him to a branch to enjoy a long, cool drink of water and then tied him to the wagon. Jack and I curled up on the seat to rest. I thought about Robert and silently wept, allowing some of my hurt to go.

How am I going to live without you, Robert!? How? I hugged Jack as he seemingly knew I needed him. One thing I knew for sure was the farther I got away from home the clearer my thoughts became. Seeing mother, Cole and Mike would help so much. I closed my eyes and said a prayer for strength.

The chirping of a bird woke me up with the rising of the sun. Stiffly, I sat up rubbing the sandy feeling from my eyes, remembering that I was headed for mothers and no longer home. Jack and I went to the creek to freshen up and then I hitched Fella back to the wagon. We were back on our journey…

"Want some jerky, boy?" Jack instantly barked, and I laughed for the first time in so long. It almost seemed to be a new experience in itself! Come to think of it, I don't remember the last time I laughed.

"I know you don't want this old cellar pear!" Jack sniffed it and of course, was not interested. I knew Jack was hungry. I really couldn't recall the last time I had been hungry. Mother, Cole and Mike are going to have a fit seeing how my dresses hang on me like a sack!

"Well Jack, it doesn't matter what I look like, mother will be relieved to see me."

If anyone will understand about loss, mother will. She will pamper the daylights out of us. I haven't seen her in almost three years, I thought, as I rubbed Jack's furry neck. Mother was exactly what I needed!

"We should reach Smith Grove tomorrow night or early the next morning, if we are lucky, Jack." Jack tilted his head listening, trying to understand like a child and I laughed, thanking God for him.

Traveling so far and being alone was dangerous for anyone, especially a woman. However, I did have Robert's gun. I have only shot it a few times, but I knew enough to fire and reload it. The reality of it was, the fact that I knew I couldn't hit the broad side of a barn! The only hope I had was...I would never need to use it!

"I know, Robert, I have to be brave!" I sighed.

I decided we were not going to stop until we got to Smith Grove

"The sun is setting faster today." The moon was already out with a few stars appearing in the dusky sky. This had been another long day...

~ Chapter 2 ~

We arrived in Smith Grove just as the sky darkened, staying the night in a small hotel. I wanted Jack to stay with me in the hotel, but no pets were allowed. It was the only hotel in town, so Jack and Fella stayed in the town stable down the street. The next morning I bought a few things at the general store for the rest of our journey.

In the late afternoon the sound of a horse thundered from the distance and to think, all this time on the road without ever seeing a soul! 'Feeling safe' had instantly vanished!

I quickly looked in all directions but could see no one! I scrambled for Robert's gun, placing it on my lap in hopes to ward off anyone with bad intentions. The gun was so heavy and I prayed I wasn't going to have to pick it up and try to aim it! I knew I couldn't hold it long enough to hit anything or anyone!

"Where is the rider?" I looked at Jack, tightening my grip on the gun. Jack's ears stood at attention, looking behind us. The horse was getting closer and now, to make matters worse, I could tell there was more than one horse! I swallowed hard and prayed they would go another direction.

My heart pounded harder as the sound of hoofs hit the ground like thunder, becoming louder and louder! I held my breath as I turned to see two enormous men in uniforms, approaching quickly. I stiffened with a deep breath and put my hand on the gun, trying not to appear afraid.

The riders slowed their horses as they came along the side of us. I took another deep breath, mustering up courage. If the truth were known, I was terrified! Jack was barking, placing himself between me and the riders.

"Good evening, Miss." Their voices were deep and flat. They tipped their black hats at me.

"Good evening." I nodded back, trying to remain calm. My heart was in my throat and my knuckles turned white from tightly gripping the gun.

"Looks like you've been traveling a long way." One of them said.

"And, you the same." I glanced at them both with a nod.

The men were very dusty, spattered with mud and had a few days growth on their faces. Their uniforms were unusual, but somehow familiar.

"I am Nicholas Baptiest, and this is, William Andrews. May I ask you your name, Miss?" The man with the black hair closest to me forced a smile.

"It's a pleasure to meet you both. My name is Rebecca Grayson." I forced a smile back at him.

The one named Mr. Baptiest looked rather ominous with green eyes that seemed to glow under the shadow of his brim.

"Might I inquire where you are heading?" Mr. Andrews leaned forwards with a genuine smile. His blue-green eyes seemed to glow as well, but he looked friendlier and warmer than the other.

"I'm going to Oak Grove, to see my mother." I stiffened, suddenly aware that I was alone… very alone! I squeezed my hand on the gun.

"I'm surprised that your husband would allow you to ride alone." I spied Mr. Baptiest looking at my wedding band…

"My husband trusts me and …and I am a dead shot with the gun." My throat was as dry as dust and I swallowed hard.

"I see…then, are you moving to Oak Grove?" Mr. Baptiest looked in the back of my wagon.

"Yes…yes, I am." Why did I feel this was more like an inquisition? Why didn't they just go on their way?

"Is your husband waiting for you there or is he to follow?" Mr. Andrews looked at me again with a bright smile and then looked in the wagon. Mr. Baptiest looked at Mr. Andrews as if they were talking without words.

"Not to worry about me. I assure you. I have everything under control and do not wish to keep you. It appears that you two were in a hurry yourselves." I was hoping they would leave me be! I was in no mood for the questions!

"I'm sure you do. No woman would travel by herself if she didn't know how to use a gun." Mr. Baptiest looked down, slightly narrowing his eyes. I instantly licked my parched lips.

"We're headed to Lawrenceburg and would be happy to escort you to Oak Grove...." Mr. Andrews offered as Mr. Baptiest glanced at Mr. Andrews again.

"I wouldn't want to slow you down and besides, I'm taking my time." Maybe that will give them a hint.

"We are going the same way and I would think that your husband would appreciate the escort." Mr. Baptiest frowned a bit and Mr. Andrews still had a kind smile on his face. However, I was beginning to feel very frustrated.

"Are you two in the service of some kind?" I tried to change the subject.

"One might say that." Mr. Baptiest looked blankly ahead, acting as if I had asked a classified question.

"You've heard of the Union Corps?" Mr. Andrews smiled, leaning forward with one hand on top of the other pressing on the horn of his saddle.

"Yes... my husband was..." Instantly realizing I said the word 'was'.

"I mean, my husband is a friend of a Corpsman named Douglas Brent. Perhaps you have heard of him?" I was hoping they did not catch my almost mistake.

"Yes, we know him well." Mr. Baptiest looked ahead.

"We were in the Corps with him long ago." I smiled nodding.

"Douglas is a fine man." Mr. Baptiest flatly stated.

"Yes, he is...I mean, I've never met him, but Robert talked about him often and I felt as if I did." I was getting uncomfortable feeling Mr. Baptiest staring. Oh! Why don't they just be on their way? I've done nothing wrong!

"What does your husband do?" Mr. Andrews sat forwards in his saddle still smiling warmly.

"He did farming and blacksmith work, after his tour." I sighed hoping they wouldn't ask me anymore.

"Well, then, he should do well in Oak Grove. It's a large place, a busy stopover for folks going to Wellington or Lawrenceburg." Baptiest slightly smirked.

"I'm sure it is but, like I said before, I don't want to keep you. I will be just fine. I'll be in Oak Grove in a few hours and I thank you for your concern." I hoped they would leave me alone.

"Very well, it was a pleasure to meet you, Mrs. Grayson." Mr. Baptiest tipped his hat.

10

"Yes, this road is a long one and not too friendly at times. Keep your eyes open." Mr. Andrews tipped his hat as well. They kicked their horses and rode off with their hair blowing and whipping behind them, vanishing in a cloud of dust.

I let out a deep sigh of relief thinking I handled that well, but realized that this was the first time...I had had to lie about Robert. Jack laid down on the seat next to me letting out a big breath of air.

"Some watchdog you are!" I shook my head at Jack.

Well, he did bark a few times, but after I started to talk to them he had not made another sound or even growl. They seemed like nice enough fellows, but that Baptiest seemed a bit suspicious about me. Andrews, on the other hand, was very nice and more personable.

"What did Mr. Baptiest think I was doing? Did he not believe me? Oh well," I sighed out, "who cares what either of them thought. I was doing nothing wrong and was on my way to my mother's."

I cleared my head and thought about my current situation. I needed to keep my mind and thoughts clear and focused. This was truly a dangerous road and being reminded of that...didn't help either!

~ Chapter 3 ~

It was about half three in the morning when we arrived in Oak Grove. I was amazed at how the town had grown in the past few years, appearing to have doubled in size! A new hotel jutted out at me as I pulled in front of it. I'm home! HOME!

I decided I would stay the night at the hotel and go to mothers tomorrow after I had a long hot bath and a good night's sleep. I knew Jack and Fella could use a good rest too!

The hotel appeared to be very modern and so large for a small town, but then again it had been almost ten years since I left. Even so, I was amazed that it had grown this much! Well, however big this town had gotten, it had to wait until tomorrow! I was too tired to think any more and walked toward the door. A man opened the door, bowing to me as I entered. He directed me to the stiffly standing man at the front counter. His graying appearance added to his uppity one, I thought.

"Good morning, may I help you?" I did not recognize him.

"Yes, I need a room for a couple of days, a stable for my horse and wagon, and I also have a dog." The man's eyes widened and his eyebrows rose up in a snooty way when I said 'dog'.

"The stable is across the street and as for your dog...we don't allow pets in this hotel." He put his nose in the air and pursed his lips slightly.

"Then I have no choice but to go down to the old hotel." I confidently turned to walk out, knowing he would stop me.

"Ma'am, if you are sure you will walk your dog before retiring and first thing in the morning, I will allow him to stay in the room with you. But make no mistake, you will be held completely responsible." He tilted his chin down, peering over his glasses with a look of warning.

"Well, of course..." I smiled slightly.

"I'll have the bellhop get your things and take care of the horse and wagon for you, Ms..." He smirked at me.

"Grayson...Rebecca Grayson." He nodded and wrote my name down in the ledger. Then he tapped on the bell twice. Two men appeared out of nowhere.

The man behind the counter instructed one of them to see to Fella and the wagon. The other man picked up my bags and led me to the stairs.

The hotel was a beautiful place adorned in deep reds and gold on the walls. Lanterns and crystal globes projected beautiful beams of light that softly lit the room with a warm glow.

"Here you are, Ma'am." He opened the door, putting my bags down and lighting the lanterns. He said if I needed anything to not hesitate to ask and softly closed the door behind him.

Jack sat by my feet as I looked about the huge room.

"Well, boy, time for me to take a hot bath!" I patted his head and grabbed my small bag as Jack found a soft rug by the fireplace. As he lay down he let out a huge breath. I completely understood how he felt and I was that tired, too!

The white washroom had running water in the tub, just like in Port Knoll where Robert and I went on our honeymoon. I started the water and wondered if this aching would ever stop. Even though it had been months since Robert died, memories such as these made it feel as if it was only yesterday. At least it seemed as if the pain of his death had lessened and I did have more control over my emotions. Still, it comes in waves and some days are better than others. I remember Robert saying 'time heals all wounds'. There's only one thing for certain, because of Father's passing, mother will know exactly what to say to me to help with Robert's death.

I took out my nightgown and, glancing at the rest of the room, I saw the bed was huge, made of dark rich wood with four towering posters and a huge backboard. Not like Robert's and my old iron bed. I hoped to sleep well tonight and looked over at Jack sleeping already.

"What a dog!" I laughed and went into the bathroom to shut the water off and undressed. The room was filled with heavenly steam and felt so welcoming and warm as I gratefully slid into the hot water, allowing my tired muscles to soak up the heat. It felt so good not to be jostled around.

As I relaxed I thought about Mr. Baptiest and Mr. Andrews. Nicholas Baptiest was so suspicious with the way he looked at me, asking questions, but maybe that was his nature. It does not matter, besides I'll never see them again. Now, mother will be a different story. When Robert and I decided to go west, she wasn't happy. She had wanted me to run her coffee and tea shop with intentions of one day taking it over. Now that I'm back, she probably will suggest me working there. It will be hard to see mother and tell her all that has happened and even more so, I'm going to have to tell his family as well and can only hope that they received my letter. I was not looking forward to tomorrow afternoon.

I finished my bath, dried off and dressed for bed. I sat at the vanity brushing out my hair, which, always seemed to take so long to do. I finally had it braided and then finally crawled between the welcoming cool sheets. I prayed that the Lord would give me strength to get me through the next few days with all the people I must face and I know it will be draining and very hard...very hard...

The sun peeked through the window waking me. I blinked my eyes only to see Jack at my feet waiting for me.

"Good morning, Jack!" I said to him as I sat up on the edge of the bed, stretching.

"I wonder what time it was." I held my watch in my hand, smiling at the last gift Robert had given me. It was a beautiful gold pocket-like watch on a long gold chain and engraved on the inside of the lid read, 'In God's time'.

Robert was the son of the preacher in Oak Grove. His father passed on about five years ago, but his mother has been ill for a long time. Just a few months ago, I received a letter from mother saying that she was doing better. I suspect that her illness was because of the loss of her husband. I could understand that all too well, feeling sick sometimes as well. A broken heart from the loss of your spouse is enough to make anyone ill. The watch said half seven.

"It's time to get on with this long day, Jack." I sighed, not looking forward to most of it.

I freshened up and dressed in a nice dress, and even though it was brown with dark brown trim, it was acceptable. These days, I've seen women wear even blue.

I fixed my hair and went down to the lobby with Jack. I'll take Jack and Fella to mother's house today knowing they could stay there. The man at the desk nodded at us as we walked out the door. I tilted my chin higher and nodded back.

The sun was so bright and warm this morning. I took in the fresh air with a deep breath. Jack suddenly ran out in the street almost getting hit! I called for him to come back and, thank goodness, he did without injury.

"Good boy, Jack! You can't run like that here. We're not home anymore!" Poor thing, he was not used to this either! I cautiously walked him across the street keeping him close to me as we headed for the stables.

"Morning, Ma'am. May I help you?" An old man appeared out of the office.

"I arrived late last night, or should I say this morning, and have the wagon and horse." I smiled at the old man.

"Yes, your horse was tired and hungry. I took care of him, but your wagon needs a new wheel." He wiped his hands on a towel.

"Thank you very…a wheel?"

"Yes Ma'am." He nodded with one eye squinted.

"Can you do the work? If so, can you do it with all that on the wagon or do I need to unload it first?"

"You might think about unloading it first…it's pretty heavy. Do you have a place to unload it?" He smirked slightly.

"Yes, at my mother's. Do you think it will go another couple of miles to unload it and then back?"

"I'm sure it will." He smiled looking at Jack.

"Alright, after I get something to eat, I will return." He reminded me of my own father and I warmly smiled at him.

"May I ask who your mother is?"

"Martha Glenn." I smiled proud knowing most everyone knew who she was.

"I know Mrs. Glenn pretty well, but I don't recall you, my dear." He took his hat off, tilted and scratched his balding head, squinting his left eye.

"I moved from here about two, almost three years ago, I married Robert Grayson." I nodded.

"Oh yes, you're Rebecca! Well, my! You've sure grown up! How's that husband of yours doing?" He laughed shaking his head in disbelief.

"He…well, Robert…died." I looked to the ground, afraid I would start to cry. This was a hard day already and I could feel it wasn't going to be getting any easier.

"Oh…I'm sorry, dear, when did he pass on?" He took my hand.

"Months ago, a storm came through this past early spring and lightning hit a tree and it fell. He hit his head on the well house." Tears rolled down my cheeks, knowing this wouldn't be the last time I would cry today.

"I'm so sorry…Honey, you've returned to tell his mother?" He had such a sad look on his face.

"Yes, I promised Robert I'd come home." I wiped my tears from my cheeks as the old man patted my hand.

"In God's time, all will be known. There's a reason for everything." He sweetly smiled.

"That's what Robert used to say. What's your name?" I liked this man.

"George Thomas." He smiled.

"Well, I thank you, Mr. Thomas. Would you mind if Jack stays here with you for a little bit?"

"Sure, I'll feed him for you. I'll give him some of Bill's food." He smiled and patted Jack on the head.

"Bill?" I looked at him wondering who Bill was and how Bill would feel about losing his breakfast to my dog.

"Bill's my dog. Eats and sleeps, that's all, he's as old as Moses." He laughed.

"Well, thank you, Mr. Thomas. I'm sure Jack will appreciate it." Bill the dog? What an odd name for a dog!

"It won't be any trouble. Bill won't suspect a thing." He laughed looking over at a soundly sleeping old hound.

"I'll not be long, I promise. Jack...you stay." I patted Jack on his head as he sat down, then smiled at Mr. Thomas and started out the stable doors.

"Take your time, no hurry!" He called after me.

There were so many people running up and down the street now. I was wondering where they all came from! Where are they all going?

There was a break in the stream of people on the road and I took my chance to cross but a carriage flew by that came out of nowhere, barely missing me.

Dust flew, blinding me and I lost my footing! I felt a hand envelope my arm, steadying me as I stepped away from the road.

"Are you alright?" I heard a very deep man's voice and looked up but couldn't see for the sun was in my eyes.

"Yes... thank you... heavens! That was close! This town wasn't so busy a few years ago!" I brushed my skirt off, feeling a bit embarrassed.

"Oak Grove has grown due to the train business coming to town." His hand still held my arm.

I raised my hand to shade my eyes. Oh, my… the man was huge and dressed in a fine black suit.

"I tried to hurry but I gather everyone else does as well! Thank you again for your help." I smiled at him.

"It was my pleasure." He slightly bowed.

Smiling, I turned to walk into the hotel and bumped right in to him again!

"Oh, heavens! I'm so sorry!" I blushed, feeling this was now an awkward situation!

"No, pardon me!" His eyes were wide open and then we both laughed out.

"After you, Ma'am…" He held the door open for me.

"Why, thank you." Still laughing, I walked into the hotel.

The dining room was to the left and I found myself right next to him again and we both laughed. His eyes caught me off guard. They were so blue, like blue crystals, and seemed to sparkle when he smiled! I felt my cheeks warm with the situation at hand.

"Really, we must stop meeting like this." I laughed.

"I'm terribly sorry, again." He looked embarrassed as he too laughed softly.

"It was my fault, as well." I couldn't help but laugh also.

"Are you meeting anyone for breakfast?" He softly smiled, still laughing.

"No, I was just going to get a cup of coffee." I walked towards the door to the dining room.

"Would you like to share a table with me, Miss…?" He smiled warmly as he tilted his head a bit.

"Mrs. Rebecca Grayson, and yes that would be nice, and you are?" I smiled, seeing no harm in sharing a table over coffee.

"Gabe McCray." He paused and looked down at my hand with my wedding band and with a slight frown he looked back at me.

"I see you're married. Where is your husband?" He offered his arm to me.

"He recently passed on." My smile and laughter faded and I saw him look down at me sadly.

"I'm sorry, what you must be going through!" We walked into the dining room and saw the host was waiting.

"Good morning, Lord McCray, your table is ready." The man smiled at him with a strange look of surprise on his face.

"Lord?" I looked at him shocked.

"Yes, but I don't really care for it when people address me as such. Please, will you call me Gabe?" He smiled so sweetly that no one could ever refuse his request.

"Yes, and please call me Rebecca." The host led us to a nice table in the back of the room.

It seemed very private, almost too private, I thought. Coffee and rolls were already on the table and a waiter standing ready, to boot!

"Good morning Sir, would the Lady like something special this morning?"

Lady? My, it's been a long time since anyone has called me that!

"Just coffee, thank you..." I smiled at the waiter as Gabe held my chair for me.

"Thank you, Gabe." I felt rather strange at the way this was going. Almost as if I was too comfortable with this Lord McCray already.

"Your paper, Sir..." The waiter laid the paper down in front of Gabe on the table, then filled our coffee cups.

"The usual this morning, Sir?"

"Rebecca, wouldn't you like something more than just a roll?" He smiled at me and I wondered if he was having the same thoughts I was having?

"No, I have never eaten a big breakfast." He's also a lord. I've never met a lord before and yet this one didn't act the way that I always pictured a lord would act.

"Very well, but you know you should eat breakfast, it's the best meal of the day." He winked at me and then nodded at the waiter.

"Yes, Stan, the usual." He nodded and Stan bowed, then hurried off. I felt Gabe's eyes on me and had to think of something to say.

"So tell me, how does one become a lord? And what are you a lord of?" I poured cream in my coffee and stirred it. Good heavens! Is that all I could think to ask! He must think me simple!

"By inheritance and taking over Father's business. My brother, Seth, is in the Union Corps and Council." He answered without batting an eye while he sipped his coffee.

"How interesting." I was still taken with the fact that he was a lord.

"How was your trip here?" Gabe looked over his cup at me.

"It was nice and quiet most of the time. However, I did come across two men in Corps uniforms. I believe they were on their way to Lawrenceburg. A Mr. Baptist and Mr. Andrews, I believe." I smiled over my cup, looking at one of the most handsome men I think I have ever seen in my life.

"Ah, I know those two, good men and loyal to the Union." He sipped his coffee, still staring at me as Baptiest had. Was he suspicious too?

"Yes, they were quite concerned about me traveling alone." I shook my head.

"That's their nature... to be of assistance when needed." He smiled at me, setting his coffee cup down, resting his elbows on the table and clasping his hands together in front of his coffee cup.

"They offered to escort me but Mr. Baptiest made me feel uneasy and didn't appear as friendly as Mr. Andrews." I explained as he still stared at me with a grin on his face.

"Yes, Nicholas is more suspicious than William. So, Rebecca, tell me, why are you here?" He smiled softly, appearing to be genuinely interested.

"As you know, I am here to see my mother and my husband's mother. I had not returned home since my husband's death and I promised him I would come here if something... went wrong. So here I am." I looked into my cup, fighting to stay composed. The last thing I wanted to do was fall apart in front of anyone.

"What you're saying is... you've moved back?" A pleased smile crept across his full lips.

"Yes, though I don't know what I'll do yet. There are a lot of things to take care of." I tried to smile, but it would have been much easier to cry, and I willed myself not to.

"Robert was a blessed man to have a wife who loved him so." He looked so sympathetically at me. Gabe took my hand and rubbed his thumb over the back of it. I was shocked at his touch, not having any other man so attentive with me except Robert. I wasn't sure how to act. Perhaps this was his nature to be attentive and as helpful as the Corpsmen I had met on the road.

"It was hard at first, but with time the hurt stops hurting so badly." I softly smiled, trying to convince myself as well.

"If I may be of any assistance to you I'd be more than happy to help in any way. I have many interests here." As he released my hand and sat back his broad shoulders hid the back of the chair, goodness!

"Thank you, but for now I have things to attend to first." I sipped my coffee, looking through my lashes at him.

"Well, Rebecca, I have a feeling you're a fighter. I have no doubt that whatever you do, you will be successful." He smiled and winked.

"Well... I hope you're right!" I laughed, not knowing what I was going to do or not going to do.

"Do you have children?" He took a deep breath.

"No, I have no children, unless you count Jack and Fella." I smiled, trying not to be trapped in his blue eyes.

"Jack and Fella are...?" He sipped his coffee, listening intently.

"My dog and horse." I laughed out, seeing his face wash over with relief, and then Gabe laughed in a deep tone.

"Where do you live, Lord McCray?" His eyes lifted open at my question as if he was shocked for some reason.

"Here and there, mostly here. I have many homes, however, I like it here the best. I have a house outside the town about ten clicks north. It isn't huge or extravagant like most people would think, but it's my favorite. My other homes are huge, drafty old places." He stared at me as if he was trying to read my mind.

"Well, that is one of those things I need to do. I don't want to live with my mother too long. She'll have me working at the Tea Shop if I stay in her house too long." I laughed, knowing I was absolutely right about that!

"Your mother wouldn't be Mrs. Martha?" He sat back holding his breath with his eyes wide open. I laughed as shock fell over his face. If you knew Martha Glenn, you knew everyone or would soon enough!

"Then... that makes you... little... little Rebecca?" He... he knew me too? But, I don't recall him at all!

"Have we met before?" I looked at him wide-eyed.

"Not exactly, but I went to church when I was in town to hear the most beautiful singer I had ever heard in my life. Then one day, she was simply gone. I only found out that you were the Tea Shop owner's daughter, and your name was Rebecca Glenn and that you had just married." He paused.

"I always sat in the back." He put his hand over his mouth and stared deeper, shaking his head in what appeared to be disbelief.

"I don't recall ever seeing you or meeting you." I was just as stunned! I knew I would have remembered such a man as Gabe McCray. To think he wanted to know my name back then!

"We never did meet. I always left the church after the singing and preaching to make it in time for meetings." He sat back in his chair with his hand over his mouth, still obviously amazed

"Do you still sing by chance?" He smiled behind his hand.

"No, not any more... well, just to Jack and Fella." I laughed out. His eyes twinkled and stared at me in a way that made me blush.

"Well, those two are the luckiest creatures I know." He laughed.

"I'm not too sure about that!" I laughed, feeling my cheeks warm with his compliment.

"I am! For now... I'm ridiculously jealous of a dog and a horse." He roared a thunderous laugh causing me to laugh out as well. Good heavens! His laughter filled the room!

He stared deeper, listening more intently than he had before as I drank another cup of coffee, telling him about my home and the storm. I don't know if he was really listening or not, but when I told him that I had to leave he stood with a frown.

"Must you leave already? I was enjoying your company immensely." He held my chair as I reached for my handbag.

"No, no...allow me." He laid his hand on top of mine as I tried to open it.

"Thank you, Gabe, I too enjoyed your company, as well." I smiled at his warm face.

"Perhaps we shall have the chance to do this again?" Hope filled his eyes.

"Perhaps..." I smiled at him as he bowed over my hand.

"Allow me to at least escort you to your wagon, if you don't mind." He smiled.

"No, that's alright. You stay and enjoy the rest of your breakfast. I'm sure we'll meet again." I smiled, turning quickly to avoid his stares, feeling his eyes on me the entire way out.

What an interesting man that Lord McCray was and, not to mention, he knew who I was! Well, it was a lovely cup of coffee, to say the least. I smiled, laughing to myself, recalling him saying he was jealous of a dog and a horse! Funny that! I hadn't laughed like that in so very long and it felt simply wonderful!

I carefully crossed the bustling street to the stable seeing Mr. Thomas waiting for me with my rig ready.

"Thank you for watching Jack and for taking care of Fella."

"Well, Ms. Grayson, it was my pleasure, Ma'am. I shall see you this afternoon, then?" The kind bald headed man with a trimmed white beard smiled warmly.

"Thank you, Mr. Thomas. I shall return this afternoon. Come, Jack." Jack hopped up on the seat and we were off to mothers.

Entering the busy street, I still could not believe that there were so many people, as we rode through town. I did see a couple of people I knew, but most I didn't know and wondered where they all came from.

Mother's coffee shop was about three blocks down on the corner from the stable and we soon pulled to the back of the shop. I told Jack to stay as I walked in the back door through the kitchen.

"Excuse me, Missy... this isn't the front door, you know! May I help you?" A woman as round as she was tall wiped her hands on a towel, walking towards me in a hurry. I didn't know her either!

"Yes, you can, but shhh... I'm Martha's daughter, Rebecca. I want to surprise her." The woman's face instantly softened as she covered her lips with her fingertips.

"Let me have the next order and tell me where it goes. I want to take it out." The woman's face lit up with pleasure. Her brown eyes twinkled as she wiped the hair out of her eyes with the back of her wrist.

"Oh, heavens child, she'll be so surprised! Here are two coffees and two rolls to the first table on the left. Your mother should still be at the table! Hurry, I'm going to peek out the door so I can watch!" She shuffled me to and through the door.

I held the tray up to conceal my face and took the coffee to the table. I heard them talking to each other about Lord McCray's breakfast date and how beautiful she was with her auburn hair and no bigger than a minute.

"Why, she sounds like my little Becca." The sound of my mother's voice was wonderful to hear, but I saw that news still travels so quickly in this town! It had only been twenty minutes since I left Lord McCray! This town never changed and I doubt it ever will!

"Here you go… two coffees and two rolls." I sat them down on the table and mother didn't look up and neither did my Aunt Marie.

"Would you like anything else?" I smiled, amused with their gossip.

"No, however, table four needs..." They both looked up and their eyes almost flew out of their sockets.

"Rebecca!!!" Mother about knocked over the table as she flew out of her seat. I laughed and hugged her, kissing her cheek. Aunt Marie followed.

"Surprise!" I hugged them both and Aunt Marie instantly was in tears…as usual.

"Oh, Rebecca, dear, sit down… sit down!" She ushered me into the seat next to her.

"I got your letter. I am so sorry, my darling, my heart breaks for you. How are you?"

I took a deep breath and began the story. Our tears fell faster than we could wipe them as I explained everything to them.

"When did you arrive?" She kept her arm around my shoulder and held my hand in hers.

"About half three this morning, I stayed in the new hotel." I wiped the tears with my napkin.

"Oh, honey, stay with me, please…you know… 'til you get things sorted out." She wiped her tears with her napkin.

"I'm staying one more night there. I've already paid for tonight, but I have a wagon, horse and a dog that I would like to take to the house. I need to store some things in the barn too. That is, if you don't mind?" I knew I didn't need to even ask.

"Well, of course, dear, whatever you want. I'll have Mike take you to the house and help you right away. Have you seen your brothers?" She patted my hand, tightening her arm around my shoulder and kissed my cheek.

"No, not yet, I only had coffee at the hotel and came right here. How are they?" I noticed her hair was almost all white now and she had aged a little, but she was still the same mother as always.

"You know your brothers, Mike is here somewhere and Cole is at the mill. You do have to go see them." She smiled, hugging me again. Aunt Marie just nodded, still crying…same old Marie!

"Aunt Marie, how are you?" I laughed.

"FFF…INE…" She cried as I laughed to myself. She'll never change and I hope she never does.

Mike walked through the door carrying a big box. I got up and walked behind him and whispered in his ear.

"I bet I can catch more fish than you, little brother." He stopped dead in his tracks, dropping the box on the floor.

"Becca?!!!" Mike quickly turned around, instantly picking me up, swinging me in circles and hugging the breath out of me as he kissed my cheeks.

Everyone laughed and Mike swung me around again before finally setting me down. My little brother had grown up! He had grown so tall and was about as big as Cole and ever so handsome too.

"Bec, when did you get here?" He hugged me again.

"Mike... I can't... breathe!" I laughed, trying to push away from his grip.

"Oh, sorry, Sis... when?" He smiled and laughed.

"This morning." My hair swung out of its bun.

"I'm sorry about Robert, Sis. It must have been rough on you all alone these past months." Tears filled his big blue eyes as he took my hand in his.

"Yes, but I'm dealing with it one day at a time and it's getting better..." I patted his hand.

"Mike, I want you to take Rebecca to the house and help her with her things and horse, then bring her back." Mother smiled so happily, she was glowing!

"Sure, let me get this box of table cloths put in the storage and we'll go. It's so good to see your homely little face again!" He teased and kissed my cheek. I threw a napkin at him as he picked up the box, hurrying to the kitchen.

"Mother, has Cole gotten married?" I took a deep breath hoping he didn't marry that Annette. Then, I saw mother looking down in her coffee.

"No, Anne moved with her parents. She gave Cole a choice to marry her or she would move. It hurt Cole deeply, but he just couldn't marry her not being sure that she was really the one." She smiled slightly and looked in her coffee cup, poor Cole. Mike interrupted my thoughts of Cole.

"Ready, Sis?" Mike smiled, looking so grown up. I thought, Cole is thirty-two, I'm twenty-six and that makes Mike twenty-four. Time sure does fly! Mike's hair was a lot darker, close to a mahogany. That made his blue eyes pop out more and he was truly handsome.

"Mother, we'll be back as soon as we can." I kissed her and Aunt Marie, who was still crying. Mike put his big arm around my shoulder and we went back through the kitchen and the woman winked at me as we made our way to the wagon.

"Hey, nice rig!" He walked around the wagon as Jack snuck up and licked Mike's face.

"What's your dog's name?" He laughed, patting him on the head.

"Jack, he's three. Robert got him for protection." I laughed.

"He looks like he could do just that!" He took Jack's paw when Jack offered it to him.

"Sure he will! He'll lick you to death!" I laughed, shaking my head.

"Oh... that kind of dog!" He laughed as he helped me in the wagon and hopped in next to me and took the reins, clicking his tongue.

"My horse's name is Fella." I winked at Mike, knowing he would remember.

"Ah...you always wanted a horse named Fella." He laughed again.

"Yes, and then I'd have my own Fella!" We laughed and the feeling came over me as if I had never left. It felt so good to be home! I snuggled my arms around his now large one.

"Mike, has mother been ill?" I looked at his handsome face, still amazed at how he had changed.

"No, but she was sick with worry over you! Had you not shown up soon, I was bound for your house to bring you back home." He looked straight ahead, nodding with certainty.

"Well, now you don't have to, but I bet Cole wanted you to go." I looked up at Mike. His hair tasseled about as the sun showed the red in his hair.

"You're right as usual, Sis. Cole had so many orders for lumber that he would have shut down his lumber yard to go get you himself, but as usual, I offered." He smiled.

"He'll probably try to run my life again now that I'm back and Annette is gone. You know, I didn't much care for her. I always felt she only wanted Cole's money." Which I knew was true.

"Right again, and Cole knew it too, but don't tell mother, she thinks Cole wasn't ready to settle down, she liked Anne." He winked at me.

"Mother tolerated her and anyway, we don't have to worry about her anymore, now do we?" I smiled to myself knowing that Cole needed someone special and could do better.

"I guess you're right there!" Mike smiled.

"Did you notice how big the town has gotten with the railroad here?" He sighed, looking down at me. He was now shaving a full beard. Last time I saw Mike, he could barely grow a mustache, for heaven's sake!

"Yes, I had coffee with a man that owns the train line."

"You did?!! How?" Mike looked down at me with his eyes wide and shocked.

"Why are you looking at me like that?" My brows furrowed.

"Well... because!" He didn't want to answer me.

"Because why?" I sat up looking at him trying to read his face. It always held the truth.

"Well... um... well the whole town was talking about this woman with Lord McCray this morning having breakfast." He took a deep breath.

"Yes... what about it?" I felt my temper starting to brew thinking small towns never change.

"Well, he never is seen with any women... you know... the devout bachelor." Mike nodded as to imply he agreed with Lord McCray's way of life.

"Well, he must see someone in the other places he goes, maybe just not here. We had a wonderful time this morning." I stiffened.

"Don't worry, Sis. No one will dishonor you in any way. I give you my word on that!" He sat up a little taller in the seat. There it was! My protective brother to my rescue!

"No one will! I do not plan on ever getting involved with another man for a long time, if ever! Robert's death almost killed me and I couldn't handle going through that ever again!" I was adamant about that!

"I'm sure you'll feel different about that one day, Sis, but if you meet the right one, you'll fall in love again. I do understand you not wanting anyone right now though." He patted my leg.

"So, little brother... what do you know about Gabe?"

"Gabe is it? You're on a first name basis, are you?" He grinned and teased me like he had just eaten the mouse. I felt my cheeks warm.

"Look here..." I was getting flustered now with him even implying that!

"I'm just teasing you, Sis!" He laughed hard. So he was teasing me!

"Well, you know how I feel... so don't be reading anything into this!" I warned him with a glare. His eyes told me he really wasn't teasing me after all.

"Lord McCray is a very wealthy man and owns everything in town, even the hotel. He has a lot of business with the railroad and is in charge of many other businesses as well." He raised his eyebrows.

"All the single ladies in town fall all over him. He could have his pick, but no one ever sees him with anyone." He shrugged his shoulders.

"Maybe he's secretly married." I flatly stated.

"McCray? No, he's not married, but I heard that he was interested in a lady a long time ago who broke his heart." He shook his head and made me think of Cole.

"Well then, that explains him saying he's a bachelor." I still thought he was an interesting man.

"Well... for someone 'not' interested in anyone... you sure have a lot of questions!" He smiled down at me teasing me like he used to and leaned away as I swatted his arm.

~ Chapter 4 ~

The outskirts of town had even changed. There were more houses than I ever dreamed! We talked about all the new businesses and people coming to Oak Grove due to the train coming to town. We drove the rig into the driveway and I instantly felt I was home. The house was just as beautiful as it's always been and a welcome sight. I noticed right away that it had been recently painted and a new roof had been added. There were flowers all around the house too. The barn had a fresh coat of paint as well.

"The old house looks... beautiful!" I smiled, feeling suddenly so relieved.

"Well, it's changed some. We did a lot of work this past summer and Cole worked every night to add mother's sunroom on to the back of the house. I slaved on it every night too." He pulled next to the barn, leaped down and opened the barn doors.

"We'll put your things in here, they'll be safe." He nodded.

"Let's get this unloaded, I want to see Cole!"

Jack leapt out of the wagon barking and sniffing everything in sight. I knew he would be just fine while we unloaded, which didn't take that long at all!

"It took me twice as long to load it!" I wiped the sweat off my brow.

"That's how it always seems. Let's go freshen up and get something to drink and we'll head to Cole's." He walked me to the door with his hand on my arm. Jack would be alright. He was busy checking everything out and wouldn't go far.

"The house looks like new!" I took a peek at each newly decorated room as I went through to the kitchen.

"Yep, like I said, Cole and I worked our tails off." I looked at the freshly painted walls and the new kitchen table, but still, it felt like home to me.

"Here you go, Sis." smiling as he handed me a tall glass of sweet tea, which I drank almost all of it down not realizing I was that thirsty.

"I can't believe how nice it is, mother must..." Father's coat caught my eye, still hanging by the back door and his hat on top of the hook.

"I know... the coat. Well, mother says she tried to put it away, but felt closer to him if she could see it there." He frowned, turning his glass up, finishing the last of his tea.

"Whatever works!" I knew all too well how she felt. I had slept in Robert's nightshirts for two weeks. I could smell his scent and it somehow made me feel better.

"Whatever works! Done?" I put my glass in the sink and splashed cool water on my face to freshen up a bit and then patted off with a towel.

"Best get a move on!" Mike opened the door and took a deep breath of country air. Jack was waiting by the door having sniffed all he could. I laughed to myself and patted his head.

"Jack, stay." Jack instantly sat.

"You know. I have a feeling that if anyone would approach you in a forceful way, Jack here would protect you." He patted Jack's head too.

"I don't know about that." I shook my head.

"He watched my every move in the barn and when I walked you to the house." Mike raised his brow.

"I guess there was never a need for Jack to protect me, there wasn't anyone to protect me from out in the middle of nowhere." I rolled my eyes as we climbed back into the empty wagon and started back to town.

We road in silence for a short while and I took in the scenery. How I missed this place! I was home!

"So, little brother, tell me of your love life." I smiled poking him in the ribs with my elbow.

"Love life?!" He laughed out.

"You got to be kidding me! I don't have a moment to spare for a love life! After I work at mothers, I go to the mill and help Cole." Something told me that there might be someone. His eyes held regret.

"Not even someone you'd give a second look to?" I smiled, looking at his handsome tan face.

"Of course, there are many available ladies, but I'm telling you, I don't have time." He frowned, sighing.

"Well, maybe I can get you some time off now that I'm here. I will have to do something for work." I smiled, knowing there was someone he was interested in.

"Yes, maybe, but I know Cole will want you in the office and mother will want you in the Tea Shop." He laughed.

Maybe I would do something completely different? There were so many new businesses that there were now more opportunities than ever.

We drove the rest of the way laughing at old times with Mike telling me about the new preacher in town and telling me I had to meet him soon. There was also a saloon in town that all the women hated with their husbands always going to it and getting foxed. I laughed at all his stories. Finally, we pulled in to the lumberyard and went to a big new office.

"Cole built this last year. He said with the train going through, he'd need more office space." He lifted me down.

"It looks really nice!" With the mounds of lumber and all the wagons full of wood, business looked like it was booming!

"Come on, let's go see big brother. He won't even recognize you!" He took my hand and pulled me into the office leading me through a large comfortable waiting room. Chairs lined the walls and there were two tables in the middle of the room for meetings, I supposed. Then Mike took me down a hall with four doors on each side saying they were file rooms and then a lunch room and offices for some of the assistants that worked for him. At the end of the hall was a door, Cole's office I figured. Mike didn't even knock and walked right in.

"Oh, excuse me, Cole. I didn't realize you had someone here." I stood behind Mike trying to surprise him.

"Mike... this is Lord McCray, Lord McCray, this is my brother, Mike." His voice was deep and sounded hard and cold... business like yet. It was music to my ears.

"Yes, I do believe we have met a few times, good to see you again, Mike." Gabe McCray was here?

Gabe's voice was deeper than Cole's. I remembered how it went through me, especially when he laughed.

"Who do you have behind you, Mike?" Cole's voice was a bit harder. He wasn't enjoying this at all.

"Well, I have a surprise for you, brother." Mike laughed.

"Look, Mike... at the moment, Lord McCray and I are..." I peeked around Mike's side and Cole stopped dead in his tracts, his face went blank and then shock washed over his face completely.

30

"Becca... my little Becca? Is that really you?" His hard look suddenly faded to the most beautiful smile that lit his entire face. He shot up from his desk walking around Lord McCray with his eyes twinkling just as I remembered.

"Cole!" He picked me up and hugged me, kissing my cheeks.

"Oh my little Becca, God, I was worried sick about you!" He held me close, my feet were off the ground about three feet!

"Cole... PL... E... ASE... I can't breathe." He smiled and sat me on my feet staring into my face. He frowned,

"Beck, you look to skinny, but so beautiful!" He then smiled again.

"Yes, she is quite beautiful." Gabe smiled and winked at me causing my cheeks to warm.

"Oh, please forgive me, Lord McCray, Lord McCray, this is..."

"We've met Cole... this morning at the hotel, a pleasure to see you again, Lord McCray." I smiled shyly at him. His eyes warmed as his smile grew.

"I assure you, Mrs. Grayson, the pleasure is all mine." He took my hand and bowed over it with a slight smile sliding to one side of his lips.

"I see you have, please sit." Cole's brow arched.

He pulled chairs out for Mike and I and we sat around Cole's big dark wood desk piled with paper work. Cole relaxed, sitting back, just smiling with a relieved look across his face.

"We were going to send Mike after you if we didn't hear from you soon." I looked at Gabe, and he, too, was smiling.

"I know. I saw mother and Aunt Marie. They told me all about it, Aunt Marie cried the whole time." I laughed.

"Gabe, I don't want to keep you waiting. Was there anything else you needed?" Gabe looked at me and smiled.

"No, I think you have filled the order. I do not wish to interfere with your sister's home coming." He smiled at me strangely and gave me a feeling that I would be seeing him again.

"This was the best surprise. We've missed her so much." Cole frowned.

"What is it, Cole?" I leaned forward seeing the sadness in his eyes.

"Robert... how... where did you..." Tears filled his eyes.

I took a deep breath and looked down knowing Cole would want to know everything.

"Robert is buried under the tree in the back. I fenced off a small place and made a wooden cross." Unable to hold my tears back or stop them, I gave into them. Gabe held out his handkerchief for me.

"Do you mean to say that you..." Gabe's eyes grew in horror at the thought.

"Yes, she took care of Robert by herself... there wasn't a soul within thirty miles around." Mike frowned, looking at Cole.

Cole's eyes held so much regret.

"Becca is a brave one indeed and too damn hardheaded!" He smiled softly as he wiped his eyes.

"She is a special woman indeed. I knew that the first time I laid eyes on her." Gabe smiled as I took his handkerchief.

"Well, I'm not and it was what I had to do, what anyone would do..." I wiped my tears.

"Well, she's back and we'll take care of her now." Cole rubbed his thumb over my hand. I smiled at my big brother's warm tanned handsome face.

"Say, let's have a dinner at the house. I'm sure mother will enjoy having a welcome home dinner for Beck." Mike's eyes lit up.

"Yes, that's a fine idea, how about Saturday at six. Mother will have plenty of time to get the place ready. Gabe, you'll come, won't you?" Cole smiled down at me taking over my life already.

"I don't..." I tried to tell them I wasn't up for a dinner party so soon.

"I would love to come." Gabe's eyes lit up.

"Fine then, we'll see you Saturday evening." Cole had the deal set and done! I crossed my arms over my chest feeling my temper rise.

"Until Saturday, my Lady..." He took my hand blowing a kiss over it.

"Yes, and bring your Corpsmen and whomever you'd like as a date." Mike smiled, looking at me with the teasing look. Perhaps he wasn't teasing? Oh!

"Of course, thank you. I'm looking forward to the evening." He bowed to my brothers and smiled at me. I forced a smile back. Gabe closed the door behind him as he left.

"Thanks a lot! You two are already trying to run my life! Maybe I'm not in the mood for a 'PARTY'!" My temper was at the boiling point.

"Look, Sis, mother was going to do this anyway after Mike returned with you. This way you'll have time to prepare. So which would you rather have, time to be prepared or not?" He was too smart for his own good I thought.

"Well... I guess you're right. Knowing mother, I would have walked right into a party! Yes, I'd rather have time." I sighed, feeling thankful that I did have a few days to get use to the whole idea.

"I wouldn't be surprised if she isn't working on it as we speak!" Mike laughed.

"But mothers place won't hold a lot of people!" I questioned the thought.

"You haven't seen the back of the house yet. Mother has a bigger sun room, remember? Well, it's huge!" Mike laughed.

"How huge?" I did forget about that.

"Big enough for one hundred of her closest friends, in addition, the French doors open up to a huge patio. It's quite the place now." Mike laughed.

"It will do!" Cole laughed.

We talked about Robert and my trip here and the two I met on the road.

"I know those two, they're nice fellows. They are in the Union Corps and one is a high ranked officer." Cole smiled.

After I told them everything there was to tell, we decided to go see mother to see if she was ready to go. Cole was done for the day after his meeting with Lord McCray. He closed the lumberyard and Cole took his wagon and followed us to the Tea Shop.

"We're back, Mother..." Mike called out as she came bustling out of the kitchen.

"Well, I'm almost done for the day, why don't you two take our girl home and let her freshen up for dinner and I'll be home soon." They simply nodded, kissing mother, and then took me home. We took Cole's wagon, leaving mine at mother's shop.

The ride home was just like old times. I laugh every time we talk about the old days. I was so glad to be with my brothers again and it felt good, very good! My thoughts went to Lord McCray as my brothers rambled on about the town and the lumber company. I knew I had to keep Lord McCray at bay, seeing the intent in his eyes. As handsome and charming as he is, he could have anyone he wanted and I was just a simple woman with a lot to do. I needed time to heal myself and just be all by myself. I know they only wanted to help, but I needed to do this on my own.

"So, what do you think Beck?" Cole smiled down at me.

"Fine... whatever you think..." Thunderous laughter cracked my thoughts causing me to look up at the two. Their faces were frozen in open laughter.

"What?!!" I looked at them.

"Oh, Beck… It's so good to have you home!" Mike's arm went around my shoulder.

"What did you say?" I looked at Cole. Oh gosh I wasn't listening and they know it!

"Nothing important… I know you've a lot on your mind." Cole leaned down and kissed my cheek.

"I do at that, but what did you say or ask?" I was getting frustrated at them as they were being their old selves again, but it felt wonderful!

"Cole asked you if you thought that you would enjoy Lord McCray's company or that Lawrence that was always after you. You know the handsome critter." I cut Mike off, disgusted.

"Oh, you two! Lawrence is a nice fellow…he's just on the heavy side and NO! I don't want the attentions of either!" I crossed my arms and sat stiff. Now they were getting on my nerves.

"Beck… we were only kidding. You know though, Lawrence will be eager to see you and he has grown up since you last saw him." I looked at Cole with a glare and both of them burst out in laughter.

"I swear you two are more trouble than you're worth!" I know they were only trying to make me feel better, but I feel like nothing would ever be Alright again.

"Cole, mother told me about Annette… I'm very sorry." I hugged his arm.

"Oh, don't be! She was money hungry." He shook his handsome head and smiled down at me. I could see the hurt in his eyes.

"You'll meet someone one day that will be perfect." I patted his leg.

"No, I'm happy just the way I am. I don't have to answer to anyone but myself, and besides, you and mother are enough for any man!" He sighed deeply and grinned wickedly, but still, I knew it did hurt him.

"You two need a woman to keep an eye on you!" They both looked down at me at the same time in shock.

"Yes… you do!" I was certain of this!

"Well, you're back now and I know you're perfect for the job… and enough for both of us, God help us!" They both nodded and laughed.

"Well!" I huffed and then laughed with them. It felt so good to have my brothers next to me. I smiled even though the two were relentless in their teasing!

As we continued home, Mike told of how the town had grown right after I moved away and what was still in the works. I was looking forward to going shopping in some of the new shops in town. I did need

34

a few new things. I wondered how long it would be before they both tried to be 'helpful'.

"Here we are... whoa..." Cole pulled the two brown horses to a stop.

"When I go back to the hotel, I have to take my wagon to the stables to get a wheel fixed."

"Alright, but I assumed that you would stay with us?" Mike smiled with concern in his eyes.

"No, I intend to enjoy one more night in that fancy hotel and enjoy a little rest before you two and mother start to run my life again!" I laughed as Cole lifted me down from the wagon.

"All I know right now is... you need to eat!" Cole laughed as he set me on my feet.

"I'm looking forward to some of mother's roast beef and potatoes." I smiled though I was not the least hungry.

"We'll have you back to normal in no time, Sis." Mike put his arm around me as we went in the house.

Normal? What was that like? I wouldn't even know what normal meant! All I knew is I was different now and I think they could see it as well. I looked for Jack, but he was probably busy, exploring his new surroundings.

As we entered the kitchen, I started to prepare for dinner so mother wouldn't have to. I got out the old hickory knife and started to peel potatoes, Mike put some coffee on and Cole took the meat out of the icebox. I sat watching them and thought how nice it was to be back and doing something I was sure of and could do without thought. Cole talked about the orders that came in, needing more men to fill them. Mike told Cole that he was glad I was back so he would be free to work with him.

"Well... that didn't take long!" I looked up at the two as they tried to look like they had no clue what I was talking about.

"What?" Mike batted his eyes and looked away.

"You know what!" I shot Cole a glare. My mood suddenly became defensive.

"Now look, Beck... a woman..." Cole started and I stopped him!

"Coleman Lee! I'll not have you taking over my life...you didn't even ask me what I had planned or what I might want to do!" I frowned at the both of them and looked at the potato in my hand taking out my frustrations on peeling it.

"I'm sorry, Beck, but I guess that running your life was something I did before Robert. I am only looking out for your best interests." Cole frowned, taking a deep breath and placed his hand on my shoulder.

"I know, Cole, but I am a grown woman and I think I know what I want...and don't want." I put my hand over his knowing that he was only being my big brother.

"Beck, I just want you to take the time you need for... you know... getting used to life again." He kissed my cheek and my arms went around his neck as I gave in and cried. He tightened his hold.

"It's alright, Beck... go ahead... let it all out." Cole's deep voice sounded so comforting to me that I just let the tears fall, needing this so badly.

"Will you go with me... to Mrs. Grayson's?" I looked into his green eyes.

"Of course I will, Beck." He hugged me tightly.

"Beck, I'll go as well if you'd like." Mike's deep voice came from behind me.

"I don't know what I'd do without my brothers. I've missed you both so much!" I hugged them both tightly. I was indeed home!

"Well, now! This is what a mother likes to come home to!" Mother's voice sung out from behind.

"Hello, Mother!" Cole smiled brightly and then glanced at me to see if I was. I nodded with a bright smile.

Cole and I have always talked without saying a word to each other. Mother use to always say we could have been twins!

"We have dinner almost ready to cook and all that's left is the carrots." I smiled at mother as she came over to me and gave me the best hug I had had in such a long time. There is nothing like a mother's arms around you to fix whatever is wrong.

"Now, Rebecca, honey, I want you to take your time and I don't expect you to get back to your old self right away. I know all too well how you're feeling. Robert was a good man just like your father." She whispered in my ear as I hung on to her neck.

"Thank you, Mother." I whispered back to her. I knew that she did indeed know how I was feeling.

"Alright... let's make dinner!" I was feeling much better. Mother winked at me.

As dinner cooked, we talked more about the lumber company and the Tea Shop. Cole mentioned that Lord McCray was in the office when Mike brought me in to surprise him. Mother's eyes lit up.

"Really?" She smiled at Cole.

"Yes and he was, or should I say, looked quite taken with Beck." Cole winked at me. Here he goes again. Trying to help!

"Coleman, I am not ready to even…" I cut Cole off and mother cut me off.

"We know, dear, but it is nice to know that a man of Lord McCray's stature finds you interesting and not to mention, he is quite the looker!" She winked at Cole and Mike. They both were holding back grins.

"He is very interesting, but like I said, I am not interested in, nor will I be interested in, a man for a long time, if ever. Now please!" I frowned at all of them. I know they all loved me and meant well.

"Beck…" Mike smiled at me with sorrow in his eyes.

"Mike, believe me when I say that I plan on never having my heart broken again! Now let's talk about something else, please!" I smiled at them all, trying to hide my heartache.

I know them… they will all eventually try to talk me into seeing someone. I rolled my eyes at the very thought!

"She's right, I know I will never replace your father, so you boys leave her be!" Mother's voice boasted no reply. For once, I was in shock.

When dinner was ready, we all sat at the dining room table, Cole holding my chair and Mike mother's chair. Mike said grace…

"Dear Father in heaven, thank you for bringing our Rebecca home safely. Lord, watch over her as she goes through this time of change. Bless mother and Cole in their business and me as well, for now Rebecca is home and I will need ALL your help! Amen!" He laughed.

"Well, Michael!" Mother laughed. I just rolled my eyes at him again.

"Mother, I know you are planning on a dinner party for Beck. We, Mike and I, already have planned on Saturday evening" Cole smiled at me with a knowing look. Cole's arms rested on the table.

"Oh, you boys always are one step ahead of me!" She laughed and wiped her mouth.

"So you agree on Saturday?" Mike smiled at mother, then me.

"Yes, I have already gotten together several menus and some of my dearest friends are fixing some of the trays. I do have a caterer coming as well, but they don't make some of the things I want to have, so I'm having Greta Kimball and Lucy Givens make those wonderful chocolate puffs and apple turnovers with icing. Lucy won't give that recipe out for anything!" She shook her head and laughed.

"Well, you won't give her your recipe for your chocolate pie!" Cole laughed, taking a bite of roast beef, knowing darn well that mother was just as bad about the family's secret recipes!

"I think it's all a big game." Mike laughed.

"It's no game, son! That recipe has been in the family for two hundred years. I'll not be the first one to let it leave the family either!" She shook her head.

"I'm sorry, Mother. I guess I didn't realize that chocolate pie held the world together!" Mike and Cole looked at each other and laughed out. I understood mother. I guess it was a woman thing.

As we all ate dinner, mother, Mike and Cole talked about the party and who would come. I listened and smiled, loving to hear the sound of their voices and how they all were running things again!

"So, Beck, what are you going to do about the homestead?" Cole, always the businessman!

"Well, to be honest, there isn't much left of the place after the storm. I took everything that was usable and don't ever want to go back there. Cole, you and Mike can do whatever you want with it." I looked down and suddenly felt like the room was closing in on me. I looked at all their faces and Cole looked at me.

"Beck, is something wrong?" He looked worried.

"Excuse me please… I need some air." I hurried from the table as tears welled in my eyes, feeling suddenly overwhelmed. I went out the back door and into mother's new garden, not paying attention to it. I found myself at a waist high wall and stood looking at a beautiful fountain and then I looked up into the sky and closed my eyes. All I could see was Robert lying on the ground and then in the house. His last words... oh, God!

"Beck?" Cole walked towards me with his brow down.

"I'm alright… I just needed a little air." I wiped my tears from my cheeks.

"Well, it doesn't look like you're alright." He put his hands on my shoulders, tilting my chin up.

"I am really… It's just my heart has a hole in it… and I can't seem to… it comes in waves, you know?" Tears and sobbing took over as I searched for some sort of peace.

"It's alright, Beck, honey…go ahead and cry." Cole wrapped his big arms around me and held me to his chest.

"I hope I didn't upset you." Cole's voice was soft and soothing.

"No, it wasn't you Cole, it's just everything… I don't know what to think or say or do and I don't want people to walk on egg shells around me. I promised Robert that I would come here and go on with my life but…" Tears fell unceasingly from my eyes.

"But what, honey?" Cole's deep voice reminded me of Robert's so much and they were best friends as well. I almost had forgotten that. I looked up into his eyes and he, too, was crying quietly.

"Oh, Cole… I'm sorry… I had forgotten that he was your best friend." I suddenly felt so selfish!

"Shhh now… it's alright. It's just all going to take time. I know none of this makes sense, but one day, it may. Until then, we just have to do the best we can." He kissed my forehead, hugging me tight. I was so grateful for Cole.

"You always know the right thing to say. That's why Robert wanted me to come home. He knew you would take care of me till I got strong enough." I hugged his big chest and cuddled my cheek against it.

"I made him swear to me that he would, if he could."

"You did?" I looked up at my brother with my eyes wide.

"Yes. I agreed not to stop you from going if he gave me his word that he would send you home." I hugged my big brother for all he was worth.

"I love you, Cole." I kissed his cheek.

"I love you too, Sis, now let's go finish dinner and we'll go to Mrs. Grayson's and then see to your wagon." He didn't say any more and we walked back into the house arm-in-arm and I gave no argument.

The look on Mike and mother's faces told me they were worried about me but I saw Cole nod his head meaning it was alright and it was… for now. They both nodded slightly.

After dinner was through, I washed dishes for mother and Mike dried. Cole and mother went out on the terrace to look at her flowers and have a brandy and of course, to have a little talk. I knew they were talking about me. I also knew Cole was reassuring her that I was as fine as could be expected and that he would take care of me. I took my apron off and went out to the garden after finishing up with the dishes.

"You ready, Cole?" I wanted to get this over with as soon as possible. I didn't want Mrs. Grayson to find out I was home by someone else telling her.

"Yes, Ma'am, lets ride." Cole kissed mother's cheek and handed her his snifter.

"Mother, I won't be back tonight, I'm staying at the hotel one more night." I kissed her cheek and before she could answer, I added, "I'll be here tomorrow. I just want to be alone after I talk to Mrs. Grayson." I smiled, hoping she wouldn't push the subject any more.

"I understand." was all she said with a look in her eye that said she did.

"Well, let's get a move on."

Mike decided to stay with mother since Cole didn't know if he was coming back to mothers tonight. Cole often stayed in a bunk at the office for early morning orders.

Cole took me to mother's shop to get my wagon and he followed me to the stable. I was getting apprehensive as I thought about Mrs. Grayson and the family. We pulled up at the stables.

"Mr. Thomas?" I called as Cole walked behind.

"Howdy…I'll be right there." Mr. Thomas called out from the tack room and a moment later he came out, wiping his hands on a cloth.

"Well now, I see the wagon made it back." He nodded with a warm smile.

"Cole…." he shook Cole's hand and smiled.

"George…" Cole smiled at Mr. Thomas.

"Yes, we made it. I hope it wasn't any trouble for you last night."

"Nah…Lord McCray saw to everything this morning. He said to fix whatever it needed and…"

"What did you say?" I looked at him, then Cole in shock.

"Ah well, Lord McCray told me to fix everything wrong with your rig and you're not to worry about the bill." He suddenly looked unsure.

"George, are you sure?" Cole scratched his head in disbelief.

"Yes, that's what he said!" Mr. Thomas was stuttering at this point.

"Well! I'll not have anyone paying my bill!" My temper was gone!

"Now, Ma'am…I think he was only trying to be…" Mr. Thomas was trying to defend Lord McCray's actions.

"I don't care what he was trying to be, Mr. Thomas. I will, and always have, paid my own bills. For that matter, do you know where he is at this time?" I crossed my arms and looked him dead in the eye waiting for him to tell me.

"I…." Mr. Thomas started to speak.

"Now, Beck… this isn't George's fault. Calm down and I shall…"

"You, Cole... shall mind your own business. Now, Mr. Thomas, do you, or do you not, know where he is?" I demanded. There was no way that anyone was going to pity me!

"Well, Ma'am... I believe that he is at the hotel's restaurant right now... but he is with..."

"Thank you, Mr. Thomas." I didn't allow him to even finish and turned towards the hotel. There was no way that any man was going to take care of a bill for me. Why, I don't even know him! How would it look to the others in town if they caught wind of this? There would be talk! I don't care how handsome and charming he is, I had to let him know that I could not allow anyone to pay a bill for me! I am married... was married... No, I am still married, but now a widow. He'll not feel sorry for me!

I heard Cole calling for me but ignored him and kept going. I started walking across the street and was so mad I didn't pay attention to the traffic until I heard yelling coming from someone else!

"Watch out, lady!" A man yelled from a carriage. I looked around and found myself in the middle of the street. I finished crossing, then entered the hotel and went right to the restaurant looking for Lord McCray.

"May I help you?" It was the same man who had been here last night. He smiled at me and I nodded back at him.

"Yes, would you happen to know where Lord McCray is at this time? Never mind, I see him!" I started for Lord McCray.

"But, Mrs. Grayson... he's..." He began to protest and I ignored him, walking to the back of the restaurant, finding Lord McCray at a large table full of men! I was startled when they all suddenly stood as I walked up to Lord McCray. They all towered over me and it was then that I realized that this was probably a huge mistake....HUGE!

"Why, Mrs. Grayson... What a lovely surprise!" Lord McCray walked towards me and suddenly I was fighting to recall what I wanted to say! Heavens!

"I'm sorry... I didn't mean to disturb... you..." Yes, I did! That is just what I wanted to do! I wanted to disturb him and tell him! Keep focused!

"Mrs. Grayson, you are always welcome." He took my hand, bowing over it with a smile and my lips were suddenly dry. I nervously licked them as I watched his eyes go to them. A slight grin appeared across his lips as I felt my cheeks warm and I realized I had stopped breathing! Focus, keep focused!

"Mr.... I mean... Lord McCray..." My voice betrayed me as my words came out in a whisper. I cleared my throat and licked my lips, took another deep breath and raised my chin higher.

"Gabe...Please." His voice was soft and calm as he smiled, squeezing my hand. Realizing that he was still holding it, I slowly pulled it away and held my hands in front of me trying to will my cheeks from getting any redder than they already were!

"Lord McCray... I see that I was interrupting... but I do wish to speak to you." I hoped he couldn't tell how nervous I was! Of course he could! His grin told me he was pleased at my discomfort! Blasted man!

Then I looked at the men standing at the table. They were just as big as Lord McCray. Some of them were older than he was and some looked about the same age and all were very well dressed. They smiled and nodded at me as I looked at them. Now, I was very nervous. This was a bad idea, very bad idea, but I had come this far and might as well say what I needed to say and get it over with.

"Ms. Grayson... no, you could never interrupt anything. What would you like to speak to me about? Do you wish some privacy?" He smiled, calm as a cucumber, and could see he was truly enjoying this!

"Yes...I mean, no... I mean... would you mind stopping by my room when you are through?" I smiled and then... horror washed over me from head to toe! I just realized what I just asked of him in front of all these men! His eyes widened with delight! I tried not to show emotion, but it was too late!

"Of course! I'd be delighted... Mrs. Grayson! May I have the pleasure of introducing to you the Inner Union Council Members of this Region?" He smiled softly now.

"This is Lord Winston Chambers." A tall older man in his late fifties with salt and pepper hair and brown eyes bowed and smiled.

"And this is Lord Thomas Winthrop." He was another tall man with white hair and light blue eyes in his fifties and very handsome still. He smiled and winked at me. Something told me he must have been something else in his day, if not still.

"And this is Lord Benjamin Thatcher." This man was younger than Lord Winthrop with black hair graying on the temples, sporting a salt and pepper beard and gray eyes, very handsome and older than Lord McCray. He smiled and bowed.

"This is Lord Jacob Jefferies." Another older man with white hair and dark eyes frowned as he bowed to me, though I still smiled.

"And here we have Lord Brigham Charlton." He was very handsome and much larger than the rest of the men at the table. His jet black hair was shorter than the rest of them but his blue eyes were beautiful.

"It's a pleasure to meet you, milady." He bowed and smiled. I nodded to him, smiling.

"Lord James Crawford." This man had golden blond hair and beautiful light blue eyes. He smiled and bowed. His enchanting smile made my cheeks blush and he seemed to be about the same age as Lord McCray. Very handsome indeed!

"And this is Lord William Andrews." He looked like the man I met on the road.

"It's a pleasure to see you again, Mrs. Grayson." He bowed, deeply smiling, never taking his eyes away from mine and made me feel funny, but I was comfortable with him.

"And of course, you have met Lord Nicholas Baptiest." His eyes took me in as he bowed, smiling at me with that look of suspicion again. They both were lords! Heavens! Where do all of these lords come from?

"Mrs. Grayson, it's a pleasure to see you again." His eyes never looked away from mine.

"And you, Lord Baptiest." I smiled nervously at him. Something about him made me feel on guard and I really didn't like it too much.

"And finally, this is Lord Douglas Brent." His smile was breathtaking as he bowed, taking me in. His jet black hair was long and in a leather strap. He looked to be around the same age as Lord McCray, maybe younger by a couple of years. His beard hid dimples that I could see as he smiled a warm confident smile. His eyes held mine like Lord McCray's did. I could feel my stomach flutter and my cheeks warming. Heavens! All these men were so tall!

"Milady, it is an honor to meet you." He took my hand and bowed deeply.

"And you, as well." I was so overwhelmed at all these men before me that I needed some air and fast. I did this to myself and yes, my temper had gotten the best of me again!

"Please, gentlemen… forgive me. I know that I have indeed interrupted a meeting. It was nice to meet all of you." I wanted to simply melt into the carpet as Lord McCray took my arm and escorted me out of the dining room.

"Lord McCray…Please… forgive me… I'm… my temper…" I was still not speaking straight.

"Not at all, you may interrupt me any time you wish." He covered my hand with his.

"I…wish to…" I looked into his eyes and they looked like crystal shining in the sun and my thoughts jumbled up. I tore my eyes away from his and looked down. I must not look into those eyes!

"I will drop by your room this evening and we will speak then." He smiled, speaking so softly I had to look up at him again or it would be rude. I had to nod for the words would not come.

"Beck!" I blinked away from his smile and heard Cole calling for me and heading towards me. Thank heavens!

"Hello, Gabe… I hope she…" Cole's face looked so sympathetic toward Lord McCray that I wanted to scream!

"Cole, Lord McCray will stop by later." I had to stop him from embarrassing me any further than I had already done myself.

"To… your room?" Cole was in an amused shock.

"Yes and… no…" Oh! How did I get myself into this mess! Cole was trying not to laugh at me. Lord McCray had that grin on his face!

"Then what, Beck?" Cole crossed his arms at his chest, smirking and was almost laughing! I could have thrown something at him!

"I tell you what, Mrs. Grayson. Why don't you and Cole meet me in the dining room for breakfast in the morning instead? I can see your dilemma." He had seen it indeed and was finally letting me out of this embarrassment! Yet, he was being so kind and understanding. I was quite relieved. I stepped back a few steps for a little privacy, Gabe followed.

"No, that's alright, I shall tell you now." I took a rather large breath and started.

"I do not wish you to pay for my wagon being fixed… why, why it isn't proper and I don't even know you! I'll not have anyone take pity on me nor think they can do what they like…" Cole helped me to regain my resolve back. I was feeling more in control of my emotions and focused.

"Mrs. Grayson… I was…" He sucked in a deep breath looking shocked.

"That does not matter! You, Lord McCray are a dangerously assuming man and I do not wish to be taken care of by anyone! Thank you all the same. Good evening, Lord McCray." I turned to walk away and Lord McCray called out after me.

"You are quite beautiful when you're angry, Rebecca!" I turned and glared at them both, seeing Cole and Lord McCray laughing. Cole would hear about this! How dare they! I felt my temper rushing to the point of explosion! I huffed, wanting to blast them both, but it was best that I left the hotel and go to Cole's wagon before I did something else I would later regret. I pulled myself up the wagon and waited, thinking what all of those lords must have thought of me asking Lord McCray to stop by my room! My temper had gotten the best of me this time! Now, I was mad at myself more than anything. I needed to learn more control! It seems like everything goes blank and it doesn't matter who or what is in the way! I took some deep breaths and calmed myself down, waiting on Cole. I was not going to say one word to him… not one! That would surely give him his due!

"Beck, I'm sorry about that." Cole stepped up into the wagon taking the reins.

"I know." That is all he would get out of me!

"What? You know? That's all you're going to say?" I could feel and hear the shock in his look and words. He clicked his tongue and we were on our way to Robert's mother's.

"Oh, you ARE really angry, aren't you? I see how it is." He charged but I still said nothing.

"You know… I do believe Gabe is interested in you." He leaned forward to look at me. I gave him no response.

"Yes, as a matter of fact he said something about how he would love to take you to dinner." I knew he was trying to get to me but I still said not a word.

"Beck…come on, say something please. I was only teasing." His voice was true regret, but I still kept silent.

"I know I can make you so angry but, honey, really, I was only playing along with Gabe." So! They were playing!

Now I really won't let him off the hook! I sighed deeply, trying to act as if what he said didn't matter to me in the least! I was not talking to him for the rest of the evening and that was that!

"Beck… Please, say something!" He sighed deeply and gave up, finally. Playing along with Gabe? Ha! Men!

We sat in silence as Cole drove the wagon toward Mrs. Grayson's home. He never tried to talk again, but as soon as the wagon pulled up in front of Mrs. Grayson's house, I was at the door knocking before Cole had a chance to get around the wagon to help me.

The quaint home looked the same with its stone structure and ivy over growing most of it but just as I recalled, the flowers were beautiful. I sighed, silently remembering when Robert had planted them, almost picturing him planting them.

"Rebecca!" Robert's youngest sister, Annie, now about eighteen, was at the door. She had grown up so much! Her big brown eyes of a child were now that of a young woman with her hair now long and a beautiful shiny brownish red. Her soft pink and white lace trim day dress wasn't like a little girl's dress. Yes, she was grown. I wrapped my arms around her and hugged her tightly, dreading what was about to take place.

"Tell me… it isn't true!" She looked behind me seeing Cole behind me.

I said nothing as tears welled in my eyes. She pulled away from me and looked into my eyes blinking as tears filled hers.

"Where's Mother Grayson?" I softly asked as I blinked tears down my cheeks.

"She's… not well… Rebecca… has Robert really…" She held my arms in her small hands squeezing them tighter by the passing second.

"Where are James and Sarah?" Tears started to flow as her grip was almost hurting now.

"They're all inside with mother… in the parlor." She shook me slightly, seeing her eyes begging to know.

"Let's go into the parlor." Cole took her arm and wrapped his other around her waist. She knew it was true.

As we entered the parlor, their faces looked surprised, but just as quickly, their faces paled.

"Rebecca…dear Rebecca." Mother Grayson held out her hands to me as I stood before her, taking in deep breaths with uncontrolled tears streaming down my cheeks.

"Rebecca?" Sarah's eyes welled up as mother Grayson's did. Mother Grayson looked down then put her face in her hands. I dropped to my knees.

After what seemed an eternity, I began to tell them about the storm and what happened to Robert. We all cried mourning his death and once again, I had relived it all over again. I laid my head in her lap. I had no words to say or nothing that could take away their pain.

"Rebecca…" Mother Grayson took my chin in her fingers turning my face up to hers.

"I know he loved you with all his heart and soul. You loved him the same, but I know my son, he'd want you to go on with your life." She tried to smile with her lips quivering.

"No… I can't." I cried, hugging her waist.

"Now, you look here, young lady! Robert is with his father now and until you are happy again, he will mourn as long as you do." She wiped her fingers over my cheeks.

"But, Mother..." I couldn't speak. My heart ached for Robert!

"Now, no buts about it! We want Robert to be happy now, don't we? We all must be strong and, Sarah... you know I'm right!" She grabbed her eldest daughter of twenty-eight by the chin as well, then Annie's chin.

"We are Grayson's! James is the man of the manor now and being so, he must have all of our support. We may cry in our own rooms, but not in front of James. This will be hard enough on him being the eldest son. You, Rebecca, will always be my daughter and as my daughter, I want you to do as your husband asked of you. I know his last request was for you to go on and find someone who will love you as he had and you, as his wife, you must honor his last request." She hugged me to her tightly and rubbed my back.

"We will tell the pastor at church about this and we will send word of the service on Sunday for Robert. Child, I love you and am proud of all that you endured for our Robert... go now." She kissed my cheek and stood, pulling me up with her.

"Mother Grayson... I am so..." She put her finger on my lips.

"Never be sorry that you loved and were loved." She kissed my cheek and I hugged her tightly wondering how she had the strength to endure another great loss in her life. Robert was her heart.

"Annie, see our Rebecca to the door, won't you?" She nodded, wiping tears and walked me to the door.

"Rebecca, I love you still as a sister and always will." She hugged me, crying with all her heart.

"I love you, too." I hugged her, then opened the door and stepped out. I paused turning to her, and we both nodded to each other, feeling the strength we both needed.

Cole came out from around the side of the house alone. James must have gone in the back way. Cole didn't say a word as we left or all the way back to the hotel.

Instead, he wrapped his arm around me as he held the reins and that was all I needed. Cole squeezed my shoulder as I looked to him for strength and I knew that I could always count on him for that.

To me, Cole was the strongest man I have ever known and was always there when I needed him the most. That's probably why I married Robert in the first place, they were alike.

We pulled up to the hotel and Cole saw me safely inside my room and closed the door. He gathered me into his arms and just stood quietly, holding me, allowing me to cry.

"Go take a nice relaxing bath and I'll stay until you're in bed." He whispered.

What would I do without Cole? I cried thinking that must be what Robert's Sisters feel like. They leaned on Robert as I did Cole.

I wiped my tears and got my soft nightgown out and took my bath. I didn't want to take too long knowing Cole was tired as well. I'd make short time of it.

When I was through I took my brush and went out to the bedroom and crawled in bed. Cole came and sat next to me and took the brush in hand. He quietly brushed the back of my hair like he used to long ago and it felt wonderful. When he finished, he braided it and sat the brush on the nightstand. He held the covers up as I lay down and tucked me in. I couldn't imagine my life without Cole.

Cole quietly went to the fireplace and placed another log on the slow burning fire. I felt so safe with him in the room. Soon, my eyes were heavy…

~ Chapter 5 ~

I stretched as I opened my eyes seeing the sun peep through the heavy curtains. I laid still, thinking about last night and having to tell Mother Grayson about her son. All I could feel was the ache in my heart for everyone. I rolled over thinking about all I had to endure burying Robert myself. I never thought I would have to do such a thing! I tried not to think about that part even though it all seemed like a bad dream and I was grateful that it was a blur.

I rolled back over and looked to the fireplace and saw Cole! He was still here! I sat up and blinked my eyes again seeing he was truly there! I hopped out of bed and went to him. Bless his heart! He stayed with me all night! No wonder I slept so well! I didn't have one dream about Robert or the storm. I gently touched his shoulder and he opened one eye, looking at me.

"Are you still angry at me?" He smirked with a sleepy smile.

"Yes I am, Coleman, but since you stayed with me all night, I will let this one go. But, I warn you, you better never do that again!" I recalled his words, 'Playing along with Gabe' and my stomach cringed with the thought that I thought Gabe was even remotely interested in me.

"Truce?" Cole raised his brow.

"Yes, a truce." I shook my head, watching him stand stretching to get the kinks out of his neck.

"Let's get you dressed and I will buy my little Sister breakfast." He called going into the washroom.

"I will." I chose another dark dress to wear.

I needed to buy some more dresses and would do so this morning after breakfast. I waited for Cole and I went in next.

Soon, Cole and I made our way to the restaurant sitting at a nice table in the back.

"Well, what do you feel like this morning?" Cole looked at me as the waiter poured us coffees.

"I think just toast and coffee. I'm not that hungry. No, a roll and coffee…" He nodded and that surprised me, he usually fussed at me for not eating.

"Well I'm starved! I think I'll have the special." Cole smiled and winked.

We ordered our breakfast and I told him that I planned on doing some shopping this morning before going to mother's, needing more dresses.

"Beck, you don't need to wear those dark things for too long. Robert wouldn't have wanted you to." He looked into his coffee cup.

"I know, but I must wear them for a while. I wouldn't feel right if I didn't." But he knew I was right.

"Beck, about yesterday afternoon…"

"Cole, I don't want to talk about it anymore!" I shot him a warning glance.

"I meant what I said." His eyes narrowed.

"Oh, Cole… you know I can't stand that when you start to say something and then you stop! I know you're going to tell me anyway." I rolled my eyes. He could be so frustrating at times!

"I know McCray is interested in you…he…"

"I don't care what he said! The man was planning on paying for my wagon being fixed and I don't even know him." I didn't need this right now!

"Well, I do know him and it is very unusual for him to pay for something like that." He shook his head which told me that he really didn't believe it.

"What do you mean?" I sipped my coffee.

"Gabe is a devout bachelor and I've only seen him once with a woman on his arm in the last year or so. Though, I can't say that when he leaves town, he may have other interests elsewhere." Cole sipped his coffee as well.

"I don't care about the man in that way and it doesn't matter what he does or doesn't do. It is none of my concern!" But now I knew. The thought of Lord McCray's interest in me was quite the compliment. I searched Cole's face to see if he was 'playing' again or not, he wasn't.

"I know it's only been a very short time…"

"Please Cole…" I was on the verge of tears.

"Well, good morning." A deep voice rumbled behind me and right through me. Instantly I knew it was Lord McCray.

"Morning, Gabe..." Cole stood and shook his hand.

"Ms. Grayson..." He bowed taking my hand and bowing over it.

"Please join us, Gabe." Cole waved his hand at the empty seat.

Great, that's all I need! I took a deep breath. Cole just had to talk him up!

"If you two will excuse me for a minute, I must speak to Mr. Wilson about his order, it's ready." Cole nodded and walked to the other side of the restaurant. I watched him stop by an older man who was short and heavy with black balding hair. Then I glanced at Lord McCray. The silence was quite disturbing.

"Ms. Grayson, I wish to apologize for yesterday's happenings." He laid his hand on mine and I smoothly slid it away from him.

"Lord McCray, I meant what I said yesterday. I shall have no man take care of me. I found your assuming that I needed your assistance an embarrassment, though I thank you for your offer. In the future, would you refrain from trying to be so...so..." I took a sip of coffee.

"So? What?" He was trying to hide a smile.

"So... So Lordly!" I laughed to myself, knowing how absurd that sounded.

"I guess I can be a little assuming at times myself. Truly, I was just trying to ease your distress for some reason that I can't explain. I had an overwhelming need to. It was rather strange, I just found myself at the stable telling Mr. Thomas to charge it to my account." He shook his head as if he truly didn't understand it himself and by his reaction, I knew he was telling me the truth.

"Well, no harm done except..." I blushed.

"Except what?"

"Well, the embarrassing moment that I asked you to stop by my room." I looked at his eyes twinkling like stars and then burst out laughing at the same time he did.

"Not to worry, my lady, they all knew that you weren't that sort." He laughed.

I was feeling a bit more at ease and relieved that he thought no more of it than I did.

"I must confess something though." He sipped his coffee and looked deep into my eyes. It felt as if his eyes were touching me.

"I did mean it when I said you were quite beautiful when you are angry." He winked at me.

"I…" I was speechless.

"And when you're speechless as well" He smiled and gazed deep in my eyes.

"Lord McCray, it is not proper to address…" I was suddenly breathless. How strange! It was as if his eyes were actually hypnotizing me!

"Ms. Grayson, a man would have to be a rock to not notice that you are intelligent and very brave, not to mention a beauty as well. Lord Baptiest was quite interested how I knew you and asked about your town connections. I told him that you were Cole's sister and he instantly changed his tone. I believe you have a small court already, Ms. Grayson, whether you want one or not!" He smiled and his eyes told me that he indeed had his own agenda!

"Lord McCray, I am in mourning and it isn't proper to…" My cheeks flushed with frustrated anger.

"My lady, I am in no hurry. I am a devout bachelor…for now…" He winked at me! My temper was at the boiling peek!

"Lord McCray…I will not…" I wanted to throw something at his assuming…

"Ms. Grayson…I will not speak of this again, for it will be you that comes to me next time." He was not smiling at me, but gazed in my eyes deeply and with intent. What he was saying and his eyes were telling me was a warning and a promise!

"Lord McCray…I shall never come to you or any other man. I lost the only love I have ever known and will be a widow for the rest of my life. I will never marry again, nor do I ever want to." I huffed at his words. He infuriated me! I could not believe he was being so forward!

"So, Ms. Grayson, what are your plans?" He sat back acting calm and cool as if the conversation we just had never even happened!

"I…I don't know." I was speechless again. Oh! How I detested this!

"Will you work with your mother or brother?" He sipped his coffee, staring at me, waiting for me to say something profound. Why was he doing this to me? I wished Cole would come back and save me.

"Good morning, Lord McCray." I was pulled out of my thoughts by another rich deep voice and looked up at a very surprisingly handsome man. It was Lord Baptiest!

"Good morning, Nick." Lord McCray didn't look very pleased at his sudden appearance.

"Ms. Grayson, you look lovely this morning." He bowed taking my hand.

"Lord Baptiest, I believe? Please, join us for coffee?" I waved at the other empty seat relieved with the interruption.

"Thank you, milady…" He sat his tall muscular form in the chair next to me.

I was surprisingly caught off guard at his smile, it was breathtaking! His eyes were a beautiful green and very different than the last time we met. They were very clear and bright and holding mine in a strange way. He had trimmed sideburns and was fresh shaven, smelling like the morning air in the spring. I saw a small sensual grin play on his rather full lips and I tore mine away from his, realizing that I was staring. I glanced towards Lord McCray.

"I thought you were to leave this morning, Nick?" Lord McCray flatly stated.

"No. We decided to stay for a few days and rest. The ride here was quite a long one." He smiled up at the waiter as he poured Lord Baptiest a cup of coffee. He seemed much more relaxed this time and I didn't feel like I was under scrutiny.

"Ms. Grayson, Gabe tells me that your brother is Cole?" He sipped his coffee. This was going to be fun indeed! I smiled warmly at him, thinking he was so different looking than he had been the other day. Maybe it was because I was so nervous about traveling alone? He was ominous looking then.

"Please call me Rebecca, Lord Baptiest, and yes, I am Cole's Sister."

"Please call me Nick." He smiled staring into my eyes like Lord McCray had. I glanced at Lord McCray, seeing he was not smiling anymore. So, he dislikes competition does he? How interesting indeed!

"Well, Nick, we're having a dinner Saturday night at my mother's, I would be honored to have you come." I smiled warmly at him again and saw Lord McCray sipping his coffee out of the corner of my eye.

"Thank you and it would be I, that is, honored to join you and your family." He smiled wider, well pleased.

"Well, well, good morning, Ms. Grayson." It was Lord Andrews!

"Lord Andrews, it's good to see you again. Would you care to join us as well?" I smiled, liking this even more and more knowing Lord McCray wasn't pleased at all!

"Thank you!" He pulled up a chair from an empty table squeezing in between Lord McCray and me. This was perfect!

"Had I known, I would have gotten a lager table!" I laughed.

"This is quite cozy." Lord Andrews smiled like the sun.

"I wish to extend an invitation to you as well, Lord Andrews. We're having a dinner at my mother's Saturday night and I hope you will accept my invitation to join us?" I smiled warmly at him and noticed that Lord McCray and Lord Baptiest were not smiling, either of them! This was fun indeed! I wanted to laugh but willed myself not to.

"Ms. Grayson, please call me William." He smiled, taking my hand and placed a kiss on the back, actually touching his lips to my skin! I warmed at his actions.

Instantly I felt that he and I would get along very well. His brown hair was so shiny in the morning sun. The golden streaks looked like the color of a wheat field and the strange contrast was almost as if someone had done this to his hair. His cologne was different from the others smelling like a musky woods. I liked that very much.

"Please call me Rebecca, if you would." I realized I was staring and stirred my coffee.

"Lord McCray, if there is any more of the Council here, please extend the invitation to them as well." I smiled at him warmly with a nod.

"I shall, Ms. Grayson." His smile appeared as if he knew what I was doing.

"Look here! I leave my beautiful sister alone for a few minutes and she is flocked by predators!" Cole laughed and sat down next to Nick.

"Not at all, Brother... They were all perfect gentlemen." I smiled at Lord McCray.

Why did I allow him get to me in such a way? He winked at me as if this was not affecting him at all, but somehow I knew better!

"They best remember that as well, or they will have your brothers to deal with!" Their laughter filled the room in a deep thunderous sound. I was enjoying Lord McCray being put in his place. I could tell he was not used to the word 'no'.

"Rebecca has invited us all to your home Saturday night." William smiled, sipping his coffee.

"I was going to invite you all as well. I've heard you decided to stay for a few days on holiday?" He looked at me, smiling like a cat that ate a mouse.

"Aye, we don't really have to be back to Lawrenceburg for another week or so, so we decided to stay for a few days. Lawrenceburg is larger and so busy anymore. I'd rather stay in a less busy town." Nick smiled at me.

"Well, it was a smart move and now you have a dinner to attend." Cole smiled, looking at Lord McCray.

"Speaking of which, I need to go to mother's shop and discuss the details, if you will excuse me, gentlemen?" I stood and they all leapt to their feet.

"May I walk you?" William held his arm out to me.

"I would be delighted to have the company." He was so tall! It felt as if I had to look up forever to find his handsome face. I wrapped my hand around his very large arm and he covered my hand with his.

"Gentlemen..." I smiled at all of them.

"William, remember... she's my sister." Cole gave him a warning glance.

"Yes, I know and shall not soon forget that, the poor woman!" William laughed as Cole rolled his eyes and escorted me out of the restaurant.

"It's a lovely morning, isn't it, William?" I loved the feeling of the sun on my face.

"That it is...that it is." His tone was so soft and deep that I couldn't help but to glance up at him. He was smiling in an unusual way. I felt my cheeks warm.

"William, I want to apologize about not telling you that I am a widow. I'm sure you know by now, I was hiding the truth."

"I don't blame you. You were all by yourself and I must say, very brave." He rubbed the back of my hand lightly.

"I had to travel...I had no choice." I looked down at the wooden sidewalk.

"I must confess, Nick and I stayed up the road for a while and let you pass and then we followed you until we knew you were safe." I glanced at him thinking that was the nicest thing anyone had done for me.

"I don't know what to say." I was speechless with his confession and he stopped walking.

"There is nothing to thank us for. We did what any man would do. I... Nick was insistent that you not see us."

"But why?" Why would Nick not want to be seen?

"He didn't want you to be afraid of us, but he thought you were."

"I see....well he was right about that. I was afraid, but strangely not of you." I smiled, feeling that for some reason I could tell William anything.

"Nick can be very intimidating. He even intimidates me at times. He is so serious about everything. However, I am surprised that he wanted to stay here for a few days."

"This surprises you?" We started to walk again.

"It's just unlike Nick, but I think he has other underlying reasons, though I'm not sure what

"Unless what?"

"Unless he is taken with you, which I could well understand." He smiled.

"Now really William, I am in mourning." I swatted my skirt with my hand.

"Yes and they all know it won't last forever…unless you plan on never…"

"I couldn't think of anyone other than Robert. There'll never be another." I sighed, feeling that it was the truth even though I had promised to go on.

"Maybe one day, someone will come along…Not that you'll ever forget him, but you are too young to be a widow. Don't you want children?" His question normally would have been too intimate but he looked truly concerned.

"I've always wanted children, but…" Why was he so concerned?

"Rebecca…I have a feeling you will have children, lots of the little ones and somehow I believe that your Robert would want you to carry on, sort of to speak. I have a year left, but after that, I intend to find a bride and have children of my own."

"It's too soon for me to think about…that." I shook my head thinking about Robert's last request. And how would he know that?

"Rebecca, if I may…" He stopped, staring off in thought and then turned to me smiling.

"Perhaps by the time I am done with the guards…you may be considering callers?" I could see he was serious.

"Perhaps, William… for now, we'll just be good friends. Besides, you're so young" I laughed, but he was so adorable and seemed so honestly hopeful.

"Very well…" His eyes sparkled when he laughed, deeply rich, as his entire face lit up as warm as sunshine. We came upon a nice dress shop.

"Would you mind if I went in here for a few minutes?"

"Not at all." He nodded.

"Thank you. I need more dresses. It should only take a few minutes."

"I'll go in with you." He smiled and opened the door. He would go into a dress shop? How odd!

"Good Morning!" An older woman in her early fifties with her salt and pepper hair and glasses on the end of her nose appeared from behind a curtain.

"May I help you?" Her voice almost sounded musical.

"Yes, I need a few dresses made." I slightly smiled as she looked at the dress I was wearing.

"I see. What a nice brother you are for taking care of your sister like this." She frowned shaking her head.

"Come, dear." I looked at William and wanted to laugh seeing his brow furrow a bit. A brother! Ha!

"I would like three for now." She took me into the back and started to measure me for the dresses.

"I have two dark dresses." I frowned, spreading out my skirt seeing the wear at the bottom.

"Not to worry, I'll have you three dresses by next Friday, you poor dear. What's your name?"

"Rebecca Grayson." My smile faded as I saw the color drain from her face.

"Robert's....Rebecca?" She breathlessly whispered, laying her hand on her heart.

"Yes." I sighed deeply.

"I am his Aunt Hannah Carson. My sister is Robert's mother." Tears filled her eyes.

"I'm so very sorry…" I looked down.

"Child, now look here, I know Robert well and Robert would not have you mourn long!" Her sad look held certainty.

"I know that is what he said and his mother as well…but I need to…"

"I know my dear, but I will not make any black dresses for you. I shall make them dark blue and dark green and one gray, but no brown and no black. I can't stand those dreadful black dresses! When my Kenneth died, I swore I'd never make another black dress for any woman again. They are hot, ugly and uncomfortable!" I looked up at her face as her words were so resolute. Then just as suddenly, she softly laughed.

"I agree, but I don't want anyone to think…" I sighed agreeing that they were hot and ugly.

"Now dear, everyone in this town knows Robert loved you and you him!"

"I know, but…"

"Rebecca, life is so short and you're so very young yet, entirely too young to be a widow for that matter!" She shook her head.

"It's only been six months but it still feels like yesterday at times." Tears welled in my eyes knowing she meant well.

"I know." She put her hands on my shoulders.

"When did you arrive here? I don't recall you being here when I lived here?" I smiled at her sweet face desperately wanting to change the subject.

"When my Kenneth died, I moved here with my sister and she helped me to open this shop."

"My family wants me to work either at the Tea Shop or at the lumber yard." I blew out hot air from my cheeks.

"You don't sound too pleased with your choices. What would you like to do?"

"I'm not sure yet, but I know I will have to do something." I sighed as she measured from my neck to the floor.

"I know that you've probably have had many offer you their advice, but if I were you…" She paused for a moment, but for some reason I wanted to know what she thought. Perhaps it was because she was the first person to ask what 'I' want to do. I took a deep breath, hoping it was truly the right answer.

"Well now, if I were you, I would stay in the hotel for another week and relax. You know, get your thoughts in order. It's not an easy thing to do in a situation like this." She nodded pursing her lips in a knowing way.

"Then, I would take a small trip to another city and, when I was good and ready to hear about working for your family, I would return. By then, you'll know if you want to work for your brother or mother or neither. That's what I would do!" Her answer really surprised me and it was a good idea!

"You know, I think I might just do that! I could stay at the hotel another week and after that, I'll take it from there." I actually felt relief for the first time in so long.

"Good for you! Take time and think. Think about Robert and what he would do and say to you, he will guide you." She winked at me.

"You're right, Mrs. Carson. I shall do just that!" I smiled and hugged her tightly, so grateful for her advice, which was absolutely the best advice I have gotten so far!

58

"If ever you need to talk…" She hugged me.

"Thank you, Mrs. Carson." I liked her right off.

"Please, call me Hannah…"

"Yes, I would like that very much, but only if you call me Rebecca." I smiled, liking my new friend very much! She nodded seemingly just as pleased.

She finished measuring me and then walked back out to the front and we caught William looking at some women's intimate underclothes. He blushed deeply seeing he had been found out.

"Tell me then, Rebecca, who is this very handsome escort you have with you?" She asked while writing in her order book.

"This Hannah, is Lord William Andrews, William, this is Hannah Carson." She smiled and winked at me as I introduced them.

"It is a pleasure to meet you, Mrs. Carson." He walked to her and took her hand and bowed over it.

"I realized now that she is not your sister Lord Andrews, please forgive me." She pouted with her cheeks a bit red.

"Not to worry and please, do call me William, won't you?" He laughed.

"Thank you I shall, but only if you call me Hannah." She laughed winking at me.

"Rebecca, I will be seeing you Saturday night at your mother's, she came by yesterday." She smiled sweetly.

"Alright, I look forward to talking more, Hannah." I nodded as William offered his arm. Hannah hurried off to the back room with a smile as we left the dress shop.

"Now where to, milady?" He smiled warmly.

"Milady?" I laughed at the sound of the word.

"Yes… milady." He smiled strangely causing my insides to feel funny.

"Well, I really should go to my mother's Tea Shop, but now that I've talked to Hannah, I don't really want to." I stopped and stared at William.

"Hannah must have said something that impressed you. Hmmm now, perhaps you would like to take a carriage ride?" William smiled sweetly.

"A carriage ride? Yes, I believe I would! You can show me what's new in town!" That sounded like a wonderful thing to do. I wasn't really ready to talk to anyone at this point and William was such a gentleman that I knew I could trust him.

"I know of a beautiful place down by the river. Would you care to see it?" His eyes were bright and hopeful I and found I couldn't say no.

"And tell me how and watch the ducks and chat. But to be perfectly honest, once in a while, if I am charming enough…" He took a deep breath as an adorable grin slid to one side.

"I may try to steal a kiss or two." He laughed looking at me as I tried to hide a smile. He knew I was teasing him.

"Is that what you planned on doing with me down there?" I looked at him wanting to laugh.

"Why yes! You've found me out! I plan on taking you to the river and charming you to a kiss." He smiled, turning his chin up in the air looking humorously arrogant.

"Well then, Lord Andrews, lead on." I laughed, you know of this place?" I smiled up at him, knowing the place myself from when Robert courted me.

"Well, to tell you the truth, I've taken a few ladies down there." He smiled, blushing, finding the wooden walkway suddenly interesting.

"You have? To do what?" I was purposely making him feel awkward. He stopped me on the sidewalk.

"Ms. Grayson, I assure you that I would never compromise you in any way." His face was suddenly serious.

"I'm sure, Lord Andrews, but what do you do with your ladies?" I tried to hide my laugh watching him become a little nervous.

"We walk or sit by the river

We walked to the stables and William rented a carriage with a driver telling the driver where to go. He helped me in and I sat down taking a deep breath.

"Now about that kiss…" He smiled and laughed as he sat across from me.

"Milord, we've not reached the river." I laughed, feeling this was a good thing.

"Oh, drats…Yes, of course!" He laughed as I did at the whole thing and felt very safe with him.

As the carriage started on its way, William sat across from me smiling, seeming to be enjoying himself. I looked out the window recalling when Robert had taken me to the river. I remembered him kissing me on a large rock that stuck out into the water.

"A kiss for your thoughts…" He smiled searching my eyes.

"I was just remembering Robert taking me to the river." I smiled slightly.

"Oh, Rebecca, if it bothers you, we could go elsewhere." He leaned forwards with true concern on his face.

"No, no it's been a long time since I've been to the river. I'd love to see it again." I smiled with a nod, as he sat back. I suppose this would be good to help me with my grieving. Yes, the river was a perfect place to begin and the river was the beginning.

"You know, William… I do think you are about the nicest man I have met yet." I looked into those warm blue green eyes thinking how handsome he was and how well we got along, so kind and charming and I do like him. If I wasn't in mourning, I think he would be the sort I would wish to have call on me.

"Lord McCray will be beside himself that you allowed me to take you anywhere! I think he is truly interested in you."

"So I've been told." I looked out the window.

"Do you find him interesting?" His tone sounded serious.

"I think all of you are quite interesting and very unusual, to say the least." I rolled my eyes. I've never met so many men that were so tall and looked at me the way these men do. Honestly, it's as if they've never seen a woman before!

"But what of Gabe?" He smiled strangely at me as if he was on a fact-finding mission.

"Well… I think…" If he wants information, then I shall give him some!

As I thought about the answer I would give, I watched his hand run through his hair then unbutton his top button of his white shirt allowing the air to blow in his shirt. I saw a hint of dark hair peek out from his collar and then he rolled his sleeves up three rolls. I noticed his huge forearms. He was very muscular indeed and I felt my cheeks warm. His black pants and riding boots fit snuggly too. Maybe this wasn't such a good idea...

"What?" He put his arm over the back of the seat and crossed his ankle over his knee and bit his bottom lip in the most intriguing way. The way his teeth held it in place was most distracting.

"I think he is handsome and, yet, as intimidating as Nick. He is arrogant and too assuming. I think I like your company much better than his." At the moment I did. Lord McCray made my temper flair.

"I think he was hoping to gain your attentions." He flicked dirt off his boot, deep in thought.

"Why are you asking me this? You know that I do not wish to see anyone…" I was getting frustrated with this conversation.

"You're seeing me as we speak...or so it seems." He shot me an amused smirking smile.

"Oh, you!" I laughed and swatted his knee. It was strange how comfortable I felt with William, but I liked it. He seemed to know what to say, just like Robert.

"Well, that is what everyone who has seen us leave together will think." He smiled, showing his beautiful teeth.

"I don't care what anyone thinks. We know the truth and that's what matters." I took a deep breath.

"But you do realize that even though we know the truth, there could be talk." He smiled wider.

"Does that bother you, Lord Andrews?" I held my chin up higher.

"No, not in the least! Actually, I am honored to be seen anywhere with you. As a matter of fact, I love it when people talk about me...It would mean they're not talking about anyone else!" He roared a deep rich laugh.

"You know, this is going to be fun watching Lord McCray all tied up in knots. I don't believe I have ever seen him or heard him ask about any woman before." He looked out the window.

"Perhaps someone broke his heart?" I wondered.

"Not that I'm aware of. He just has a problem with his time, never has any, like myself." William looked down at his boot again with a sad and longing gaze.

"Well, take me for example, I have all the time in the world and wish not to have any at all. I only wished I knew what I was going to do. But for now, I am going to take Hannah's advice and stay at the hotel another week to see if I can figure all of it out."

"Then if that is so, perhaps we can dine together so both of us will enjoy our stay." He smiled hopeful.

"Perhaps..." I looked out the window seeing the river ahead. We sat in silence but I could sense William's eyes on me.

When the carriage stopped, the coachman opened the door. William stepped out and offered his hand for me to take.

As I put my hand in his, his thumb ran across the back of my hand causing a surge of warmth to run down my spine. My first thought was, that shouldn't be happening! He smiled warmly as I stepped out. Maybe he didn't realize he had even done that.

"There we go." He kept a hold of my hand and wrapped it around his arm covering it with his other hand.

"This is one of my favorite places." He smiled, leading me to the bank of the river.

"I know this place." I looked at the large rock and smiled remembering Robert. The funny thing about this memory was it didn't bother me as much as I thought it could.

"You do?" He looked at me in a funny way.

"Yes, that's the rock Robert took me to. That very rock is where he first kissed me." I sighed and softly laughed.

"What's so funny?" He rubbed the back of my hand.

"Robert was so nervous and I remember seeing his lips twitch and his hands were shaking." I shook my head softly laughing.

"Well, I don't blame him! For a lady such as yourself! Why, any man would have cause to tremble."

"Oh stop! You men are always using such flattery!" I laughed and swatted his arm.

When we reached the rock, I sat down and put my face in the sun and wind breathing in deeply.

"Rebecca, you are quite lovely and I would be tempted to try to charm kiss from you, but I know how you feel." He smiled softly, and I could tell he was deep in thought. I smiled at him thinking he was truly a gentleman.

His hair shined in the sun and the wind tugged some of it out of his leather tie. I took a deep breath and gazed at the river as a barge floated down on the current.

"Thank you for being honest, William." I felt he did understand.

He squatted down on his haunches and took a blade of grass and placed it between his teeth. He looked up into my eyes with a serious look across his face.

"Rebecca, please be careful." His hair blew across his face.

"Of what?" I looked down at him with concern.

"Of...men... Lord McCray, Lord Baptiest... and myself." He sat down on the grass. Why should I be careful of him?

"Not to worry about me, William, I'll be careful, but what do you mean?"

"Well, my lady, though you are in mourning for Robert, I would not be surprised if someone tries to win your affections." He slightly smiled.

"But why should I be careful of you?" I started to reach out to brush his hair back from his face and stopped myself.

"Please... don't ask that." He laid back with his eyes closed and his hands clasped behind his head.

"William, that is not an answer." Though I had a feeling of what he meant.

"Rebecca, I don't want to frighten you away." He looked down as my stomach fluttered.

I gazed down at him in the sun. He was so muscular with his chest rising up in a great breath. Then he sat up.

"Frighten me, William? I... I don't understand." I saw him searching my face.

"I'm saying that we men find you... desirable." His words shot through me like lightening. I found that I was holding my breath. Oh no, maybe all this was a very bad idea!

"William... I..." He took my hand and smiled.

"Rebecca, as I've stated, I would never do anything that I know would upset you in the least." He smiled softly, searching my eyes.

"Thank you again for being honest." So, he too found me desirable?

"Though, I will admit I may still try to charm you out of a kiss...one day." He laughed and fluttered his brows up and down teasing me. His actions were charming without him even trying!

We sat quietly for a moment and I glanced at him as the wind blew a hint of his cologne in my direction. He truly did smell wonderful. He then stood offering his arm and we walked in silence enjoying the cool breeze and the sound of the river.

"This is such a nice place." I felt so relaxed and much better than I'd felt in months.

"There is no place I'd rather be." He let go of my hand and bent over and plucked a wild daisy, handing it to me.

"Me either." I smiled up at him nodding.

I felt his hand touch mine and then without a thought, my hand entwined with his as if it was natural. I looked up at him and he winked. We both liked this very much.

In silence we walked just holding hands and I recalled seeing him the first time on the horse. He looked so warm and friendly then. I was feeling guilty of how William was making me feel and the thoughts that were swirling through my head, but William was truly a very sweet and a truly charming man.

As I stole another glance, I noticed how strong his features looked with dark sideburns that lead to a square jaw that pulsed with muscles when he was in thought. His dark brow furrowed above dark eyelashes that curled up on the edges, yet, he had the look of a warrior. His hair in the front was almost all out of the leather tie and I held back the urge to touch the light golden brown strands that fell forward. God in Heaven! What was I thinking? Robert!

I was not ready for anyone, yet I had to be honest! I found myself unable to look away from William. Why? I had to stop thinking like this! It wasn't right! I gathered my reserve and stopped, taking a deep breath.

"My goodness! We've walked to southern territory!" I laughed, feeling my cheek warm from my thoughts.

"Yes, we better head back." He stood in front of me staring down into my eyes. I turned to walk back feeling him squeezing my hand. He stood still looking down at me.

"Rebecca…" He licked his lips as my eyes went to them.

"William…I…" I could hardly breathe.

"I know." He caught his bottom lip under his top teeth and held it just staring down at me. Good heavens! He reached up with his hand and tucked my hair behind my ear.

"We better go." His words were at a whisper. I could not look away from his eyes.

"Yes, we… best." I let out a breath I didn't realize I was holding.

William held my hand as we walked silently toward the waiting carriage. I was enjoying this feeling of being with someone I trusted. I knew William was a man of his word. I heard him take a deep breath and let it out.

"Rebecca? How long will you mourn?" His tone and look was serious.

"I don't know… however long it takes. I may never get over Robert. Then again, a knight in shining armor might ride along!" I laughed but somehow, I knew that if anyone could help me get over Robert, it could be the man right beside me.

"I have to leave in a week." He looked down at the ground in front of him.

"I know." I could hear the sadness in his tone.

"Would you mind if… I came back to visit you?" He stopped and took my other hand.

"William…" I started to again remind him.

"I mean…as friends." He seemed nervous.

"Friends...friends? Yes, I think that would be lovely." I searched his eyes seeing more behind his question. I could have refused, but I don't know why I hadn't.

"Good!" He smiled and we continued to walk back to the carriage.

"Yes, good..." Robert would like William, he would indeed.

"Here we go." He helped me into the carriage and sat across from me, his eyes never leaving mine. There was something about him that I was very drawn to, but what? He wasn't like the others, having a different way about him.

"I want to thank you, William, I needed this!" I smiled straightening my skirts.

"I did as well. Is there anything else you would like to do?" He smiled warmly.

"I best get to mother's. She'll send the troops out after me if I don't show up soon." I laughed.

"You're probably too late!" His rich deep laughter filled the carriage as it lunged forward.

When we reached the Tea Shop, William assisted me out of the carriage. I felt a bit guilty about disappearing, but I didn't regret it. We walked into the shop and saw mother sitting with Aunt Marie. William placed his hand on the small of my back.

"Good afternoon, Rebecca." Her tone was musical and she was glowing with a smile intently focused on William and, of course, obviously well pleased. She didn't even spare me a glance!

"William, this is my Mother, Martha Glenn and my Aunt Marie, this is Lord William Andrews."

He took mother's hand, bowing over it looking into her eyes. She actually blushed!

"My goodness!" She smiled blushing.

"It is my extreme pleasure to meet the Mother of such a lovely woman as your Rebecca." Then he took Aunt Marie's hand and bowed over it. I was amazed how his charm made them gush like school girls!

"Come, you two, have a cup of tea. I will be back in a moment." She smiled, backing into the door. William held my chair out for me and then sat himself smiling at Aunt Marie.

"Tell me, Lord Andrews, are you here long? I've never seen you here before." She sipped her tea.

"I shall stay a week and then I have to return to Lawrenceburg." I saw his smile fade.

66

"Oh, that is a shame to be certain." Aunt Marie frowned glancing at me.

"Oh, not to worry, I do plan on returning for a visit as soon as I can." He smiled at her then at me.

"That is well. I think Rebecca could use a friend...you know what I mean." She nervously laughed.

"We are just friends." I smiled at my 'concerned' Aunt.

"It's so good to see her smile and back home where she belongs. You know her mother and I were so worried about her." Aunt Marie smiled sweetly at William.

"Not to worry, Aunt Marie, I'm back and soon I will decide what I want to do." I sighed deeply.

William's knee touched my knee causing my stomach to flutter! I glanced at him, seeing his eyes blink and a warm smile creep across his lips. I found myself staring at his breathtaking smile, white teeth and a dimple! I tore my eyes away from him as his smile widened, realizing he knew I was staring....again! I looked at Aunt Marie and she fanned her face, approving of William. I shot her a warning glance.

"Here we go." Mother poured us a cup of tea and sat sweet rolls on the table.

"So, Lord Andrews, are you here long?" He had just answered the same question Aunt Marie asked!

"I was telling Lady Marie that I had to leave in a week for Lawrenceburg."

"Oh, that is sad! Our Rebecca could use a nice friend such as you." I looked at William and we both almost laughed.

"I was telling Lady Marie I planned on a visit as soon as I could." He smiled and winked at Aunt Marie. She was blushing as well.

"Are you on holiday?" Mother sipped her tea glancing at me.

"Yes, for a week... as well as several of the Council." He sipped the tea and relaxed sitting back in his chair with one shoulder slanting down.

"Then you must come to dinner on Saturday night. There will be dancing." Her eyebrows went up and down at him.

"We invited all of them to attend mother, so don't worry, you will have more than enough coming."

"My dear, it sounds like you are not looking forward to it." She took my hand and patted it.

"I am, Mother, it's just..." I looked down into my cup.

"I know what you're thinking about." She smiled and her eyes went to William.

"I shall see that she dances all night." He smiled at me and laughed softly. He knew what mother was getting at.

"Good! We have everything planned already." Mother nodded with certainty.

"You do?" I was in shock.

"Yes, I have hired everyone and just finished the last details." She sat back pleased with herself.

"But I thought you wanted me to help."

"No, Rebecca, I want you to relax." She looked back at William and he winked as if they were speaking without words.

"Have you had your things sent to the house yet?" She sipped her tea looking over her cup at me.

"No, Mother, I plan on staying at the hotel for another week and I don't want to hear any argument over it. I have made up my mind." I nodded, quietly thanking my new friend Hannah.

"That is alright by me." Her reply caught me off guard as I was preparing for battle.

"And where might you be staying Lord Andrews?" So that's why she did not give any argument.

"I…a…at the hotel." His cheeks warmed slightly and her question had caught him off guard, as well.

"Good! Then I know you'll see to her protection and let nothing happen to my girl." She was pleased, well pleased! Too pleased!

"That I will Lady Martha… that I will." He smiled warmly but had a glint of sympathy in his eyes. He sipped his tea.

"Mother, what time is the dinner party?" I changed the subject as fast as I could.

"I thought everyone should try to arrive by six." She smiled.

"If there is anything you need, I am at your service, Lady Martha." William smiled.

"Thank you, Lord Andrews, but taking care of Rebecca will be enough for you." She laughed.

"Oh, Mother!" I laughed even though I could not get any more embarrassed than I already was.

"I need to go to the stable to see about my wagon." If changing the subject didn't work, going to the stables would!

"Shall I walk with you?" William smiled warmly at me.

"Yes, that would be fine." I stood and William offered his arm.

"Ladies, it was a pleasure to meet you and I will see you soon. Thank you for the lovely tea." He smiled and bowed slightly at them both.

"Come to dinner tonight, if you'd like, and you too, Lord Andrews, we're having chicken!" She called after us as we walked out the door.

"Please ladies, call me Will or William and thank you. I would love to join you." Glancing with a smile on his face, I rolled my eyes shaking my head.

"Don't worry about what they said. I was on to them." William patted my hand.

"I'm sorry about those two…" I shook my head in disbelief, though it wasn't beyond them to be this way.

"Though I must admit, I do like the idea of being the one to watch over you." He laughed softly.

"You know… to be honest, I do as well." I leaned into his arm and laughed.

"Well, that is a good thing, for since the moment we met, it seems like that is exactly what I have been doing." He laughed softly.

As we walked to the stable to see about my wagon, I thought, he has been watching over me since we met and it was the truth! How odd!

"Why hello, Mrs. Grayson… your wagon is ready for you. I had to replace the entire axle, it was split. I don't know how you made it all that way." He shook his head.

"How much do I owe you?" I smiled at him.

"Lord…"

"Mr. Thomas, how much do I owe you?" I was instantly getting angry.

"Follow me, then." I watched William as he looked over the wagon while waiting for the bill. Mr. Thomas nodded as he handed it to me.

"Mr. Thomas, this couldn't be right?" It wasn't half of what I thought it was.

"The axle was twenty-five and the wheel was fifteen." I looked at him searching his face.

"Now, Mr. Thomas, it was more than this, I know it." I stood firmly with my arms crossed, knowing that it was more.

"Alright….alright! It was seventy-five and no more." He huffed. Oh! Lord McCray would hear about this!

"Now, here you are, Mr. Thomas, and make no mistake, no one takes care of my bills ever again! Do I make myself clear?" I raised my brow with certainty.

"Yes, Ma'am." He laughed shaking his head.

"Alright then, we're even." I nodded feeling I had won this battle!

As I walked out, I found William talking to Lord McCray.

"Why hello, Mrs. Grayson." He was all smiles.

I stepped right up to him and pointed my finger at that proud chest.

"Don't you hello me! I'm about tired of your trying to help me, Lord McCray!" I looked at William and his eyes went wide.

"But…" He sucked in air.

"If you'll excuse me, I must go to the hotel and ready myself for dinner." I took William's arm and turned to get up into the wagon.

"Mrs. Grayson. I didn't do anything…Cole…"

"It isn't my brothers concern either!" William helped me into the wagon. I glanced at Lord McCray and his eyes were angry and narrowed.

"Shall we?" I smiled at William.

"We shall." He clicked his tongue leaving Lord McCray standing by the stable. After we were out of earshot, I looked up at William seeing him in deep thought.

"William, I'm sorry about that, but Lord McCray had tried to pay for the work on the wagon and now my brother. I do not need any help from either of them!" I was so mad and embarrassed.

"Rebecca, are you… employing me to get to Lord McCray?" His brow furrowed tightly.

"Employing?" I gasped at the very thought!

"Yes, employing." He furrowed his handsome brow.

"No! How can you... NO! Why, you could have been my brother Mike and I would have done the same thing." Employing? Good heavens!

"Good, I do not like to play games with my brothers."

"Brothers?" I looked up at him. Surly Lord McCray was not his brother?

"My brother corpsmen…"

"Oh, I see! No, William, I was not employing you to get to him. He is just so assuming!" Though, I too, was assuming myself as well.

"Good, I like you too much already to have that happen!" He smiled softly.

"I would never do that to anyone, I do hope you don't think of me that way?" I shook my head at the thought.

"No, I don't, but I had to be sure of your intent. Thank you, Rebecca, that's all I needed to hear." He covered my hand.

"Well, you already know my intent... I don't have any!" I laughed as William nodded, laughing as well. I just couldn't be angry with him over the question. Normally a question like that would have angered me instantly. William's honesty was a rare thing and I knew he was protecting himself as I would do.

"Would you care to go to dinner at mothers?" I thought that would make up for his taking time with me today.

"I would be honored." He slightly smiled.

When the wagon came to a stop at the hotel, William looked around. He nodded to a boy motioning him to come.

"Yes, Milord?" The poor little filthy boy smiled.

"Would you like to take care of the horse and wagon for a little bit? I'll make it worth your while." He winked as the boy nodded eagerly.

"Yes, Milord… right away!" The boy started to lead the horse and wagon to the other side of the street when William stopped the boy.

"Oh yes, and would you go to the stables and get my horse for me in two hours. Tell Mr. Thomas that I sent you, Lord Andrews. My horse's name is Diablo. Mr. Thomas will then believe you." William looked down at the scruffy boy.

"Yes, Milord I will!" The boy squared his chin bravely.

"Now, let's go in and I'll see you to your room." He held his arm out for me to take. I was amazed William would trust a boy with the wagon.

We walked through the hotel receiving many stares along the way and as we reached my room he said, "I shall return, let's say, at four?"

"Yes… that... would be fine…" His eyes held mine.

"Two hours, then." He kissed my hand, his lips slightly touching my skin.

I turned to put the key in the door and looked to see if he was still looking at me. As he turned to go up to the third floor he stopped. I nodded and went into my room looking so forward to his return. He still watched over me, even when I went into my room! A true gentleman he is!

What is wrong with me? I was enamored with William? I shouldn't be! Suddenly the feeling of not being true to Robert washed over me!

Oh, Rebecca! It was a harmless ride to the river and to your mother's shop. You've done nothing to be ashamed of. And I hadn't! Even so, my thoughts would have loved to betray me. William was very much the gentleman. Robert would have liked him.

I went to the washroom and started the water. As the tub filled, I went to the wardrobe looking at those dreadful dark dresses and then glanced at my dark blue dress. I was so tired of the dark colors. Maybe I will stop wearing such dark clothes and I can still mourn for Robert but with not such a drab appearance?

I weighed all the reasons and couldn't find one to wear them, besides what others would think. It had been six months... hmmm.

I might wear a new dress at the dinner. I would love to wear a yellow one or light blue one. I smiled at myself thinking what Robert would say. I know he liked the pastel colors on me saying it went with my auburn hair and hazel eyes. I think he wouldn't mind if I made the day of changing dress at the six month mark. I undressed and slid into the warm bath feeling no guilt at the decision I had made.

Soon, I was dried and chose the medium blue instead of the lighter blue dress thinking I'd come out of mourning a little at a time and then sat at the vanity looking in the mirror at myself. I thought I would ask William to stop by Hannah's so I could see if she had anything already made up and tell her to change them to a medium color. I felt good about making my own decision for the first time. I brushed my hair out and left it to air dry. I powdered my nose and dabbed a little perfume on, pleased at my reflection. I still felt good about not wearing those dark dresses knowing Robert would not approve of me wearing them.

I gathered my hair from the front and put a clip in the back leaving it hang in the back. I always liked it this way the best. A soft tap at the door interrupted my thoughts.

I opened the door and saw William's face go from a smile to less of a smile. Oh no! He doesn't approve!

His cologne floated through the air as if it could hypnotize my senses. His smile grew as he took me in. He said not a word.

"You look very handsome tonight..." My cheeks warmed as I felt I had to break this awkward moment of silence.

He was dressed in a dark slate gray suit that was tailored snugly. The coat was trimmed in black and the pants had a black seam down the sides. He was freshly shaved with his shiny hair pulled back with not a one out of place.

"Tis' I... that is blessed to have such a lovely escort for dinner." His eyes twinkled. He was pleased!

"William..." I rolled my eyes at him.

"Rebecca, your hair is beautiful and your dress…" He reached out to touch the lace on my neckline but stopped.

"Thank you, William. I get tired of it being up in a tight bun all the time and my dress and well...I'm slowly coming out of mourning…" I smiled, turning to grab my shawl and hand bag.

"That's a perfect idea, Rebecca. I wasn't too early, was I?" He stood in the doorway almost filling it.

"No, I was finished and I feel wonderful tonight and thank you! I think the little trip to the river cleared my mind." He took the shawl and laid it over my shoulders slowly. His fingers touched my neck, causing my breath to catch.

"Your perfume is... wonderful." His hands rested on my shoulders. I closed my eyes trying hard not to feel what his touch had just done.

"Thank you…again." I took his arm and a deep breath as he shut the door.

"Ready, my lady?" His eyes glowed with a look of being well pleased. He said my lady…not milady?

"That I am, but if Hannah's is still open, would you mind stopping for a minute?"

"No, not at all…" His hand covered mine as we walked down the stairs and out to the wagon and there was the little boy with William's horse! I was amazed!

"Well, I watched the wagon and got that devil of a horse for you. He's a wild one, ain't he?" His brave little dirty face was adorable!

"Yes, he is and you have done good work, young man. And for your troubles you have earned this." William gave him an entire ten dollars. The boys eyes lit up and he looked at it in shock.

"If you ever need anything…" He could hardly speak.

"Alright son…I'll ask for the man I trust and know can do the job." He nodded with a laugh.

"Joey McKinney is the name." He proudly spoke his name as if William was not to forget it.

"Joey, it has been a pleasure to do business with you, Sir." William shook the boy's hand.

"And you, too, Milord." Joey put his hand into his pockets, turned and ran into the alley across the street.

"Poor little guy, I bet he's homeless." I saw something in William's eyes. Such pain and sadness!

"Surly he is not, a boy that cute and sweet?" He helped me up into the wagon by slipping his hands around my waist.

"I believe… he is." He looked down the alley deep in thought as he tied his horse to the wagon.

"We can keep an eye out for him." He was truly concerned about the boy.

William leapt up into the wagon taking the reins in his hands and we were on our way, but he was obviously still deep in thought with his jaw pulsing. I watched him lick his lips and bite it.

"William…Hannah's." He blinked at me and smiled slowing the wagon. Hannah was just closing her shop.

"I'll be one minute…" William was about to get out of the wagon to help me down but I motioned him to stay.

"He's only a friend." Hannah's eyes twinkled as she stood in the door.

"Of course, but my oh my! What a friend indeed!" She whispered and laughed softly.

"Hannah, would you change the colors of the dresses, if it's not too late?"

"Oh, my girl… I already have! Wait till you see!" She laughed.

"How did you know?" I was surprised!

"Well, when you've been around as long as I have, sometimes you just do!" She winked and looked at William.

"I'll see you in the morning." I shook my head.

"Yes, yes." She waved at William and he nodded.

"Thank you!" I walked back to the wagon and climbed in taking Williams hand.

"Is everything alright?" William clicked his tongue.

"Yes, wonderful." I smiled excited about my decision.

"I'm pretty hungry and hope your mother cooks a lot of chicken, it's one of my favorites." He laughed.

"I'm sure she did, and probably enough for an army!" I could smell his cologne drift by on the breeze. Heavens! He smelled wonderful.

"It's a lovely evening." William glanced at me. The sun was starting to set in the sky.

"Yes, and it feels heavenly out." I glanced at William, seeing he was still deep in thought.

What could he be thinking? Was he thinking about Joey? His brow was furrowed deeply, but I didn't know if I should ask him what was bothering him. He looked almost angry.

74

"I do hope you'll save a dance or two for me at the dinner party. I'm sure you'll not be sitting very much Saturday night." He took a deep breath. Was that what he was thinking about?

"I'm sure there will be plenty of room on my dance card." I laughed.

"I seriously doubt that." He furrowed his brow again.

"I hope you will save me a dance or two as well! I know when the ladies see you that you'll be swarmed with all the dances you could ever wish for. You might even meet one that you would take to the river and charm." He looked at me with surprise on his face. His blue green eyes went wide and his mouth opened slightly.

"What did you say?" His voice was hoarse.

"You heard me, Lord Andrews." I laughed and then looked into his eyes, but he was not laughing.

"I think they will be quite disappointed. I think..." He paused.

"Think what?" I glanced up in his handsome face smiling.

"I think it will be a wonderful night." He looked straight ahead.

"That is not what you were going to say." I nudged his elbow.

"I was going to say your mother had appointed me to guard her daughter which is such a ghastly and insufferable job. I'm not sure if I'll be able to accomplish that mission or not." He laughed and I rolled my eyes laughing with him.

"Honestly... William!" I rolled my eyes.

His laughter rumbled through my body like thunder...My heavens! I had not been so drawn to a man like William since Robert. This was truly a strange feeling as I had always loved Robert, no other. The possibility of actually caring and loving another man was unimaginable. Yet, as I looked up at him and studied his face, he made me feel things that I thought I'd never feel for any other man. I had to keep myself and my emotions in check. William... was a real threat! I knew it and felt it! Good heavens!

"Are you pleased?" My breath caught as I saw a slight grin slide across his lips. He knew I was staring again!

"I was just... lost in thought..." Thinking that I need to control myself!

"I hope it was a good thought." He smiled, biting his lip again. I wish he wouldn't do that!

"Really, I was wondering what you did for the Guards." Lord, forgive me!

"Really?" He smirked as if he knew that was not what I was thinking.

"Yes, and where you are going to go after Lawrenceburg."

"Really?" He softly laughed at me as if he knew that wasn't what I was thinking at all!

"Yes...really!" I shuttered a breath to calm myself down.

"Well, I have to be in Lawrenceburg for about a week or so, then honestly, I don't know." He frowned slightly, glancing at me.

"Oh..." I sighed then realized that had come out a little too revealing!

"I'm glad to see that my departing disturbs you." He smiled, still looking forward.

"Well... I... I enjoy your company." And I truly did! That wasn't a lie!

"And I do yours as well." His tone was lower than usual.

We finally came to mothers and Jack barked and jumped for joy at the sight of us.

"Jack... here, boy!" He jumped into the wagon and up to the seat licking my face so happy to see me.

"Jack, this is Lord William Andrews, but you can call him William." I rubbed Jack's neck and kissed the top of his head.

"Well, hello, Jack..." William patted his head as Jack licked his hand and gave William his paw.

"Well that was strange!" I looked at William then Jack.

"What?" He laughed as Jack licked him again.

"Jack rarely warms up this fast to anyone!" Maybe he was just excited?

"Animals like me, always have and I love dogs." William jumped out of the wagon with Jack following him.

I held my hand out for him to take but, instead, he took me by the waist looking in my eyes as he lifted me out of the wagon. My hands slowly slid down his chest and his eyes never wavered. My stomach fluttered and my heart pounded as I looked into them and they seemed light green now. I tore my eyes away, hearing Cole call out.

"Rebecca!" Cole approached the wagon with Mike in tow.

"Will, thanks for coming." Cole shook his hand as he smiled at him.

"William, this is my other brother Mike, Mike this is William." I smiled.

"Mike." He shook Mike's hand.

"William." Mike nodded shaking his hand.

William was about a head taller than Mike. Cole was almost as tall as William but not quite. My brothers were freshly shaven and dressed in suits and both looked very handsome. Cole and William took care of the wagon and horses. I smiled up at Mike, taking the arm he offered.

"Mother says you're staying at the hotel another week." Mike frowned, not liking that!

"I need time, Mike." I watched the steps as we went up them.

"I know Sis, but I was hoping that you would stay here with us." He sighed.

"It's just a week. I'll see you every day, please be patient with me." I rubbed his arm.

"I'm just glad you're home." He smiled finally.

"Me too, Mike, me too!" He opened the door and we went inside. Mike took my shawl and hung it on the coat rack.

"I can't believe all the work you've done on the house. It's lovely!" Mike showed me the sitting room on the way to the dining room. The walls had been freshly painted in a soft yellow with white trim. New curtains with soft golden flowers with light green leaves and a lighter yellow background had been hung and mother had also gotten a new settee and chairs.

The dining room was redone as well in rich, deep colors of gold, green and yellows with lighter hints of each color. The walls were a golden color but not too dark. It was warm and welcoming. Her new chandelier cast sparkles of color all over the room. I was pleased with all the renovations that they had made. Cole and William came in.

"Cole... it's beautiful!" I smiled, hugging him as he wrapped his arms around me kissing my forehead.

"Mike and I worked long late hours to do all this. We had a decorator from Wellington come to consult with mother about the colors and had the curtains made. It was for her birthday." He smiled.

"Well, it's lovely!" I looked at William as he nodded.

"I think I'll check on mother now."

I found her very busy cooking and asked, "Mother, do you need help?" She turned and smiled.

"You're here! Did you bring that fine young man with you?" She glanced at me.

"Yes, Mother, William is here as well. He said chicken was his favorite." I put on an apron and started to mash the potatoes.

"Now you shouldn't be doing that!" She scolded.

"Mother, I want to help." I laughed shaking my head.

"All I have left are the rolls in the oven and this whipped topping." She smiled as I smelled chocolate pie!

"Chocolate pie?" I could only hope!

"What else is there?" She laughed as I finished up the potatoes and she the topping.

She placed the rolls in the basket, got out the serving tray and placed the chicken, mashed potatoes and the gravy on it and I carried it to the dining room. The men were having brandies and turned as I entered with the food, placing it all on the table. I gave them a warning glance to not touch a thing as I went back in the kitchen for more. Mother had also made corn on the cob and green beans.

"It smells wonderful!" William smelled the air.

"I wish I could take the credit!" I laughed, as mother walked in with the butter and a pitcher of tea.

"Well, sit, sit!" She laughed.

"William, I'm glad you came tonight. Please, make yourself at home." He walked to her taking her hand and bowed over it. His smile made her blush again!

"It is the hostess that makes a house feel like a home, Milady." He smiled and held her chair as she sat. Mike held mine and sat next to me. William sat properly across from me. Cole sat at the head of the table and without a word, Cole bowed his head and we all took hands for the blessing.

"Lord, thank you for this bounty you have provided for us and bless mother's hands for preparing it. Lord, we thank you for our sister's safe return home and hope that she finds happiness once again. We thank you for all you have given us and will... Amen...

"Amen." We all chimed.

"Well, let's eat before it gets cold!" Mother smiled at William and then me. She passed the chicken to William. I took my napkin and placed it in my lap. We all filled our plates and I bit into the chicken.

"Mother, this is wonderful!" I closed my eyes. She made the best chicken I have ever had.

"I've gone to heaven!" William closed his eyes as well. Mike and Cole moaned, tasting her chicken.

"Well, thank you all." Mother blushed.

"So, William... What do you do in the Guards, if I might ask?" Cole asked William with only a glance.

"I'm afraid that is classified and I cannot divulge that information." He gave Cole a strange look.

"Oh my! Is it a dangerous position?" Mother looked at him and then me with concern in her eyes.

"Yes, it can be as with all the ranks of the Special Forces."

"Can you tell us your rank?" Mike looked up at William and narrowed his eyes. He was very suspicious.

"I am... a Colonel." He looked down into his plate and took a roll tearing it in two. Cole stopped his fork in midair.

"You're too young to be a Colonel!" Cole narrowed his eyes at William too. Oh no!

"I am older than I look." William was still looking down.

"Why, William, you don't look any older than our Rebecca!" Mother was just stunned as I was! At this point everyone stopped eating.

"I am older than... Lord McCray." He smiled at everyone and then took his brandy swirling it deep in thought. William is older than Lord McCray?

"Now you have my curiosity on the run. Just how old are you, William?" Cole put his fork down, picking up his brandy as well. Oh heavens... the inquisition is about to begin! Lord, help William!

"I am thirty-seven." William took a sip of his brandy then looked at me searching my eyes.

"I would have lost the farm if I was a betting man." Cole laughed. William's eyes stared deeper into mine and I back into his.

"Have you any land or home?" Mother's question was so personal...Perhaps too personal.

"Yes, I own a home, though I don't see it very much, which I hope to change in the near future."

"And where is that?" Mike sat back as stunned as all of us.

"In Winchester. Actually, it's outside of Winchester." His answers we getting shorter.

"I think you have interrogated the poor man enough!" I smiled nervously, feeling as if he was under scrutiny now! Thirty-seven?

"Rebecca, it's alright. I'm used to the way people react when finding out my age and rank."

"I thought Colonels were older, and Lords, for that matter?" Cole asked.

"I started out very young and worked my way up to my rank in time."

"Well, how interesting! How old were you when you enlisted?" Mother was still full of questions. I felt sorry for William now.

"I was young." He didn't want to answer that question. I wonder why?

"Mother..." I gave her a warning glance.

"Let's finish dinner. I have made a surprise for you." She smiled and winked at me knowing I knew what it was.

"William? One last question, if I may?" Mike put his fork down and held my breath. I just knew Mike was being too quiet too long.

"Yes, Mike?" William put his brandy down as if he knew Mike's question would be most serious.

"What are your intentions towards my sister?" I gasped at his question.

"Excuse me?" William appeared just as shocked as I was.

I glanced at William and William's eyes held a hint of amusement! He thought it funny? Heavens!

"Michael, please! I hardly think…" William cut me off with the raise of his hand.

"No… I want to answer, Mike." William wiped his mouth and laid his napkin down resting his forearms on the table edge, then clasped his hands together.

The look he gave Mike was intent, one I've not seen before. Mike looked back at William as if William's answer would be the defining decision.

"Look, I can see his interest all over his face and we hardly know him. Beck doesn't need any more hurt in her life." Mike looked at Cole and mother, then back to William. I know Mike was only looking out for my best interests, but this was too much!

"William, you don't have to answer that." Mother laid her hand on William's forearm.

"It's quite alright. I'd like to answer his question. It's a loving question and I respect Mike for caring enough for Rebecca to ask it." He took a deep breath in letting it out.

"Well… then answer it." Mike was not being very friendly at all!

"First of all, I'd like to say that I think Rebecca is a wonderfully intelligent person. Secondly, I would never disrespect Rebecca in any way. After all, she still is in mourning. And thirdly, yes Mike, yes, I am very fond of her already. I think… if it is alright with you and your family, I would like to be her friend and enjoy her company." His answer made Mike smile and Cole as well.

"A… friend?" Mike laughed softly.

"Yes. I'm aware she is not ready for callers and if she were, she would be the one to tell me herself. But until then, I only wish to be a friend and honor that." He smiled at Mike and Mike smiled at me.

"Perfect!" Mike laughed with relief while I, on the other hand, was embarrassed completely!

"Rebecca, now don't be hard on your brother. He only loves you and doesn't want to see you hurt." I could see his age and wisdom now. Why hadn't I seen this until now?

"I... I don't even know what to say." His answer was absolutely perfect, I sighed.

"I think a friend like you is exactly what she needs." Mother smiled.

"Are you sure you only want to be her friend?" Mike asked again.

"Mike! That will be enough!" I stood and walked into the kitchen.

I couldn't bear them interrogating William like that! Did they think that I couldn't take care of myself? What did I do before? I did fine without their help!

"Beck..." Mike followed me.

"Oh, go away... you've done all you could ever do to humiliate me." Tears welled in my eyes.

"Beck, I'm sorry, but I saw the look in his eyes. He has feelings for you and I don't want him to rush you into anything. You've been without a man..."

"I will not stand here and listen to you or Cole tell me something I am all too aware of... Now please in the name of God... stop this!" I pleaded as I ran out the back door, down the steps and around to the barn. I needed to get away from that. Jack came running.

"Jack..." I patted his head and hugged him close with tears unceasingly falling.

"Rebecca?" A soft rich deep voice called my name.

"Rebecca? Ah, there you are." William stood with his hands behind his back.

"I'm sorry, William...my brothers can be..." I couldn't even look at him!

"What? Loving... caring... concerned?" He walked over and squatted on his haunches and Jack went right to him. I couldn't figure out Jack liking him that fast and so much!

"They would like to run my life and..."

"Rebecca... it's alright." He laid his hand on my shoulder and tilted my face to his.

"No, it's not. What I do know is that I'm glad I'm staying in the hotel for another week. I need time to adjust to... them!" I looked at William and he tried not to laugh, but I couldn't hold back and we both fell out in laughter.

"What I said was true. I am very fond of you already, but I..." He looked down and furrowed his brow.

"But what?" I looked up at him.

"I can't wait to charm a kiss from you." He stood and held his arm for me to take.

I laughed as I took his arm but he was not laughing. He stopped and raised his hand to my face and wiped my tears away with his thumb. His gaze was deep and my heart thundered in my chest.

"I would never hurt you, Rebecca." His tone was soft and deep as he took a deep breath, staring into my eyes.

"I know you wouldn't." Somehow, I did know that.

"Good, then we agree on that. I think I better get you back into the house." He smiled softly.

I licked my lips that had suddenly become dry. His eyes dropped to them and he took another deep breath as we turned and walked back to the house and into the dining room. Mike and Cole were drinking brandy and mother was waiting at the table for me.

"Beck, William...we're sorry and please forgive us. We love Beck..."

"Not another word. If I had a sister, I would do the same." He smiled and started to clear the table.

"Stop that right now!" Mother swatted William's hands.

"But I wish to help." He insisted and took all the plates into the kitchen while mother and I carried the rest in. I started the water and washing. Why does William affect me so much? There's a saying about widows but as for me, it's not true. William's not like those that just come along. No... he's different and, I believe, special.

"A kiss for your thoughts." William had the dishes I had washed already dried.

"What? I'm sorry... What are you doing?" I looked at him holding a towel.

"Drying dishes!" He laughed.

"You... you don't have to do that!" He was a guest, not to mention a Lord and a Colonel!

"I wish to help." He smiled down at me.

"Ah... I know why! You fear my brothers!" I laughed rinsing another sink full.

"No, I just want to help. There isn't much I'm afraid of." He laughed.

"Really?" I smiled.

"Really... but there is one thing I do fear." He pursed his lips looking at me.

"And what could you possibly fear?"

"I don't do well with rejection." He looked at me in a devilish sort of way.

"Well, I don't do well with that either!" I laughed at him.

"There's another thing we have in common then." He laughed.

"I suppose so!" I had rinsed off the last of the dishes and took some small pie plates out.

"Would you take these to the sitting room?" I was nervous at the thought of asking him.

"Of course..." His hands covered mine, making my eyes go right to his. Heavens! Why must he look at me that way!

"I'll...be right in." I turned quickly away from him and heard the door swish shut.

"Men!" I laughed.

Who would have guessed he was thirty-seven! Somehow knowing he was older made my cheeks warm. I was just being silly about the entire thing. I took the pie out of the oven and then into the sitting room.

"Is that chocolate pie?" William smiled.

"Yes." I smiled at mother.

"It's been years since I have had a homemade chocolate pie! I think I have fallen in love with your mother!" He smiled wickedly at her fluttering his brows up and down causing mother to blush again!

"Rebecca can make the very same dinner and has." Mother smiled and I gave her a warning glance.

"She cooks as well?" William asked as mother cut him a big piece.

"Oh yes, and sews and sings." Mother bragged.

"She sings?" William glanced at me with surprise.

"Like an angel!" Cole smiled.

"I haven't sung in years." I blushed.

"She used to sing at church." Mike nodded, taking the plate from me.

"I would love to hear you one day, Rebecca. You surprise me more and more." William laughed, shaking his head as he took his first bite of pie. He closed his eyes with deep pleasure.

"Good?" I laughed.

"Now I know... I am in love with your mother." We laughed at his face.

"Like I said, Rebecca makes a better pie than I do." Mother smiled with a wink.

"I shall take note to that!" He grinned as he took another bite.

You'd think he'd never tasted chocolate pie before! I watched him eat as he chewed his food slowly, enjoying every morsel as his jaw muscles flexed with every bite. His lips softly closed around the fork…heavens! What was I doing? Watching him eat! I looked up into his eyes and he was slightly smiling! I felt my cheeks warm knowing he had caught me staring again!

"Beck, are you sure you want to stay at the hotel for another week?" Cole frowned.

"Yes, I do." I looked at William thinking about what I had said in the barn. I almost laughed out.

Cole frowned and knew by my tone he was not going to change my mind. We enjoyed the rest of the evening without another incident and everyone soon relaxed.

All too soon it was getting late and I covered a yawn, but William noticed it and without a word, William stood offering his arm to me with a nod.

"Mother, thank you for dinner, but I need to get some sleep. Tomorrow will be a busy day." The dinner party was at six. I needed to be at Hannah's in the morning early.

"Yes, and I have a lot to do as well. I shall see you two tomorrow night then." I kissed my brothers and William shook their hands knowing he had done well with them.

"Mrs. Glenn, thank you for the finest evening I have had in years and one I'll not soon forget, nor you and your cooking! You wouldn't be looking for a husband now, would you?" He smiled as she blushed bright red.

"Oh! Heavens no! I've already had one and care not to have another!" She laughed and shooed us out the door giggling. William had her wrapped around his finger.

"Cole, Mike, see you tomorrow night. If you need me for anything I'll be in room four fifteen." They nodded and with that, William took me to the barn.

"I hope you don't mind riding with me on my horse?" He smiled, raising a brow, knowing I had no choice.

"No, I don't mind… but he's huge! What did you say his name was?"

"Diablo." He patted his neck and between his ears giving him a good itching.

"Well... he's big!" I swallowed hard.

I knew Diablo meant 'devil' and he looked the part, very big, sleek and blue black.

"He's as gentle a lamb as long as I am on his back." I didn't question him at all.

"Diablo... trecho." Diablo stretched his legs out to lower himself.

"Diablo... arco." Diablo put his head down between his legs and brought it back up.

"Diablo...quedarse quieto." Diablo did not move a muscle!

"Ready?" William put his hands around my waist. My legs weakened with his touch and I placed my hands on his shoulders.

His eyes deeply searched mine as he sat me upon the back of Diablo.

"Are you sure you want to ride? We could take your wagon."

"I'll ride with you as long as you are sure about me riding with you." His hands still held on to my waist.

"I am... Diablo...quedarse quieto." He took the horn and with one single movement swung up on Diablo's back and was behind me. His thighs touched mine as he moved to get comfortable in the saddle. He wrapped his arm around my waist lifting me as he put my legs over his left leg. I felt his heart in his chest beat against my arm.

This was the closest I had been to any other man except Robert. My stomach fluttered at the thought!

"Diablo... vamos." Diablo walked forward out of the barn. My arms went around his neck as Diablo stirred underneath us.

"Diablo... pórtate bien!" Diablo calmed down right away. I saw Diablo ears go back listening to his deep voice.

"Are you alright?" His lips were so close to my ear, I could feel the warmth of his breath. His cologne was almost too much as I breathed it in. I closed my eyes as Diablo trotted a little slower allowing me to release my arms around his neck. William still held on snugly, but knew I wasn't going to fall.

"Yes, much better. I'm not use to such a big horse." I looked up into his face and he down at mine.

Our lips were only a breath away from each others. I quickly glanced down at my skirt, feeling nervous, hardly being able to breathe... I had to breathe! His natural scent permeated through his cologne the longer I sat on the saddle and his lap. I won't look up at him again. It's too close and it isn't right.

"Diablo is a well trained horse and you are quite safe. You have my word." He tightened his hold around me and his hand on my stomach fanned out covering it all. His thumb went almost to my breastbone!

"Here, you'll be more comfortable if you wrap your arm around my waist." He took my hand and put it behind him. I could feel how muscular his back was. My heavens! The man was like a rock! Diablo jerked again causing my other hand to fly to his chest.

"I'm sorry… it's just that we're so high in the air. Fella isn't this big. Was that Spanish you were speaking to him?" Oh Rebecca! I was rattling nervously on!

"Yes, I trained him so he will only know my commands." I could feel William's chin brush the top of my head and his breath in my hair.

"He's a beautiful animal."

"That he is…" His words faded. I felt him take a deep breath in.

"You smell… wonderful Rebecca… like lily of the valley." He took another deep breath in. My cheeks warmed.

"Thank you…" He smelled so wonderful that it was hard to think. I shook my head.

"What's wrong, Rebecca?" The way he said my name was like music.

"Nothing, I guess I'm a little tired." He rubbed my arm.

"We forgot your shawls… are you cold? The night air is rather cool."

"No, I'm fine." He took his coat off and wrapped it around me, pulling me even closer into his chest. His white shirt felt like the finest silk money could buy, so soft against my skin.

"How's that?" The warmth of his breath caressed my cheek.

"Much better, thank you." But, not really! For now his cologne and natural male scent was overwhelming! My head spun as I tried to compose myself but I couldn't control all the warmth that was running through my body.

"It's a breathtaking night… look at all the stars, Rebecca." He softly spoke.

I slowly looked up to make sure he was too. He was looking way above his head with his head back and his face to the sky. I looked up into the vast darkness of the heavens.

"It's breathtaking…" I was looking away from his face.

"Yes… it is." I knew he was no longer looking up. I looked down at my skirt and saw out of the corner of my eye that he had reached up and was unbuttoning his top buttons and pulled his shirt out of his pants a little.

"Ah... there! That's more comfortable." He was more relaxed. He rested his hand that held the reins on my lap and shifted in the saddle.

"I had a wonderful day, Rebecca. It's been a long time since I have enjoyed myself so much." He tightened his hold.

"It seems as if so much has happened in just one day. I can't imagine that we actually just met this morning." I felt as if I've known him a life time.

"Yes, strangely I have felt the same all evening." His tone sounded different, almost peaceful if I were to guess.

"I could ride all night with you in my arms..." He softly rumbled rubbing my arm.

"It is nice." I yawned, what did he just say? I could see the town lights about a mile away.

"We're almost there." I heard him softly say.

"What?" I looked up at him realizing that I was falling asleep! He wasn't smiling and I watched him close his eyes, breathing in and letting it out.

"I was saying that we are almost there. Shhh, it's alright." He pulled me closer.

"I'm sorry. I think I was drifting off." I covered a yawn.

"I'm glad you feel that comfortable with me, either that or you are quite bored with me." He softly laughed.

"No, I'm not bored with you at all! It was just a full day...a wonderful relaxing day. Well, until my brothers interrogated you...that is." I smiled, feeling more awake.

"It's alright, but I must admit I've never been interrogated by brothers before." He laughed a deep soft rumbling laugh.

"What do you mean?"

"I've never been to a woman's house and met her family. I've always tried to stay away from that quandary all these years. You know... being tied down." He glanced down at me.

"You have never been invited to go to dinner to someone's house you were calling on?" I cleared my voice realizing that he didn't avoid the 'quandary' of coming to my house this time.

"I didn't say that I wasn't invited. I was, many times." He smiled biting his bottom lip. Heavens! I wished he wouldn't do that!

"Why didn't you go and…" My voice gave out on me for I wanted to know why he came to my mother's house and not anyone else's before.

"As I've said, I've tried not to get involved with any one woman. With my work and settling down, it simply was not an option." He sighed deeply.

"I see."

"Do you?" He whispered in a softer voice.

"Yes, or I think I do." Did I?

"Well, my Lady, I believe you should be advised that your invitation is the first that I have accepted." His eyes took in my face.

"Then I owe you a thank you." I smiled up into his handsome face.

"It was an honor and a pleasure."

We rode the rest of the way to town in silence. Resting my head against his chest, I could hear his heart beating a slow relaxing rhythm that made me even sleepier. I had enjoyed his company all day and thought he was the perfect gentleman and guardian for me. To think he was thirty-seven still amazed me and because of that, I was now noticing that he was considerably more mature than I first thought, but why hadn't I seen it before?

"We're here." He whispered.

We rode into the stable and stopped in front of the stall. He swung down and held his hands up to me. He gently put them around my waist and slowly lifted me down to my feet…his eyes never leaving mine. I blinked my sleepy eyes.

"Thank you, William." I could barely breathe.

"You know, I rather like you calling me William. I never much liked that name until I heard you say it." He softly spoke gazing down at me and then turned to Diablo.

"I like William better than Will. Perhaps that is why I thought you were younger than what you were. Will is a little boy's name to me." I laughed as he took the saddle off of Diablo and shut Diablo in the stable.

"You might be right about that theory." He laughed, offering his arm to me.

"Tomorrow night will be fun, don't you think?" I was looking forward to the dinner party suddenly.

"I am looking forward to it." He covered my hand with his.

We walked across the deserted street to the hotel and went inside. The hotel was still full of activity with many people coming and going up and down the stairs.

"Would you care for a cup of tea before retiring?" His smile was hopeful, but I knew if I stayed with him any longer he might just charm that kiss from me, which had almost happened a few times today already.

"Thank you, but I must decline your offer. I have an early appointment in the morning and there will be much to do, but perhaps another night?" I smiled hopeful that he wouldn't be too disappointed.

"You're right, my Lady, would you like me to escort you to your appointment tomorrow?" His brow rose slightly.

"It's at Hannah's, the dress maker." I covered a laugh thinking he was truly adorable.

"That's right. We stopped at the dress shop earlier." A breathtaking smile lit his face as he escorted me up the stairs.

We passed several beautiful women on the way up and he smiled, nodding at them. He looked at a couple of them, taking them in, and surprisingly a feeling of heaviness filled my chest. What was that? Jealously? I wasn't a jealous type and I hardly knew him! Why would I be jealous? We've only just met!

He walked me to my door, number three fifteen. He did say his was four fifteen did he not? If that was so, then he was right above me.

"May I?" He held out his hand for me to give him the key. I smiled softly and handed it to him. He opened the door and swung it open, but did not step into the room.

"William, I had a wonderful day. Thank you." I smiled, holding on to the door handle.

"I did as well and I am looking forward to that dance you are saving for me." He took my hand and raised it to his lips allowing them to linger. My breath was instantly stolen and I laid my other hand on my chest as if it was going to help me to breathe.

"So….am I…" My words were breathless as he held my hand, rubbing his thumb across the back of it. My stomach rolled over fluttering.

"Again, thank you. This day, I shall always remember." He kissed my hand softly again.

"I shall see you tomorrow night then." I smiled into those beautiful blue-green eyes that one could drown in.

"Until tomorrow then…" He bowed and smiled then turned to walk away.

I watched him walk down the long corridor, stopping and turning to look back at me as if he knew I was watching him. He smiled and nodded. Blushing, I backed into my room, amazed that he was such a gentleman and that I actually wanted him to kiss me! I felt my cheeks warm at the thought of his lips touching mine. I wondered if he felt the same thing. Then I realized that I wasn't feeling bad for wanting William to kiss me.

Robert... I'm sorry, but I don't feel sorry. I hope you're not disappointed in me. It just seems like a life time since you've been gone.

I wish I had some kind of sign that would tell me that you approve and that I should go on with my life now. There's something about him that feels right and his kindness and sense of humor remind me so much of you. I took a deep breath, thinking that it was so hard to go on with my life when I didn't know if it's right to do yet. What was my life all about now? I'm glad I decided to stay here for another week.

I undressed and hung my dress up, taking my bed clothes and putting them on while thinking of his handsome face smiling down at me with small strands of hair falling out of his tie flooded my thoughts.

Oh, God, I need a sign. Yes, I wanted him to kiss me and to feel his arms around me. How I missed being just held. The way his eyes looked at me stole my breath! Sometimes they looked blue, and other times green, which was strange, and all I know is I loved how they took me in and then smiled. Heavens!

To think...he's thirty-seven! Thirty-seven! I just can't believe that! He must think me too young. I'm twenty-six and that's an eleven year difference. I think... I can care for someone now and to be honest with myself, I knew already that I did. Oh heart, watch out! I crawled in bed...

~ Chapter 6 ~

The morning came without me remembering my head had even hit the pillow. I stretched yawning and looked at the timepiece on the nightstand.

"Nine thirty! I'll be late to Hannah's!" I jumped out of bed and dressed as fast as I could and attacked my hair, then washed my face. I was ready in less than twenty minutes! That was a record! I grabbed my handbag and flew down the stairs and out to the sidewalk. I hurried to Hannah's shop and walked in.

"Hannah…" I panted.

"Oh, Rebecca…you're here!" She came over to me with a smile, and then her smile faded.

"Lord Child! Are you alright?" She placed her hand on my back with a worried look across her face.

"Yes…" I licked my lips still trying to catch my breath.

"What's wrong?" She patted my back.

"Oh, I had to hurry… I slept too late… I didn't… want to be… late…" Lord, help me to breathe!

"Here…have a drink of water. You know, I would have been here all day." She laughed, shaking her head.

"I just didn't… want to be late in case I had to come up with something else." I was catching my breath.

"It's alright. You're not late! You're a hoot!" She laughed and went into the back room.

"I've got six dresses that I think you'll like." She called out to me from the back.

"Alright…" I called back to her, finally catching my breath.

"Now then, Rebecca, I will show you the ones I don't think you would wear and save the best ones for last." Hannah held up a red and white stripped dress. I shook my head no and with a knowing nod she smiled.

Then she held up a nicer one, but it was pink. I shook my head no again
and she nodded agreeing. Then she held up a pretty light blue dress with
white trim and I thought I would wear that.

"No, child… I think these last three will suit you the best." She held up
a rich blue gown with a darker trim in blue and a higher neckline. I
nodded and smiled at that one. Then an off-white one that was very
pretty, but looked like a wedding dress too much.

"Now, this is the last one." She held up a beautiful pale yellow dress
with no trim and no lace. It was rather plain, but there was something
about it that I liked. It was satin and a small portion of crinolines showed
at the bottom. The sleeves were long, but not too loose looking and not
too tight.

"May I try it on?" I smiled.

"Of course, my dear!" She took me and the dress back to the back
room. She helped me into the dress and smiled.

"I can have it fixed in about two hours. All I have to do is take it in a
little here and here."

She pulled the waist from the back and at the top.

"Are you sure it won't be too much trouble?" I looked at her over my
shoulder.

"Heavens, no! No trouble at all! I'll fix it and have it sent to your
room." I thanked her and took the dress off and put mine back on, then
went back out to the front.

"That dress was the one I picked for you myself. It goes with your skin
and hair. Speaking of hair, would you let me come to your room and fix
it for you?" She smiled not looking at me.

"You want to fix my hair?" I was surprised!

"Yes, I would love to." Robert's aunt wants to fix my hair? That has to
be a sign!

"Yes, please!" I hugged her tightly.

"Good! I will bring the dress myself, then. I will be there at….three. I
will get ready with you and we'll go together." It was as if she had this all
planned!

"That sounds wonderful, Hannah!" I smiled for the first time with true
hope and peace in my heart. I was feeling better about everything and it
was nice.

"Now, go and buy some pretty things at Carla's store across the street
and tell her Hannah sent you and she'll know what you need." She
smiled showing me to the door.

"But, I have to pay for the dresses." I argued as she pushed me toward the door.

"We'll settle that later. For now, you only have a few hours to get what you'll need for the dinner party." She scooted me out the door.

I took a deep breath and I walked across the street to Carla's and went in.

"Good morning! May I... are you Hannah's niece?" A small tiny woman with black hair swept up on top of her head walked up to me smiling with the biggest brown eyes. So pretty! Cole came to mind instantly!

"Yes, and you must be Carla." I smiled, offering my hand. She nodded as she took my hand shaking it.

"I am." She smiled so pretty.

"Hannah said that you would know what I need? Well, what does she think I need?" I couldn't believe she would.

"Rebecca? Is that right?"

"Yes." I saw that she was so petite and yet well shaped. I believe Cole would find her very interesting! Very!

"I have taken it upon myself to choose several different perfumes and nail polishes to match your dress and some wonderful oils that will compliment your perfume. Also, some shampoo and special rinses for your hair." She smiled, waving her small delicate hand out over a small counter filled with all different sizes of bottles. My eyes popped!

"How did you know I would pick out the yellow dress?"

"I didn't, Hannah said you would." She laughed. Her fingers went to her lips. I saw two dimples on each cheek. She was just perfect! I must ask her if she knows Cole! If she did, Cole must be blind!

We went over all the colors of polish and the perfumes and then went to the oils and face powders. I chose the same ones that Hannah told Carla I would. I was speechless! This has to be another sign!

"Now, let's do your nails now and by the time were through, the polish will be set and you can relax in your hotel room for a while." I just nodded and let her do the work.

She buffed and filed and clipped and worked my cuticles. I was at her mercy for over two hours. I had never experienced anything like this before and, to tell you the truth, I loved every minute of it! Carla asked about my family and I felt at ease telling her anything she wanted to know as she worked.

"There we go! I always put a coat of clear on the color so it will last." She smiled not really looking at me and kept on working.

"I can't believe that you are doing all this!" I was still feeling a bit shocked.

"Hannah is good to me." Her smile told me that she cared a great deal for Hannah as I already do. There isn't anything that I didn't like about Hannah.

"She has been good to me too." I thought how sweet she is and her words were truthful.

"She tells me that you are still in mourning?" She frowned slightly.

"Yes, but I think the change in my dress will be the first step in coming out of mourning." I still felt good about that choice.

"She also tells me you have quite a court already."

"What?" I looked up at her.

"Hannah says that several men, enormous in stature, had come in to Hannah's store to find out if you were having a dress made and what color it was." She smiled.

"What? Several men?!!" I had never heard of such a thing! Who could they be? The only men I know besides my brothers are Lord Baptiest, Lord McCray and Lord Andrews...oh yes and Lawrence.

"I think you'll have a fun time finding out who they are and what they're up to."

"Why would they come in to find out if I ordered a dress and what color it was?" I've never had this happen, let alone know why.

"Men often try to impress the one they have their sights on by wearing the same color cummerbund. Sometimes it's for flowers." She smiled at me. Her light blue eyes twinkled with delight.

"But, I haven't come out of mourning officially." I tried to defend myself and the only one that I could even say I would consider was William!

"That doesn't matter to men! They want you to know they're waiting." She laughed as blush ran through her cheeks.

"Well, doesn't that seem rather forward?" I really thought it was assuming of the men to do that. My goodness! They act more like vultures in waiting.

"It seems that way, but what can you say? They're men! Hannah said she believed they were all like Lord William."

"Hmm..." This was going to be a very interesting night indeed.

"Are you coming?" I smiled at her.

94

"I'm not sure. Your mother did invite me." She was in thought with her brow furrowed.

"Are you married?" I asked with a slight smirk on my face.

"No, but perhaps one day my prince charming will ride into town!" She softly laughed and then sighed, a deep dramatic sigh. What I saw was the longing in her eyes.

"Then that settles it, you must come! I shall need you to assist me with all the Lords and who knows, you may meet your prince tonight! I have two brothers and they are very handsome and very single, though you must know them already, Cole and Mike Glenn? How old are you?" I looked at her.

"I'm twenty-eight." She blushed and smiled nervously biting her bottom lip.

"Well, you're old enough for Cole. Do you know him?" I grinned, knowing she was perfect for my big brother and she would keep his attentions while I was trying to sort my own life out.

"I think I know of him. He owns the lumber yard, right? He's the big one with dark hair and hazel eyes?" She looked directly at me with interest. She knows his eye color? Then why hadn't he noticed her?

"Yes." I grinned, thinking Cole would fine her so appealing.

"But I'm an old maid, or so some would say." She frowned slightly, sighing.

"Now look here, Cole is not married and not seeing anyone. He's your age and you are not a rock! I think you should fix yourself up and come. Please say you'll come!" I leaned forwards pleading with her.

"Well, alright... if you're sure?" She smiled shyly blushing.

"I am. Now be there at..." I thought for a moment and changed my mind.

"I tell you what, come to my room at the hotel and ride with Hannah and I. We'll leave at five thirty. My room is three fifteen." I was so excited and loved to play matchmaker! Cole has been a bachelor long enough! I was now on a mission!

"Yes, I'll be there." She smiled so sweetly. She is perfect!

"Wear your hair down...it's beautiful. Cole loves long hair." I was feeling like a school girl going to my first ball. This is going to be so much fun!

"I will! Come to think of it, I have a new dress I was saving." She smiled and two of the cutest dimples appeared on her cheeks. She looked like she was as excited as I was now.

Carla finished up my nails and told her I'd see her soon and gathered the oils and perfumes and went back to the hotel. It was lunch time and I thought I best eat now or I will be too famished tonight.

At the counter, I asked one of the bellhops take my things up to my room and went into the restaurant. I was seated at a nice table by the window and ordered a tossed salad, rolls and coffee. Staring out the window I watched people coming and going thinking there are so many beautiful women in this town, I couldn't understand why William was so interested in me?

I watched a mother and child walk hand-in- hand on the side walk and painfully envied them. Maybe I wasn't meant to have children? Then my eye caught the small boy named Joey McKinney coming out of the alley across the street. He was talking to a little girl half his size and then he pointed back down the alley as if he was telling her to go. He ran his hand through his reddish hair and wiped the dust off his clothes and then walked up to a man saying something to him, but the man turned his back on him. Then he walked up to another man but this time the man pushed him down and I was instantly horrified! I jumped to my feet rushing to the front calling to the waiter that I would be back.

I ran out to the front of the hotel and across the street looking up and down the street for the boy but lost sight of him. I looked down the alley and still saw no one. What if he is homeless? Was that little girl his sister? I wasn't sure if I should dare walk down the alley but they were children! I took a deep breath and started down the long alley.

The odor was appalling and there was so much trash everywhere! Rats ran across the damp path as I slowly and carefully made my way down the alley quietly as not to make too much noise, but I couldn't hear a thing. There were all kinds of doors, but I could see no one. Where did the little girl go?

When I reached the end, I gave up. Must be they do have a place to live. Thankfully they weren't in the alley! I turned to walk back and saw something move out of the corner of my eye. I stopped and stood still listening. I looked towards a large pile of boxes and slowly stepped towards them.

"Hello?" I softly called. I listened, but I didn't hear a thing.

"It's alright...you can come out. I want to help." I called again, but nothing. I decided it must be a cat or possibly...a rat!

At that thought, I hurried back out of the alley slowly and went back to the hotel to the powder room to wash my hands. They felt dirty even though I didn't touch a thing. I returned to my table and the waiter asked if everything was alright. I nodded and stared at the alley knowing that a small girl and Joey came out of there. I would watch for them from now on.

The waiter brought my salad and rolls and I picked at my lunch not hungry any more thinking about Joey and the little girl. I know I saw them! I left my barely eaten salad, half eaten roll and my coffee. I looked at my timepiece and it was two! I only had an hour to bathe and be ready for Hannah, I hurried to my room.

When I opened the door I froze seeing a large bouquet of yellow roses on the table. I closed the door and took one of the roses, holding it to my nose taking the fragrance in and then took the card off the table opening it...

Please save a dance for me,
Your, Knight

I held the card to my chest and smiled to myself. See, Robert? He is a very sweet man. I placed the card back by the flowers and went to start my bath. I picked out a wonderful smelling oil and a perfume to match and sat the perfume on the vanity. I poured the oil in the water and undressed. Soon the room was full of the wonderful aroma of flowers, like a spring morning, lily of the valley. I slid into the water and shampooed my hair, then put the special rinse on it and left it wrapped up in a towel for a few minutes. I washed, being careful of my nails, and rinsed my hair out. I dried off, put my underclothes and robe on and went out to sit at the vanity to brush out my hair. It felt like silk! I couldn't believe how soft and shiny it looked! I heard a soft tap on the door and I looked at my timepiece, three on the nose! It must be Hannah!

"Rebecca, it's me, Hannah." I smiled so glad she was here and opened the door.

"Good, you're about ready to do your hair...Oh... how beautiful!" Hannah saw the roses and went right to them.

"Hannah? Who came by your shop today?" I crossed my arms over my waist.

"Well there were a lot of people." She laid the garment bag on the bed. Her tone made me know that she knew very well what I was referring to.

"You know what I'm talking about."

"Oh, you mean your court?" She turned with a rose in her hand, smelling it deeply and dramatically.

"Yes, or I mean no…no, not my Court! But yes, the gentlemen!"

"They didn't leave their names."

"Well, what did they look like? Was one of them William?"

"No. William wasn't in the shop today. I can say honestly it was just three of the largest, handsomest men I have ever seen in my life!" She smiled, placing the rose back in the vase. She then walked over to the vanity.

I sat down looking at her reflection in the mirror. I only knew of three and maybe it was one of the other lords at the Council meeting. Nevertheless, I knew I would soon find out but in all honestly, I only wanted it to be William. I felt safe with him…strangely safe.

"They all had dark hair and that's all I know and they asked if you ordered a gown and what color it was. Of course I said, no." She laughed and winked.

"Thank you, Hannah, I'm grateful. I want it to be a surprise, I'm no longer wearing dark clothes, not even mother knows. By the way, Carla should be here at five thirty. She's riding with us!" I smiled very excited at that thought!

"Good! I think she and Cole would like each other." I looked up at her as she brushed my hair.

"That was my thought exactly! But you know it is strange that she has never really met Cole before. I mean it is not a huge town like Lawrenceburg."

"That's true, but I don't think there is a call for Cole to have his nails done that much!" We both laughed at the thought.

"Well no, I doubt that, but maybe he should have!" I was glad Hannah saw the match as well!

She soon had my hair wrapped in rag rolls and did my face powders. As she took the dress out of the garment bag, I thought it looked too small and just knew it wasn't ever going to fit me, which made me nervous. Hannah went into the washroom while my hair was drying and came out in beautiful lavender floor length dress with ruffles on the neck, sleeves and hem of the dress. It was beautiful.

"Hannah, you look beautiful!" And she did! This was going to be a fun night!

"Thank you, but you're going to even be more beautiful than you ever imagined!"

"I only hope that dress fits, Hannah, it looks too small for me."

"Shush now. It will fit, I'm never wrong." She laughed.

"If you say so, Hannah, I'm in your hands!" I sighed and then shook my head, not really believing it would really fit.

"Now to finish your hair…" She hurried over to me and unwrapped the rolled rags out of my hair letting long curls hang down. She took the sides of my hair and pulled it all back into a clip. She left a few curls on the sides and pulled the front so it was loose. Then she pulled out two pieces of hair on the front and took out scissors and I gasped. She smiled a 'Trust Me' smile and cut them so they would hang to the corners of my eyes. They cork screwed in beautiful spirals. I was simply amazed.

"There! Now, let's get that dress on."

She held the crinolines as I stepped into them and then tied the front up tightly. She held out the dress and I stepped into it very carefully. Then she pulled it up buttoning the back, it fit perfectly! The neckline was a bit low, yet not to revealing. She finished the back of my hair and fluffed it several times. Then she stood back smiling at me as if I was her own daughter.

"Perfect… simply perfect!" She put her hands on my shoulders and turned me toward the mirror and I gasped at my reflection! I stood with my mouth opened and my eyes wide.

"Hannah… I don't look like… me!" I moved to see if it really was.

"Indeed! It's you, my sweet!" She laughed, clasping her hands together under her chin.

"Oh, Hannah! I don't believe my eyes!" I turned sideways and saw a waterfall of curls down my back and how the 'v' shaped bodice made my waist look so tiny. The soft yellow of the dress matched my hair, nails and skin. I couldn't believe what my eyes were seeing. Then a soft tap at the door made us look at each other. We both smiled wide.

"That must be Carla!" I whispered to Hannah as she answered the door.

"Ah… Carla… you look simply beautiful!" Hannah clapped.

Hannah was truly enjoying this herself. Carla came in the room dressed in a beautiful dark green satin gown with black trim. The bodice was like mine in a 'v' with black lace trim in the sleeves. She looked so tiny, like a porcelain doll.

"Oh, you both are beautiful!!" We all squealed in excitement.

"Ladies... its half five.... time to go!" Hannah was giggling like a school girl and went for the door.

"Wait!" I put my slippers on and dabbed my perfume on my neck.

"Alright, now I'm ready!" I took one last look in the mirror still not believing that it was me!

~ Chapter 7 ~

We walked down the stairs seeing several men smiling, nodding and tipping their hats. I secretly looked for William as we made our way out to the front. I had not seen him all day.

"Excuse me, but is my carriage ready?" Hannah smiled at the porter.

"Yes, one moment please." The porter waved at a driver and a nice black carriage pulled up in front of us. The porter opened the door helping Hannah in and then Carla and me. I glanced down the street to see if I could see William but no sign of him. I wasn't used to him not being close.

"This is a lovely surprise!" I smiled, running my hand across the red velvet seats. Carla sat next to me and Hannah across from us. She smiled with excitement. We were on our way!

"Have you seen your William today?" Hannah smiled.

"No, I haven't." I admit I missed his company.

"I know he will be there. Did you see the roses in Rebecca's room?" Hannah winked at me.

"Yes I did! Who are they from?" Carla leaned forwards.

"I believe they are from William, at least I hope." I smiled and blushed a little.

"Did it come with a card?" Carla fixed her skirt.

"Yes, and it read, 'Please save me a dance…Your Knight."

"You know it could be from any one of the gentlemen that came in to the shop today." Hannah winked at Carla.

"Yes, it could be." I looked out the window.

"Well, you'll find out soon enough." Carla smiled.

"Yes, I suppose I will and soon, very soon. My handsome brother Cole will meet you soon, as well!" I smiled and squeezed her hand. She looked down as if the very thought scared her to death!

"Carla, don't worry, Cole is a very sweet man." I smiled at her and patted her hand.

"But what if he doesn't find me…" She bit her bottom lip.

"Oh, he will!" Hannah and I chimed together and then we all laughed!

We pulled in front of the house and it looked like everyone in town was here with all the black carriages.

The coachman opened the door and one by one, we were helped out. Together we walked up to the back terrace with the path lit by small lanterns. Music and laughter floated through the evening air and became louder the closer we approached.

Servants with trays of wine and champagne were being run all over. Well Mother, I thought, you've outdone yourself this time! It looked wonderful with streamers and lights floating above everyone on tall iron poles that resembled shepherd's hooks. Flowers were placed on every table with candles floating in bowls of water. The back patio was surrounded with small round tables leaving a huge place to dance in and the orchestra was off to the side on the higher part of the patio. It was beautiful!

We looked at each other and giggled like school girls. Finally, I saw mother and walked toward her. She glanced toward me and away and then back again, looking at me in disbelief. Her eyes widened when she realized it was me.

"Cole, come here! Mike!" Mother hurried to us and hugged me tightly looking me up and down as Cole looked twice at me as well and then Mike did the same.

"Well… I don't believe my eyes! You're beautiful, Sis!" They both kissed my cheek.

"Beck! I'm glad to see you out of those ugly dresses! Now you look like you." Mike hugged me tightly.

"I took it upon myself to take the first step and not wear the dark clothing. It has been long enough." I smiled, noticing Cole taking a double look at Carla!

Yes! I smiled to myself. I knew it! I was right!

"Mike, mother, Cole… You all know Hannah, but this is my newest friend, Carla." Hannah whispered in my ear, Taylor.

"Carla Taylor, Carla, this is my Mother, my Aunt Marie Glenn and my brothers, Mike and Cole." I watched Cole's face closely.

His eyes were locked on her and he slowly took her in from head to toe. Yes!

"It's a pleasure to meet you, Carla, nice to see you as well, Hannah." Mike bowed over both of their hands. Cole took Carla's hand and was immediately lost.

"Hannah, it's good to see you." Cole never took his eyes off of Carla. He just stood gazing at Carla. She blushed even deeper and looked at me for help. Mike saw it too, rolling his eyes.

"A... Cole... either ask the lady to dance or let go of her hand." Mike laughed at Cole.

"Oh, pardon me, Carla." He bowed over her hand and blew a kiss over it.

"Have we met?" Cole was still holding her hand.

"A... no..." She laughed a nervous laugh then looked at me for help again.

"Cole..." I looked at him and then his hand holding hers.

"Oh, please forgive me." He finally let Carla's hand go.

He looked so tall standing in front of Carla. She only came up to the middle of his chest and was even about three inches shorter than me and Hannah. His cheeks blushed! My brother Cole blushed! I looked at Hannah and laughed, winking at her. A servant came up to us with a tray of drinks.

"Would you care for wine or champagne?"

We all wanted the wine and Cole handed us each a glass.

"Rebecca dear, that handsome William was looking for you earlier. Last I saw him... he was by the fountain down below." Mother smiled softly.

"Thank you, Mother dear." I laughed, teasing her, but so very pleased he was really here!

"Oh, you!" Mother smiled as she took Hannah by the arm, walking off smiling.

"So tell me, Rebecca, where did you two meet?" Cole was smiling, but not at me! He was still entranced with Carla.

"On the moon and then on the sun." I knew he wasn't actually listening and Carla looked at me and almost laughed out loud.

"That's wonderful... where did you say?" He looked at me knowing I had said something.

"She owns the bath and beauty shop in town." I laughed as Carla did.

"Oh, no wonder I've not had the honor to meet you. How long have you been there?" I could tell that he was expecting her to say that she just arrived.

"Almost two years." Carla softly spoke. Cole's eyes went wide with shock.

"What? Two years and we've not met?" He was truly shocked.

"Yes, two years and no, we haven't met, but I have seen you in town a couple of times." She shyly admitted.

"Well, I'm glad that we have officially been introduced." He smiled at her so softly that I could hardly believe it was my brother! I looked around for Mike but didn't see him.

"Would you care to dance, Carla? May I call you Carla?" He stood with his arm out to her.

"Yes and yes." She softly laughed and took his arm. Cole led his lady out to the dance area and never once took his eyes off of her. I glanced at Hannah as she knowingly winked.

Now was my chance to look for William and I started towards the steps that led to the lower terrace. As I reached the top of the steps there he was just like mother said, leaning on the edge of the fountain with his legs crossed at the ankles. He was dressed in a black suit with black satin trim and a white shirt with a small straight collar where only the corners folded over the slender black tie.

His evening jacket fit his wide shoulders down to a tapered short wasted double-breasted jacket with two rows of gold buttons in threes. His slacks had black cording running down the sides, but they weren't as fitted as the jacket. However, he did look like a prince! I closed my eyes and took a deep breath, trying to slow my pounding heart down as it tried to push the air out of my lungs.

I looked up at William again, seeing him twirling a flower in his hand, looking very deep in thought. I started down the small set of steps and tried to keep a watch on where I was stepping. When I looked up he was standing toward me, frozen. I saw the golden buttons sparkling on his cuffs and the front of the jacket. His hair shined in the evening sun warming his appearance even more. He truly looked like a prince... as if he were from another time. I licked my suddenly dry lips and took another calming breath as I stepped down reaching the bottom steps. I gazed up into his handsome face not able to find my breath and wondered if I even had a voice.

"Rebecca... I can't breathe!" He spoke in a deep whisper.

"You're stunning! I... you're... beautiful!" He slightly smiled revealing that wonderful dimple. My stomach had a thousand butterflies in it seeing that he was pleased. He was so devastatingly handsome tonight that all I could do was stare at him, but I knew I had to say something!

"Milord... you are very handsome as well." My voice had not betrayed me. I curtsied to him and he took his finger and raised my face to his.

"Rebecca..." His tone was breathless, deep and husky as he struggled for breath.

"Dance... with me." He held out his arm for me to take.

He turned towards the fountain instead of going to the dance area and placed his hand on the small of my back. Then he gently took my other hand in his. I laid my hand softly on his shoulder hoping he couldn't see that I was trembling. I took in the aroma of his cologne, but tonight he wore a different one. It seemed to mix with the evening air like a hypnotic potion.

We stood locked in each other's eyes. He took another deep breath and with the next beat he swung me into the waltz. He tightened his hold, pulling me closer to him with every turn. I had to close my eyes just to keep my thoughts from scattering and to savor the feeling of being in his arms. We floated around and around the fountain never saying a word the entire dance. When the waltz ended, he still held me, searching my eyes, not saying a word. He swung me into another waltz tightening his hold even more. I couldn't look away. It was as if I had no control!

All I knew was... this was right. That even though we only just met, this was right and being in his arms felt right. I felt safe and cared for. It felt wonderful!

When the dance ended he stood holding me. Then he raised his fingers to my hair.

"Rebecca... you are so beautiful." He touched one of the curls on the sides then ran his finger down my cheek slowly. He looked into my eyes and leaned down. My heart raced as he...

"Rebecca..." Mike called out.

I looked into Williams eyes as instant disappointment crept through them.

"Here, Mike." I stood beside William feeling his hand on the small of my back.

"Mother's looking for you. She wants you to meet someone." He smiled at William.

"Where is she?" I know my eyes held regret.

"Just follow me." He turned to walk away and William stopped me by grabbing my hand.

"Save another dance for me…" He whispered softly with a serious look about his face.

"William, did you send me roses?" I looked up at him smiling expecting him to say he did.

"Roses?" He suddenly stiffened standing taller.

"You didn't?" I felt the disappointment that it wasn't William.

"No, it wasn't me." His brows furrowed deeply.

"I don't know who it was." I was so sure, or should I say so hoping, that he had sent them. The only other one would be Lord McCray, I sighed.

"Was there a card?" He frowned.

"Yes, and it said, 'Save a dance for me, Your Knight'…and honestly? I thought it was… you." I blushed, realizing how this must look to him. He glanced up into the crowd as if he were looking for someone.

"I'm sorry, William." I looked down and then felt his finger raise my chin.

"I'm not… it goes to show you how beautiful and desirable you are. But know this… if they were from me... you would know it." He raised his brow with a slight grin sliding across his lips and somehow I believed him.

"I would?" William wasn't angry and I was relieved.

"Believe me… you would." He whispered softly leaning back down with his finger still under my chin and his thumb resting at the corner of my lips.

"Rebecca!" Mike called out.

I furrowed my brows at the interruption. He knew I was just as irritated with the interruption as he was, but he smiled holding out his arm and covered my hand with his. I shivered at the thought that he again, wanted to kiss me.

We walked up the stairs and around the patio to where we saw Mike. Mother was talking to a very tall man with black hair that was just as immense as William.

"Mother…" I smiled as she saw us approaching.

"Why there you are, Rebecca… This gentleman would like to meet you. Rebecca, this is Lord Douglas Brent. Lord Brent, this is my daughter, Rebecca." He took my hand and bowed deeply and blew a kiss over it. I heard William take a deep breath and let it out. William's hand was still resting on the small of my back and I felt his thumb move up and down.

106

"It is a pleasure to meet you, though I did meet you one morning this week at the hotel's restaurant." He too had a beautiful full smile. His beard was trimmed neatly and his gray eyes looked illuminating.

"Yes, I remember meeting you but you will have to excuse me that morning..." I blushed.

"Yes, I recall seeing a wonderful fire in those beautiful eyes." Lord Brent turned to William.

"Andrews, it's good to see you as well." He shook Williams hand as William nodded.

"Ms. Grayson, may I have the honor of this dance?" He held out his arm. I was about to refuse, but I looked at William and he nodded to me to accept.

He took my hand and wrapped it around his arm and escorted me to the dance area. I looked back to William and he winked at me as he turned to mother offering his arm to her. William led mother to the dance area with her cheeks still blushing. She was so fond of William already and I was glad.

"Ms. Grayson, I must say you are exquisitely beautiful tonight." This Lord Brent was truly handsome and just as charming. I couldn't believe just how big these 'Lord's' seem to be!

"Thank you, Lord Brent, but please call me Rebecca."

"Rebecca, please call me Douglas." He smiled. Good Heavens! Did they all look into your eyes so deeply and intensely?

"Douglas... do you know my brothers, Cole or Mike?"

"Yes, I know both of them." His tone was as deeply rich as William's.

He tightened his hold and swung me around to the other side of the dance area. I saw Cole still dancing with Carla. He was staring down at her like William had me.

"How do you know William?" He danced me around in circles.

"I met him a couple days ago." My head was getting dizzy from turning in circles so fast.

"Only a couple days ago, you say?" His eye widened raising his right brow

"Yes... he's quite charming and very funny." So handsome and with eyes I could just drown in.

"What? Andrews... funny? Charming?" His eyes widened and his brows both went up in obvious surprise.

"Yes, do you think not?" William was wonderful and so handsome!

"The Lord Andrews I know is quite the opposite." He furrowed his brow in thought.

"To me he is quite witty and very charming." And how I love how he makes me feel in his arms!

"Yes, charming he can be." Douglas smiled and when we were finished with the dance he escorted me back to mother. I saw Lord McCray coming our way.

"Well, my heavens! You are a sight to behold, Ms. Grayson." Lord McCray smiled walking up to us.

"Thank you, Lord McCray." I tipped my head. William stepped closer to me.

"Care for a sip of your wine?" William handed my glass to me, but it was now full.

"Thank you so much, I'm parched." I tipped it back and took another from a passing waiter's tray.

"You better be careful, that will go to your head!" Mother gave me a warning look.

"I know, Mother. I wished it was water. I think I'll go into the house for some."

"Nonsense, waiter!" Mother called to one of the servants.

"Yes Ma'am?" A young man appeared before us.

"Please get my daughter a glass of ice water, thank you."

"Yes Ma'am, right away." He hurried into the house.

"See, Rebecca, just that easy." She smiled as she snapped her fingers.

"Really, Mother, I could have gotten my own." I sighed, but it was nice.

"Well, I think not… this is all for you, my dear. You're supposed to be enjoying yourself."

"Oh, I am!" I glanced at William, feeling overwhelmed with everything.

"Rebecca…" Lord McCray held his arm out for me to take. I took his arm as William smiled and winked. I truly didn't want to dance with all these men, but that would mean that my intent was more than it should be.

Lord McCray smiled down gently taking me into his arms. My breath caught when I looked up into his eyes, seeing a fire. I knew his look appeared to be rather bold at the moment and intimidating.

"Rebecca…I can't believe how lovely you are tonight. Milady, you have stolen my very breath." He swung me into a slow, beautiful waltz. I looked over his shoulder at William and he smiled nodding. I somehow felt better with him watching me.

"Thank you, Lord McCray." I tried to keep my sights on William.

"Rebecca, please call me Gabe. It tears at my heart hearing you call me Lord... It sounds so cold and impersonal and I do think we are beyond all that." He laughed softly.

"Alright, Gabe... But please call me Rebecca and not Ms. Grayson. It makes me sound so old." I laughed wishing I felt more at ease, but I wasn't.

"Well, you are far from that my love." His eyes searched mine so deep that it made me feel uncomfortable.

"Why thank you, Gabe." I thought him the most handsome man I ever saw in my life that is, until I met William.

"I see that William is quite interested in you." He bit his lip.

"He's very charming and witty." I wanted to see what he thought about that comment as well.

"Yes, he can be both of those things. He is generally as busy as I, entertaining is very rare." Gabe's honesty was like Williams and I liked that.

"I saw you dance with Lord Brent as well." He watched my every emotion it seemed. Why was he interrogating me like this?

"Yes, he is charming as well." But still not like William.

"Yes, he has slain many hearts." His eyes widened as he raised his brow.

"Thank you for the warning, but what about you, Gabe? Do you collect hearts as well?" It was time to turn the tables on him. Both his brows now were raised in surprise at my question.

"No... I have not the time as I've said before... but one day I hope to win one heart and only one heart. What of you, Rebecca? Do you wish to marry again?" He smiled warmly.

"At the moment, I can't even imagine that. I was married to Robert for so long that right now, I just couldn't fathom being married to another." My smiled faded, for that was true. Being a friend to someone was one thing, but marrying another man? Yet, I found my thoughts on William so much.

"Perhaps one day?" He simply said.

"Perhaps..." I sighed... perhaps.

"I know that you spent the day with William." He did know!

"Yes I did and it was a wonderful day indeed. " I smiled wondering why what I did interested him so much.

"I was wondering if you were thinking about considering… well… if you would allow any gentlemen callers." He smiled with hope in his eyes.

"I'm not sure yet. I just recently arrived. William and I are friends and agreed to be so. I do enjoy his company very much and know Robert would have liked him as well."

"I didn't know Robert, but I do know that he was well respected, according to Nick." Gabe was deep in thought now. His brow was furrowed.

"Yes, he was in the Guards." His hand moved on my back and I could feel the cool air instantly where his hot hand had been. The waltz ended but he kept his hold and swung me into another.

"Nick tells me that Robert was a Lieutenant." He smiled down at me.

"Yes, he was." His eyes went to my lips as I licked them as I was getting parched.

"Then he was older than you by a few years?" He softly grinned to one side.

"Yes… he… was ten years older than I." I tore my eyes away from him and looked at William. He, Lord Brent and Lord Baptiest were talking.

"That is a considerable age difference. You must have been young when you married?" His tone remained so soft and soothing. I know he really was interested in what he was asking.

"Yes… but I feel age is just a state of mind."

"Yes, I agree… I can hardly believe my eyes at how lovely you are this evening. I'm afraid that you have stolen not only my very breath but all my thoughts as well." Gabe warmly smiled as he moved his hand again.

"And you, Gabe, are quite the charmer, whether you have time or not." I laughed wondering why it seemed that all the Guards were paying so much attention to me. There were a lot of beautiful women here. Then I saw Lord Brent swing Hannah out o to the floor. She was blushing. I saw mother dancing with Lord Baptiest.

"I'm trying to be." He softly whispered, leaning down. My stomach tightened.

We danced to a slower waltz and I finally relaxed in his arms. He was a very fine dancer and I was enjoying it very much but I wasn't used to all of this attention.

When the waltz ended, he looked at me with regret in his eyes.

"Please, save a dance for me?"

110

"Did you send me the flowers, Gabe?" I had to thank him properly. He smiled softly.

"Did you like them?" He smiled holding me still looking into my eyes.

"I was so surprised when I walked into the room. Why did you send them?"

Another waltz started and without answering, he tightened his hold and swung me into another, this was three in a row! I knew two meant simply friends, but three in a row showed intent.

"Gabe, I thought we were going to..." I bit my bottom lip looking for William.

"I sent them so you would know I wanted to dance with you. I knew you wouldn't be sitting very long and I wanted to tell you how very sorry I was for the other day, please forgive me, Rebecca. I really was not trying to embarrass you...instead it was me that ended up being put in my place." His eyes pleaded for forgiveness. How could I not?

"I forgive you, Gabe, it was a nice gesture. But as you can see, I have, and can, take care of myself." I smiled up at him. His breathtaking blue eyes searched mine.

"I've taken note of that and I do admire that." He tightened his hold pulling me closer to him as he turned me in a circle.

"Rebecca..." I looked down at his huge chest. His finger turned my face up to his. My hand that he was holding went to his other shoulder. My heart pounded.

"Rebecca... would you consider." Gabe paused, looking at me searching.

"Consider?" I was afraid of what he might ask and I held my breath.

"Would you consider me calling on you in the near future? I mean not right away... but..." He was serious!

"Gabe..." I was about to say I wasn't ready.

"Just think about it... don't turn me down yet... I would love to take you to dinner. We did have such a lovely time the last time we enjoyed a table together and frankly, I wish you hadn't departed so fast." In his eyes I saw he was speaking the truth.

"Perhaps...." He was being so kind!

"Ah... good..." A huge smile lit up his face and as the waltz ended he stood still holding me.

"I'm in need of refreshment." My heart was pounding and I fought to breath. I needed space and wanted to be with William.

"Thank you, Rebecca." He smiled, taking my hand and wrapped it around his arm. We went back to where mother was standing with Hannah. They both smiled as we approached.

William was talking to Lord Baptiest and when he saw me, his smile warmed my heart. Gabe retrieved me a glass of wine and I drank it down a little too quickly, feeling it go right to my head. I looked for my water but one of the waiters must have picked it up. I excused myself and went to the kitchen and saw a flurry of activity. It was wonderful! There were women making up dishes and men cutting meat on platters with one man giving the orders. He noticed me and stopped. He was tall and not so muscular but not too small. His skin was olive in color and his hair was long in a tied tail. He had a clean shaved face and was very handsome.

"Ah... may I help you... ma belle ...." He's French!

" Oui, puis-je avoir un verre d'eau glacée ? I had asked for ice water.

"Ah... Oui, Mon Cheri!" He smiled sweetly and barked orders to a woman and she got the ice water for me.

"Merci beaucoup!" I smiled to myself as I walked out. It had been years since I had spoken in French.

"Ah, there you are." Cole smiled. His eyes were somehow different. He was still with Carla and she, too, was all smiles!

"Are you enjoying yourself Carla?" Giving her an 'I told you' smile...

"Oh my, yes! I think your brother is coming in for a manicure!" We all laughed.

"Well, that would be a first!" I shook my head in disbelief at how my serious, never smiling, no time to waste, brother was acting... and it was wonderful!

"And what about you, Rebecca? I see you've been quite the belle of the ball." He smiled and covered Carla's hand with his.

"Well, I think Carla here is the one in demand. I saw Lord Brent dance with her as well."

"Yes, he did and I had to steal her away from him." He laughed as she blushed.

"Where's Mike?" I looked over the crowd and saw William dancing with a beautiful lady whom I didn't know.

"He's helping mother."

"Who is that woman dancing with William?"

"Oh, that is Mr. Nelson's daughter, remember Clarissa?" Cole smiled knowing I wasn't too pleased at seeing her in his arms. I drank my water.

"Yes, I remember her... Lawrence's cousin." I tried to hide my disappointment.

"He's here as well, over there with Mike as we speak." I looked in the direction he pointed and saw a tall light haired man talking to Mike. Lawrence had indeed grown up.

"You should say hello to him" Cole winked.

"No, that is alright. I will run into him soon enough!" I rolled my eyes.

"Rebecca..." I turned almost into Gabe's chest.

"I'm sorry... we seem to do that a lot!" He laughed and I did as well recalling that we had done this several times!

"Yes, we do!" He placed his hand on the small of my back.

"Let's get something to eat, shall we, Carla." I smiled at her and took her arm.

"I think I could nibble on something." She smiled at Cole and I shot him a 'stay here' look.

We went to a buffet table and chose vegetables with a spread and a small finger sandwich while leaving the men to talk amongst themselves.

"Carla, I see you've not been disappointed with my brother." I smiled and looked at her. We sat at a small table.

"He is charming." Her tone softened.

"I think he is very interested in you, not to mention that I've never seen my brother quite so taken with anyone so quickly before." I shook my head thinking, I was right about the two of them. They were perfect for each other!

"Do you really think so?" She looked at me with her eyes wide.

"I know so!" I laughed.

"He is as sweet as you said he was. I'm so glad I came, thank you Rebecca." Her face simply glowed.

"I am glad you came as well, but it is I that should be thanking you for coming." I laughed and nibbled on a carrot.

"Do you think he will want to... call on me?" She shyly asked.

"If he didn't, I would be totally fooled and I think by the end of the night, he'll ask you." I had a good feeling he would.

"I'd like that very much." She blushed so sweetly.

While we ate, we watched everyone dancing and talking. I saw William still chatting to Clarissa, smiling down at her the way he did me, and my stomach turned over with a dreadful feeling.

"Rebecca... it bothers you that William is with Clarissa, doesn't it?" She must have noticed.

"A little, but I have no right for it to bother me." I sighed knowing that was the truth.

"He is very handsome." She softly spoke.

"Yes… he is." I watched him move hair out of her eyes.

"I saw Lord McCray dance with you as well and he is very handsome too." She smiled and looked into her plate.

"Yes, he is," which was true.

"I too can tell that William is interested in you Rebecca. I see it in his eyes as well as Lord McCray's." She glanced at William.

"I know, but there is something about William that interests me, and I can't put my finger on it. Lord McCray is charming too but he makes my blood boil. I don't know why, maybe it is better that I don't see anyone yet, maybe I'm not ready?" I blew out a big breath.

"Oh, Rebecca, you're more than ready, it's just that two of the most handsome bachelors are interested in you at the same time." She giggled softly.

"For someone that never courts anyone, you sure are smart!" I laughed knowing she hit it right on the head.

"How do you think I've stayed single for so long?" She laughed.

"Oh Carla, you're simply a hoot!" I burst out in laughter then looked back at William and his eyes locked on to mine and he whispered something in Clarissa's ear. She laughed putting her hand on his arm. He smiled down at her and looked back at me again. I batted my eyes, looking away telling myself it did not bother me, but it did. I didn't like how my heart ached and my stomach felt like it was sinking.

"Rebecca, are you through?" Carla stood smiling as Cole walked towards us.

"Yes, I am." I was and was through with feeling anything. I didn't like this feeling and I knew that I was too close to William entirely too fast. I looked at him and he laughed at something she had said and again, my stomach rolled. This was too much…too much!

"Beck, are you alright?" Cole's brow furrowed slightly.

"Yes, of course." I smiled my best smile.

"Beck, will you dance with me." Mike smiled, walking up behind Cole.

"I would love to." I took his arm and Mike swung me into the waltz.

I tried not to look at William, but couldn't help myself. Clarissa was smiling so sweetly up at William. He would be a rock if he didn't notice how beautiful she is. She wore a low cut dress in light blue. Her brown hair hung in a mass of curls like mine and she was prettier than I

114

remembered... not to mention petite, shorter and also shapelier than I. I've always thought she was a nice girl when I was young. Why wouldn't he find her desirable? He is a man after all!

"Beck... Are you alright?" I heard Mike's voice interrupting my thoughts.

"Yes, I just drank the wine too fast," which was true.

"I think William really does care for you Rebecca and I like him." My stomach fluttered when he said that.

"It seems that he has found another that interests him just as much." I frowned, admitting the fact.

"Why, Rebecca! You are interested in him!" Mike's face went wide with a smile.

"Why wouldn't I be? He's charming and sweet and quite the gentleman." He looked at him talking to Clarissa.

"Oh, I see what's bothering you." He laughed.

"What?" Heavens! Was I that transparent?

"You're jealous!" He smiled.

"I am not!" But I was! It bothered me to see William holding another woman.

"You are, too." Mike laughed.

"Honestly Michael, I hardly know him." But I wanted to know him more and admitted that to myself as well.

"Yes, but I know you. Remember, I'm your brother!"

"Meaning what?" I was now focused on what Mike was trying to accuse me of.

"Meaning that you're not one to just 'fall' for anyone and I can clearly see that William is different. You are fond of him... admit it." He laughed then winked at me.

"Alright, I do care for him... but only as a friend." I gave him a warning look. He rolled his eyes and we both laughed. After the dance Cole asked me to dance.

"Beck, are you having a good time?" Cole took me into his arms and Mike danced with Carla.

"Yes, I am." I tried to sound believable, but his eyes told me that he knew I wasn't really.

"Don't worry about Clarissa... She's..." I interrupted Cole and did not want to know how sweet she was or beautiful.

"Clarissa is a very nice woman... how come you never called on her?" I smiled up at my handsome brother.

"She's not my type." Cole flatly stated.

"And Carla is?" This was my opportunity to pry and get the focus off of me!

"She is beautiful! Thank you for asking her to come." He smiled looking at her dancing with Mike.

"She really likes you Cole." I smiled, looking at my handsome brother smiling at a woman.

"She does?" He gave me only the slightest glance then turned back to look at Carla.

"Yes and she hopes you'll call on her." I watched his face.

"She does?" His eyes widened as he just watched her.

"She asked me if I thought you were interested in her." I knew he would be interested in her!

"She did?" He looked at her and smiled the sweetest smile that took my breath.

"She's within your age range." I wanted to laugh as I've never seen my brother so tied up in knots! It was priceless!

"She is?" He smiled, sparing me only a glance.

"Yes, and you might consider calling on her. I know she would like that very much."

"She would?" He nervously licked his lips and looked back at her again.

"Yes!" I laughed for I couldn't hold it back anymore.

"What?" He furrowed his brow.

"Oh Cole, you really do like her!" I was so pleased!

"Yes… yes, I do." He rolled his eyes in admission and swung me into the last part of the waltz with such joy. I was happy for him.

After the waltz ended Cole took me over to where mother was. Hannah smiled as we walked up to them.

"My children are so wonderful." Mother smiled kissing Cole and Mike's cheeks then she hugged me tightly and kissed my cheek.

"Mother, I think you're enjoying the wine." I laughed.

"So what if I am?" She laughed.

"Mother, thank you for all this, it's wonderful." I hugged her.

"I would do anything for you, Cole or Mike. I love you so much." She had tears in her eyes.

"Carla, Hannah? Would either of you like to go to the powder room?" I smiled.

"I would." Carla smiled.

"I've just been." Hannah smiled shooing us with her hand.

"Come on then Carla." I took her hand and walked to the front of the house and went upstairs.

"Rebecca, this is a beautiful house." Carla smiled.

"Mother just had it redone. Cole and Mike did most of the work and speaking of Cole, he admitted he is quite taken with you. He also thanked me for inviting you."

"He did?" She was blushing.

"Yes!" Here we go again! I laughed to myself.

"He was very interested and I believe he plans on asking you if he may call on you."

"He did?" She looked up at me wide-eyed.

"He also said that you were beautiful."

"He did?" She blushed and shyly looked down.

"He said that you were the kind of woman he looked for... his type."

"He did?" I couldn't hold my laughter back any longer.

"Yes and you two talk the same way."

"We do?" She smiled and laughed.

"Yes, you do!" I laughed at how the two of them seemed so much alike.

We both powdered our noses and fixed our hair and headed back down to the party.

We walked the long way around the house avoiding most of the crowd. I looked at all the flowers mother had planted. How beautiful! They were all fall colors.

"You know, Cole wants to build a house on the other side of the property, in the back woods."

"He does?" I laughed again.

"I think he has started to clear out a parcel of land. I think he wants it stone."

"Stone is beautiful, but doesn't he own the lumber company? One would think he would make it of wood." She furrowed her brows and she made perfect sense too.

"You know, I think that because he does work with wood, he wants stone, like a chocolate maker doesn't eat chocolate." I smiled looking at her in thought.

"I see, yes that makes sense." She agreed as we came to the lower patio and the water fountain.

"Oh, this is beautiful." She ran her hand in the water.

"I, too, was surprised when I saw the fountain. Cole made this."

"He did?" She was amazed.

"Yes, and he handmade the doves from wood and poured a mold for it."

"I'm impressed." She nodded.

"Cole is very talented, and he is very sensitive as well, but you didn't hear that from me!" I laughed, shaking my head.

"No, I didn't!" She laughed too. I liked her very much.

We walked up the steps and around the dancing area and I didn't see William or Clarissa. My heart suddenly sunk.

"Let's find Cole." I silently sighed, feeling sad.

We went back to the place where we last were. They all were standing like princes as we walked towards them. William was standing next to Clarissa and her hand was wrapped around his arm. My heart sank even more and she smiled warmly at me.

"Oh, Rebecca, how are you?" She hugged me.

"Thank you for asking, I'm fine and it's good to be home. You've grown up so lovely." I had to be honest.

"Thank you, I'm so sorry about Robert." Oh! Even her frown was adorable! I hated admitting that!

"Thank you." I smiled and glanced at William then saw Cole was looking at Clarissa as if his eyes couldn't take her in.

"Clarissa, please excuse me, but I must talk to Rebecca." She smiled and nodded at William and he patted her hand.

"Rebecca? Would you care to go for a walk?" My heart skipped a beat as he bit his bottom lip and smiled, causing that dimple to show. I took a deep breath and let it out, taking his arm but wasn't sure if I wanted to. I was afraid of what he wanted to talk about. He retrieved two glasses of wine as we walked down to the lower terrace. His eyes were on me the entire time.

"What is it that you wish to talk to me about?" I looked up feeling unsure feeling my heart pounding the inside of my rib cage. I had to stay calm.

"I watched you dance with Gabe." He looked troubled. Like what he was about to say was hard.

"Yes?" I licked my dry lips out of nervousness.

"Well …" He stopped by the fountain setting the glasses down and took my hands in his.

"Well… what William, I saw you dancing and laughing with Clarissa." My heart aching.

"You did…" Not him too! Was he taken with Clarissa!

"Yes, and I saw you enjoyed her company immensely." I said in a cool tone, but kept my head about me even though it was as if my heart was breaking.

"She is very charming." He looked up into the dusky sky and the stars starting to come out. I searched his eyes when he looked back down into mine.

"Then you like her?" I looked up into his face and saw what was in his eyes! Tears threatened and I turned and looked away.

"Well yes… she's…" I couldn't hear this. I turned to walk away.

"Rebecca?" He called after me as I went up the steps, grabbing my skirts, wanting to run. My heart was aching so much. No! I couldn't even look back at him. I couldn't allow him to see the pain in my eyes. I knew this was too soon and of course he was a devout bachelor. I shouldn't have allowed myself to get involved with anyone. It was too soon. For that matter, I really didn't even know William and we had only just met! I was feeling foolish allowing myself to even think about someone else right now!

"Rebecca!" He followed me.

I willed the tears that tried to fill my eyes not to. I saw Gabe and walked to him.

"Rebecca, would you care to dance?" I nodded, afraid if I said a word I would cry. I had to get my emotions in check!

Gabe led me out to the dance area. He swung me into the waltz. William likes Clarissa. How could I be so foolish! How could I think that he would be interested in me? How could I care so much already? Yes, I was foolish indeed!

"I was waiting to dance with you again." He searched my eyes.

"You were?" I collected myself and put my resolve up again.

"Yes, I could dance with you all night!" He laughed a deep rich laugh.

"I love to dance." I could feel my smile trembling and wanted nothing more than to leave.

"As do I…" He swung me in circles and I closed my eyes thinking about William.

Oh, Robert, what a fool I must have looked like. We danced two more dances without talking and I was thankful for that. I needed the time to regain my composure. When I had, I begged him for refreshment and found an empty table and sat relaxing and sipping wine. My feet hurt, my body ached and my heart? Broken, but how could that be? I hardly knew

William! All I did know was I was tired of hurting and that was all I had done since Robert had died. I wanted not to feel anything, especially what my heart was feeling now. I tried to focus on what Gabe was saying, but my mind thought back to the look I had seen in William's eyes. He liked Clarissa! That was all there was to that!

"Rebecca, would you like more wine?" I nodded to him and he had two more glasses brought to the table.

"This hits the spot!" I tilted up my glass and smiled.

"You better be careful..." Gabe warned with a smile.

"I know." But I didn't care, all that I had been through in the past months, I couldn't stand anymore! The waiter left a whole bottle at the table and after a couple more glasses I was feeling much better! My head felt light and I felt all soft and warm.

"Well, you're right, Lord McCray. This does go to your head!" I laughed.

"You know, Rebecca, you are quite desirable." I heard him but didn't look at him.

"And you, Lord McCray, are quite the charmer." I laughed, sipping from my glass.

"You know you make that wine look so good. I would love to taste it on your lips." He leaned closer as his eyes devoured my lips.

"No, you wouldn't want that." I thought about William.

"Oh, but I would!"

"You Lords are all good for a woman's ego!" I laughed and finished another glass.

"Would you sing?" He leaned too close.

"What?" I leaned back away from him and opened my eyes wide.

"Would you sing with the orchestra?" He smiled.

"Why, I haven't done that in so long. I wouldn't know what to sing," or if I could even stand still at this moment...

"What is your favorite song?"

"Oh, I don't know." I thought about it, but not concentrating really. All I could think about was the roses and the thorns that come with the beauty of it, just like my life!

"Please, Rebecca, sing any old song but please, sing... for me?" He was being so sweet and truly wanted me to sing.

"Let me drink another glass and then I will."

I surprised myself in saying yes, what had I gotten myself into? Gabe went to the Maestro and whispered in his ear and he nodded. He walked back to me and I tipped my glass finishing it and went to the front of the dais and whispered into his ear. He nodded and the orchestra began playing the old melody 'Roses are like love'. I started to sing and everyone stopped and turned to listen. I scanned the crowd and saw William watching me with an intense stare. I tore my eyes away and closed my eyes and sang my heart out.

Before I knew it, I was through and was startled by a thunderous applause. Hearing them begging for one more, I sang another one and knew it would be my last one. I looked at mother and she was crying. I whispered to the Maestro and whispered to the orchestra. They started to play 'Deep from the heart'. I closed my eyes and sung to Robert, and yes, to William. I sung with all my heart tears ran down my cheeks as I felt the music run through my veins and into my heart. Then when I was finished, I heard the thunderous applause again. The conductor shook my hand and asked if I wanted to sing later. I told him I'd think about it. People swamped me and told me how beautiful it was. Mother came up to me crying and held me tightly.

"Oh, Rebecca... How I have missed that!" She cried.

"It felt wonderful." I smiled wiping tears.

"Rebecca, thank you!" Gabe kissed my hand softly. I looked for William and he was gone.

"Dance with me, Rebecca." He didn't wait for me to respond and took me into his arms and swung me into the musical version of 'Roses and Thorns' I closed my eyes as tears ran down my cheeks, then I felt Gabe's fingers touch my cheek. He wiped the tears from my cheeks with his thumb. I opened my eyes and looked into his. Chills ran down to my feet.

"Rebecca, you've put a spell on my heart." He smiled.

I couldn't say a word. Where did William go? Gabe tightened his hold, our bodies almost touching. I pushed on his chest but he kept his hold.

"Please..." I looked into his eyes as they held desire.

"Please what?" A sensual grin played on his lips.

"I..." The back of his fingers ran down my face.

"Rebecca, please let me call on you." His plea was so sincere and heartfelt that if I hadn't met William... Well the fact was, I had and now I was paying for it with my heart, again.

"I..." I should say yes, but I wanted so much for William to ask that of me, but he hadn't.

"How about going to a play and dinner?" He smiled down so sweetly.

"Perhaps…" My heart said no.

"I shall ask you until you agree."

"Please, Gabe, I don't know if I'm ready."

"Then you'll think about it?"

"Yes." I finally had to say something. I was worried he may do more than just beg!

"Good!" He smiled and swung me into a huge turn and when the music ended I asked for something to drink. I was parched! He walked me back to the table and held my chair.

"You know, I thought that I may have to spar with William over you." He poured me a glass.

"What are you talking about?" I drank down the whole glass of wine.

"He obviously is very interested in you. I watched while you sang and his eyes never wavered, but when you sang the second song he vanished." He sipped his wine.

"I didn't see him." I sipped the wine. William vanished?

"Well, I did. Your song affected me. Well, everyone for that matter. I still have the feeling I will have to pull out all the stops to win your affections." I looked surprised at him.

"Like I've said, I still need time." I looked down.

"Time I have." He sipped his wine and poured me another glass.

I sat watching all the people dancing and enjoying the night. The sky turned a deep midnight blue blanketed with a million stars and the moon was almost full as it hung looking down on us. Listening to the music, I allowed my thoughts to float away. William, where did you go? I looked around the dance area and saw Cole and Carla. He was looking at her in a dreamy state and she was looking into his eyes the same way and they were very close. I didn't see Clarissa or William. I sighed deeply and drank another glass of wine and another. I didn't want to feel anything and realized I couldn't. I stood and Gabe hopped to his feet.

"Gabe, dance with me." His eye shot wide open and took me to the dance area swinging me into the waltz, and another…then another. I was relaxed beyond being relaxed. I wanted to see mother and check on her. After the waltz ended I found mother and hugged her.

"Why, Rebecca… you best not drink any more either!" She looked worried for me.

"Oh phooey, Mother! I feel wonderful." To be honest, I couldn't feel anything!

"Rebecca…" She laid her hand on my arm.

"Don't worry, Mother… I'll not drink anymore." Which, I couldn't or I would surely be sick.

"See that you don't!" She scolded, tapping me on the nose. I laughed and hung on Gabe's arm.

"Water… I need water." I smiled at Gabe.

"I'll be right back." He smiled so prince like and bowed going into the kitchen.

"Mother, have you seen William?"

"No dear." She looked at me strangely.

"Hannah?" Hannah knew I was fond of William.

"No, I'm sorry, dear." She frowned.

"I miss him." I pouted. Maybe I have had too much wine.

"Have you seen Carla?"

"No…" They both shook their heads. I frowned slightly.

"Well, I'll be right back." 'Powder room', I mouthed.

I walked around to the front of the house feeling like the world was spinning and saw Clarissa and William on the porch sitting. The world suddenly stopped and he looked up at me and stood. I turned to walk away and a large hand had a hold of my arm.

"Oh, do let me go, Lord Andrews!" I spat.

"I will not…" His tone was firm. I stiffened and turned to him squaring my chin and looking him square in the eyes

"Yes, you will!" I clenched my teeth.

"No… I won't!" He took my other arm in hand as well. Why was he doing this to me? Oh God, how much more can I take? The wine was making it worse and I knew it!

"Yes, you will… or I'll…" I tried to free myself by wiggling my arm, but his hold was very tight and he wasn't going to let go.

"Why… you're foxed!" He smiled with his eyes opened wide.

"So if I am and, and you'll… let me go now." I felt very sober at the moment.

"And if I don't?" Why, he was almost smiling! Blasted man!

"Then… I'll…" What kick him? I don't think a bear could escape!

"You'll what?" Oh! The man was smiling! I was so angry!

"I'll do something, you won't like." I saw Clarissa walk away and around the house.

"I want to talk to you." His brow furrowed.

"You better make it fast for your lady is walking away." I was so angry and my heart ached.

"My Lady? Oh, you think? Ah… but that is where you are wrong, my lady." His brow relaxed.

"What are you talking about? Oh! Do let me go!" I pulled from his grip and walked into the house.

"Rebecca!" He called after me, but I didn't stop and huffed up the stairs and into the powder room. Men! Why was he doing this? He was playing with my heart like most men do. I was such a fool and it's my own fault. I should have never let myself come out of mourning tonight. My face was a mess and I tried to fix it and groaned.

I stood looking at myself in the mirror and breathed in and out slowly. I took a drink of water and suddenly I felt almost back to normal, thankfully. I took another deep breath and walked back down stairs. I peeked outside and no one was in sight as I stepped out and down the stairs.

"Now I have you!" Two large arms caught me around the waist. I could smell William's scent all around. I stopped myself from taking it in. I needed to be strong.

"Let me… go!" I wiggled, realizing I wasn't touching the ground. My backside pressed against him.

"No! You, Rebecca… are going to hear me out." He carried me out into the dark yard by the big oak. I could hear the crunching of leaves under his feet! Blasted man! He sat me on my feet but still holding me.

"No, I will not! You've made your self very clear." I spat as he spun me around so fast that my hands landed on his chest.

"Well, apparently… I have not!" His eyes seemed full of anger.

"Yes, you have! You said you liked Clarissa… and well… you can have… "

Suddenly his lips crushed mine covering them as his arms pulled me into his chest, pinning my arms against him. I pushed on his chest enough to free my arm and pulled away from his lips. I gasped, slapping his face hard!

He clenched his teeth as the muscles pulsed in his jaw. He tightened his hold and crushed another kiss on my lips. I fought to pull away but he held his grip and even tightened it more. He deepened his kiss making my knees weaken from under me. I stopped pushing on his chest and I felt my hands sliding up around his neck and into his hair as if I had no control.

His lips burned the thoughts out of my mind as his tongue touched my lips as they opened on his command. Deepening his kiss, my heart pounded out every breath I fought to regain. His lips burned mine as searing heat rose from the ground to my head. He slowly pulled back from my lips, breathing hard. His eyes searched mine deeply, tears welled into my eyes.

When he saw my tears, he loosened his hold. He searched my eyes and I, his. He was about to release me completely, but I was tired of fighting this feeling and pulled him back to my lips and kissed him matching his passion. He tightened his hold again. I melted against him not being able to stand on my own. His natural scents permeated through his cologne…my senses were intoxicated. I pulled away slowly trying to breath. He stared into my eyes not saying a word, not smiling though his brows were furrowed. He brushed his lips across mine and then covered them softly and tenderly, then slowly pulled away. He bit his bottom lip as he raised his head and looked at me still holding me tight.

"Rebecca… this is what I wanted to talk to you about." He shuttered a breath.

"You wanted to capture me and kiss me senseless?" I was trying to catch my breath. He brushed his lips across mine again.

"I was trying to tell you that when I saw you dancing with Gabe and I didn't like it."

"Oh… well I…" I felt my cheeks blush. His lips brush mine again. My legs were gone.

"When I saw how he was looking at you my heart pounded in my chest… Do you have feelings for him?" His lips were a breath away from mine.

"No!" Oh William, if you only knew!

"What about… me?" He bit his bottom lip again but not smiling. He was serious, very serious!

"You?" Oh, William! Yes!

"Yes… me." He was holding his breath and brushed his lips across mine again.

"Well… I didn't like you dancing with Clarissa." I brushed my lips across his.

"You didn't?" He smiled still feeling the warmth of his breath on my lips.

"No." I had revealed too much but now I cared no longer.

"I… Rebecca…" His lips covered mine again with such desire and passion. I melted where I stood. I could feel his powerful legs touch mine and my head spun as his lips burned a trail down my neck. Then slowly back to my lips. Oh, how I wanted this man in my life!

"Rebecca... please... let me call on you." He whispered softly in my ear. His breath was hot and made every part of my body cry out.

"You have feelings for me?" I barely could speak. He brushed my lips with his. My head was spinning and was feeling a different kind of drunk.

"God... yes!" He kissed me again letting his lips still linger across mine.

"Yes..." Without thought I replied as I brushed my lips across his.

"You'll allow me to call on you?" He looked into my eyes, his lips still touching mine so lightly.

"Yes, William." I whispered, smiling, feeling my heart just soar.

He smiled and kissed me tenderly. Then he took my hand and wrapped it around his arm and covered it with his warm one. As we walked back to the party, I almost tripped I was feeling so dizzy.

"Are you alright?" William steadied me around my waist.

"Too much wine." I laughed.

"I've had quite a bit as well." He laughed.

We joined Cole and Carla. Gabe frowned as we walked towards them. I smiled and covered a yawn. I knew my lips had been thoroughly kissed and William's face had my hand print on it. What a sight we must look! I wanted to laugh.

"Why, Rebecca. I had wondered where you slipped off to." Gabe smiled.

"We had to discuss... matters." William smiled down at me.

"That we did." I smiled squeezing his arm.

"I think I need something to eat." It had been several hours since I nibbled on the carrots and a finger sandwich.

"I agree, I need something as well." William led me to the buffet table where we filled a plate with everything from sandwiches to desserts. We found a table to sit at way in the back. He held my chair as I sat and then sat across from me.

"Rebecca... Thank you."

"For what?"

"For saving my heart, I thought it was about to be shattered." He took a finger sandwich and held it to my lips. I took a bite and he smiled. Gabe was watching and turned and walked away.

"I think Gabe is a bit upset. " William frowned.

I nodded at William as I also saw Gabe. He winked at me, nodded, and then smiled a knowing smile. Though I couldn't help but feel sad for Lord McCray as he, too, was looking for someone to share his life with. I took a carrot and nibbled on it and sipped the wine.

"I think I've had too much of this." I laughed.

"And I, as well..."

"Why did you leave while I was singing?"

"It was the song you were singing and the way you were singing. I felt something strange. Then I looked at Gabe and he was looking at you in a way that made my blood boil. I just couldn't take it. The thought that you were singing to him was not acceptable to me."

"I wasn't singing to him." In truth, I had chosen that song for William. I laid my hand on his.

"I know that sounded silly." He blushed.

"I was singing to you." I smiled.

"You were?" He smiled his eyes twinkling.

"Yes... I wanted you to know how I was feeling. I was hoping you were feeling it too."

"I was... believe me... and you sing like an angel!" He smiled looking deep into my eyes.

"Thank you... I use to sing all the time."

"I could listen to you all night." William held out a big bite of strawberry shortcake with lots of whipped topping. I opened my mouth and he put the whole thing into my mouth! I had whipped cream all over and we laughed at my face for my cheeks were puffed out and my eyes were tearing as well. I almost choked on it from all the laughing.

"I'm sorry, Rebecca!" He roared a rich laugh. I wiped my mouth.

"Really...you should be." I laughed.

"Let's dance." He stood holding his hand out.

"I would love to." I laid my hand in his and felt such a strong connection to him that I hadn't felt before. It felt warm and familiar and this was wonderful!

He stood in front of me and took me into his arms. Our eyes were locked and he took my breath away. The music started and he swung me into a waltz, a slow waltz. His arm almost surrounded me holding me so close and then turning me around in smooth turns and circles. I closed my eyes and let him take me away, feeling as if I was floating on air. His hold tightened and he swung me into another, then another... and another. I didn't care about the proper amount of dances. I was enjoying the wonderful feeling of being in his arms. When I opened my eyes he was smiling down at me with twinkling eyes. My heart skipped a beat as he swung me into another. Now people were noticing William and I and whispering quietly back and forth. This was this the fifth waltz, sixth? It didn't matter to me in the least. I was where I wanted to be, in William's arms.

"Rebecca... you are breathtaking." He smiled, a little winded.

"And you, my Lord, are handsome... too handsome!" I smiled, very winded.

When the waltz ended he read my thoughts and nodded. We walked to where mother was. I smiled at her as William went for a glass of water.

"I see that you found your William." Mother smiled approvingly.

"I did." I smiled at mother and then looked up at William.

"And I see that you are feeling much better." She laughed.

"I am." I smiled and kissed her cheek.

"I see that you are indeed quite interested in him." She was interrogating me.

"I am." I smiled feeling glorious!

"That's wonderful!" She clapped her hands.

"I told him that he may call on me." I whispered.

"You did?" Now she was shocked.

"Yes and please, don't you tell me that I should wait." I warned her, still smiling.

"I would never do that. I think you should have snatched him up the first you saw him." She hugged me tight.

"Honestly, Mother... I said he could call on me... not marry me!" William came back with water.

"Here you are, my lady." He was smiling so sweetly.

"Oh, it's 'my lady' now?" She winked at William.

"Mother!" My cheeks blushed.

"Well, child... He's a fine specimen." Hannah winked at me.

"Hannah! Honestly!" Now I was beyond embarrassed!

We all talked and laughed at Mike being flustered at the girl he 'wasn't seeing', Gail Cropper. She was not a small woman, but not heavy either, though she was quite pretty, but I was surprised to see that she was his 'type', as Cole put it. Where were Cole and Carla? I looked around and they were not in sight. That was good. Very good!

"Mother, what do you think of Carla?"

"She's lovely! Perfect for Cole and I think he has taken to her." She nodded at Hannah and Hannah nodding back.

The Maestro announced the last waltz gathering everyone for the last dance. William took my hand and led me to the dance area. I saw Nick and William nod to the Maestro.

When the waltz started William danced me down the stairs to the fountain area where Carla and Cole were. We shared the area and danced to the last note. When it ended I looked up into William's eyes. He wanted to kiss me, I could tell. I saw Cole bend way down and kiss Carla on the steps.

William took me into his arms kissing me tenderly, pulling away slowly and glanced at Cole and Carla still in an embrace.

William took my hand and we quietly walked around them so we wouldn't disturb them. We reached the top and saw that most everyone was leaving. I wondered if mother needed help and went to see all the guests off in the front of the house. Mike and Gail, the woman Mike wasn't seeing, stood next to mother. I smiled to myself thinking this was a very good night. Very good indeed!

We thanked everyone and some praised me on my singing and many wanted me to sing at their affairs that were coming up. I said I'd consider it and, last but not least, Gabe walked up to me looking not as bright as he had earlier in the evening.

"Well, Rebecca... I see that I need not to ask to call on you any longer." He kissed my hand and shook William's.

"I also see that you have found your place, brother." He smiled shaking William's hand.

"I have." He simply nodded, turning to walk to his carriage.

"Are you alright?" William tone was at a whisper.

"Yes." I looked up at William smiling, feeling my heart slowly being filled and it was a wonderful feeling. I took a deep breath and turned to mother.

"I'll help you clean up." I smiled at mother and Hannah.

"No... the caterers will see to everything. I myself will not have to lift a finger except to lock the door. By the way, where is Cole?" She looked over my shoulder and behind her.

"He's..." I started to tell her, but his deep voice interrupted.

"I'm right here." Carla was on his arm, with her lips swollen from being kissed so much, and I couldn't help but blush for her.

"Well son, I see you have had a wonderful night as well." She smiled softly, laughing as she kissed Cole's cheek.

"Yes, I have and one that I'll shall never forget." He looked at me with thank you in his eyes. I smiled up at him, nodding in silent understanding. Then he looked at tiny Carla, smiling warmly at her.

"I think we should be going." Cole glanced at Hannah.

"Well, alright." I kissed Hannah's cheek, whispering 'thank you'. She was Robert's aunt, after all.

"I'll see you tomorrow if you stop by the shop, that is, if you're not busy." She laughed as Cole helped her into her carriage.

"Yes, tomorrow." I laughed, rolling my eyes at her.

"Well then, you young men best get your ladies home soon." Mother teased kissing Cole and I on the cheeks and she and Hannah quickly disappeared into the house.

"Shall we?" William held his arm out.

"Thank you." I took his arm and he covered it with his hand. Cole and Carla went to the other side of the yard to the swing.

"I think Carla and Cole are a perfect match." I watched them sit on the swing.

"I believe you are right." He spoke softly as we walked into the barn and opened the stall leading Diablo out. Jack was put up in the other stall and I let him out. He jumped excitedly.

"Oh, Jack!" I laughed as he pushed me down in the hay.

William held his hand out and pulled me up to my feet and into his chest as his arms went around me.

"Thank you, William. I believe Jack acts like a little child." Jack ran out the door.

"Well, you make me feel young again, as well." He laughed, raising his hand up and pulling hay from my hair and looking deep into my eyes.

"I know what you mean." I laughed.

"It's been a long time since I've felt this way." Was he implying that he had felt this way before?

"I'm just glad to be feeling... well...feeling anything for that matter." I started to laugh and suddenly his lips covered mine.

"A hmm!" I jumped away from William's lips and Mike was standing with his hands on his hips smiling.

"Sorry to interrupt, but I have to make sure the horses are taken care of."

"Where's Gail?" I blushed.

"She went home."

"I guess I should be going as well." I laughed.

"Hmmm…" Mike looked serious, but then a slight grin played on his lips.

"Alright, ready?" William smiled as he placed his hands on my waist.

"Yes." I still wasn't too sure of Diablo. He lifted me up in the saddle as if I weighed nothing.

"Diablo…detenerse." Diablo didn't move, acting much better than he did the first time.

William swung up on his back and lifted me like he did before and put my legs across his left leg and I automatically wrapped my arm around his waist this time.

"Good night brother." I smiled at Mike thinking he, too, had had a good evening.

"Good night, be careful with her." Mike warned and then smiled at William.

"Fear not, I would never let anything happen to her, good night! Diablo… Salir a dar un paseo." Diablo walked out of the barn and to the road.

I saw Cole sitting on the swing with Carla holding her hand. I thought he would not wait long if she indeed was the one he would marry.

"I had a wonderful night, Rebecca." His breath warmed my neck and chills ran down my body.

"So did I, but it was after you abducted me and kissed the sense back into me." I laughed.

"I won't apologize for that! I saw McCray was trying to win your affections and he gave me no choice." His voice was stern.

"Why couldn't you just have told me?"

"I tried, remember?" He looked down at me.

"Oh, yes… I do… but why did you not have a choice?"

"I didn't want him to kiss you. I wanted to burn my name into your heart before he tried." His words melted my heart.

"You think he was going to kiss me?" I was surprised to think that William would know or feel something like that.

"Yes, I do! Why? Did you want him to kiss you?" He suddenly looked down at me with his eyes wide open and brows both up.

"Hum… did I want Lord McCray to kiss me?" I was teasing him, pretending I was truly thinking about it.

"Well?" He stopped Diablo in the middle of the road. His brow furrowed.

"What if I did?" I teased.

"Then you would not be on this horse with me, you would be with him!" He was short and his tone sounded flat.

"How do you know I would be with him and not you…does he kiss better than you?" I teased.

"How should I know that?" He was tied up in knots and was raising his voice.

"Well, do you think one kiss is going to make a woman decide who she wants to have call on her?" I almost laughed.

"No, but a woman should not spread her kisses. She should save them for the one she truly wants." He tone was less than pleased.

"And you think that 'I' was going to kiss him then?" I looked up at him in shock myself.

"I was hoping that you didn't want to." He looked away with a great sigh.

"And what of you?" I crossed my arms over my chest.

"What?"

"I saw the way you looked at Clarissa Nelson and how you and she were sitting on the porch so nice and cozy." I looked up into to his eyes searching them the way he did me. I could play this game as well.

"Rebecca… I tried to tell you."

"What?"

"I am very fond of her because… she is my cousin." He softly laughed.

"Your cousin?" Now I was truly embarrassed.

"Yes! My cousin and a first one at that! Here…" He swung down from the horse and pulled me down by the waist.

"Let's walk." I nodded and he breathed a sigh of relief. He took my hand in his, entwining his fingers with mine with Diablo's reins in his other hand.

"So you were jealous?" He looked well pleased.

"No… well… I didn't like thinking that you were interested in another." I lifted my chin knowing that I really was more than just a little jealous.

"I thought you were or you wouldn't have ever said 'I could have her'." He grinned.

"Well… I…" I was speechless.

"It's nice to know that another beautiful woman like Clarissa would upset you and make your blood boil, and over me, to boot!" He smiled and ran the back of his fingers down my cheek.

"To tell you the truth, when I saw you dancing with Clarissa, I realized that it did bother me and knew I was fonder of you than I had thought. I saw Lord McCray dancing with other women and it didn't bother me." I admitted.

"What I was talking to Clarissa about was... you Rebecca. How you had me all tied up in knots and that I was worried that you were interested in Gabe. I asked her what I should do." He wrapped his arms around me.

"I... don't know what to say, but I'm sorry, William."

"What? You're Sorry? About caring for me or for tying me up all in knots?"

"Both... I know you're not ready for a relationship... you told me that at the river, at least until you're out of the Corps and yes, for tying you up in knots." I smiled.

"Rebecca... I can retire from the Corps any time I want, I am a Colonel. I could have retired at thirty if I really wanted to. Remember, I started the Corps very young."

"Yes, I remember you said you were young. Just how young were you?" He took my hand again and we started to walk.

"Well, first I want you to know, not too many people know this."

"You don't have to tell me if you don't want to."

"Rebecca, I want to tell you." He nodded in thought.

"If you are sure..." He really does trust me!

"Yes, I am. I was fourteen." He looked down at the ground.

"Fourteen?!" I stopped and looked at him.

"Yes, fourteen. I was...homeless in a sense." He sighed deeply.

"What? Homeless?" Shocked, I looked up at him.

"Yes, my parents and brother and sister died." He sighed pausing.

"Oh, my heavens!" I couldn't even speak.

"It was a long time ago." He spoke softly and calmly patting my hand.

"Oh, William, you must have been so afraid." A fourteen-year-old boy alone and homeless!

"I was at first, but soon, I found out that I could take care of myself."

"How did your family..." My heart pounded as I felt his hand squeeze mine.

"After the last war, the Corps swept the ocean waters for bombs and they successfully retrieved thousands of them. However, the ocean had renegade bombs appear every now and then. When they believed that it was safe and they could monitor the ocean, they allowed a few ships to go back and forth from Europe with an escort, but unfortunately they missed a few. My family was lost at sea, presumed drowned and there were no survivors found. Some say the bombs floated up from the bottom or possibly floated up from an undercurrent. My family was heading to England and then to Paris but I had stayed behind. I was needed to tend to the place, the live stock and the crops." He took a deep breath and he wrapped his arm around my back and I, his. I was so absorbed in his story. I could do nothing but listen.

"I was young, but I had run the estate on occasion before, but this was my father's way to see if I could truly run the entire place for longer than a few days, a test if you will.

Early one morning, as I was working a horse in the corral, about two weeks after my family left, the Corps came to the house. I watched them walk up the path to the corral and the look on their faces told me there was something wrong. Both men made me sit down on the tack box and stood in front of me, though their names escape me. I remember the gut feeling I had and swallowed hard knowing my life was about to change before they ever told me a thing. I sat trying to prepare myself for whatever they had to tell me. Then... they told me about my family and immediately took me to Lawrenceburg without allowing me any rebuttal. They told me I wasn't old enough to be on my own and was too young to be taking care of the estate." He took a deep breath again and I listened to him, trying to imagine this all happening to someone as wonderful as William! My heart ached for him.

"My Uncle Clarence, Clarissa's father, took me in for a while and promised to take care of everything... along with... my Uncle's brother, Carl Nelson." I could tell he hated this man and watched William's eyes grow cold and angry.

"Since my Uncle Carl was the eldest brother of my mother's family, the Union awarded him the estate to oversee until I was twenty-one. My uncle had complete control. My father was an only child so Mother's eldest brother, Uncle Carl, was appointed control of the estate. Well, you see, Uncle Carl was a closet gambler and a drunk. He put the estate up for a bid as collateral and lost everything." William paused and I saw a look wash over his face as if he was there at this very moment

"My Uncle Clarence promised to do everything to try to save the estate, but his resources were not enough. He did try his best and spent his own money on attorneys. My Uncle Carl was killed one night. Reports told he fell off his horse, which to this day, I don't believe. Rumors say he was murdered for his debts. I only know one thing, a dead man doesn't talk." He stopped and turned to me, seeing tears falling down my cheeks. William raised his hand to my cheek and softly smiled.

"Please, Rebecca, don't cry..." I was so overwhelmed with all he was telling me that I couldn't believe how William, as a boy, must have been so terrified!

"Please, tell me what happened." I wiped the tears away and took hold of his hand and made him walk again.

"At the findings of Uncle Carl's death they said that there was nothing I could do, or anyone else for that matter, and I was angry. I had no family of my own and no home to call home. Everything I ever knew or loved was gone!

After weeks of waiting, the court allowed me to retrieve any personal things. I could take family papers of personal importance, pictures and personal belongings of my family but was denied furniture, horses and livestock as they would be used to repay Uncle Carl's debts.

For about a week at Uncle Clearance's, I tried to figure out what I should do and finally decided. I took my birth certificate and changed the birth date to sixteen. I knew I was taller and stronger than most and I knew I could pass for sixteen. You see, Rebecca, I didn't want to burden my Uncle Clarence and his family any longer so I told him I was going to join the Corps. He never gave me any argument, though Clarissa and my Aunt Chloe fussed. They tried to change my mind but couldn't and a few days later, I thanked them, kissing them all goodbye, and never looked back.

I worked every step of the way to get to Port Augustine and it was a long way from home." He smiled, stopping again and covering my hand with his.

"Oh, William! That is so tremendously sad!" I couldn't stop the tears.

"Rebecca, it's alright! Let me finish the story!" He held my face in his hands and wiped my tears away.

"Alright..." I sighed, thinking what a brave boy he was, as we started walking again.

"As I said, I worked all the way to Port Augustine. I did odd jobs that I could find telling whomever that I was only here to make enough to make it to the next place. I slept where I could and once in a while, I got a nice cot in a stable and a warm meal. Finally, I got to Port Augustine and enlisted in the Union Corps immersing myself into the life and way of life in the Corps. I love it and to me it was strange, it felt as if I was born for that exact moment! Somehow, I knew I was where I was supposed to be! It felt wonderful! They all became my new family.

When I turned twenty, a letter from the territory of Tennessee was sent to the Department Head and I was called off the field. I was a heading for a promotion and thought that was what they wanted to see me about. When I reported to the office, the Colonel said nothing and handed me a letter. It stated that upon my eighteenth birthday, I was allowed to have access to all my father's accounts in the bank and anything that the bank held. The Colonel was angry that I had lied to the service for so long and had no choice but to demote me. I was offered an option to leave if wanted to, but refused deciding to stay since the Corps was the only thing I knew at the time and the only thing I could count on. I worked for the respect of myself and my Colonel to get my rank back. Little did I know, the Colonel had respected me for doing what I had done I was assigned one thing then the next. That went on for several years until the age of twenty- six. I finally regained my rank and a higher rank rather quickly after that. By the time I was twenty nine, I was next in line to a Colonel. I had been in the service for fifteen years already, and at thirty I was promoted to Colonel. At thirty-three, I was knighted because of my involvement in a special part of the Corps for several rescues and many missions I successfully accomplished. They are still confidential and I cannot expose anything about them." William smiled at me knowing I was trying hard to take all this in. My heart still ached for that fourteen year old boy as he continued.

"When I was thirty-four I looked into father's estate and by my word, I was going to buy it back. That whole experience of loss and making my way to Port Augustine was enough for me that I swore I would never be homeless again."

"But that is sad… you have no family!" I could hardly breathe.

"I have Uncle Clarence and Clarissa and Aunt Chloe, but here's the most important part..."

"What? Please tell me this story gets better?" I couldn't believe all he was telling me.

"I found out that I could purchase Father's estate back, but that took another whole year to do. In the meantime, I needed to look into Father's bank dealings and was quite surprised at my findings. I had allowed Father's bank dealings to sit for years untouched really having no idea what they were about and when I looked into them to see what was there, that's when I knew I could purchase the estate back, all but 200 acres. So when I had purchased everything back that was taken from me, I looked for the loyal people who used to work at the estate and asked them if they wanted to return. Some were too old and settled where they were at and some sadly gone. The ones that could return and wanted to return were so happy to come home. That's what most of them said, they were going home.

You see, the two hundred acres that I would never want back was land that I gave to the people that I've known as far back as I can remember, loyal people who used to work on the estate for my Father and built homes on the land. They were ones that were too old to work but had served Father for so many years. We together as a family, built homes for them so they would never again have to leave. Many honorable Lords who have estates do this for their faithful ones. We all take care of each other and are now what I refer to as my family... all of them. So in essence, I have a rather large family." William smiled, looking so at peace.

"William... I... That is wonderful and so amazing!" I was still trying to comprehend all that he had gone through and held a new respect for him.

"I want you to come see 'Castillo en la Árbol', the name of the estate. It means, 'Castle in the Trees." His eyes twinkled telling me that he truly loved this place.

"The name sounds beautiful, is it made of stone?"

"Yes and it is huge!" He laughed deeply.

"William, I would love to see it." I smiled up at him.

"Then, my love… you shall." He smiled and stopped again looking deep into my eyes.

"I have lots of horses and land and a dog named Loco, who is truly crazy. He runs the cattle, but he's also good company."

"Well, it doesn't sound uneventful in the least." I laughed.

"It never is. I also have a few oil wells on the property that I found after I bought it back. One of them yields quite well and the others are used for the estate as a reserve." He nodded.

"God knew what he was doing after all." I smiled up at him.

"Yes, he does... he sent me you." He looked deep into my eyes as his lips gently covered mine. My hands went into his silky hair loosening the tie. His hair fell all around his face and shoulders touching my face. A soft rumble escaped from his lips. He deepened his kiss taking my breath in with his. I had never been kissed in this way and my flesh began to scream out to him wanting to return his passion. He pulled away from my lips slowly. His eyes darted back and forth looking into my eyes as if he wanted to say something.

"William... are you alright?" I searched his eyes.

"We better go." His tone changed.

"What's wrong? Did I do something wrong?" His face was tense. His jaw muscles flexed and brows furrowed deeply.

"No, Rebecca." He lifted me up on the horse and the swung up behind me.

"But why are you angry?" He put my legs across his.

"I'm not angry, Rebecca." His answers were short.

"Diablo...Vamos!" Diablo bolted down the road.

"William?" I looked up at him.

"I need to get you back to your room, it's late." He was deep in thought.

Diablo ran into town. What had happened that made William's mood change? Had I done something to offend him? My heart pounded against my ribs. He didn't say a word all the way back.

We reached the stable and led Diablo to the stall and then he reached for me, setting me on the ground, looking into my eyes as if I was supposed to know what he was thinking. This look he had I didn't know! He put Diablo in the stall and closed the stall door. Then he turned to me and stopped. He took a deep breath and then offered his arm and I took it without saying a word. I stole a glance at him as we crossed the street, seeing now his face more relaxed.

"William, please tell me what I have done to cause this change of tone and mood in you." He still didn't say anything till we reached my hotel room door.

"Rebecca, it was nothing you did or didn't do... It was me." His jaw flexed and rippled and his eyes were so different.

"What are you saying?" I felt my heart start to pound again.

"Rebecca... I'm sorry." His eyes searched mine and he pulled me into his arms.

"William... tell me, please?" I pleaded.

"Rebecca... you consumed all my thoughts... just know, one day..." He couldn't speak the words and struggled to speak.

"Then you're not angry with me?" I put my hand on his face.

"Rebecca... no I'm not angry, very much the opposite. I would never want to hurt you in any way." His tender look warmed my very soul.

"Nor I you, William..."

"Then, Rebecca, please trust me?"

"Yes, William." I whispered.

"Rebecca, I respect you more than you know." His eyes were saying more than his words as his heart thundered under my hand.

"And, I, you..." He held me close and leaned down covering my lips, holding me in his arms gently. He pulled away slowly and his hand touched my face.

"I have never before met someone that stole my every thought. The thought of Gabe or anyone else for that matter, holding you was driving me out of my mind. I have never been so taken with any woman in my life... until I saw you on the road." He took a deep breath, still in deep thought.

"On that note, we should say good night." He sighed deeply.

"Yes, we better... it is late." I looked down wanting to sigh as well.

"Thank you for a wonderful night." I looked back up into his handsome face knowing not to press the issue.

"Shall I meet you for breakfast?" His eyes darted back and forth.

"I would like that." I handed him my key and he opened the door.

"Then, will you allow me to escort you down?"

"If you would like to..." I couldn't believe this man standing right before me.

"I would." His arms surrounded me as he kissed me deeply and tenderly. My arms went around his neck and into his silky hair. I pulled away looking into his unbelievable changing eyes.

"You... better... go... Lord Andrews." I smiled and blushed and could see him blushing as well.

"I think you're right." He cleared his deep husky voice.

"Nine?" I whispered, eyes locked on his.

"Nine..." His voice was hoarse. He smiled and gave me a quick hard kiss and walked away.

I closed the door and raised my fingers to my swollen lips smiling to myself. He seemed too good to be true! How could I be so happy? Was all he said true? If I didn't know better, one would think he was falling in love with me. Robert, what do you think? I smiled knowing Robert would approve of William and think Robert would have been pleased with Gabe McCray, but not like William. My stomach was still fluttering thinking about the entire evening!

I took out my nightshift and as I did, I thought William's kiss was so passionate, so tender. Robert was the first and only man that ever kissed me and his were short and quick. But at that time, I had had nothing where I could have compared kisses. I thought all men kissed like that. Robert never left my lips swollen, but to be honest, I rather liked how they were feeling right now. Robert never kissed me deeply though it was enough that Robert loved me and cared for me.

Robert was so controlling with money and even time, but I loved that about him. He was so well disciplined, having everything in order and on time. Robert and I would talk and laugh and do small things, like pick wild flowers and he'd put them in my hair or he would sweep me off my feet and dance in the kitchen with me singing his favorite song. 'Let me call you sweetheart', which was one of the oldest songs in the world to me, but when Robert would sing it, it was his song to me.

Suddenly I realized I wasn't missing Robert so much. Was that wrong? Robert would say no, time is too short. You must do whatever you can with the minutes of each day because you can never get them back. Time was so important to Robert. Everything had a time and a time for everything. Robert would have told me that I wasted months mourning over something I could not get back.

Now William was in my life and I smiled to myself, feeling free to possibly take a chance. I do like him and maybe even a little more than just liking him I thought.

I'm glad that he kissed the wits back into me at the party and even the way he did that, I slapped him and hard! I laughed out recalling his face and him cursing, then the crushing kiss. I was now glad he was brave enough to take the chance and show me how he felt. Brave indeed!

Dressed for bed and crawling under the covers I recalled his comment about how he thinks me beautiful! I was never considered beautiful like Clarissa, his cousin!

William makes me almost believe that I am beautiful and tonight I felt beautiful. I closed my eyes and yawned. He wants to take me to 'Castillo en la Árbol' the Castle in the Trees. I wonder if he wants to take me when he has to go back. Would it be proper to go? I would have to take someone with me or it wouldn't look right, maybe Cole and Carla? I think I could talk Cole into it. He has a good foreman that can run the company. Cole needs a vacation. I'll have to wait and see if William plans on taking me back with him this time and then I'll ask him about Cole and Carla. He likes Cole and I think he would feel better as well. Yes, tomorrow... I yawned... tomorrow...

~ Chapter 8 ~

The early morning sun peeked through the window as I awoke. I yawned and stretched looking at my timepiece, seven fifteen. I had plenty of time to be ready for breakfast with William. I crawled out of bed, smiling already and happily picked out a dress. I was officially out of mourning, well after church today that is. I wondered if William would go. Robert's family was going to be there and officially announce his passing and I would understand if William did not want to go. I washed up, dressed and put my hair up in a bun. I was not looking forward to this morning knowing the whole town would be there. A soft tap on the door interrupted my thoughts and I opened the door.

"Good morning." William smiled. He was dressed in a black fitted leisure suite and as always, his cologne was wonderful.

"Good morning." I smiled as I walked to get my handbag.

"Shall we? I'm famished." William's smile was like the morning sun, warm and glowing.

"I am as well." I laughed. Heavens! He looked very handsome this morning.

"William, I have to go to church this morning and if you don't want to come, I'll understand."

"Why wouldn't I want to come?" He took my hand, wrapping it around his arm and covered it with his hand.

"Robert's mother, brother and two sisters will be there and his mother is going to officially announce the passing of Robert."

"I see." William frowned deep with concern.

"That is why I said I wouldn't blame you if you didn't want to go." I smiled up at him.

"I think you are right. It will be an emotional morning, and for me, it would be too tempting to comfort you." He rubbed my hand.

142

"I know. This will be that last thing I have to do concerning Robert." And though I had to do this, I knew it would close this part of my life.

"I will find something to do and when the service is over, we could meet back here if you'd like?"

"Yes, that would be lovely." I could feel his warm hand on my back as we entered the dining room.

We were seated at a nice table by the window. The waiter poured us coffee and gave William the paper.

"Thank you, Stan."

"My pleasure, Milord…" The waiter, Stan, smiled at me.

"Anything special for your lady, Milord?" I looked at William wide-eyed, seeing his eyes twinkling!

"What would my lady like this morning?" He leaned forwards beaming.

"I think I shall have one of your wonderful cinnamon rolls." My eyes were locked to his, I could not look away.

"Very good!, and for you, Milord, the usual?" He smiled at William

"No, I think I'll have what my lady is having." He smiled and gave me a wink as he took his napkin, flicking it out and laid it across his lap.

"Very good, Sir, I shall be right back." He bowed and smiled at me and hurried off.

"Thank you, Stan." William still smiled and our eyes not wavering from one another.

"Did you sleep well?" He spoke in a soft tone.

"It took a while." I took my napkin laying it on my lap.

"I took me a while also." He slightly smiled in thought. He was having trouble sleeping as well?

"What is it, Rebecca?"

I was about to stumble all over my words when Stan approached the table! Thank goodness!

"Here you go. Would you care for anything else?" Stan sat two huge rolls in front of each of us. I was thankful for Stan's interruption!

"No, that will be all, thank you, Stan." He bowed with a smile.

"This is a cake! Not a roll!" I laughed.

"It is rather large, isn't it?" He sipped his coffee looking at me over his cup.

"We could have shared one!" I laughed shaking my head.

We fixed our coffees and I looked out the window at the alley, thinking of Joey.

"I recall you saying you sent word to Robert's mother about his death?" William interrupted my thoughts.

"Yes, but I had to be sure she got the message and she did. It was about a month after he died that I finally gathered my thoughts well enough to compose a letter." I hardly remember writing a letter!

"I see." He nodded, looking at me over his cup.

"What will you do this morning?" I took a bite of the mouth-watering roll.

"I'll find something to do. Perhaps I'll just wait for you and when you are through, you can come to my room and tap on the door?" His eyebrows fluttered up and down teasing me as he's never done before! William was feeling very comfortable, very comfortable indeed!

"Mother may have something planned or Mother Grayson."

"I thought about that as well, but don't worry. I may find a beauty and take her to the river." He laughed, teasing me again, and I rolled my eyes.

When we finished breakfast he walked me out to the front of the hotel.

"I'll see you soon." He kissed my hand softly.

I nodded, turning to walk down the sidewalk and couldn't help but glance back at him seeing him watch as I crossed the street. He nodded and I smiled, nodding back.

I finally reached the church with ten minutes to spare.

"Well, Robert, here we go." I took a deep breath and entered the church.

It was over filled with people, seeing some that I knew and some that were familiar. I saw mother, Hannah and Mother Grayson. I nodded and slightly smiled to mother and Hannah as I went to the front to see Mother Grayson. She stood and we hugged each other.

"Mother Grayson…" I felt tears threaten instantly looking at her face so sad, yet so strong. This was a very hard day for everyone!

"I have one request, Rebecca." Tears welled in her eyes.

"Anything for you, Mother Grayson…" I bit my lip, fighting not to cry.

"Will you sing Amazing Grace?" Her eyes begged me.

"Of course…" I hugged Mother Grayson then turned to walk back to mother as my eye caught Lord McCray sitting in the back.   "Good morning, dear." Mother whispered.

"Good morning, Mother, Hannah." I squeezed both of their hands.

"Mother Grayson asked me to sing Amazing Grace." Mother and Hannah nodded and smiled.

"Are you?" Hannah whispered.

"Yes." I hoped I could!

The new preacher, I was told about, walked out and opened the service with a lovely prayer. After the prayer, he announced that Robert Grayson had passed away and thanked God for my safe return. He held out his hand to Mother Grayson and she slowly walked up to the podium. She held her handkerchief in one hand and held the podium with her other. She took a deep breath and looked directly at me with a nod and then the mass. She cleared her throat...

"I know most, if not all, of you knew my son, Robert, and sadly, I am here to tell you all he was killed in a storm six months ago. I want his young loving wife Rebecca to know that we all know Robert loved you more than his own life, but... if anyone knew Robert, they also knew how he felt about early passing. He would tell his wife to live, love and go on with living and not waist precious time on mourning.

As much as he loved you, he would sadden with your mourning over him for too long. I want you to know that as your mother-in-law, I release you from mourning and ask you to not waste one more day! I do not want to see you weep nor cry, or spend another day in those dark clothes! Six months is long enough! Knowing my Robert, he would have said, 'Even one day is too long!'

When he died, you took care of Robert by yourself and I know of no other woman who's endured what you have." She stopped for a moment and looked at me, wiping her eyes and then looked across at all the loved ones in the church.

"I want you all to know, Rebecca put my son, her husband, to rest without help from anyone!"

I glanced up hearing gasps and seeing women and men cover their mouths looking in my direction. I silently wept, remembering.

"To you, Rebecca, my brave Rebecca, no one could ever have loved a husband any more than you loved Robert. I am aware of Robert's last request to Rebecca. He told me before he left home that if something happened to him there was a box for you. I have no clue of the contents, but he said it would be buried on the land close to the house under a rock. Did you get the box, Rebecca?" I nodded to her.

Mother Grayson paused, wiping tears again, taking a big breath as she gave me a slight relieved smile and a reassured nod. My heart ached for Mother Grayson and I could see where Robert got his strength from!

"Now in saying all that, son... rest well in the Father's arms, we shall miss you, but one day be reunited. Until then, Robert, look over us and know we love you. Rebecca... would you sing please?" She nodded, stepping away from the podium.

I stood with the sound of muttering all across the hall. I kissed Mother Grayson hugging her as she whispered...

"Rebecca, be strong... live!" Mother Grayson's son, James, helped her back to her seat.

"For you... Mother Grayson, Sarah, James, Ann." I closed my eyes and waited for the pianist to start, then took a deep breath and sent my voice all the way to heaven, to God and Robert. The church echoed with my voice and it was as if many angels were singing along.

I sang to Mother Grayson and her family, to Robert and myself saying one last goodbye. My heart slowly released all that bound me with each word, each note, each teardrop that fell. For the first time I felt as if I was truly allowing myself to let go.

When I was through with the song, I asked if I could sing Robert's favorite song and the preacher nodded. Robert's favorite song was an old one 'Let me call you sweetheart'. I opened my eyes and motioned the choir and members to sing with me.

After the song was through, I smiled to Mother Grayson and her children sitting arm in arm.

"Family and friends... I want to thank you with all my heart for coming to share here today. Robert was a strong-willed, wise and kind man and I want to share one of the last things he said to me... 'I promised to love you all my life... and I did.'"

I stood smiling, knowing that Robert did keep his promise, now I must keep mine to him. The preacher came up to the podium and shook my hand, patting the back of it. I returned to my seat.

"Everyone... I think we will just close our services for today. Sometimes the Lord has his own plans." The preacher bowed his head and prayed for the Grayson's and for me. When he was through, we all chimed 'Amen'.

The service in the church only lasted for a half hour. On the way out, everyone came up to Mother Grayson and I, hugging us and wishing us well. By the time we walked out of the church, it had been an hour and a half.

Mother, Hannah and I watched everyone leave. Mrs. Grayson looked at peace and I felt at peace, as well. Lord McCray slowly walked to us.

146

"Rebecca, I am truly sorry for your loss, but it was a beautiful service."

"Thank you, Gabe."

"How was your ride home with William last night?" He asked, helping Hannah into their wagon.

"It was nice." I smiled slightly.

"You know Cole was already gone this morning to Carla's. He was taking her on a picnic." Mother smiled as Gabe helped her in the wagon.

"He really does like her, doesn't he?" My heart jumped for Joy. Cole needed someone to love and someone to love him.

"Oh yes! He was awake, shaving and singing this morning. He wore his nice casual suit today."

"Singing? That's wonderful!" Cole was happy and Cole singing was a very good sign.

"And just to think Hannah here, has kept her to herself all this time." Mother teased.

"Me?" Hannah laughed.

"Well, I should have invited everyone to a dinner party long ago. Then my Cole would be married to her already." Mother smiled at me.

"You think so too?" I laughed.

"I'd bet the farm on it." Mother never said anything like that before!

"Well ladies, I have some things to attend to. I shall see you later, Rebecca…" His slight smile and eyes showed he had intent!

"Thank you, Gabe…" I nodded as he kissed the back of my hand. He winked and turned walking away.

"What are you doing today?" Mother straightened her skirt.

"I'm going to meet William at the hotel."

"You are, are you?" Mother smiled widely.

"Yes… and Hannah? Thank you for changing my dress order." I hugged Hannah.

"Well, I had a feeling!" She laughed out and winked at mother.

"Oh, Hannah! You're something else!" I laughed out.

"Well, you best hurry off to your room. I have had one sent to your room already… Well go on child! Your mother and I are going to go for tea." I hugged and kissed them both and walked quickly to the hotel thinking that Hannah was a life saver!

I looked to see if Lord McCray was lurking, but he was gone. I hurried up the walkway excited to see the dress! I reached the hotel and walked briskly through the entrance and up to my room. I opened the door and stopped in my tracks. My room had what looked like hundreds of roses in it. This was William, without a doubt! I saw a card on the table and my hands shook as I opened it…

Rebecca,
Thank you for saving my heart and bringing love into my life….I'll be waiting for
you…
Estoy enamorado de ti
William

"Oh, William!" But what does that mean? Estoy enamorado de ti? I held one of the roses taking in its sweet fragrance and closed my eyes…estoy enamorado de ti sounds so beautiful. I smiled looking at all the roses and thinking how wonderful he was! Then saw the box on the bed! The dress!

I carefully opened it and gasped. Oh Hannah! It was another soft light blue day dress, but this was out of practical cotton and looked very comfortable. The light blue wasn't as light and had a hint of checks trimmed in a small white trim. The neckline was comfortable with a bow tied in the back of it. I loved it! It was a simple dress but perfect!

I hurried to change, letting my hair down and pulling it back with a clip. It felt so good to let it down and free, besides wearing it up all the time gives me headaches. I freshened up my face with a little face powder and looked at myself in the mirror and my heart leapt for joy. The dress was perfect! I couldn't wait to see William now!

I glanced back at the roses and laughed, thinking he had found something to do alright! There were so many roses he had to have bought out the local flower shop! Shaking my head in disbelief, I put my shawl on, grabbed my clutch, shut the door behind me and headed to the fourth floor. With a deep breath, I tapped on the door.

"Just a minute…!" I heard him call. Then with a click, the door opened slowly…

"Rebecca… a… please come in. Forgive me for not being ready. I'll only be a moment… please have a seat." My eye flew open wide for he was wringing wet and in a robe and drying his hair with a towel. The top of his robe was opened in the front, exposing his damp chest. My heavens! He must have just gotten out of the bath! Oh HEAVENS!

"I'll…come…back…..when…or you can…" I closed my eyes tightly. OH MY! He's not dressed! I must leave!

"Oh, don't be silly." He grabbed my wrist and pulled me into his room.

"All I have to do is…" He wrapped the towel around his neck and I froze, staring at him. This is not a proper situation to be in, my thoughts raced.

"I…" My voice betrayed me as his eyes took me in from head to toe.

"Rebecca… You're lovely! Beautiful!" He walked around me then took my hands in his.

"William… I think… I better… I turned toward the door… I have to leave." He's not… dressed!

"No, don't leave…" His smile was so genuine.

"William, the roses… are… beautiful." He was wonderful!

"I told you that you would know if I sent you roses." He smiled with a nod.

"I did, but they must have cost you a fortune! I know the local shop didn't have all of those… How did you…" I couldn't even imagine how he could have done this.

"I ordered then from Lawrenceburg and from here. The florist here set it all up." He smiled, crossing his arms over his huge partially exposed chest. My cheeks flushed as I tore my eyes away from him. I should leave.

"Thank you, William… they're beautiful." I could hardly breathe! I had to go! Seeing him this way was making my head spin.

"Seeing you smile like that is worth every rose in the territory!" He took my hand and kissed it softly.

"Well… I…" I tried not to look at him and started to stand. This was more than just intoxicating!

"Rebecca, please sit. I'll only be a minute… and I'll be right out." He held his hand up.

I bit my lip nervously and slowly eased back down as he went to the washroom. He acted as if it was the most natural thing for me to see him in his robe! After all he was covered up… for the most part.

As I waited for him, I looked around his room. His wardrobe was open and I saw a uniform hanging up as well as several very expensive suits. A clean shirt was lying across the bed and I wondered if it was the one he planned on wearing today?

"Are you hungry?" He called out from the washroom, seeing the door was ajar. Suddenly, I caught a hint of his cologne drifting around the room. HEAVENS!

"Yes, I could eat a bite of something." I can't believe I'm sitting in his room while he is dressing! How scandalous!

"Good! Then I have a treat for you." He called and his tone was excited.

I loved how his eyes lit up at something that interested him or surprised him. I heard his curse under his breath.

"Pardon me, I forgot my shirt." I couldn't help blushing, seeing him half-dressed. I tried to act unaffected as I smiled, waving my hand at him to go ahead. I couldn't even breathe…let alone talk. Thankfully, he had his dark blue denim jeans on, but still, they were form fitting, showing off his large muscular legs.

The shirt he wanted was not the one on the bed, it was in the closet. He smiled and he went to the wardrobe and it was then I saw the scars on his back! Good heavens! What were they from? How did they happen? Who would do such a thing? Surly it wasn't his Uncle? I wanted to gasp out! They were so long and some were tattered looking. How he must have suffered! Why hadn't he mentioned them? They were definitely lashings! I just couldn't imagine someone doing that to William! All I could do was stare! Perhaps, one day he would tell me about them.

He chose a blue denim shirt and that made me wonder why he was dressing so casual. His hair was still wet hanging down over his shoulders and his back. I swallowed hard when he looked at me, trying to keep my smile on my face as my tongue was stuck on the roof of my mouth. He softly laughed, shaking his head and showing teeth that looked so white against his tanned bare skin. To make matters worse, I could smell his intoxicating cologne. I was a tea total mess!

Finally, he went back to the washroom while I sat, melted to the chair, knowing I couldn't walk, breathe or think, with my eyes bugged out, my mouth no doubt hung open with my cheeks fire red. Oh, and let's not forget my fingers embedded into the arms of the chair, a tea total mess! No wonder he laughed. He walked out of the washroom moments later.

"Rebecca, I am truly sorry about that." His hair was brushed and tied into a tail bound with a leather tie.

"That's alright… I've seen… a man's… chest before." Oh, right! Not like his! Robert's wasn't as muscular and William's was so much more defined. There wasn't an ounce of fat anywhere. His stomach was like a wash board. His chest muscles jumped when he reached up to get his shirt. His chest was covered in a soft silky cover of dark hair. His arms were huge and sculptured and no doubt, like a rock. My cheeks would never go back to their normal color. Of that I was sure!

150

"That's what I thought... you were married... I mean to a man... I mean..." He took a deep breath and looked up with his hands on his hips.

"I know what you mean." I laughed smiling, not being able to do much else!

"Well, are you ready?" His eyes held a bit of mystery.

"Yes." I managed to hoarsely whisper out taking his hand.

"I think you will love this." Whatever he had planned I was sure I would.

"Can you tell me where we are going?" I smiled.

"No, it's a surprise!" His face lit up like the sun as he wrapped my hand around his arm leading us on our way.

Waiting outside was a beautiful sleek black carriage and I looked up at him surprised! He helped me into the carriage, but this time, he sat next to me! His cologne instantly filled the carriage and my thoughts went back to him in the room shirtless, with my cheeks warming again. I thought about his hair still wet and hanging down. It was rather wild looking with it flowing all around his face, down his shoulders and back, but what of those scars? I frowned, thinking that someone would do that to him. I hoped he would tell me one day.

Where could he possibly be taking me? I wasn't overly dressed, but he was rather under dressed. He smiled and put his arm around the back of the seat behind me. Heavens! He smells wonderful! His eyes were twinkling with mystery! I took a calming breath in.

Suddenly I could smell food. Then the carriage lurched forwards and wherever we were going we were on our way.

"So, will you tell me where you're taking me now?"

"No, I wish to surprise you. It won't take long to get there... here, just relax and enjoy the ride." He looked adorable being mischievous.

He softly chuckled as his arm, behind me, move to my shoulder pulling me closer to him.

"Your dress is so pretty Rebecca. I'm glad you're finally out of morning," He tilted my chin towards him with his finger.

"Yes. Mother Grayson gave me her blessing in church this morning. She said I'm not to waist one more day and that she didn't want to see me in anymore dark dresses, that it had been long enough."

"How did you and your family react to that?"

"Well no one said anything really, but the whole congregation heard Mother Grayson and no one will test her word, her husband was the pastor of the church and she is well respected." That was the truth.

"And what of you? How did you feel?" His tone was serious, very serious.

"Mother Grayson requested me to sing 'Amazing Grace' and while I was singing, I got a wonderful feeling, a peaceful one, a sense of release… it was amazing. I knew that it was time to end the mourning and go on with my life and I knew somehow in my heart that Robert was telling me that enough was enough." I looked out the window feeling sad that indeed I was closing the book on Robert's life and mine. However it was a wonderful chapter in my life even though it wasn't perfect at times.

"Does that bother you?"

"No, it is wonderful. I finally feel at peace… but now what do I do? I'm still left with not knowing what I will do." I sighed out loud.

"You know, I found out that sometimes it's best to let the good Lord take care of those kinds of matters… besides, he took care of me when I had no clue what was going to happen to me." He lowered his chin raising a brow.

"You're right." I sighed softly.

"Sometimes we don't know why God does what he does and sometimes we never find out why, but sometimes we do and it all makes sense when we finally see why. Whatever Robert's job on this earth was, Robert must have completed it. I believe that the Lord doesn't needlessly take some one home unless he has reason." He nodded with sureness.

"I see what you're saying, though I never thought about that in that way."

"We base our brotherhood on His word and honor Him with the utmost reverence."

"I heard you say you were knighted." I looked up at him and he looked forward and didn't say anything for a moment then he smiled and looked down at me.

"Yes, I am Rebecca. I am a knight in the Special Forces under the Territory and governing rule."

"I thought knights were only a fairy tale."

"Please do not speak of what I tell you about the knight's it is guarded and reserved for only a few to know... wives." William paused. He stared deep into my eyes, as if he was searching for something.

"We are real… and each knight has a special gift or talent that they do or can perform, if you will. When you are given the opportunity to or asked to go through training for the Special Forces… and pass… then you are knighted, but the test aren't to be talked about ever, so I cannot tell you any more about that. Just know that only a chosen few people know about the truth that knights are real… I'm surprised that your husband didn't tell you about us."

"No, he didn't. He was in the guards, but he did say that there were some things better for me not to know about." I smiled thinking how strange that Robert would not mention the Knight's. Why, was it that dangerous? William slightly smiled at me.

"Then your Robert was truly an honorable man and true to the guards. He did know about the knight's as well as Special Forces. The knights are the Special Forces… a code name if you will." He smiled down at me.

"Then why are you telling me if only a selected few are to know?" I looked at him seriously and bewildered.

"I trust you, and besides you'll find out why I told you... one day." He smiled kissing my forehead.

"You really do trust me, don't you William?" My heart leapt for joy that he truly did.

"Yes." He looked down at me in a way that instantly took my breath and added,

"With my life…" His eyes narrowed from the bottoms. What was this look? Strangely, Robert use to say that to me as well.

I looked out the window and realized we were by a pond, a large pond. Then the carriage stopped.

"We're here!" His eyes held excitement as he leapt out of the carriage taking my hand then lifting me out.

"Look…" He pointed to the weeping willows and the pond and it was beautiful! He went to the back of the carriage to the travel carrier and took out a blanket and a large basket, a very large basket. Then the driver led the carriage away leaving us alone.

"William this is a lovely surprise indeed!" I met his smile as he took my hand leading through the tall grasses and under the umbrella of the huge tree and then in a nice spot, he spread the blanket out. He helped me to sit and then sat next to me. He opened the basket and took out a bottle of wine and two glasses, opened it, and poured us each a glass.

"I knew you would enjoy this. Here's to a beautiful day and a woman whom I admire more than I have any other." His glass touched mine and we both took a sip.

"That was lovely, William. Thank you." I smiled surprised again with William.

"Tis the truth, my lady." He smiled warmly.

"I am speechless!" I smiled sipping the sweetly fruited wine.

"I was trying to think of something to do for you after church today knowing it most likely would be a hard morning for you." He smiled and dug around in the basket.

"You were right and I thank you for being so kind." How considerate he was!

"With you... it's an easy thing to do." He smiled up at me then dug around more in the basket.

"What do you have in there?" I tried to peek.

"You'll see." He laughed with that mischievous look creeping across his incredibly handsome face.

"Cheese..." He took out a tray of three different kinds of cheese. Vegetable sticks. Then a basket of chicken and chocolate cake!

"My goodness! That's a lot of food! When did you decide to do this?"

"After you left for church this morning..."

"Well, I am completely taken that you would do such a wonderful thing for me... you are so considerate and kind." I was in complete awe of his kindness.

"And loving?" He grinned simply wickedly.

"Yes... and loving... are you trying to charm me?" I laughed as I took a bit of cheese he held to my lips.

"Oh drats! That's right! You're on to my ways! You are very clever Ms. Grayson... very clever indeed!" He smiled and ate the rest of the cheese that I didn't.

"Why yes... Lord Andrews and I do believe you have ulterior motives in bringing me here." I glanced at him in a playful way as he leaned closer to me and raised his brow grinning.

"Are you going to flee?" He said in a low husky tone.

"I... well I'm not sure!" I laughed thinking he indeed was being extremely charming!

"Well then my lady, I guess I will have to pull all the stops out and charm the day lights out of you!" He laughed and relaxed on his back, stretching his long legs out crossing them at the ankle.

"Try this…" He handed me a piece of chicken and I took a bite.

"This tastes like mother's chicken!" It really did!

"That's because it is! Your mother prepared this wonderful basket." He grinned as if he ate the mouse!

"How did you… But she was at church." Mother was in on this.

"As I was saying, I didn't know what to do. Cole stopped by the hotel this morning holding a basket. He told me he was taking Carla on a picnic by the river after church and I told him I had planned on doing something for you as well. Cole wanted to be alone with Carla and I told him that I wasn't going to the river and that I want to take you another place. His face lit up and he handed me a basket saying that your mother would want me to have the basket, that your mother made plenty, that he would get another basket. Cole was the one to help me figure out what to do for you. So, it all worked out wonderfully I could not have planned it better myself! Funny though, it was as if your mother knew." His face was glowing with pleasure.

"I wouldn't put it past her either William and I thank you for thinking of me like this, it was rather a nerve wracking morning and this is perfect." I smiled up at him seeing he was well pleased.

"Your most welcome my love." He patted my hand then held it for a moment rubbing his thumb across the back of it.

I looked towards the pond seeing the willows that hung over the water. The branches full of leaves made it appear like a massive green waterfall pouring into the water. The gentle breeze lazily bent the long branches that dipped into the calm water with small ripples. I heard several fish jumping on top of the water. All around birds were singing and enjoying this lovely day just as much as we were. I tilted my up face towards the sun feeling the warmth kiss my face.

"Ah…to be the sun…" William smiled staring at my face as he bit into a carrot. The things he says! I softly laughed smiling warmly at him.

"This is truly wonderful." And it was!

"Would you care for more wine and cheese?" He held out the plate to me. I took two pieces and curled my legs under me. If the truth be known, I wanted to lie down and stretch out in the sun!

"William?"

"Hmmm?" He took a deep breath in.

"Do you still have to go on missions?" I didn't know what I could and could not ask.

"No, the last one was about three years ago." He unbuttoned his sleeves, rolled them up and undid the top three buttons of his shirt. He took a bite of cheese and smiling at me now looking totally relaxed.

"Do you wish to go on missions?" I took a bit of cheese.

"No. I train new recruits. One out of a thousand I see, may possess the potential to be in the Special Forces. I push them sometimes almost inhumanly, some would say." He frowned slightly.

"You hurt them?" I looked wide eyes at him.

"I am... very hard on all the men, but they all have to be prepared for any mission or attacks and the ones that are chosen for the Special Forces, I have no choice but to be hard on them." He looked down frowning still.

"But William... I could never see you as an inhuman person! It doesn't match the person I'm looking at or know!" I couldn't believe what I was hearing.

"When I am training my men, I'm not the way you know me now." He frowned again but this time there was something different in his eyes. Something that frightened me enough to give me chills realizing there was a lot more to this man that I didn't know. His age was definitely clear with the look on his face now. He looked older and his face was like stone, cold...

"I would have never thought." I looked at him not believing what I'm seeing in William.

"My job is to train and see that they can and will and do what they must...on my order." I could see in his eyes that he didn't want to talk about this anymore.

"Tell me of 'Castillo en la Árbol'." I knew it was time to change the subject.

"I would love too." He took a deep breath and I saw instant relief. I finally did lay down on my stomach as he took out the chocolate cake and one plate two forks and poured our glasses full again then laid along side of me. I listened while he talked.

"Let's see, where did I leave off the last time? Oh yes, after I bought back the estate, it was rather run down from lack of care. I rehired all the old workers that wanted to come back and we all poured ourselves into redoing, remodeling and fixing the entire estate top to bottom and for their work. I gave them the land they were still paying for as payment for their loyalties to me, plus the use of another several hundred acres connecting to all the small farms. I wasn't going to use the land so I let them have it. They make their own money. I want nothing in return, except perhaps for apple pie and pear pie and maybe strawberry and pumpkin! I love fruit pie!" He laughed out.

"After several months we had the place almost finished and I began to replenish the crops, livestock and horses. Little by little we started to make a profit on the estate. I devised a plan for profit sharing for the workers so that they would never be put out again... should something happen to me, which at that time was a reality due to my job. I also had my lawyers put my Uncle Clarence as the overseer on my Will so that I was insured that it would never be lost again. I thought about adopting a child to be my heir so that there would be a Lord and name sake, but I'm still in the Forces and still not allowed." He looked down and could see the sadness wash over his face.

"You want children?" I smiled as his eyes shot up searching mine.

"Yes! More than you'll ever know." He looked up then back down quickly with his cheeks slightly blushing.

"Go on... tell me more." I ate another bite of cake trying not to be too obvious that I was happy that he did want children.

"Oh yes, well, I left Nicholas in charge of the estate if I had to leave and if we both had to leave like this time, I have another corpsman that I leave in my absence, Jon Luke Baptiest. Yes, Nick's little brother. I have two of the best cooks, six kitchen assistants and eight house maids and one very pushy, aggressive, overbearing, but wonderful Butler, Jules Burke. He was Father's butler. No one knew where he was located, but finally after I searched for him, a passerby over heard me talking to the grocer in town, that I hadn't found Jules and the man had just come from South Bend and knew of him. He told me right where to find him. I was off the next morning to South Bend and found him in no time. He was working for a very wealthy man that treated him poorly. The moment I looked into his face, he asked if I got the 'Castillo en la Árbol' back and without a word, Jules turned and walked into the den telling the man he was leaving and came back with me. He was more like an Uncle to me than my own Uncle. Jules was glad to be back and approved of how 'Castillo en la Árbol' was shaping up. In no time Jules was back ordering everyone around." William smiled warmly at his memories of Jules and I could tell he loved Jules as family.

"The estate has three floors and all the modern conveniences. We had water put in the house. I hated to fetch water as a boy. It was one of the first things I had to have done. My head cook, Libby Walters, and her kitchen staff were overwhelmed, so much so they cried, hugging me to the point my shirt was wet!" He laughed out shaking his head. He loved them, I could tell!

"All the floors have a sitting parlor and library. The third floor has ten bedrooms with full baths. There used to be more, but when we renovated the estate, I wanted all the bedrooms to have their own baths, which eliminated several rooms. The second floor is for family and friends that I want close to me. There are eight bedrooms as well on that floor including mine. On the first floor is my office, library, sitting room, sun room, billiards room, tea room, a weapons room, ballroom, dining room, formal family room and every staff member has their own room on the back side with their own kitchen library, sitting room and game room if they choose to live in the estate. There is an inner court as well with pool and a fountain in the center of the pool and a place to wield swords for practice.

"You really use a sword?" My eyes flew open.

"Why yes!" He roared out a thunderous laugh.

"Well, your home sounds like a castle!"

"It is a castle!" He laughed at the look on my face.

"It's stone like a castle?" It sounded beautiful and I had no doubt that it was.

"Yes, but it's not cold and drafty as a real castle, except when Jules gets going... God love him!" He laughed out.

"It sounds utterly amazing!" I was truly surprised with William. The more I found out about him, the more I saw his heart, except the matter of his Special Forces training. It just didn't seem to be something that I could ever imagine William to be involved with and to the degree he claimed.

"It is..." He was staring without words again. His hand went to my cheek.

"How many acres do you own?" I took a slow deep breath. His touch did something strange to my insides with all the fluttering, that it was so hard to breathe at times. I've never felt anything like this before! Not even with Robert.

"Minus the two hundred, I own thirty eight hundred acres." He smiled at my face as it was in shock.

"That's enormous!" I thought.

"It is but, some people own a lot more. It's a little more than the average." His eyes took my face in.

"Then you have workers for the grounds as well?" The way he talked about it, made me want to see it even more!

"Yes, I have my stable master, Lord Victor York, and five other men to handle the rest. We hire workers when the crops come in." He nodded.

"What crops do you have?" He was gazing into my eyes, I could not look away and was entranced drowning in their depths.

"We have a bit of everything, Corn, soy beans, wheat, oats and potatoes. We also have apple trees, pear and peach trees." He took a bite of cake.

"It sounds very profitable." His eyes went to my lips as I licked them and a sensual grin crept across his lips.

"It is and self-sufficient. We don't have to rely on anything or anybody. It's perfect." His voice was softer.

"Your father would be proud." As I was to even know such a man.

"I think he would." He leaned down and held my chin with his finger and pressed his lips to mine and pulled away slowly.

"Let's walk…" He stood and held out his hand. I felt the warmth flood my body as I laid my hand in his. He took our glasses and the wine with him.

"You know, this truly was a wonderful surprise." I smiled up into his handsome face.

"I hold many surprises." His eyes twinkled.

"This is all the surprise I need." And it was. I couldn't believe he would think to do something like this for me.

"Ah but, my lady…I wish to surprise you even more." He wrapped his arm around my waist as we walked to the edge of the pond. We stood for a moment just looking at the beautiful pond, enjoying the warm sun and cool air. He led me around the pond reaching the huge weeping willow on the other side. He took his hand and cleared the long green branches aside so we could go beneath the canopy of lush green branches. It was like a special secret place. The green branches surrounded us all around like green walls. I looked up into the tree and it was beautiful! It was glowing green all around as the sun hit the leaves. I had never seen anything like this before!

"Oh William, this is wonderful!" The air was cooler under the tree.

"Rebecca…" I turned to him and his lips covered mine. My heart pounded as his hands covered my back holding me against his muscular body. He lifted away and smiled down at me. I loved the look in his eyes right as they are now.

"I have a few ponds on my property, like this with the giant willows around them. You would love them and they are just as big as these. I can't wait until you come home... with me." He helped me to sit. What did he say? He couldn't wait to take me home? Home...with him?

"Your brother is in love..." He looked at me with something more in his eyes, but what?

"What? But they just met!" I was surprised to see that he noticed it as I had. He poured me a glass of wine.

"Do you not believe in love at first sight?" He smiled looking at me in a strange way and again, I felt my breath leaving me again and butterflies.

"Well... Yes... I think it can happen... but Cole is not one to jump into a relationship falling head over heels. He called on one woman for a few years, but never married her. Love at first sight? No, not for Cole..." I was almost sure about that, then maybe not. He did look at Carla like no other I have seen before.

"What if I told you I knew differently?" He smiled and bit his bottom lip.

"Do you?" I looked at him hoping by chance Cole had confided in him.

"Yes, I do. Cole told me that he has never felt this way for a woman ever. All he can do is think about her. She makes his knees weak, his head spin, his thoughts scatter and his heart pound in his chest. I'd say that is love." He sipped his wine as I stared up at him in thought. He made me feel the same things! My breath indeed was stolen at that very moment! Love? Could I to, be in love? Love at first sight? I thought about the card he sent with the roses. I had to know what the Spanish words he wrote before his name meant.

As I looked at him, I was so deep in thought I hadn't noticed that he had laid back on his back with his legs stretched out and hands clasped beneath his head with his eyes were closed. I looked at him in awe. The wind blew his untucked shirttails up exposing his washboard stomach. Silky hair trailed down his stomach and then vanishing. The longer I looked at him lying there the more my mouth became dry and my cheek warm with my body getting warmer. I took a drink of wine.

"William?" I took a shuttering breath looking away. I had to know what it meant about the note.

"Humm?" He smiled softly not opening his eyes. The sun made his golden skin glow.

"The card you sent with the roses?" I still couldn't look at him.

160

"Um hum." He still did not open his eyes.

"What did the Spanish words mean?" I looked at him waiting, but he didn't respond.

"William?"

"Estoy enamorado de ti." He took a deep breath in and let it out. I watched his wide chest rise and fall. I had to take another sip of wine.

"Yes... What you just said... what does it mean?"

"Estoy enamorado de ti." He slowly sat up and took my hands in his.

"Rebecca, I don't know if I should tell you." He looked down.

"Why? Is it bad?" I bent down to look into his eyes.

"Not in the least." He looked down at my hands.

"Then, tell me please." He looked up into my eyes searching them in a way that he never had before, deep, very deep, then he looked back down.

"Are you blushing Colonel?" I teased seeing he was so serious.

"Me? NO!" He suddenly stood and paced in the grass running his hand through his hair.

"Then are you afraid?" Now I really had to know!

"I fear nothing." He looked down at me with a strange look as if it were me he was afraid of.

"Perhaps you are?" I was smiling teasing him.

"No." His tone was rather horse and defensive.

"You said you were afraid of only one thing."

"I did?" He stopped pacing and looked down at me with his hand still in his hair.

"Yes, rejection..." I smiled holding my hand over my eyes to shade the sun from them.

"I did, didn't I?" He ran his hand through his hair again.

"Well if you're not going to tell me... then why did you write it?"

"What the words mean could change the way you feel about me, even look at me." He paced back and forth again. I stood up and went to him and took his arms in my hands and stared him right in the eyes.

"Then it must be a bad thing for I am extremely fond of you William." His eyes widened. I laughed, for his cheeks indeed had a hint of blush on them again. Whatever the words mean, this was very hard for William.

"Oh, William, you command entire legions of men do you not?"

"Yes..." He was about to say something, but I cut him off.

"And you are a Colonel... are you not?" He was at least apprehensive.

"Yes, but…" He looked deep into my eyes wrapping his arms around me.

"Then why do…" I counted on my fingers the number of words I thought there were four words, Estoy enamorado de ti and continued.

"Then why do four words scare you?" They weren't the three little words… there were four.

"I shouldn't have written them…" He sighed deeply.

"Then you've changed your mind in some way?" I was about to give up. I looked down at the ground thinking.

"Yes." He tilted my chin up. He looked deep into my eyes.

"I see." I looked away recalling he hadn't kissed me the way he did last night, so he has changed his thoughts about me.

"No, I don't believe you do." He took in a deep breath.

"William it's alright." I tried to smile my best smile but couldn't help notice that my heart was hurting as if it was breaking. I swallowed hard still trying to smile.

"Rebecca… I don't believe you do." His tone was absolute.

"William… I understand… Last night was wonderful and we got ahead of ourselves and…"

"NO!" He pulled me to his chest and crushed his lips on mine in a consuming passionate kiss. My thoughts flew and my legs weakened my head spun as his kiss became more passionate. I heard myself let a small moan escape from my lips. A rumble came from deep within his chest. My arms slid around his neck and his arms crushed me against his body. I could smell his natural scent seduce my senses as the soft breeze blew around us. I felt him slowly pull away and opened my eyes finding him looking deep into mine.

"Rebecca… I have never been so… so utterly overwhelmed with a woman in all my life. You do things to my thoughts. I think things I know I shouldn't think. I desire so much more… with you." His lips covered mine again in a passionate kiss and I returned his passion. He raised his head again looked deep in my eyes and my face.

"The words I wrote mean…" He bit his bottom lip deep in thought.

"Yes, William?"

"The words I wrote mean… I'm in love with you." He searched my eyes all the way to my heart, tears welled in my eyes.

"William…" I pulled him to my lips and kissed him tenderly. My heart pounded against my chest feeling his beat along with mine. Tears fell down my cheeks as I pulled away from him slowly.

"Rebecca... why are you crying... I shouldn't have told you...I've upset you!" He raised his hand to my cheek and wiped the tears with his thumb.

"No... I'm not upset! William, when you told me about what Cole said all he could do was think about Carla and his head spins, his knees weaken, his thoughts scatter?"

"Yes..." His voice was husky.

"That's how... you make me feel." I smiled shyly through the tears.

"Then you... feel the same way... I do?" He released a breath he was holding.

"William... Estoy enamorado de ti." I smiled up into his handsome face repeating the same words. His eyes softened and he lowered his head and deeply kissed me. My heart was so full, as my thoughts floated. I knew now I was truly free of Robert, feeling no guilt for my actions. I pulled away from him slowly and placed my hand on his. I brushed his hair out of his face.

"I'm elated you didn't reject me." He looked up and then down.

I smiled up at him seeing a very relieved man.

"I would have had to resort to drastic measures to secure my position." He smiled a devilish smile.

"Like what?" His eyes went to my lips.

"I would have you captured and keep you in my protective custody." He laughed softly.

"Well then, maybe I should have rejected you then." I gave him a devilish look of my own.

"Ah... but my lady... you do not know what you speak of or what that would imply." One black eyebrow went up and a sensual grin played on his lips.

"You think not?" I raised my eyebrow as well.

"Then I shall order a covert operation right away and will not risk anyone infiltrating and attempting to capture my intended's heart." He smiled down a breath from my lips.

"Intended?" I pulled away from him at his words.

"Of course! Do you think once I captured you, I'd let you go?" His grin widened.

"I..." I wanted to laugh, but played along with him.

"I plan on being the only one you allow to call on you. Then I shall court you, which I think I have called on you enough for you to know that I have been trying to court you already. When I have thoroughly courted you, I will marry you." His grin went to a wicked smile. I could not say a word!

"Ah… and then I shall keep you very busy." His smile turned back into a very sensual grin.

"Busy? Busy how?" I nervously laughed for he was being so silly or was he? All I knew was I was warm from head to toe.

"I shall keep you bare foot, with child and throw away all your shoes." He tried not to laugh, but he could see the shock on my face I'm sure!

"Why bare foot?" I looked at him wonder why he would throw out my shoes and keep me barefoot. That didn't make sense at all!

"Well, my lady, if you're pregnant you'd be slow, escape would futile and you would be easily captured." He laughed and so did I.

"Everyone knows pregnant women can't run." He chuckled.

"And the other?" I tried to look serious and not laugh, thinking he had to be teasing.

"Throw away your shoes? Well… you wouldn't get too far without shoes!" I looked at him in shock at the thought then burst out in laughter as he did. He was being so silly. Marry me and keeping me bare foot and with child! Suddenly the thought was very real. To carry his child, which would mean I would know him and him me. My body warmed as a heat wave flowed throughout my entire body, was he serious? I searched his eyes as I saw he was not laughing any more. He was deeply staring right to my heart as if he were touching my very soul… I was fast drowning.

"William, you are so funny sometimes, that I don't know what you'll come up with next!" I smiled and boldly touched his lips with my fingertips.

"Ah but my lady… you think I'm not being serious? I am very serious! You have my word on that and my word is my heart." His face suddenly lacked a smile.

"Does that frighten you?" He raised his brow.

"What?" I was speechless.

"That I'm serious?" He looked at me intently.

"No, but I am surprised." I admitted and truly, I was in nothing short of shock!

"Rebecca, I am too old to 'beat around the bush' and you are the only woman to ever tie me up in knots and the first woman I ever considered to spend the rest of my life loving and taking care of. You are the one I know I could talk to till the wee hours of the morning and one who challenges me with her every word. You stole my heart the first time I saw you, that woman on the road, alone and so brave. I admired you so much and you reminded me of myself. Then when I saw you sitting with McCray that morning, my head spun. I knew there was something to it all and knew I had to keep you away from him. Then at the dinner party, McCray was about to kiss those lips of yours. Those lips were going to be mine!"

"I don't know what to say... this is so... sudden..." My heart was so full. Was I dreaming?

"Is it McCray?" He held me back.

"No, William, no..." Oh heavens no!

"Do you wish me to court you or do you want to see others?" He furrowed his brow.

"No, I wish to see no others, William." Only you, William.

"Then, Rebecca, may I court you?" He held his breath.

"Yes, William, yes." I wrapped my arms around his neck.

"Rebecca..." His lips covered mine with a deep and tender passionate kiss as his arms engulfed me completely. I was falling for this man by the minute deeper and deeper. He was everything Robert wanted for me and Robert would have liked him and was perfect for me in every way.

He deepened his kiss then trailed his searing lips down my neck and back up to my chin and covering my lips again. It was like the night after the party when he had kissed me on the road and had to take me home. The desire was just as strong and deep and wanting as that night. My hidden thoughts were running wild. His kisses were so much different and nothing like Robert's.

I wanted to know what it was like to be loved by him. He scooped me up in his arms and took me back to the blanket laying me down. He laid next to me and pulled me into his arms. He reached up and unclipped my hair. It fell all over the blanket.

"I love your hair." He ran his hands through my hair and spread it out behind me and then he leaned over and covered my mouth with his lips in a very breathtaking kiss. His hand lay on my stomach and then he put it on my cheek.

"Rebecca... I know you will complete me." He kissed me softly and then looked at me.

"I want to take you home with me next week. I want you to see the Estate. I want you to see what I wish to give you, to share with you. You will be the first woman to ever come to the estate with me. My staff will not know what to think!"

"I would love to, William. The only way I could go, is if I ask Cole to go and I think he would say yes, if we invited him to bring Carla." I smiled a devilish grin.

"Yes, I think that would be fun. It's been a long time since we've had guests and it's about time! Yes, let's ask Cole and Carla. I am very fond of them both." We heard the carriage coming and I sat up and fixed my dress and put the clip back in my hair.

"Please... leave that out?" He pulled the clip back out.

I nodded thinking Robert always wanted my hair up in a clip.

The carriage reached us just as we folded the blanket and packed the basket. I smiled at him seeing he was well pleased.

"Where do you think Cole is?" He asked putting the basket and blanket in the back.

"We could try mothers." I smiled.

He nodded and helped me into the carriage and hopped in and sat next to me, taking my hand softly kissing it. He was as truly as excited as I was.

"He still might be at the river too." I thought.

"Well, if he's not at your mother's, then we'll wait for his return." I nodded as he kissed my hand again.

We were soon at mother's house and Cole was there with Carla. William helped me out of the carriage and we went to the back and found Carla and Cole sitting at the patio table drinking coffee. They smiled as we walked up to them.

"Well hello you two... a beautiful day isn't it?" Cole was smiling ear to ear. It was so good to see him smile again.

"Yes indeed." William smiled winking at Cole.

"Come sit and have some coffee." Cole raised his brow as if he knew what kind of day I had.

"Thank you, that sounds wonderful." William held the chair as I sat.

"William, you remember Carla." I smiled up at him.

"Of course... you are the one who stole Cole's heart over night" He took her hand and bowed over it.

"Yes, and I remember you, you are the one who stole Rebecca's heart over night." She smiled and winked at him making us all laugh.

"Another beauty with brains!" William laughed.

"Yes brother... a dangerous combination." Cole agreed.

"But neither of you would have it any other way!" I laughed.

"You are right my lady." William smiled tenderly.

"So, it's my lady now is it?" Cole looked at me and then William.

"Yes, she has agreed to allow me to court her." He smiled taking my hand.

"Is this true?" Cole's brow furrowed.

"Oh, don't you be like that Cole. You asked me the same thing!" Carla looked at him and he blushed.

"He did, did he?" I crossed my arms.

"Yes, today." We looked at each other and burst out laughing!

"So then, William and I have a question to ask the both of you." I looked at William and his eyes held excitement, they were twinkling.

"I have invited Rebecca to Winchester on Friday for a week and we would like it if you two would join us?" He smiled at Cole.

"Well…now. I would have to arrange all the orders that come in this week and have Wilson take care of everything." He sat back with that look on his face scratching his head. Then he looked at Carla and she smiled and Cole melted right before my eyes!

"I think that is a wonderful idea! I haven't had a vacation in…"

"EVER!" I laughed and waited for him to try to deny it!

"Yes, I think it will be a good thing and yes we will join you… that is, if my lady can have her helper cover for her?" Cole looked at Carla with hope in his eyes.

"Of course! I own the place and I can do what I want to. I am the boss you know!" Cole and William looked at each other and raised their brows.

"Good for you Carla! I bet you haven't taken a vacation since you opened the place either."

"That is very true! Yes, I would love to join you." She smiled winking at me.

"Wonderful! We all leave on Friday morning. I can't wait to show Rebecca…"

"Well, well… what are you four planning?" Mother smiled as no one noticed that she was even there.

"Hello Mother!" I smiled and sipped my coffee.

"Cole? What is going on here?" She crossed her arms trying not to laugh, but I think she knew what was going on.

"Well, 'We', Carla, Rebecca and I, are going to Winchester on Friday at the invitation of William."

Her mouth hung open and she put her hand over her heart. She looked like she was going to faint with her hand over her heart and one on her forehead. William and Cole stood, one on each side of her holding her arms.

"Mother, are you alright?" I stood as Carla did.

"Should I call for the doctor?" Cole looked worried sick!

"Heavens NO!" We all looked at each other confused.

"Mother?" Cole looked at me bewildered!

"What is it Mother?" I looked at Cole and we both got the grave impression that she was teasing us.

"Cole... Cole going on a vacation? Slap me quick... I think I've died!" She laughed out.

"Oh, Mother!" I laughed and sat in the chair.

"Mother! That was not funny in the least!" Cole sat with his brows furrowed again.

"Funny? No. A miracle? Yes! And thank you God!" We all busted out in laughter.

"I thought so too!" I laughed.

"So how long will you all be gone?" Mother sat down next to me.

"I shall return them safe and by Sunday." William smiled at her and she instantly blushed!

"I think it's wonderful." She patted Cole and my hands.

"Now if I could only get your other brother to realize that Gail thinks he hung the moon!" Mother sounded like that too was a miracle. I rolled my eyes.

"Where is he?" Cole looked at her.

"Fishing... always fishing." Mother rolled her eyes too.

"William... would you tell us about your home?"

William told them everything he told me about the land and the estate home and they were just as amazed as I was when William told me about it.

"And as I've told your daughter, she is the first woman I have ever brought to my home, 'Castillo en la Árbol'." He smiled and looked at me tenderly.

"Castillo en la Árbol sounds so romantic. What does it mean?" Mother smiled at William.

"It means Castle in the trees." He looked at me.

"Oh my!" She smiled and winked at me.

"I too would love to see it one day."

168

"If you would like to join us…" He smiled at her.

"Heavens, No! You kids go… I'll see it soon enough!" She winked at William with a knowing look.

"If you are sure?" He laid his hand on mothers.

"I am very sure Lord Andrews. All I really want is for you to sweep my Rebecca off her feet and you my dear, indeed have my blessing!" She laughed and stood. William and Cole stood with her.

"Mother!" I blushed.

"Where are you going?" Cole laughed and looked at her.

"I'm going to throw something together and we'll all have dinner out here it's a wonderful evening."

"I'll help you." I stood still blushing and so did Carla.

"I will too." She smiled at me.

"Well then come with me my daughters." She turned to go into the house and I looked at William then Carla and we looked at each other and laughed softly.

"Is your mother one of those…" Carla whispered.

"Nuts? Yes." I whispered and laughed and so did she.

"I heard that Rebecca!" Mother chuckled too.

"Of course you did." I laughed.

We went into the kitchen and pulled out everything and warmed it all up. We put the food out on the center counter and had all the leftovers ready to eat. I fixed a fresh pitcher of sweet tea and a fresh pot of coffee and called the men in, Mike followed. He had returned while we were in the kitchen.

"Look what the cat drug in." I smiled at Mike.

"How's my son? Catch anything?" Mother smiled pouring tea.

"No they weren't biting." He huffed.

"You spent all this time drowning worms and you didn't catch a thing?" Cole teased.

"Well Cole, if only there was a real job fishing, your brother here would be rich!" Mother teased back.

"I'd take the job too!" Mike laughed.

"I love to fish. Our ponds are well stocked." William smiled at Mike.

"Well it sounds like you have it all under control up there." Mother smiled.

"I do and it runs itself." He smiled filling a plate.

"This looks better tonight." I smiled looking at all the food.

"Well, you didn't even see it, you were foxed!" Mother laughed.

"I was…" Not finishing.

"I think you were!" Mother gave me a, 'I know for a fact' look.

"Well maybe a little." I laughed giving William a warning look for he knew why.

"Well, let's go outside and William? Will you say grace?" Mother hooked her arm around his and he rolled his eyes this time. It was contagious.

"That I will…" He smiled down at mother and patted her hand.

We all sat down and held hands and bowed our heads.

"Father in heaven, thank you for all this wonderful food, Lord we know we wouldn't have it if it weren't for your grace and mercy. Father, we thank you for our families, friends, new beginnings and the things that must end. Father bless this wonderful family I have been recently honored to have in my life, you know it has been a long time since I have heard the sounds of love and laughter of family and pray that I will for a long time to come. Keep us safe on our journeys. All that we have is yours and all that you will bless us with in the days ahead we are eternally grateful for and Lord, thank you for Rebecca and you as well Robert. In Jesus' name we pray, Amen and Amen."

"William…that was beautiful!" Mother wiped her tears. Carla and I did as well.

"Women!" Mike laughed.

"It truly was William…thank you…" He took my hand and kissed it.

"Well, let's eat… or are you women going to cry all night?" Mike laughed.

During dinner, we talked about the trip to Winchester. Mike was as dramatic as mother was about Cole taking a vacation.

"I don't believe my ears!" Mike shook his head.

"It's true! They're leaving Friday!" Mother told Mike.

Mike asked William a lot of questions about the estate and they were very good questions about business and production, profits verses losses. I hadn't realized Mike was so astute in the business world and I believe Cole was astonished too.

William explained the profit sharing and how that worked, Cole was interested in that very much. William said it gave the workers incentive and incentive produces better quality and more devoted workers and they take more pride in their work. Cole liked the idea very much! Cole wanted William to write a comprehensive plan that he could study. William told him that he had one better. When we got to his Estate, he would show Cole the paper work and how to convert it to apply to his business. They both were a lot alike! That was it! Now I know who William reminded me of! William reminded me of Cole's ways and Robert's. If I were a betting woman, I would bet that William and Cole could talk of business all night. I looked at Carla and she smiled so sweetly at Cole and he returned a sweet smile back to her. Cole was in love already. His eyes say it all. He never looked at Annette that way and I think mother could see that as well.

"There's more food in the kitchen and dessert." She laughed at their faces.

"Dessert?" All three men said at once. Looking at each other, they smiled and went to the kitchen all at the same time.

"Boys will be boys!" Mother laughed.

"Mother... do you like William?"

"Heavens, yes! He's perfect for you and can the boy pray!" She shook her head.

"It was beautiful." I thought about what he said about love and laughter of the family. He hadn't had that since he was thirteen thinking about his very own family. Tears welled in my eyes.

"Rebecca?" Mother put her hand on mine.

"I'm alright, I was thinking about William not having his family since he was thirteen."

"What?" She squeezed my hand in disbelief.

"That's right! He didn't tell you he lost his entire family when he was thirteen?" I told mother and Carla about William's life story and we were all in tears when the men came back... sobbing.

"What in the world?" Cole looked at all of us and all three of us stood and went to William and hugged him.

"What happened?" Cole put two plates down.

William looked totally lost and confused. He was balancing three plates above our heads looking down at three crying women.

"Now, what did I do to deserve this?" He smiled a confused smile and put the plated down and wrapped his arms around all three of us.

"Women! See why I'm in no hurry?!!" Mike laughed and huffed.

"Shut up, Mike!" All three of us turned to Mike and said it at the same time.

"Well, whatever it is... I'm Sorry... I didn't mean to... or I won't do it again...I forgive you...you've forgiven me?" I looked up into his strong handsome face and cried harder.

"My goodness! I only brought cake!" He hugged us and gave in.

"Go ahead and get it all out." He shrugged looking at Cole and held us.

"Mother please, what is it?" Cole begged.

"My poor, William." Mother laid her hand on William's totally lost face.

"Yes, you poor thing!" Carla cried.

"Oh, William... you are the strongest man I have ever met and I love you." I cried.

"You truly do... don't you?" He stopped hugging everyone and looked down at me.

"Yes, I do." I cried.

"She does and I do too!" Mother cried.

"I know I will... too." Carla cried and hugged me.

"I'm so happy!" I cried and hugged mother.

"Me too!" She hugged me smashing Carla in the middle leaving William standing confused.

"Lord, help me, but I love this family!" He laughed shaking his head. Cole started to laugh then Mike did.

Soon when we heard the men laughing with deep rich laughter that filled the house and we all started to laugh as well wiping tears away. When we all settled down Cole and William looked at all three of us and had the same question in their eyes.

"Would you mind telling us what that was all about?" Cole insisted as William was looking at his shirt. It was almost wet with tears. I laughed.

"I shall never wash or throw this shirt away for it is now the most blessed shirt I own!" He laughed.

"Rebecca was telling us about your life.... and about your family."

"Oh I see." He shook his head.

"Well, I don't." Cole looked at William waiting for an explanation.

"Neither do I." Mike was still laughing.

"Well, it's rather a long story, but in a nut shell, my family drowned on a ship at sea when I was thirteen, I lived with my cousin Clarissa Nelson for a year then joined the Guards, worked my way up to Colonel and bought back my father's estate after another uncle gambled it all away. There that's it..." He shook his head.

"Rebecca tells it much better." Mother smiled still wiping tears away.

"I don't know about that, but I do know that I'm not crying and hugging William!" Cole laughed out.

"And you better not either, brother!" William laughed.

Then we all laughed at the thought of coming out and seeing the men crying hugging William. We laughed until it hurt!

"I think I know why I think you two are so perfect for each other." Mother smiled.

"Why is that?" William smiled at her then me.

"You both are survivors." I looked at William and he looked at me and she was right! We both realized it was true. We both lost everything we knew and fought back surviving it all. I looked at William and he was deep in thought. He looked at me and took my hand smiling and put it to his lips. Mother smiled softly then she stood.

"After I get this cleaned up, I think I'm going in for a nice hot bath and a good book." She stood gathering up dishes and taking them into the kitchen. Carla and I helped mother, the men went into the den to have a brandy.

"You know Rebecca, William is truly in love with you." Mother smiled and looked down.

"How do you know that, Mother?" I looked at her and she was being very serious.

"It's in his eyes, words and actions." Mother smiled softly handing me the drying towel.

"And you, Carla…" She put her hands on Carla's shoulders.

"You my dear are the perfect match for my Cole. He has never been so taken with any woman as he is with you." She took her finger and lifted her chin and looked into her eyes.

"Ms. Glenn, I just met him." Carla shyly smiled.

"You know, one thing I have learned in my life is this, we never know when God puts a person into our lives. It's His timing, not ours and sometimes we tend to analyze everything to death! We need to enjoy who the Lord puts into our lives when it happens. Rebecca's Robert was a very wise man. He always used to say that time was a gift and what we did with every second was very important and that we can never get back a second wasted. What I'm trying to tell you and Rebecca is that, you two have had very special men brought into your lives and you need to just enjoy and thank God for putting them into your lives and don't try to do what is 'proper' to society, for society doesn't have to live your lives. I've been on this planet long enough to see and discern a few things and I know my children better than they think I do. They forget I was once young and have been through things and seen things they can't."

"Mother, thank you, William is a special man and I know Cole is as well. After this morning at church, I felt that my life with Robert was like a chapter in a book of my life and I finally reached the end of the chapter. Now I'm starting a new chapter, new start and life." I smiled at Carla and mother

"Carla, I know Cole as a brother and a friend. I can honestly say that Cole has never acted like this and he would never go on a vacation without analyzing it to death! He was spontaneous and so quick to decide to go. I told William that I thought he would go, but in my heart I wondered if he would tear himself away from his company and all it took was one look at you and he said yes."

"And as his mother, I know that it would take a miracle to get him away and I think you are just the miracle that he needed. That man has never acted this way even with Annette, whom he called on for four years. He still did not marry her when she gave him an ultimatum, which was to either to marry her and keep her here or she would move with her parents. He let her go."

"Cole told me a little about her, but not that he was with her for so long. He said he did love her, but not enough to marry her." Carla looked down into a cup of coffee mother poured for us.

"That is right. He is the kind to keep things in and doesn't show his feelings in the open." I sipped my coffee.

"He did tell me that he wanted to start on his house at the end of the month." Carla sipped her coffee.

"He did?" I looked at mother wide eyed.

"Yes." Carla was lost to why mother was so surprised.

"Well, well! It looks like our Cole is very taken with you my dear!" She shook her head.

"Why do you say that?"

"I'll tell you why… Annette tried to get him to start building his house two years ago and he always had an excuse why he couldn't."

"He really said that?" Mother waited.

"Yes!" Carla shyly smiled.

"He asked me if I liked stone houses, how many bedrooms it should have, if sun rooms were a desired thing, if a stable for horses would be a desired feature and… if I would help him with the interior, colors and patterns and about flower gardens…" She looked at us and stared for mother and I stood looking at each other in shock with our mouths hanging open.

174

"What? Is it that unusual that a man asks a woman for their advice on decorating and what is important to have included in his house?" She looked at us both wide eyed.

"When it comes to Cole… that is a resounding, YES!" I smiled and looked at mother and she looked at me and smiled back.

"Well my dear… I feel confident enough to tell you that when you have to order your next year's supplies of letter heads concerning your business or even personal stationary, I would suggest you put Mrs. Carla Glenn as the name." Mother laughed softly.

"What?" She almost dropped her cup and nervously laughed.

"Mother's right about that… Mother do you believe what Carla just said?"

"No… but I do know it's a true blue miracle we have just been a witness to."

"I think you two are wrong." Carla shook her head.

"Carla did he not ask to call on you and to be the only one who did?" I smiled and sipped my coffee.

"Yes."

"HE DID?" Mother's mouth hung open again.

"And has he ever asked you about children, if you wanted them and how many you would like to have?"

"Well… Yes… but…" Carla was looking rather shocked herself seeing a pattern here.

"And when he was talking about the bedrooms in the house he planned on building… he asked if there would be enough bedrooms to have as many rooms as children on the family side of the house including two spare bedrooms?" I looked at Carla as she was deep in thought as if she was counting in her head. Then her eyes flew open wide. Her mouth hung open this time!

"See? Mother and I are right!" I laughed and nodded to mother and she agreed with a nod.

"Oh, my goodness! He… also… asked… me what particular furniture I liked and about bedroom suites." She was blushing so red. I wrapped my arm around her shoulders and hugged her and then mother turned her chin up and looked her in the eye.

"I would love to have you as a daughter." Carla's eyes welled in tears and we all started to cry again.

"Are you…" I heard a deep voice and looked to find Mike standing and shaking his head.

"Men... do not go in there! I warn you!"

"What? What is it?" I heard Cole call to Mike.

"Oh, No! They're crying again." Cole looked at William and William looked at me and I smiled and we all went to Cole and hugged him.

"What did I do?" Cole laughed and put his arms around us.

"Nothing and everything... We just love you too..."

"My Lord..." Cole laughed.

"I think I'm going to bed... I don't want this to happen to me next!" Mike laughed and rolled his eyes and left the room.

"Carla..." Cole took her in his arms.

"Rebecca..." William took me into his arms and I looked up at him and smiled wiping the tears away with his thumbs.

"I think you need to go for a long walk." He laughed and hugged me to his chest.

"Well children... I'm going to go for that bath and a book... I think a good love story is in order!" She winked at all of us and left the kitchen.

"I think I shall take Rebecca back to her room as well."

"I think a bath sounds wonderful!" I admitted.

"Cole... will you see me home as well?"

"I wouldn't have it any other way." He kissed her forehead and walked her out.

"Shall we my love?" He looked into my eyes tenderly.

"Yes." I whispered as William and I walked to the barn taking Fella out of the stall.

"Does he ride well?" He looked at me with question in his eyes.

"He's as gentle as a kitten." I smiled putting his harness on and no saddle. He took me by that waist and sat me on Fella's back and with one smooth move swung up on Fella's back behind me arranging my legs across his leg.

"Ready?" He smiled as I put my arm around him kissing his cheek.

"What was that for?"

"For being so wonderful..." I laid my hand on his chest.

"I didn't do anything." He looked down.

"Yes you did."

"Whatever it was, remind me to do it more often." He softly laughed.

"I think you just do it automatically."

"And what wonderful thing are you accusing me of doing?" His eyes were soft and tender looking.

"You my love are guilty of making me happy."

176

"Well then…" He tilted my chin up to his lips and he covered mine in breath taking tender kisses then slowly pulling away looking deep into my eyes.

"Oh my! What was that for?" I couldn't breathe.

"For allowing me to love you, loving me back, and making me the happiest man in the world."

"Well then my lord…I'm afraid that we're at an impasse." I bit my bottom lip.

"What do you mean?" He looked at me in a serious way.

"We'll just have to deal with both of our guilt's!" I laughed and he rolled his eyes as he nudged Fella's sides.

We rode in silence for a little while enjoying the night, it was beautiful. The stars hung in the sky twinkling brightly and the half moon was high in the night sky. The sounds of night creatures were all around us as Fella walked back to town.

"You're going to love our home."

"I know I will…" I couldn't believe that only a couple weeks ago, I was so sad and lost. He just said our home!

"I want you to think of it as your home." He spoke in a soft tone.

"What?" I looked up into his eyes not being able to breathe.

"I will marry you, Rebecca… and…" I reached up and pulled him down to my lips kissing him deeply, passionately as I pulled on his leather tie.

"Rebecca… I…" He tried to speak but I pulled him back to my lips. I searched him with my kiss as passion ran through my body like wild fire. He deepened his kiss and wrapped his arms around me.

His hair fell all around my face and I could smell his cologne a musky woodsy scent with his own natural scent pervading through. His hands seized the clip out of my hair allowing it fall all around me. He pulled away slowly and brushed the hair away from my face. His look was full of desire and was entrancing. I could not look away. He touched my lips with his thumb.

He did not say a word, but he could see what my eyes were saying to his heart and I could see what his eyes were saying to mine. I laid my head against his chest and closed my eyes. How I needed to be loved, held, to be touched and needed to return it in the same way. We rode for a while in silence, words were not needed.

"Rebecca…" He took a deep breath and tightened his hold and slowly let it out.

"I'm sorry, William…" I whispered.

"No… don't ever be sorry for… wanting me." He took another deep breath.

I took a deep breath as well. This was the hardest thing to endure.

"Rebecca… look at me." I looked up at his handsome face with his eyes tenderly looking into mine.

"William… I…" I was ashamed not of loving him, but how I acted.

"Shhh… I know… I feel the very same thing! It's all I can do not to hall you off to the nearest preacher!" He took in a deep breath and slowly let it out.

"How can this happen so fast? How can I feel so strong about you in this sort of way in such a short time?" I looked down at my skirts.

"I have been fighting this for days now. I am only human and I find this… almost too hard… nothing has ever provoked me so much." He took what seemed to be a bottomless breath. What were we going to do? How were we going to make it through this without… Oh Lord, help us! He has had the same feelings I have had in my most secret thoughts.

"So… you feel it as well?" I looked up at him thanking God I wasn't the only one feeling this.

"God yes… since the first time I saw the fire in your eyes when you were angry with McCray." He looked up into the dark night.

"Rebecca… when I smell the bath oil you use or scent of your hair and the feel of it, your skin, it's so soft and smells like flowers and your eyes, I drown in every time I look into them and those lips that take my breath away every time they touch mine. I can't sleep at night knowing you're right beneath me… I mean your room is right below mine. God this is the hardest thing I've ever had to endure… I've never wanted to make love to a woman more than I do you, but… you… are just not anyone…" He took another deep endless breath.

"I can't deny I feel the same…" I whispered.

"Rebecca… I am a knight…" He looked deep into my eyes.

"What shall we do?" I sighed.

"That, I cannot tell you." He sighed, a great sigh.

"Well, then we will do our best." I tried to calm myself.

"Yes." The tone of his voice was as if he didn't believe that he could keep a promise or give me his word or he would have offered one or the other. I couldn't do it either.

"I want you to know that I would never do anything that you wouldn't want me to do. I would never hurt you Rebecca as God is my witness." His eyes were telling me the truth.

"William, I want you to know that I realize, you know that I was married for a long time for someone my age, but I am…" I was about to tell him my deepest secrets.

"Rebecca… I do understand what you were going to say…and like I said we can only try… Remember I am thirty seven and not an innocent." He laughed.

"Tell me about some of the types of ladies you have encountered."

"No…" His tone was flat.

"Why not?"

"Because… I have never been close to any woman… I've always kept them at arm's length."

"But, surly there was one?"

"No, I'm more like Mike than you think!" He laughed.

"Not even one?" Was he telling me the truth? Not even one?

"The women I've experienced were for… a medicinal purpose only." He looked up to the dark sky again.

"You have never been in love?" I looked up at him still thinking there has to have been one.

"No."

"I just find that hard to believe! In the barn you said it had been a long time since you've felt this way."

"I meant as a teenager… alright… I will tell you something." He took a deep breath and let it out. Now he will tell me about at least one.

"Rebecca… I believe that God has the perfect mate for each of us. Some of us choose to rush into a relationship and others wait until God sends them their mate."

"How do you know who is the one?" I looked up into his eyes. I wondered if he truly thought that God sent me to him like he said.

"Well…when I saw you the first time on your way to Hickory Hill, I felt that God was telling me 'She's the one'… Of course I said to God… She's married. Then, I felt him tell me again 'She's the one… Trust me'… Of course I didn't think so at the time, but then all I could do was think about you and I had to follow you. I don't know why, but I felt it… Rebecca… you are the one and only one."

"If I'm the one for you… then why did God put Robert in my life and not you right away?"

"I've pondered that myself, but if you think about it… When you married Robert, how old were you?"

"Eighteen…"

"And how old are you now?"

"That's right you don't know how old I am!" I'll tease him.

"No… it never occurred to me." He looked down at me.

"I'm twenty two."

"What? Twenty two?!" He had a horrified look on his face! Then he thought for a few seconds and laughed. He knew I was older than Mike.

"I'm twenty Six!" I laughed and then he tried to tease me and look horrified again, but he laughed shaking his head.

"That was eight years ago… eight years ago I was twenty nine and still working my way up the ranks, I hadn't even bought my father's estate back, so you see I was in no way ready for you."

"But… that would mean that Robert's life was for not." I couldn't believe that!

"No, Rebecca… Robert was very important in God's plan… The fact that God chose Robert for you was evidence in itself for me."

"Why do you say that?" I welled in tears.

"I know this is hard to understand Rebecca, but I believe that you'll understand why I think as I do and it might just make sense to you when I'm through." He took a deep breath.

"Go on…" I needed to hear this!

"Now, the reason I think Robert was chosen for you is because Robert was a well-disciplined man. He took care of you and taught you about love and marriage. He provided everything that you would need. He moved you out in the middle of nowhere and gave you a home and everything you could possibly want or need… except, he waited for me to finish his statement.

"Children…" Which, that was true.

"Yes… children… Robert probably didn't want children because he wanted something for you that he didn't have at the time. Am I right?"

"He said that he wanted to build a room for a child and was saving the money and buried it."

"After Robert passed, the savings happened to be enough to keep you going and move you home and for a while longer right?"

"Yes… How did you know…?" Now I was really intrigued.

"Listen, what month did Robert pass away?"

"April." I was getting a little frightened.

"That was six months ago right?" He looked down at me. I nodded up at him.

"A little over six months ago was when I returned to 'Castillo en la Árbol'... to stay."

"But I thought you said that you had bought the place way before that?"

"I did, but I still was active in my duties until the first week of April. I was still handling things from Lawrenceburg, but it was inactive. I was considering retiring and getting out of the service all together.

On October eighteenth, I will have been in the Services for twenty three years. I could have retired last year if I wanted to."

"October eighteenth... April Eighteenth is when Robert died." Chills ran down my spine.

"So I think Robert was more than your husband to you and for you." He smiled down at me tenderly.

"He was a guardian as well... It's so hard to think that that could be possible!" I stared out into the night not seeing anything, just thinking.

"When Robert's job was through, whatever God had for him to do... on April eighteenth... Robert's work was done." William looked up to the night sky.

"Then why did I have to bury him by myself and go through the loss by myself and almost not make it myself?" If that was God's plan, it was cruel!

"The word is 'Almost'. But you did make it." He kissed my forehead. This was a lot to take in!

"It was awful... I had to build a box and..." Tears welled in my eyes. It was truly awful! I loved Robert so much.

"Even though it was so awful and heart wrenching... you wouldn't be who you are right now had you not gone through what you had nor would I be who I was either if God didn't take my family away." He smiled softly down at me. I hadn't even noticed, but we were at the stables already. William swung down and lifted me down off of Fella's back and he led Fella into the stall.

"William, Mr. Thomas said he didn't know how I ever made it all the way here with the broken axle." My heart pounded and in a strange way this all made sense.

"And Mr. Thomas has said 'In God's time all will be known... for there's a reason for everything'. I've heard Robert say that and you and mother and Mother Grayson!"

"I just know that you're the one I have waited my entire life for." He smiled and wrapped my hand around his arm and took me across the street into the hotel.

"Let's have some coffee, say in twenty minutes?" I looked at William.

"I'll tell the host at the restaurant to send up coffee and pie?" William's eyes grew wider.

"Yes... pie! Alright I'll see you in twenty minutes!" William kissed my hand as I watched him go up the stairs, taking two at a time. I went to the host in the restaurant to send up coffee for two and two pieces of Apple pie. He smiled and I saw Lord McCray walking towards me smiling.

"I couldn't help but over hear you order coffee and pie for two?" He smiled.

"Yes... Gabe." I felt honestly sympathetic for the man.

"I wish to say that William is a very lucky man." His smile was genuine.

"It is I that am blessed." I corrected.

"Have you thought about letting me call on you?" He smiled so handsomely.

"Gabe, I am allowing William to call on me and William only." His smile faded and he tried to bring it back. It had to be said.

"I really knew that last night, but I had to ask once more."

"I'm sorry, Gabe... you are quite a wonderful man and have so much to offer a woman, but William and I have something that we can no longer deny." I bit my bottom lip.

"Then... I wish you well." He took my hand and bowed and kissed it closing his eyes.

"Thank you, Gabe... You are a kind man and one day..."

"Oh, I hope not too soon! You were too close of a call for me!" He laughed and walked away. I shook my head amazed he could bounce back like that! Maybe God does have something to do with this!

I walked up to my room and opened the door and the scent of roses was wonderful! I lit the lantern and stoked up the fire then went into the washroom to freshen up thinking this was a wonderful day! So much has happened that it made my head spin.

I lit the lantern in the washroom and the thought that Robert was more than just my husband made me feel better. God protected me for William? I had to think about that, and the timing of everything was strange. I washed my face, brushed my hair and put new face powder on leaving my hair down and taking my shoes off, putting my slippers on.

Ah! That was much better. I wished I had something I could wear that was proper to be comfortable, but my dress would have to do I thought as I went back into the bedroom. I dabbed on a little perfume and I felt much better. As I looked into the mirror, there was a soft tap on the door.

"Room service..." I hurried to the door and the man had a big cart with too much on it!

"There must be some mistake... I didn't order but coffee and pie..."

"You are, Ms. Grayson?" The man looked confused.

"Yes... but this is too much!"

"Let me look at the order." He dug into his pocket and pulled out the order.

"Yes, it the right room and oh... A Mr. Andrews ordered this."

"Oh... well alright then." Why did he change his mind? He must be really hungry.

"You beat me here, Tom!" William stood in the doorway.

"Sorry, Lord Andrews. Where would you like this?" He smiled at William.

"I'll take care of that." He smiled at the man taking the cart.

"Very good, Sir." He bowed towards me and William showed him to the door and shook his hand. Tom smiled and thanked William and he closed the door.

"I know this is not what you had ordered, but I was suddenly hungry for more than just pie. I hope you don't mind?"

"No not at all." I sat in one of the chairs by the fireplace.

"There is apple pie here somewhere, but I wanted something more. Ah... here you must have a bite of this." He took his fork and cut into a pie that looked wonderful.

"What is it?" I smiled.

"Here open up!" He laughed. He fed me the most delicious mouthwatering thing I had ever eaten. I closed my eyes.

"Oh! This is heavenly!" I closed my eyes again savoring the flavor.

"It's a breakfast Quiche, but I like it at night. It's a sin, is it not?" He smiled and sat back.

"Yes, and now I am hungry!" I laughed.

"Well then..." He sliced me a piece and put it on a plate with a crescent roll smothered in butter.

"You do know how to eat!" I laughed.

"When I get you home... I want to cook you 'my' Quiche... home made." He smiled softly. He said take you home...he cooks?

"You can cook too?" What couldn't he do?

"Of course! Why wouldn't I?" He laughed.

"I don't know, though the thought of you in an apron would be a thing to see." I laughed and smirked. He rolled his eyes. I took another bite of heaven.

"Coffee?" He smiled and I nodded for my mouth was full. He poured me a cup of coffee and put sugar and cream in it like he knew exactly how I liked it. He stirred and place in front of me.

"Thank you! I can't believe how this tastes and you say that yours is better than this?"

"Of course! Do you doubt me?" He sat back and smiled.

"No, but you must be an exceptional cook to beat this!"

"I am, my love... I'm exceptional at many things." He smiled a sensual grin and winked! That is not fair! He is teasing me!

I took a bite of Quiche and let my lips surround the fork and pulled it out slow. I closed my eyes and moaned a soft 'mmmmm'

"That good huh?" He laughed shaking his head.

"Oh yes!" It was.

"So, have you thought about what we talked about on the way here?" He sipped his coffee.

"Yes." I pulled my legs up under me and sat with my arm on the arm of the chair.

"Well, you have to admit it is rather unexplainable."

"Yes, and the more I think about it, the more I think it could be true." I smiled and sipped my coffee. This was good too.

"Want your pie too?" He leaned over.

"No thank you, maybe later. So then if there is something to this, then that means we will be..."

"Married?" He smiled at me the fire dancing off his face and shirt. He sat back in the chair so regal, like a prince. His eyes took me in as if he was touching me in some intimate way. Heavens he was so handsome! He crossed his left ankle over his knee and then his left hand went to his face placing his finger up the left side of his cheek and his thumb rested under his chin holding it up. His fingers curled in front of his lips pressing on them. He stared into my eyes not saying a word for a moment as if he was deep in thought about what to say. As he was about to speak, his right eye brow went up.

"Yes." His eyes went to mouth as a slight grin appeared on the right side of his lips.

"That's right." His voice was husky and soft. He bit his bottom lip and hid a grin that turned to a smile. My heart started to beat faster. My cheeks warmed slightly and then I thought.

"What if you're wrong?" I held my breath. The words were out before I even thought about it.

He stood and took my coffee from my hand, sat it on the table, then pulled me to my feet. He lowered his lips to cover mine and kissed me so deeply that my body melted against him and felt like a rag doll in his arms. My arms went around his neck as if I had no control of them. As he tightened his hold enveloping me with his arms. He slowly pulled away from my lips. I couldn't open my eyes for a moment feeling paralyzed. When I forced myself to open them, he was looking down into mine.

"That is why I know... no woman's lips have ever made me feel the way you make me feel after we kiss." His eyes searching mine profoundly. My heart was beating hard forcing my breath out.

"William..." His lips covered mine again.

His hand went to my hair and my arms tightened around his neck. He deepened his kiss even more taking my breath inside of him as he breathed. My thoughts were gone, my legs were gone. All my strength to fight was gone! I was at his mercy and knew I would not say no. My head started to spin and my hands ran into his hair pulling the tie out. His hair fell down all around my arms and face. I ran my hands back down his chest and could feel his heart thunder under my hands. I could feel his muscles flex and move. I have to stop! He pulled away from my swollen lips. His scent lingered surrounding me as I tried to catch my breath.

"Rebecca... We have to stop." He was breathless and his voice was hoarse.

"I know." He rested his head on my forehead trying to breath. He had his eyes tightly shut. He was fighting... I was fighting. He straightened and looked at me biting his bottom lip. He released me and then stepped back. His eyes said 'I have to go'. I put my fingers to my swollen thoroughly kissed lips. I stood feeling my body scream out for him to come back, hold me... love me... He ran his hand through his hair as he fought to compose himself. He breathed deep in what seemed to be an endless breath. I stood not moving looking at him unable to trust my weakened legs. His eyes were so different tonight. They looked so consuming and noticed every move I made. I just stood saying nothing watching him. I could not tear my eyes away. I could not speak! Oh God why?!! I need him right now I thought swallowing hard. He stood just staring at me. What was he thinking?!! He ran his hand through his hair again and backed up towards the door. Oh Please! Don't leave, my heart cried. Tears started to well in my eyes. Was I supposed to say something? Is that why he stood there? William… say something… don't just walk out… He opened the door and stood with one hand on the door knob and one on the door frame. His head was down… I still could not move. I wanted to run to him. He started to turn to look at me and stopped and walked out shutting the door softly. My body screamed out in pain for it missed his arms, his touch and his kiss.

I went to the door and leaned on it. I felt like he was still here. I opened the door and to look and he wasn't there. I softly closed the door and leaned against it. I don't know if he was angry or not or was I supposed to tell him to stay? No… he 'had' to go! I wiped the tears away from my eyes and went to grab my nightshift thinking that was so close! He knows that I have had a man for eight years and thinks this is very hard on me. Maybe we should not be in the same room alone like this again. I thought that we could handle it and almost failed terribly! I wanted him so badly! To touch his face…his lips…his chest and to feel what it is like to love him. To simply lie in his arms and feel safe.

Oh God, why do I have to go through this? I wish he would have said something! Anything, but he will… tomorrow… we will agree not to be alone! He is a knight and he is an honorable man and wants to do this right! I want to do this right! I took a deep breath and started to relax. His kiss said so much more than words could ever say and I was in love with him, madly in love with him so much that it hurt! How could it be so fast? Everything happened so fast, maybe too fast? No! William and I are perfect for each other. I love his laugh, his smile, his wit, his eyes, how he kisses me, how he treats me, I am in love with him! I smiled to myself feeling proud that I was taken to the very edge and did not fall off. I dressed and crawled into bed blowing out the lantern. I laid awake in the bed thinking about William and how badly we wanted to be together and how strong he was to walk away. I was truly in love with him for there is only one thing that makes you so crazy like this and that was love. Soon, I yawned and fluffed my pillow… and yawned again…

~ Chapter 9 ~

A soft tap on the door woke me. The sun was up! What time was it? I listened to see if I was dreaming and looked at the door listening. Then I heard another small tap on the door. I leapt from bed threw my robe on and ran to the door. William! I opened the door and a young man stood holding out a note.

"Yes?"

"Lord Andrews asked me to give you this." He bowed and walked away.

My hands shook as I stared at the white paper and shut the door, staring at the paper. I walked to my bed sitting on the edge staring at it. Taking a deep breath, I gathered all my courage and slowly opened the note,

"My Darling Rebecca,

I do not wish to alarm you, everything is alright, but I want to tell you that I've left for Winchester this morning. First of all I want to tell you that I am going to Winchester to prepare my home for you, your brother and Carla. Rebecca, I want everything perfect when you arrive.

But the truth is, last night, I came so close to taking you in my arms and to my bed. I was so engulfed with desire and so much so, that I came back to your room an hour after I had left. That is one other reason why I had to go. I need to regain control.

I love you and know that every day that passes with you, my love for you only grows. However, when the day comes that you and I become one, I don't want any hindrance.

I respect you too much and love you too much to not be your husband when you give the greatest gift you possess to me for the first time. I know it will be a challenge for both of us, but we can and will do this and we will be better for it. I hope you understand. I barely do myself!

God only know how I ache for you. Please try not to be angry with me. You have my word that I'll see you Friday morning. I pray you'll be waiting for me.

Forever Yours, Until Time Is No More, Estoy Enamorado De Ti
William

I held the note to my heart and cried anyway. What was I going to do for four days? I missed him already! But there was no sense in staying in the hotel any longer. Hannah was right about knowing what I was going to do before I left. I do. I'm to marry Lord William Andrews.

Thank you God! I took a deep breath and dressed for the day. I gathered up my things and packing everything and went down to the front counter. I told the man at the front desk that I wished my things to be ready for my brother to pick them up.

"But Lord Andrews has taken care of everything till he returns on Friday Ms. Grayson." I thought for a moment. He has taken care of me until his return!

"Alright, I will stay, but I shall pay up to this day Sir." He smiled.

"Lord Andrews expected as much, and insisted that if you paid till today, then he would pay for all your breakfasts, lunches and dinners, room service and all." He smiled as if he ate the mouse!

"Alright, what does he want me to do?" I rolled my eyes.

"He would like you to stay and enjoy yourself and he said that if you needed anything from his room to give you his key." He handed me William's key.

Why would I need anything from his room? The man behind the desk was smiling at me rather strangely.

"Well alright. Then I guess that I shall go to the dress shop for now." I was so confused. What does William have in his room I may need?

"He also said to give you this…" The man handed me a note!

"Thank you Mr…." I was so confused.

"Mr. Matthew's at your service." He smiled as I took the note and walked out of the hotel. I feel like I have lost my mind! I took the note and opened it…

My Darling Rebecca,
I had guessed that you wanted to go to your mother's this morning, but please stay. I don't want you to go because of me. I want you to enjoy yourself and know that I will

return. There is something in my room for you. When you get back from Hannah's go
to my room and see.
  See you soon, Te amo,
  William

What in the world could William have in his room that he would want
me to go in there for? I wished he didn't go, but if that is what he had to
do, then that was what he had to do. Wait a minute… How did he know
I would go to Hannah's this morning?!! That is right! I had said to
William that I wanted to tell Hannah about the dresses…or did I?
Nevertheless I did want to talk to Hannah. She has been so good to me
and seemed to know what I need and how I felt about things. Then I
may go to Carla's. I should have gotten a cup of coffee.

I smiled at some people that looked familiar as I headed for Hannah's.

"Hannah…" I called as I walked in her shop.

"Rebecca… Good morning! And how are you this beautiful morning?"
She smiled as she came out from the back.

"Well, I don't know…" I looked down.

"What is it dear?" She walked over to me and put her arm around my
shoulder.

"William went to Winchester this morning."

"He did? I thought that you two…" She looked surprised and frowned.

"Oh no! William went to prepare for Cole, Carla and I to visit. We're
leaving on Friday and will be gone a week."

"Well, that was wonderful of him, wasn't it?" She didn't look too sure.

"Can I talk to you about something rather…delicate?" I had a feeling
she would know what to say.

"Of course…" She led me to the back room to sit on one of the settees.

"We'll have a cup of coffee while we chat." She went to a side cart and
fixed a cup of coffee and brought hers and sat next to me.

"So tell me, what has you so distressed?"

"To tell you the truth… I am a bit uncomfortable…" I looked at her
through my eyelashes hoping she would understand.

"Oh, I see." She took a deep breath.

"Well there's more to it than just that. Last night William brought me
back to the hotel and we agreed to have coffee and talk about 'us' and
well it was almost too much…"

"Oh I see!"

"When I woke up this morning there was a note brought to my door and…"

"Yes… go on… what did it say?" She patted my hand.

"Well here, you read it… I'm not embarrassed of it." There wasn't anything bad in it, besides Hannah would understand I was sure of that. I gave her the note and she sipped her coffee while she read it. She folded the note up and handed it back to me and looked at me smiling.

"Well, what do you think and what should I do? I am the first one he has ever brought to his home and the first woman he has claimed to ever love. He said that he believed that God has someone special for everyone and he waited for me all his life! Hannah, he is a Colonel and a knight and he stands on the word of God. It's just when we're alone! We can't… Please tell me you understand and don't think me less…" Tears filled my eyes.

"I can tell you this Rebecca, William is in love with you and he respects you very much. If he didn't, it wouldn't have mattered to him, but it does. William is a strong willed man and an honorable one, but he is human, just like you. If he wants you to become his wife and wants to wait until he's your husband, then I suggest that you try your very best not to be alone for too long together. You are only human as well. I don't know if I would have shown such self-control as you and he did. I do know this… there are only two things you two can do." She took my hand in hers.

"What is that?" I took a deep breath.

"Well, you could stay away from each other and never be alone together when you are together, which I don't think either of you will be able to do and the only other thing is to get married right away."

"What?!!" I looked up at her in shock!

"Do you love him?"

"Yes…but…"

"Does he love you?" She smiled.

"Yes but…"

"Do you want to marry him?"

"He is the most wonderful man I've known since Robert. I know Robert would like him well, but it would be too fast!"

"Would you marry him today if he had it all arranged?"

"I believe I would, but…"

"Then what is the problem?" She waited.

"He hasn't really officially asked me. He has just said he is 'going' to marry me." I sighed and wiped a tear that slipped down my cheek.

"Rebecca, no man would say that unless they mean it!"

"But I'm wondering if I should even go to his home now, the temptation would be enormous!" I looked down into my cup.

"God puts people together when he sees fit, not when we do. If he asks you, do it... don't wait. There is nothing to wait for, besides, you and William are ready. I have never seen two so in love before. It doesn't matter if you met only a few days ago or not!" She patted my hand.

"I was with a wonderful man for eight years... and ..."

"You don't have to say any more, I know." She held up her hand.

"I know you do but he makes me be so... well bold! I don't want him to think less of me."

"Just take it day by day and if you and he... well, are together, I believe he will do the right thing. You can only do your best." She laughed and shook her head.

"You know you're right. Thank you Hannah, I know you are right and feel so much better." I kissed her cheek and stood putting my cup on the side cart.

"I have to go back to the hotel. He gave me his room key and said there was something in there for me. What, I've not a clue." I laughed feeling much better.

"Oh how mysterious... and romantic!" She clasped her hands together.

"I will stop by later and let you know what it was." She nodded and shooed me out the door.

I did feel much better and Hannah was right about William. He did say he never was in love before. I smiled to myself and went back into the hotel walking by the front desk and the third floor with the key in my hand and stood at the door for a second thinking to myself that I was about to go into a man's room. I was about to go into William's room without him here and the entire idea was rather exciting. I held my breath and put the key in the door and turned it taking a deep breath and slowly opened the door.

I looked around the room and the bed was made, everything looked clean and in order. I could smell his scent everywhere the minute I stepped into the room. I shut the door taking the key and looked around and not seeing anything that appeared out of the ordinary.

I walked by the wing back chairs and then stepped into the washroom feeling strange being in a man's room with all his personal things here for me to look at, but nothing was in there, though his cologne was on the counter promising his return. His hair brush was by the sink and ran my fingers down the wooden carved handle and then I saw his robe was on the chair. I picked up his dark blue satin robe and held it to my nose. I breathed him into my senses closing my eyes almost feeling his heartbeat. I laid his robe back down thinking how strange this feels, William allowing me to look at anything I wanted to. I looked at the bathtub and could almost see him in it…relaxing back, his hair wet and shook my head stopping my thoughts and took a deep breath.

In the bedroom, I looked over his vanity and then sat on the bed where he slept. My heart was pounding even though he wasn't here, I blushed feeling silly.

At the end of the bed I saw a blanket but that was all. I didn't see a thing. I thought what did William want me to see? Surly he didn't wish me to go through his personal things! Maybe it's just that his things are still here as a promise of his return?

I looked around the room trying to figure out what I missed. I ran my hand across his pillow feeling something crunch underneath the covers and pulled them back. There was a dark blue night shirt and a pair of night pants with a note on top of it.

"Rebecca" How did he know I would sit on the bed? I ran my finger over my name in his hand and unfolded it.

My Dearest Rebecca,

You have found this note, which means you walked in my room by the chairs. I can see you now going into the washroom and touching my brush and picking my robe up holding it close to you. You then walked to my bed, sitting down wondering if you missed something and then running your hand across the pillow where I lay my head. Now you are sitting in disbelief on the bed wondering how I could have known what you did when you came in the room. It is that I feel as if I've known you all my life and know you well enough to know what you would do.

Last night I wore these night clothes and wish for you to take the shirt and wear it every night till I return. My arms were in the sleeves and they shall hold you till I return. I know you think this strange, but I know you will sleep well and when I return, we will need to have a serious talk. It cannot wait another day. Know that I love you and am thinking about you right now and that I will return in three more days.

Estoy Enamorado De Ti De lo mi
William

He was so mysterious at times and another thing I admired about him. It matched that grin! I laughed to myself seeing his grin.

I lifted the night shirt off the pillow and held it to my nose. There wasn't any cologne on his night shirt. I took it in again... his scent! My heavens! I didn't realize how wonderful his scent was without his cologne! I breathed in deeply smelling such a sweet light musky scent that made my head spin. I wanted to wear his night shirt tonight even more.

"Yes, William, I shall do what you ask." I felt so wonderful and still in disbelief of all that was happening to me. I couldn't wait till he returned!

Taking his nightclothes with me back to my room, I spent the day relaxing and reading a book. A tap at the door interrupted my concentration and went to the door and called out...

"Who is it?"

"Room service..." Room service? I opened the door and it was a cart full of food. For a moment I thought that William would suddenly appear.

"Where do you wish me to put it?" The young man smiled.

"That's alright. I shall take care of it." He smiled and I went for my purse.

"It's not necessary Ma'am, it's all been taken care of."

"Let me guess, Lord Andrews?"

"Yes Ma'am." He smiled and shut the door as he left.

I could smell something very good as I pushed the cart over to the chair. I lifted the lid and smiled to myself... Quiche! He must be smiling to himself about now I thought.

As I ate, I wondered why he had to prepare for our arrival. I wondered what he had planned. He did say he was full of surprises and would talk when he returned for me on Friday.

I looked back down at the cart thinking William had seen to every last detail, even what I was sleeping in! I laughed, so amazed. I took another bite of the wonderful Quiche thinking about how excited he was, wanting me taste his Quiche.

Well, tomorrow I will go see mother and also Carla, to get the update on her and Cole.

After I ate, I took a long hot bath relaxing and scrubbing my hair. The whole time I thought about William wondering what he has planned and when I was finished, I dried myself off and slid my arms into the nightshirt, buttoning it up and looked into the mirror laughing at the sleeves that went to my knees! I rolled them up and up and up! I laughed as for all my work, the sleeves fell anyway, but the silk felt wonderful against my skin. I brushed out my hair and put it into a simple braid down my back. I slid on my slippers and went to the chair not bothering to put on a robe as the shirt was so long. I curled my legs underneath me and grabbed the book I wanted to finish. I nibbled on the Quiche thinking it was just as good cold as it was hot.

After a couple hours, I had grown tired and blew out the lantern as I crawled into bed. I snuggled up under the bedclothes and was fast going to sleep with William's scent all around, hearing him saying he truly loves me.

~ Chapter 10 ~

I jumped out of bed in the morning, bright and early, feeling so refreshed. I hadn't slept that well in so long! I was hungry and wanted to go down for breakfast this morning. Two more days I thought and couldn't believe how much I missed him! I made fast work of dressing and my hair. I was excited to see Carla this morning and hear how their plans were progressing. I was soon in the restaurant and was seated at a table by the window. I was in such a good mood and felt so wonderful! Tomorrow my dresses should be ready and in perfect time to go on our trip!

"Good morning, Beck." Cole and Carla were standing by the table.

"Wonderful! I was coming to see you Carla! Can you two stay for breakfast?"

"That's what we came in here for. May we join you?" Cole smiled.

"Well of course!" I rolled my eyes.

"Where's William?" Cole smiled at the waiter as he brought two more cups and filled our coffees for us.

"He went to Winchester yesterday to make sure things were in order and prepare for our arrival. He'll be back on Friday saying we should be ready in the morning." I smiled at Cole and Carla.

"I didn't know he was gone." Cole sipped his coffee.

"Cole, do you like William?" I smiled softly.

"Yes, I do." He nodded with a wink.

With Cole's approval, I felt even surer of William and me. We ordered breakfast and it was served in no time. Carla and Cole ordered the special, two eggs, hash browns, bacon, and toast. I told them about the Quiche and they said they would wait for William's. I couldn't believe that Cole was actually excited to go on a vacation! He truly was surprising everyone!

"So Carla, did you figure out what you are going to take with you?" I looked over to her sipping my coffee.

"Yes, I think we need to get together and discuss things." She gave me that 'we should talk', look.

"Yes, I think that is a good idea. How about I walk over to your shop this morning and we can plan what we need and I can pick up a few things." I nodded.

"That's a good idea. I'm sure Cole will have to get to the lumber yard right after we eat." Carla looked at Cole nodding as he chewed a mouth full.

"I still can't believe the story you told us the night before last. Poor William! It was quite a haunting story." She frowned, thinking about it.

"Good morning." A deep voice that wasn't familiar spoke from behind me.

"Ah, Nick…good to see you! Sit down." Cole smiled waving above my head for Nick to sit.

"Ms. Grayson." He took my hand and bowed over it.

"Why, Lord Baptiest, what brings you here? I thought you would be with William." My heart pounded thinking that maybe William was back.

"I'm staying until William returns" He smiled and winked. His tone was baritone deep… very deep!

"It's nice that you could stay." I smiled.

"He is a great man, honor to work for, but right now, he's a little, let's just say, bossy, demanding and very particular about things. I know he has everyone running around the place like Jesus is coming!" He roared out a great laugh as we all did!

"So, how did you luck out not having to go back?" Cole roared out as well.

"I have an assignment." He raised his brows.

"A real assignment?" Carla's eyes went wide.

"Yes, and one of the most important ones I've ever been assigned." He avoided my eyes.

"Really? Is it a matter of life and death?" I looked up at Lord Baptiest.

He was the biggest man I had ever seen in my life and he was sitting down! He must be close to seven feet tall and just as broad shouldered with black hair and beautiful blue eyes. When he picked up his coffee cup, it looked like a teacup! His smile was surprisingly beautiful too. One thing was for certain, he wasn't like the man that was on the road at all!

"Indeed, milady." He smiled then looked at me.

196

"Are you in danger?" I looked at him.

"Milady, I am always in danger." He didn't look very old now that I studied him closer. He actually looked younger than me. He was just so big I assumed that he was at least my age.

"My goodness!" Carla gasped.

"But, as you all know, I am not at liberty to discuss anything about my assignment." He tipped his head down as if to warn me not to ask.

"Well then you be careful Lord Baptiest!" I smiled softly.

"Not to worry, I was trained and instructed by Lord Andrews." He smiled and winked at me.

"You all enjoy your visit to Will's, I'm glad to see him so excited about something other than the Special Forces or corn!" He let out a thunderous laugh we all laughed as well.

"He's truly excited?" I sipped my coffee.

"Yes, and wants everything perfect for his Lady." Lord Baptiest blushed. I couldn't believe a man that huge would blush.

"Is it true that he has never had an interest or brought any to his house?" Carla smiled. Oh she was very good!

"I do not like to talk about William if he is not here to defend himself, but I will answer that question. William is a very devout man and keeps his word. He is the epitome of a true man of honor, and would never jeopardize it if his intent wasn't serious. I do know for a fact that William has never had anyone other than family at his estate and yes, William has waited for God to give him a wife." He blushed and smiled at me again.

So, William has told Lord Baptiest about his intent. Now I was the one who blushed! That's interesting and means he confides in Lord Baptiest. That tells me that William trusts Nick and so would I.

"So, he confides in you?" I looked at him, squinting my eye.

"Yes, Ms. Grayson." He wasn't smiling now.

"Please, call me, Rebecca." I smiled and sipped my coffee.

"Rebecca, please call me, Nick." He smiled back.

"Then you know his intentions towards me?" I looked at his sweet face turning bright red and didn't look so dangerous any more.

"Yes, Rebecca, he has told me." He looked down.

"Then you must know what his plans are?"

"I do, but that is not for you to know right at this moment, it is for him to tell you. I will say this. He is full of surprises and I know you will be pleased." He smiled. So he does have something planned. How intriguing!

"I hope it isn't anything too much. I wanted to rest and just enjoy time with William." I purposely said that to watch Nick's face. I watched his reaction... nothing!

"Now, Beck, don't interrogate the poor man." Cole laughed shaking his head.

"Not to worry, Rebecca, it won't be anything you can't handle." Nick winked at Cole. Does Cole really know something? I looked at Carla and she was smiling at me and Cole.

"You're right, Cole. So Nick, what do you do on the estate?" I asked before eating the rest of my roll.

"I over see everything for William, as well as whatever needs to be taken care of and, I do it and make sure it gets done." He smiled sipping coffee.

"So he keeps you busy then?" I sipped my coffee.

"Yes Ma'am. I don't think you realize just how big thirty eight hundred acres is Rebecca. There's more than just land, there's houses and barns and stables not to mention all the crops and livestock." Nick sipped his coffee.

Cole about spit his coffee out.

"Thirty... eight... hundred?!!"

"Aye, Sir." Nick sipped his coffee.

"Holy Mary, Joseph and John!" Cole's eyes were as big a saucers!

"Coleman!" I shot him a scornful look! Carla covered her mouth.

"Forgive me ladies. I didn't realize he owned that much!"

"Yes Sir, he's quite the business man, but not the sort to tell anyone much about himself. He's quite private." Nick laughed at Cole.

That shut Cole up until we all were through with breakfast.

"Thank you for joining us Nick, but Carla and Cole and I must be going." I nodded to Carla.

"Thank you for allowing me to join you. I shall see you soon." Nick nodded to Cole and smiled in a strange way at me.

We walked out together and Cole kissed Carla's cheek before he went off to the lumberyard. Carla and I started to go to her shop, but stopped at Hannah's first and went in.

"Well, hello you two." Hannah smiled brightly.

"I've come to check on my dresses and to see when they'll be ready." I hugged her.

"Well my dear, your dresses will be ready tomorrow evening, I will send them to the hotel. I can tell you how much they will be."

"Alright, I'd rather pay for them today if it's alright?"

"Sure, but are you sure you want to pay for them before you see them?"

"Yes, I'm absolutely positive, for if they're like the one I wore that other day, then I know they'll be beautiful." That was the truth too.

"Alright then, and your dress will be ready as well Carla."

"Whatever are you talking about?" Carla looked lost.

"Cole ordered a dress for you and he said not to give it to you, but I could tell you that he had one made for you as well...I tell you two, my helper and I have been covered up."

"But... I..." Carla was about to reject such a gift.

"Now, Carla, don't take this away from Cole. He has never done anything like this before and it would be a shame to deny him this. He needs this, please allow him spoil you. I wouldn't be surprised if he didn't sweep you off your feet and marry you this weekend!"

"What?" Her eyes went wide as saucers and I laughed seeing her jaw hanging.

"I just have only met him." She blushed.

"Oh please, Carla! I can see that you have feelings for Coleman already." I smiled at her.

"Yes, I think your brother is very charming and handsome, and yes, I do like him very much." She was looking at the ceiling as she talked about him.

"To think that Cole is taking you on vacation and that he's even going on a vacation in itself tells me it's more than just an 'I like you' kind of thing." I smiled looking at the bill. Then my mouth hung open.

"Hannah! This can't be right!" I ordered three dresses! This will only pay for one... not even one!

"William and Cole were here at the same time... it was rather a funny thing!"

"When?"

"It was the night before last and I had to come in the shop to pick up some seam work and I saw both of them coming from both directions just flying to the shop. I had yours almost done and told Cole I could get one done in two days with help from June, but it would be pushing it. I've done a dress in three days, but never two. We will have it done by tomorrow night...if not the last touches by Friday morning early... I promise..." She smiled.

"Well, Cole best be paying for it dearly!" I crossed my arms thinking how hard Hannah must be working!

"Oh he is, he is and if I had it my way, I would work under this pressure all the time for what he's paying." Hannah laughed.

"Good!" I laughed.

"Now, about mine, I don't want William…"

"What makes you any different than me? I'm sure William has never bought a dress in his life either so you're going to have to deal with it too!" Carla crossed her arms and tried not to laugh, but she couldn't hold it back and neither could Hannah and we all laughed knowing she was right!

"Men!" I laughed.

"Yes, Men!" Carla laughed.

"Alright here you go, but I hope you got more for them out of William!" I paid the bill.

"He tipped me a hefty tip to allow him to buy them, don't worry about me. That tells me a lot about both of your young men." She smiled and wrote me a ticket.

"Now, you two need to go on your way, I have an order to finish by tomorrow night! Shoo!" Hannah waved her hands at us.

"We'll see you soon!" We walked out and across the street to Carla's shop. She opened the door and her helper Ann was already there. Then we both stopped at what was on the counter…roses!

"Oh, Carla! Their beautiful! Read the card!" I was so excited for her and Cole! Her hands shook as she opened the card.

My Dearest Carla

I wanted you to know that I am thinking of you. For like the rose, you my love, are as beautiful and just as entrancing. I do and hope you are looking forwards to this week as I am. I shall see you tonight.
Je suis tomber en amour avec vous
Cole

"Oh my, Carla! He is in love with you!" Tears welled in my eyes as I covered my lips not believing this at all! I know my brother and he is in love with Carla! If mother saw this, she'd be on the floor!

"Oh, don't be silly! It's too soon! He couldn't possibly be in love this fast! But… what does it mean?" She tried to read the French.

"I know exactly what that means! Cole, Mike and I took French in school. Are you ready for this?"

"I'm not sure." I took her hands wanting to scream!

"Oh, Heavens!" I was trying to breath.

"Rebecca, what does it mean WHAT?" She could see I was very excited.

"It means, I am in love with you!" I watched as she stumbled backwards almost falling over.

"Carla, Cole is falling in love with you! How do you feel about him?"

"Carla, are you alright?" Her eyes were full of tears.

"I..." She shook her head.

"Carla, here... drink this." I poured a glass of water from the counter.

"Thank you." She drank the water.

"Are you sure that means what you said it means?" She hung on to my arms.

"Yes, Carla...why? Are you not pleased?" Maybe she didn't feel what Cole did!

"But how can he be in love with me so fast? I thought women only did that."

"So, then you are falling in love with him too?" I looked at her with my eyes wide.

"From the second I saw him, I was madly in love with him. I even thought that I was mad! I had never done that before!" She still looked shocked.

"So, you are... in love." Now I really wanted to shout for joy.

"I know he's your brother, but he kisses so..."

"I know." I looked down thinking of William and his kisses... how he...

"YOU KNOW?" She almost yelled. I darted my eyes back up to hers.

"Oh NO! I meant... William kisses me so deep that I can't breathe or talk or move or think! It's as if I have no control!" I blew air out of my cheeks.

"I know what you mean! Cole does the same thing to me." We looked at each other and squealed with delight at the same time.

"We are going to have so much fun this coming week." We hugged and laughed.

"Oh, I hope we will!" Carla smiled so sweetly.

We talked about the trip, William and Cole telling her about the last night with William's nightclothes and how hard it was with being so attracted to one another just being in each other's arms. Carla understood exactly what I felt and meant. Apparently she and Cole had a night almost like William's and mine!

"I'm not going to worry about a thing. The men are true gentlemen." She nodded.

"You're right, Carla. I know we will all have a wonderful time." She was right. William and Cole are true gentlemen.

"I do need to go see mother, so I shall see you soon, maybe at mothers tonight?"

"Thank you for listening and helping." Carla nodded.

"I enjoyed our talk." She smiled walking to the back room.

"Me too, I'll see you tonight." I winked and started for mother's teashop.

"Hello Rebecca." A deep voice rumbled from behind me. I knew it wasn't William.

"Well, hello to you too Nick!" He surprised me.

"May I escort you to where you are going?" Nick smiled walking with his hands behind his back.

"Yes, that would be lovely and by the way, did you enjoy the dinner party?" I smiled up at him taking his arm as we walked.

"Yes, I even danced with a young lady named Clarissa." He covered a smile and looked away.

"That's William's cousin." I noticed him take a deep breath.

"Yes, I recall. I haven't seen her in a long time. She's grown up into a beautiful woman." His cheeks slightly blushed. It was simply precious to see such a huge man smitten.

"I see." Was all I could say in fear of gushing over how adorable he was.

"She dances like a princess." His eyes were glassed over and I could see he was thinking about her.

"Has she not visited William?" I bit my lips to keep from saying too much. I had to be careful as Nick was a very intuitive man.

"Yes, several times, but I wasn't there." He frowned.

"How old are you, if I may ask?" Now I'm being nosy. He took my elbow and looked both ways as we stepped off the sidewalk to cross the street.

"Thirty four." He took a deep breath and answered me! Perhaps he does want to talk about this. If anyone knows how that feels, I do!

"Do you know how old Miss Clarissa is?"

"Why? I am not looking for a wife!" He looked down at me with his brows furrowed.

"I don't know. I was just curious. Besides, I'm sure you are dedicated to William." Lord where did that come from?

"I am, but he's not everything. I mean, I have called on ladies. She's William's cousin and probably wouldn't be interested in the likes of me." He looked at the sidewalk as we approached the other side of the street.

"Why wouldn't she? You're very handsome and very strong and tall. Any woman would love to be seen hanging on the arm of such a man as yourself." I smiled up at him his cheeks blushing again.

"You think so? Do you think she would?" He was deep in thought now.

"Would what?" I knew he was interested in her. I was match making again!

"Never mind…" He stretched his neck from one side to the other and squared his chin. He truly is a handsome man.

"Nick… I think any woman would find you attractive! All you have to do is smile and secondly, try not to analyze and be suspicious of them when you first meet them." He looked at me realizing I was referring to how he was when he first met me.

"I'm sorry if I made you feel that way, but it is my duty to protect William." He pursed his lips.

"Does William know how you feel about Clarissa?"

"Feel about Clarissa? I don't feel anything about Clarissa." He looked away from me which told me he did indeed like her. We approached mother's teashop and I took a deep breath.

"Nick, please come in and have some tea with me, I know mother would love to see you again."

"Thank you, I think I will." He smiled and opened the door for me.

He wasn't uncomfortable to be around me any longer. I was glad about that too and wanted to talk with him more about Clarissa.

"Well hello… Lord Baptiest, was it?" Mother smiled walking up to me to hug me.

"Yes, but please call me Nick." He smiled taking her hand and bowing over it.

"Well, sit and I shall send for tea and or coffee?" She looked at Nick and me, asking without asking if I wanted tea or coffee. We both said coffee at the same time and laughed softly.

"Have a seat and I shall return." She smiled and hurried to the kitchen. Nick held my chair as I sat.

"Have you heard from William?" I placed a napkin in my lap.

"No and don't expect to either. So don't ask me things I cannot tell you. I shall not betray William." He smiled a devilish smile.

"I won't ask another thing and wouldn't make you tell me something you shouldn't." I looked down giving into the woman's tactics of a poor defenseless woman trick. Pouting a bit works most of the time.

"Rebecca, please don't worry. William is doing exactly what he said he was doing." He leaned forwards.

"I just wished I knew if I needed a special dress or a riding habit or maybe a ball gown." I sighed out. I was pouring it on and looked up at him through my lashes and bit my bottom lip.

"If he was planning anything extravagant or nothing at all, he would take care of everything that you would need." He looked up with one brow arched and a smirk on his face and I realized that he was smarter than I thought.

"I'm, sorry, Nick. I know you're not supposed to say." I sighed.

"Here you two go." Mother returned with three coffees and a small basket of orange rolls. I loved mother's orange rolls! Nick stood as Mother sat down holding her chair.

"How will everyone travel to Winchester on Friday?" Mother took a bite of orange roll.

"William is bringing back the coach, which is one of the reasons he wanted to return to the estate." He smiled down at me and winked.

"I see. Then what does William have planned for their visit?" She smiled at Nick and looked at me and winked. Thank God for Mother!

"I think he has several things in mind, but I cannot say if anything is in stone or not. I have not heard from him." He smiled at mother and me as if he was on to that as well. Shoot! Foiled again! I heard Nick softly chuckle.

"When Cole came in and told me William had gone back to Winchester, I thought the worst, but when Cole explained that he was preparing for their arrival, I was impressed." She sipped her Coffee.

"Lord Andrews is very serious about your daughter and would never hurt or harm her reputation. He is a man of honor." He nodded with certainty.

"He is serious about Rebecca?" Mother smiled wide. I looked at mother thinking, I am sitting right here! But I couldn't say anything. I wanted to hear what Nick had to say. I just sat listening sipping my coffee.

"Indeed. He has only the very best intentions towards her and..." He suddenly stopped sipping his coffee.

"Go on, Nick." Mother sipped her coffee as well.

"I shouldn't say this, but Rebecca knows." He looked at me as if to say, have you told her? I shook my head.

"What?" Mother was eating this like chocolate pie.

"He wishes to marry her." He smiled looking at me as if he just ate the mouse.

"What?" Mother's face lit right up with surprise.

"Yes, he is in love with her and wants her to become his wife." He laughed out.

OH! I was going to get him back and knew exactly what I was going to do! I pursed my lips! Why did he do this to me? Maybe he was testing me for William.

"Rebecca, why haven't you told me this news yet?" Mother smiled with tears in her eyes.

"I was waiting for William to come back. I wanted him to be with me when I told you!" That was an answer he did not expect! He slightly nodded his head as if he agreed in his own mind that my answer was sufficient.

"I knew you two would marry, you are just alike, but not enough to make mud!" She smiled and laughed.

"Please don't say anything until William officially asks me his self and Nick... You have a big mouth!" I laughed seeing his mouth opened wide as his eyes were. I don't think anyone has ever said that to him. If anything he was tight lipped!

"I... I'm sorry, Rebecca." He truly did appear sorry. I wanted to laugh, but I was not going to give my plan away.

"That's alright, Nick. We all say things we shouldn't." I couldn't help myself any longer and laughed out loud. Then mother and Nick laughed out as well, but Nick could see in my eyes that I wasn't through with this! I smiled to myself.

We chatted the afternoon away and soon it was time to call it a day. Mother wanted me to go back to her house with her and invited Nick to join us, but I declined wanting to relax and finish that book. She agreed, Nick went on his way and I hugged mother and promised her I would come over tomorrow night. I had a feeling that Nick was watching me for some reason. I saw him across the street watching me trying not to look so obvious and shrugged it off and went inside the hotel. The man behind the front desk called to me.

"Ms Grayson?"

"Yes?"

"A message came for you this afternoon." He handed me a envelope.

"Thank you." I took the letter seeing it was from William and my heart started to pound. I was feeling as if the balance of my life was hanging on the words inside the envelope and hurried to my room. Then I started the bath water and sat the letter on the nightstand. I didn't want to read the letter and yet couldn't wait to read his words. I was torn and decided to take my bath and ready myself for bed. The letter was pressing me to hurry in the tub and instead of relaxing and enjoying the hot water, I was washed, dried, had my nightshift on and brushing out my hair. I couldn't stand it anymore!

As my heart pounded, I groaned. I braided my hair in a simple braid down my back and a soft tap on the door stopped me from reaching for the letter. I put my robe on and called through the door

"Yes?"

"Room service…" I slowly opened the door and sure enough it was room service with another cart!

"Pardon me, Ms. Grayson, your dinner has arrived." The same young man pushed the cart into the room and bowed leaving without a word, just a simple smile.

"Thank." Before I could get the whole thank you out he was gone. I could smell something wonderful fill the room. I lifted the cover to find a wonderful roast beef and potato dinner with carrots and gravy, rolls and apple pie for dessert. I licked my lips realizing that I was indeed hungry. I thought about the letter and still decided to eat first. I was so afraid and so compelled to read it. I figured that right now, I didn't know what it said and my heart wasn't breaking. Why was it so hard for me to believe he is a man of his word! I shouldn't doubt William. That's not right nor is it true love! I laid the napkin on my lap and leapt up taking the letter back to the chair. With a deep breath, I opened the envelope and unfolded the parchment type paper. I blankly stared at the length of the letter and it was very short. Then slowly read…

My Dearest Rebecca,

I am writing to you as I cannot sleep. The entire time I have been away from you my mind has done nothing but think about you. I miss you terribly and am counting the moments until Friday. I am finding myself miserable without you and cannot believe how much you had become a part of my life already and realized that it's from depriving myself of your company. I want you to know that this to me is much harder than I anticipated. We must have that talk immediately. Until Friday my love

Estoy Enamorado Conmigo

William

"Oh, William!" My heart cried out, I had missed him just as much! He was all I could think about. These last days without him have been so hard.

Upon finishing my dinner I put another log on the fire and put the uneaten food back under their covers on the cart. I took the pie and milk to the bedside table. I wanted to read the book I started and I figured that I would not sleep very well tonight.

I crawled into bed with the book and fluffed the pillows. I reread the letter and then laid it on the nightstand. He was missing me as much as I was missing him. I can't wait to see him on Friday and after tomorrow, it will be Friday! I will have to pack what I want to take and send the rest to mother's. My dresses should be ready tomorrow as Hannah said. That poor woman must be working on them right now! I feel so close to her and thought I would have loved to have known her when Robert was alive. I am so glad I know her now. Then I thought how odd that I didn't know her before and do now.

The pie sat on the table with the milk for about an hour before I took the first bite. It was so good! As I took another bite, I thought of all the things William and I talked about concerning Robert and how God's plans sometimes aren't what we expect, even what they appear to be sometimes. Robert was so dependent on God's word for guidance and wisdom, I never thought any different about why he thought the way he did or did the things the way he did. He was strong willed and always had the answers to everything he was doing or not doing. I never questioned anything. Now I find myself thinking about his reasons for his decisions and why he made them. Even some that frustrated me and made me angry and sad at times. Robert said one day I would understand. Was he truly led by God's own hand? I took another bite of pie then sat it back on the table finding myself thinking about all my own decision. All the ones that I had made and the path I had chosen which all led me to this very place in time, from the move to Hickory Hill to this very moment in this bed eating apple pie thinking about the paths I've chosen. I know God has reasons for everything.

I yawned and laid down resting my head thinking that after tomorrow I would know what God had planned for my life. William said I would love his home and couldn't wait to show me what he wanted to share with me. I realized that I wasn't going to read the book and blew out the lantern and lay back down...

~ Chapter 11~

Morning was here and I couldn't recall even falling asleep! The last thing I remembered was starting to pray, thanking God for all the right paths I have walked down, even if I thought they were wrong. I felt wonderful and tomorrow I would see William! Tomorrow!

I made up my mind that if God truly had made William for me and William had waited all his life for me, then I was no longer going to deny myself nor him being happy and enjoying each other…and suddenly, I realized that Robert was no longer the first thing I thought about in the morning anymore! This was the first morning that this has happened! It's William! To me it was another confirmation that I was doing the right thing. Robert's hold had truly been released in earnest and felt as if I was given the gift of a second chance for happiness. I silently thanked God for all he's given me as I slid out of bed.

Soon I had packed all my things and took the food cart out to the hall. I was going to go see mother and Mike this morning and Cole later.

After I was through packing and instructed the clerk at the counter about my bags, I made my way to the Tea Shop and saw Mike sweeping the floor.

"Good morning, Mike." I smiled feeling new life inside.

"Morning Rebecca… mother is in the kitchen… You ready for your trip tomorrow?" He smiled as he picked up the dirt with a piece of paper.

"I am so excited! Do you think Cole is just as excited?"

"Oh, he is and I think he is planning on something very special for Carla."

"Why do you think that?" I had a feeling as well.

"I haven't seen hide nor hair of him since Monday."

"He's probably preparing for the trip. Carla was ready yesterday." I smiled thinking how wonderful if Cole was head over heels in love with Carla!

"Good morning, I thought I heard you, Rebecca." Mother smiled at me as she came to hug me.

"Morning, Mother!" I hugged her tight.

"Come… let's have some coffee and rolls." I nodded.

We sat at her favorite table and she had Mike bring coffee and rolls in for us. There weren't too many people here right now and the rush was over a half hour ago, so it was rather relaxing.

"Cole is looking forward to this trip. He has bought a few new suits and something he won't say for Carla." She smiled sipping her tea.

"I talked to Carla and she has everything taken care of as well and is very excited. I do know Cole ordered her a dress from Hannah's."

"Isn't that sweet? Cole has been acting like a pup in love." Mother smiled.

"I think he would marry her right now if she would say yes!" I laughed.

"Yes, he is taken with her isn't he?" Mother laughed.

"Oh he is and I think she is perfect for him."

"As well as William is for you." She winked.

"I agree with you, Mother."

"You do?" She looked surprised

"Yes." I smiled and sipped my coffee.

I spent the rest of the morning talking about what William and I had discussed. She thought that it was indeed a possibility and that there was no use in worrying about it. If it were, no one could stop the hand of God! I also thought I have seen that little boy Joey, but I wasn't certain it was him. He was running so fast and flew past the window. I still wonder about that little guy and his possible sister. I sighed thinking he was so adorable.

When the lunch crowd started to come in, she shooed me off and I went to see Cole at the lumber yard and kept an eye out for Joey.

"Good morning, Ms. Grayson." I looked up to see Nick had found me.

"Please call me, Rebecca."

"Rebecca… Where are you headed?" Nick smiled slightly.

"I'm going to see my brother Cole." This was interesting finding him here again.

"May I escort you?" He smiled at me.

"Of course, but I don't want to keep you from anything."

"You're not. Are you ready for your trip?" He offered his arm.

"Yes and I can't wait to see William. It feels as if it's been a month since I've seen him."

"Well, I know he will be most anxious to see you as well." Nick nodded.

"Have you heard from him?" I smiled up at Nick watched his brows furrow.

"Yes I have and he is quite restless to get back here and take you home." His words warmed me so much!

"He said that?" My heart leapt for joy! Home!

"He hasn't gotten much sleep, but has everything almost ready." He winked at me.

"Can you tell me if he plans on anything really big? Like a dinner party?"

"I can tell you that whatever he has planned, you will be happy." He smiled down at me with one eyebrow up.

"Alright, I won't ask anymore." I laughed as Nick covered my hand and took me across the road.

"Cole's lumber yard is busy today." Nick looked at all the full wagons and people coming and going.

"He's always busy, that is why he never takes a vacation."

"Who will run the place when he leaves, does he have a right hand man?"

"Wilson, he's very good to Cole." I nodded as we stepped into the office.

"I shall wait." He smiled and was about to sit.

"No, come back with me!"

"If you are sure?" He smiled.

"Of course I am sure!" I led him back to Cole's office and knocked on the door.

"Come in." Cole called as I opened the door. Cole was buried in paper work sipping coffee.

"Rebecca, Nick, come sit!" He smiled walking around his desk and shook Nick's hand.

"How is my beautiful Sister this morning?" He kissed my cheek.

"Wonderful! Are you looking forward to tomorrow?"

"More than you know! So Nick, have you heard from William?"

"Yes, and he will be here in the morning ready and waiting." Nick smiled.

"That is good! I am ready for a nice break." He rolled his eyes as he motioned to all the paper work.

"I know you will all have a wonderful time. I've never seen Will so excited. It is good to see him so taken with your sister and about time too!" He smiled at me and I could feel my cheeks warm.

"I have made a folder of how I run this company and am going to bring it with me. I want William to help me convert it to the profit sharing he has implemented in his businesses."

"That will thrill William." Nick laughed out.

"I want my employees to be surprised this Christmas with a little something extra that will last them a life time." Cole was so good to the workers.

"I'm sure William has everything in order as well. You remind me a lot of William." He chuckled.

"I'm sure I will enjoy his views." Cole smiled wide looking so alive!

They talked business for a while as I sat and listened. Cole ordered lunch and ate right in the office. He had Wilson ready for taking over for him and was going to make sure all the paper work was in order and caught up. As I stood, Nick and Cole did as well.

"I think I will check on Carla and then go to Hannah's, you two can talk business all day and night, but I can't, I still have to do a few things."

"I need to go as well, I have to go to the stables and see Mr. Thomas about William's arrival." Nick smiled at me softly.

"Well Cole...until tomorrow!" I kissed his cheek as Nick shook his hand.

We walked to Carla's but she had already closed for the day. I decided to go to Hannah's, but she too was closed already. Nick escorted me back to the hotel remembering that Hannah said that my dresses would be delivered to my room.

"Nick, thank you for your company, but I think I will finish up packing and turn in early."

"As you wish... I will see you at eight in the morning for breakfast. William will be waiting for you." He smiled so sweetly. I leaned up and pulled his collar down and kissed his cheek.

"What was that for?" He put his hand on cheek.

"For being so sweet and watching me this week..." I looked up at him and gave him a devilish grin.

"How..." He was flabbergasted!

"Believe me, I didn't at first, but when I saw you across the street, I knew what your 'Mission' was and to tell you the truth, I was grateful for it. Thank you."

"You are the first to ever expose my cover which confirms with what I've been noticing... It's time to retire." He looked down at me with a soft smile. I didn't realize that blowing his cover was the deciding factor of retirement!

"I just guessed if you must know!" I laughed hoping that he would feel better.

"You guessed did you?" He smiled wider.

"Yes." I hoped he believed me. I held my breath.

"Good! I wasn't ready to retire yet!" He laughed.

"Well, Nick, thank you."

"Any time, milady." He smiled happily whistling as he walked away.

I walked to my room recalling his face and knew he didn't really believe me when I said I guessed, but was trying to make me feel better, sweet man indeed!

Then I saw three boxes on my bed.

The dresses had arrived! I put my purse in the chair, hurried to the bed and opened the first box. I held up a light blue day dress with light blue lace on the long sleeves and buttons down the front and three quarter sleeves. It was perfect! The next box held a light green dress with a bow in the back and trimmed in white, very pretty indeed. The last box had two boxes. A beautiful satin cream dress with lighter cream lace and a lower neckline lay on top of a small box. The dress didn't look like a day dress, but more like an evening dress, but not as fancy as a ball gown. My heart pounded as I touched the satin and as I opened the small box and inside it were some beautiful nightclothes. Not like my night shift at all. These were more intimate. Like a wife would wear for her husband. Oh that Hannah! I laughed and blushed.

Unable to resist, I held the lacy nightgown up to me and looked in the mirror. It was beautiful! The front laced up with small thin satin ribbon. The sleeves were long and lace trumpeting out on the ends and to the floor, breathtaking! It too was cream in color.

I held another one up, but this one was more conservative in pale blue satin with long sleeves and buttoned up the front with small pearl buttons tapered at the waist and the neckline was not cut low. It was a scoop neck, I liked this one. The last was a pale pink with a low-neckline and tied in the back with long sleeves and satin as well. I couldn't believe

Hannah thought about even nightgowns. A soft tap on the door startled me as I was thinking about William.

"Yes?" I called out.

"Room service…" I opened the door and a cart of food was brought in.

"Thank you." The young man bowed and left the room.

"What do we have here?" I looked at the cart and it seemed that there was too much food on the cart. I uncovered the first one, it was a complete dinner plate, prime rib and potato with a salad and rolls. I uncovered the second plate and it had the same thing on it. Then a tap on the door made me realize the young man must have made a mistake and that this was for a different room.

"I thought you had made a mist… William!" He stood smiling wide down at me. My breath caught and my heart pounded, I threw my arms around him almost knocking him down!

"Rebecca… I could not…" His lips covered mine as he scooped me up in his arms and carried me into the room kicking the door shut. He kissed me deeply and I returned his kiss with the same passion. My William…my thoughts echoed. He pulled away from my lips and they instantly rebelled.

"Rebecca, I have missed you." He kissed me tenderly still holding me in his arms.

"William… I missed you too." I whispered softly as he kissed my face.

"You did, did you?" He smiled wide and bit his bottom lip.

"More than I ever thought!" I pulled him to my lips. My body weakened and felt so warm.

"Rebecca… I…" His eyes held an overwhelming desire in them that was undeniable. His lips covered mine as I felt him tense. He slowly pulled away from my lips and looked into my eyes.

"William, I didn't expect you until tomorrow morning!" He was here!

"I couldn't wait another minute. I had to come. I had to hold you… to tell you…"

"Tell me what?" I touched his lips with my fingers and he took them into his hand and kissed them holding them to his chest. He looked into my eyes and leaned down.

"Rebecca… I love you." He whispered as his lips hovered over mine. His eyes consumed my thoughts as his lips covered mine in a deep passionate kiss that took my breath and made my head spin.

He pulled me to his chest wrapping his arms around me and could once again smell his scent breathing in deeply taking it in.

"I missed you so much, William. I can hardly believe all that you have done for me."

"For you my love, there will be never enough that I could do for you." He pressed his lips to my forehead.

"I can't believe you're here early!" My heart was pounding so hard.

"I wanted to surprise you, but as I said, I could wait no longer." He placed his finger under my chin and turned my face to his.

"I'm so happy you couldn't! I was as miserable as you were while you were away." I laughed.

"I was hoping you were!" He laughed realizing how much I missed the sound of his laughter, voice, his smile, his arms around me, and his lips.

"Come, we have all night!" He smiled and grinned devilishly as he held my hand leading me to the chairs, but sat down and pulled me into his lap. His fingers ran down my cheek and his thumb ran across my lips. He looked tired, but so handsome! Even more than I could ever think! His eyes stared deep into mine.

"Does Nick know you're back?" I smiled and was trying to slow my heart and took a deep breath.

"Yes." He whispered.

"When did you arrive?" I brushed a long strand of hair out of his eyes. He caught my hand and kissed the palm of it. I felt my body warm.

"Not long ago. Nick was in the stable when I arrived and he told me you just went to your room." He kissed the palm of my hand again then looked at me seeing in his eyes a look I've only seen twice before… Desire!

"I am so glad you're here. I thought I would never sleep tonight!"

His arm was wrapped around my waist and the other he had my hand in as he rubbed his thumb over the top of my hand.

"I have something for you and want to give it to you now." He lifted me up off his lap and sat me in the chair. Then he went to one knee.

My heart pounded in my chest and my breath was gone! My fingers went to my lips. He reached into his pocket inside of his jacket and pulled out a small box. Tears welled into my eyes as I looked into his. They were so full of love.

"Rebecca… from the first day I saw you on the road, till this day, I have been the happiest I have ever been in my entire life. You complete me, Rebecca and I do not wish to live without you. I love you more than words can say and have from the moment I saw you, I knew you had to be mine. I do not wish to wait another minute without you in my life. Rebecca, please make my life complete and make me the happiest man in the world and become my wife… marry me Rebecca." He opened the box and my heart was about to explode as I gazed on a breathtaking ring sparkling out of a deep blue velvet box. I could not breathe or speak I looked into his eyes seeing them full of love. Tears poured from mine and all I could do was nod my head.

"You will?" His eyes welled in tears. I nodded again.

"That was a yes?" He could hardly speak.

"Yes…" I hoarsely got the words out.

My arms went around his neck and I crushed my lips on his. I kissed him deeply as tears fell from my eyes as my heart was so full of love. I wanted to be his wife! I pulled away from his lips and we wiped the tears from each other's face and laughed softly.

"Here, my love." He took my hand gently and placed the ring on my finger then kissed it softly holding my hand to his chest.

"My lady, you have made me the happiest man in the world." He stood and pulled me to him. His lips covered mine and took them in consuming every breath I had. He pulled away slowly.

"Somehow, I feel as if I have known you all my life." He stared deep into my eyes.

"I feel the same! Maybe that is why things are going so fast? It just feels so right!" I smiled up at him and it did feel right! I could see myself growing old with him spending every moment of the rest of my life with him.

"I guess that since I've waited for you all my life, I already knew the woman I wanted, and in truth, I have known you all my life." He smiled and brushed his lips across mine.

My body wanted more than just a kiss, but I was trying to keep my feelings in check. I respected William so much.

"Shall we eat, my love?" He smiled down into my eyes biting his bottom lip.

"I think we had better!" I softly laughed as he took my hand and helped me down in the chair. Then he kissed the ring on my hand again. His face was glowing with joy.

"Rebecca, you know, I am quite a bit older than you." He looked down as he sat down.

"I know, William… but, that does not matter to me. I love you… not your age." I smiled taking my napkin and placing it in my lap.

"Well, that is a good thing, though I was a bit concerned about being older." He smiled.

"You could say to you that you intend to marry a young bride. You shall be the envy of all your Ilk!" I gave him a devilish looking smile.

"Ah, I never thought about that before! Hmm…I like that! A bonus if you will." We both laughed.

"I still can't believe you're here." I smiled at him lovingly

"Do you like the ring?"

"Heavens… Yes! But isn't it a little too…" I held my hand out and looked at the beautiful marquee diamond with one diamond on either side of the large marquee sparkled with a thousand facets of lights.

"A little too. what?" His brows furrowed.

"Well… expensive?" I looked up at him and his eye widened, then he roared out in laughter.

"What?" Why was he laughing?

"Rebecca… expensive?" He roared a thunderously deep laugh.

"William! Why are you laughing?" I furrowed my brows.

"Oh, Rebecca… it's not too expensive! Though really, I'm glad you think it is."

I was really confused.

"Rebecca, I am a very wealthy man. I could have spent a million times more and still never have to worry about anything for the rest of my life." He smiled and leaned forwards.

"Well… I…" He thought this was not expensive? Goodness! I blushed.

"Rebecca…when you marry me…you'll never have to worry about anything for the rest of your life… except one thing." He smiled a devilish grin.

"What, William?" His smile turned wider and more sensual and he raised that brow of his.

"Except children… and I want a house full!" He smiled biting his bottom lip showing his dimple.

"Children? Why of course and how many is a whole house full?" I raised my eyebrow.

"How about until I can't?" He laughed.

"Meaning?" I took a bite of a roll.

"Meaning until I'm too old to move!" He roared out a great laugh.

"Oh!" My cheeks blushed realizing what he was saying.

"Yes... Oh!" He laughed.

I looked at him and with the shape he was in. Goodness! That would be a long, long time!

"What if I... can't have children?" The thought never occurred till now.

"Well, then we'll have a wonderful time trying!" He laughed out.

"My goodness, William!" My cheeks were so red and I knew it.

"Oh, Rebecca, I'm sorry, but I feel as if I can say anything to you!"

"You can and should be able to... but..." I took a deep breath.

"Robert did not talk to you this way, did he?" He frowned.

"No, he never said anything that he felt he couldn't say to the Lord." Then I thought that it made perfect sense with the theory and all that Robert wouldn't do!

"I'm sorry, Rebecca. I guess that I assumed that you and Robert talked about everything." We both started to eat dinner.

"We did mostly... but..." How could I tell him? Would he understand?

"But what my love?" He was the confused one now, I could see that.

"As you know, we had no children, right?" I took a deep breath. He needed to know the truth and I had to tell him so he would understand.

"Yes and I wondered how you avoided them all these years. Oh I see, are you afraid because you never had children that you couldn't? Or maybe Robert couldn't?" The concern on his face was true concern.

"No... that's not it. We were able to avoid having children by... avoiding..." I looked down into my lap. He isn't going to understand this!

"Rebecca?" He laid his napkin on the table and got up kneeling by my side. He took my hands in his and then brushed the hair out of my face.

"What are you trying to say Rebecca?" His voice was soft and comforting.

"We actually... never." I looked into his eyes. His eyes widened so big. He took a breath in not letting it go for moment.

"My God, Rebecca... are you telling me what I think you are telling me?" His hand went to my face. I could see his wide eyes were in disbelief. His mouth opened.

"I think I am... yes I am." I hope he doesn't think less of me!

"Rebecca... tell me... I must know... did Robert make love to you?" He looked deep into my eyes.

"No..." Tears welled into my eyes.

"Are you saying that you and he never?" His eyes wide and mouth open, I knew he didn't believe this!

"He loved me other ways." I was so embarrassed fearing that William was thinking something was wrong with me or that Robert did not want me.

"What?" He sat down on his heels and stared at his hands holding mine.

"Robert said that there was other ways to love and it was the only way to prevent having children before he could properly prepare a place for them." I couldn't look at him. I was feeling suddenly light headed.

"Are you telling me you still are... you've never..." He touched my face with his fingers.

"He was saving that for when we were ready to start a family. He said it was the only way and that it would be more of a selfish act to have a child and not have a place for the child." Tears threatened.

"I see... so you and Robert never... were one?" He was deep in thought.

"That's what I'm telling you, William." Tears poured down my cheeks.

"My God... Rebecca!" He pulled me to his chest and hugged me tightly.

"I do know what two people that are married are supposed to do, I'm not ignorant. Robert said that the one thing we couldn't do was the thing that would lead us to bring a child into this world and that a child deserved to have everything. William, he was truly wonderful. He only tried to be the best husband and then one day a father." I buried my face into his chest.

"I don't know what to say." He gently took my face in his hands and kissed my forehead.

"Don't feel bad for me, William. Robert was a good provider and husband."

"But, Rebecca... you do realize that I want children." He stared deep into my eyes with this look of shock.

"Yes... and I want them." I looked down.

"You know, this tells me even more that God sent you to me." He smiled with so much love in his eyes. They were peaceful and calm. He wasn't upset in the least!

"I thought about that too… I wanted to tell you if the time was ever right, but I wasn't sure if you would believe me or not or if you would marry me after you found out that I was still…" I looked back down.

"My God… Thank you God for this great gift!" He looked up then hugged me to his chest.

"William… You see it as a gift from God?"

"Yes I do! You have known no man that way and that is a very precious gift indeed!" He was still in disbelief as I looked back up and seeing it in his eyes.

"Robert's ways were different than most, but they were always led by the Lord. Don't get me wrong, I wanted to and I pleaded with him, but he always said no and that we had to wait. He always promised soon. Well… soon never came." I looked down.

"Rebecca, I promise that I will love you in any way you desire. I want children right away, and care not to wait. I have many bedrooms to fill!" He softly kissed my lips and pulled away from me slowly.

"I want you to just love me." I brushed my lips across his.

"I already do and only have begun to show you just how much I do." His eyes were so full of love.

"Thank you William for not being upset with me."

"Rebecca, I still find it hard to believe that a man could deny himself of you for so long! I could not, you're so beautiful and I am far too selfish." He laughed.

"Then my Lord, I will surrender all to you, you have waited so long. That was one of Robert's requests, find someone to love me as much as he did and give me all he could not."

"And I give you my word I will do just that!" He kissed me tenderly and then deeply. My knees weakened and my head was spinning.

"Rebecca, I want to love you so badly that I ache. I can't help myself." His lips crushed mine. I won't be able to stop and knew it in my heart. I loved this man as much as Robert already. He pulled back and looked deep into my eyes again searching for something.

"What is it, William?" I looked up into his eyes waiting.

"I must leave." He breathing was hard.

"William?" I wanted to say please don't go, but I understood.

"I will see you tomorrow morning my love." He pulled me to his lips and kissed me tenderly then pulling away slowly.

"Alright, William, I will be ready." I searched his eyes knowing that he must go now. He knew I understood.

"Rebecca, I promise when we are married... I will love you and never deny you anything, nor will you want to..." He grinned then released me and walked to the door.

"I shall never do that my Lord!" I licked my dry lips.

"I love it when you call me that!" He smiled and winked looking over his shoulder as he went out the door.

I stood still for a moment then looked at the ring on my hand and was in disbelief! He loves me and turned in a circle in where I stood.

I went to start a bath and as the water filled, I finished gathering my things. I hung up the new dresses, then I took a fast bath and was in bed trying to go to sleep. I could feel the ring on my finger and recalled his words he said, 'I complete him.' You complete me, William. Robert thank you for William! Just as I lay down and a soft tap on the door woke me up. I walked to the door.

"Yes?' I called.

"It's William." I opened the door and he stepped in and took me into his arms. I'm not dressed I thought!

"I just had to see if you were real and if you were, did you really say you would marry me." He slightly smiled.

"William, I'm not... dressed... I..." His lips covered mine, my nightshift started to feel cool against my skin instantly feeling so warm. His kiss deepened, full of hunger, desire and passion. Then he pulled away and picked me up and carried me to the bed. He gently laid me down and pulled the covers up around me.

"I love you, Rebecca." He kissed my lips and my forehead.

"William..." I didn't know what he was going to do next.

"Hmm..." He leaned back down towards my face.

"I did say yes and yes I'm real and I love you." I whispered.

"You did say that, didn't you?" He whispered back grinning.

"Yes." He smoothed my hair back.

"Was that why you really came to my room again?"

"Yes and no. I did want to see if you still said yes, but to be honest, I find it hard to stay away." His lips were a whisper away, his voice soft and very sultry.

"William, I think you're right. If this is a gift from God, how can we defile it?" I heard him take a deep breath.

"Soon my love we will not have to worry about such things." He kissed me tenderly.

"Soon..." I kissed him softly.

"Good night." He whispered and gently kissed my forehead smoothing my hair from my face. I closed my eyes and thought how relaxed I was feeling and then, heard the door close...

~ Chapter 12 ~

The memory of his words woke me up. Was that a dream? I looked around the room at everything and then I remembered...the ring! I raised my left hand, closing my eyes before I looked and when I opened them it was there! It wasn't a dream! He said I complete him! He loves me! There was a tap on the door and I sprang from bed... William!

"Yes?" I called.

"It's me, Carla." I opened the door and flung my arms around her.

"Rebecca? What is it? Are you alright?"

"I am simply wonderful... come in!" I took her by the hand and pulled her into the room.

"So what besides you seeing William today has got you in such a good mood?" She laughed.

"William came back last night and gave me something very special."

"He's back? I thought he was coming this morning?" She tilted her head.

"No, he couldn't wait and had to tell me something and ask me something and give me this!" I held my hand out and Carla's mouth hung to her feet and she was speechless.

"He asked me to be his wife!" I cried tears rolling down my cheeks.

"Oh, Rebecca! It's beautiful!" She held my hand looking at the ring.

"I was so surprised! He does not want to wait to be married." My heart pounded at the thought that he wanted to marry me.

"He loves me and I love him, so we're not going to wait long." I hugged her.

"Oh, Rebecca, I am so happy for you!" She hugged me back.

"So are you ready and set to go?" I looked at her.

"Yes, that is why I came up. William and Cole are in the restaurant waiting for you. Now get that behind in gear!" She laughed.

"Alright, all I have to do is change my clothes and put this in the bag."

Tamalyn E Scott

"Well, what are you waiting for? Your husband to be is waiting!" She smiled so sweetly.

"I'm hurrying!" I ran into the washroom and changed into one of my new dresses.

"I'll put your gown in the bag if you throw it out to me." Carla called.

"Here!" I tossed the gown to her and finished my hair.

I looked around the room one last time to see if I had missed anything, but I hadn't. I took Carla by the arm and we went down to the restaurant to meet William and Cole. I bit my bottom lip thinking about William and strangely, it feels as if we are meant to marry and felt so good! I don't know why I feel this, but perhaps it is God's plan! There are so many facts that enter into all of it and one day I will write down all the things that have happened and see how many things point to God.

I had the clerk retrieve my bags from the room and told them where to take them while Carla and I went to see William and Cole. They stood as we approached. William looked so handsome in his dark gray casual suit trimmed in black with a white shirt and a slender black tie tailored to fit. I smiled shyly feeling as if I could not breathe.

"Well Sister, I hear that William has asked for your hand." He smiled and hugged me kissing my cheek and then Carla's cheek.

"Yes." I smiled laying my hand in William's as he held my chair to sit. He kissed it softly then sat himself.

"I have asked Cole for your hand, Rebecca." He smiled with a new look in his eyes. It was as if they danced!

"You did?" I knew he didn't have to do that, but I'm sure he did it out of respect for our family.

"Yes, I did." He smiled softly and looked at Cole.

"Of course I said you two had the family's blessings." He smiled at me and winked.

"Thank you Cole!" I leaned over and kissed his cheek and hugged his neck.

"William says he wishes to marry you right away." Cole smiled and winked at William.

"The sooner the better!" William laughed.

"I am so happy for you Rebecca." Carla smiled.

"We have taken the privilege of ordering for you two, I know what you want. Cole ordered for Carla." William kissed my hand.

"Thank you." I smiled and sipped my coffee feeling my stomach was all in knots. I am so blessed to have a man this wonderful in my life.

224

"How long is the trip to Winchester?" Carla looked at William.

"It takes about two hours but actually we're going to the out skirts of Winchester." He smiled and sipped his coffee.

"Cole, did you see your sister's ring?" Carla sipped her coffee as I held my hand to Cole.

"Holy smokes! That's a ring alright!" He sat back holding my hand.

"It's breathtaking!" I smiled at William.

"Unfortunately, there wasn't a ring that I could find that suited Rebecca and how I felt about her. This one would have to do." He looked down at my hand and took it in his.

"William, the ring is beautiful and it's perfect! I love it!" I looked confused at him.

"Well, the fact is nothing I could ever find to put on your finger would ever match how I feel about you my love." He kissed the ring on my finger.

"Alright you two, you'll have the rest of your lives to do that. Our food is here… let's eat!" The waiter sat all the plates on the table.

"Thank you Stan." William nodded.

We quietly gave thanks to God for all that has happened and will happen, for safe journey and blessings for all those we love. We ate and listened to William saying that his staff was ready and so eager to meet Cole, Carla and especially me. He also talked about the horses at the stables saying there were new ones born last week with three to go. He also said that we could come and go whenever we wanted to, treating his home as if it was our own. After we finished the last cup of coffee William smiled as he stood taking my hand.

"Is everyone ready?" Cole followed taking Carla's hand. I noticed that people in the room were staring at us as, William escorted us into the main lobby. The clerk smiled and thanked me for staying nodding to William as well.

"Now we are ready!" He wrapped my hand around his arm and led us to the carriage. Cole helped Carla in the carriage sitting next to her. William helped me in and sat next to me.

The coachman closed the door, nodding to William and we were on our way. William took his jacket off loosening his tie and unbuttoned his top two buttons then rolled up his sleeves. He put his arm gently around my shoulder pulling me closer to him. Instantly his cologne surrounded me and his scent is wonderful!

"I know we are all going to have such a wonderful time this week." William smiled truly looking happy.

"I know we will." His eyes sparkled.

"Cole, do you have everything done and ready for Wilson?" I smiled at my handsome brother holding Carla's hand.

"That I did. Wilson could be busy for the next month if he could finish all that I need." Cole laughed shaking his head.

"You have that much business?" William asked Cole.

"Yes, and then some. I could add on to the building yet again!" He laughed.

"Do you log in one certain area?" William and Cole were going to talk about business again. I looked at Carla and we both rolled our eyes laughing to ourselves.

"Yes, do you have any thoughts about that?"

"Well, yes, if you are interested." William leaned slightly forward.

"Anything that would help catch us up would be a blessing." Cole laughed.

"Let me ask you this. Do you transport all the cut logs back to the lumber yard and if so how many at a time?"

"We cut the trees and haul them by wagon about ten miles back to the yard and then they are processed." Cole looked at William as if he was expecting William to have an answer to his question.

"Hmm..." William was deep in thought. I could see he was sorting ideas in his head.

"Do you have a thought on the matter?" Cole waited on William knowing that he did have an answer.

"I do have one idea. Would it be possible to erect a temporary pole barn where you are cutting and put a smaller mill there? That way when you're through logging that area you can move it to a new location? That way it wouldn't be so time consuming in the numerous loads you have to do per day. It would allow you to put more boards on the wagons. This would even the loads allowing less time on the road, more lumber and less work at the yard?" He waited as Cole sat deep in thought.

"You know, I think that is doable! I believe that I can get a smaller mill that can be torn down and moved without much trouble. You know, I think that is a brilliant idea William! Yes! I honestly think that can be done!" Cole was now excited!

"Well, you'll be able to rip the wood on the sight and plane it at the yard, now the one thing to remember would be, how long you intend to be in that one spot? It wouldn't pay if you were there for only a week or two, now a month would be worth the time in moving the mill." William smiled down at me squeezing my hand.

"Yes, I see what you mean. Most of the time we're at one spot for three to four weeks, but if we were to go deeper into the woods, we could cover a larger area all around and stay longer." Cole was deeply thinking about this theory.

"The wagons could be right at the end of the mill so that you wouldn't have to handle the wood so much." William leaned forwards and I could see his thoughts whirling!

"Yes and the men wouldn't get so tired as well as the animals! Yes! I think that would work!" Cole smiled wide as he sat back, shaking his head. I saw the excitement in his eyes and his thoughts racing!

"I'll work out the plan when I get back." He smiled at William and then me with a nod.

Cole looked out the window deep in thought. I looked at Carla and shrugged my shoulders. William squeezed my hand and leaned down and whispered in my ear.

"You look beautiful my love." His deep voice sent waves of heat through my body as I glanced at him seeing a sensual grin slip across his lips as if he knew. My cheeks warmed thinking how I loved feeling his lips on mine. His grin widened as he bit his bottom lip. He knew I was staring! And I was!

"Thank you, my Lord." I softly smiled at him as he raised my hand to his lips kissing the back softly. His lips lingered and I could not look away. He winked at me and raised one brow.

"William, have you planned anything while we visit? Or are we left to just enjoy our visit and relax?" Cole asked interrupting my thoughts and I was glad for that!

"I have only one small thing planned that will take only an evening and then you are free to do whatever you wish." He looked down at me and gave me a strange look.

"Will you tell us?" Carla was intrigued.

"I will say it will be something you'll not soon forget." He looked at me and winked.

"Is it a dinner party?" Carla was thinking hard.

"Yes, in a way… but not to big just a few of my closest friends I want you all to meet." He smiled at Carla.

"So, it is a party of sorts?" Carla smiled at William.

"Of sorts…" He squeezed my hand and leaned down and whispered in my ear.

"I love you, Rebecca." I could feel his hot breath on my ear.

"I love you." I mouthed to him as he kissed my hand again.

"I had such a good time at Rebecca's mother's house." Carla looked up at Cole as he looked down in her eyes with such love it was plain to see.

"You'll enjoy this just as much, I hope." William nodded at Cole.

"What day will it be on?" Carla looked at him smiling.

"Tomorrow night…" He nodded.

"I love dinner parties. I can wear my new dress." She smiled at me excited.

"I will too!" I smiled up at William seeing his brows furrow slightly.

"What is it, William?" I looked at him searching his eyes.

"We'll talk later." He smiled and kissed my hand softly… another talk?

William pointed out a few things on the way, and Cole and he talked about business again and the profit sharing. As we passed through the outskirts of Lawrenceburg and approached the town of Winchester he pointed out several points of interest. Shops of all kinds went down the main street with people waving at the carriage as we passed by.

"You are well known, I gather." Cole laughed.

"It makes me feel strange… like royalty." Carla laughed.

"And you are my love. To me you are a princess!" Cole kissed her hand.

"Why thank you my prince." She laughed out.

"Now, that red brick building right there, is one of mine. I lease it out to an architect and his company who is developing the down town area." William smiled at Cole.

"I have been here many times and every time I come here, so many things seem to change." Cole was deep in thought again.

"When the train line came through two years ago, business surged and that's progress." William nodded.

As we left the city limits and were well into the country again William leaned forward.

"We're almost there." He looked out the window, as we all did.

Trees and hills were everywhere with fall colors so brilliant. The road looked just like a painting!

"This starts my property." He sat back and smiled at Carla and Cole, then me seeing in his eyes that he was so excited. He squeezed my hand

and looked out the window as the carriage pulled up to the iron gated road. We saw two guards holding the gates open as we passed through.

"This is quite a long road, but beautiful." He smiled down at me mouthing 'I love you' raising my hand, kissing it.

"It's magnificent William!" I couldn't look away from his eyes. They were speaking to my heart telling me more than his words. His eyes softened as he ran his finger down my cheek. His face was so handsome yet this moment, so content.

"This is quite a long road." Cole turned to William.

"Yes it is." William spoke quietly still looking at me.

"Do you have lumber taken from the woods?" Typical Cole I thought.

"No, but in other areas I do have the woods thinned from time to time. I do not wish to strip any of this." He smiled at Cole.

"I can understand that…it's beautiful." Cole sat back and looked out the window again.

"We're about to the last gate." William smiled

"What…another gate?" I was surprised!

"Yes, there are two gates…for privacy." He nodded but could see in his eyes that it was for safety as well.

"There…" He motioned with his head to the gates as the carriage turned the corner. Two huge iron gates with guardhouses on either side made of huge stone blocks and two guards waiting. The men wore uniforms much like the one I saw in William's closet. They nodded as we passed by.

I heard the clopping of the horse's feet on the cobble stone road. Then saw a hint of the estate home. I took it in as we approached and looked up at William wide eyed so much that he laughed out.

"Rebecca, I warned you it was big." He softly laughed hugging my shoulders.

"William, I can't believe my eyes!" I glanced at Cole seeing he too was just as overwhelmed.

"My goodness!" Carla breathlessly whispered out.

His home was a castle in the trees just as he said! Ivy hid part of the bottom few rows of huge blocks of stone that looked gray in color. Though there were no castle towers, the corners of the home were rounded as the front entry into it. As we got closer I saw tall windows that were rounded at the tops two floors high with at least two windows per room.

As we pulled towards the front and stopped, the drive was lined with lanterns, trees and flowers. A tall older man smiled at us as he opened the door holding his hand out for Carla to take.

"Hello, Jules." William smiled warmly at the old man.

"Good afternoon, my Lord." He helped Carla out then Cole stepped out.

"Milady…" Jules held his hand out as I laid it in his. He smiled as I stepped out of the carriage. William then was at my side with his hand on the small of my back.

"Jules, I would like you to meet Mr. Cole Glenn and his lovely lady Carla Taylor." He bowed to Cole and Carla.

"It is a great honor to meet you…welcome." He smiled.

"And this is my beautiful bride to be, Ms. Rebecca Grayson." William smiled at me tenderly.

"Lady Grayson, it is a great honor and pleasure to meet you. I hope you will find everything to your liking in your new home. Welcome…" His eyes smiled and twinkled at me as he bowed. My home he said!

"Milord, I will see to their bags and have them sent their rooms." He snapped his fingers and three young men came rushing.

"Each one of you will have your own maid, so if you need anything please don't hesitate to ask." William held out his arm and leaned down whispering,

"Welcome home, my love." I squeezed his arm smiling up at my handsome husband to be as butterflies took me over. Home! My home!

We started up the walk, up five steps and towards the rounded entryway and saw the doors. They were enormous! Dark, heavy arched wooden doors with black iron hinges and handles and two life size ark angels carved into the wooden doors as if locked in battle. They looked so real! Jules slightly bowed as he opened one of the doors holding it as we entered.

The stone floor shinned like polished black, gray and white glass mirroring everything above it. We all gasped at what we were seeing. A deep red carpet under our feet led our eyes to an enormous stone staircase that was very wide with the red carpet running from where we stood and up the stairs.

On each banister, sat on half pillars, were large potted ferns. At the top of the stairs were three large windows that allowed light to shine down into the room and stairway. My eyes couldn't take it all in! All around the entryway were arched walkways that matched the shape of the doors.

Above was an enormous chandelier that dropped from the ceiling by golden chains lit with a thousand candles that sparkled everywhere. I looked to my left and there was a beautiful settee, white with small gold flowers, in front of the window draped by white curtains trimmed in gold with gold chord tiebacks. To my right sat a matching settee done in the same fashion with white curtains to match.

Large tables with lanterns and roses in vases sat along the walls in between the arched doorways. I held my breath as I took the room in. Beautiful masterpieces of art work in heavy gold framing hung on the walls from royal blue velvet material like big ribbon trimmed in gold cording. In between the art hung golden and iron wall sconces with cut crystal lamps. Breathtaking!

"William, it's simply... beautiful!" I let my breath slowly out.

"If you will follow me I shall show you to your rooms." William smiled at all of us seeing we were in total awe. He covered my hand with his as we walked up the stairs watching me. My heart pounded in my chest at all that I've seen already! He did say it was big and he did say he was wealthy, but I think he was being quite modest!

We turned to the right towards the bedrooms recalling he said they were for family and friends. He glanced down at me as I looked at all the art hung along the walls with horses, forests, oceans and many masterpieces that looked like they were so very old. Some of the women were naked with little naked babies at their mother's breasts. I knew they were treasured works of art.

"What's wrong, Rebecca? Do you not care for the art?" His eyes held concern.

"No, it's wonderful, William! I'm just...astounded with your impeccable taste!" I softly whispered to him. He smiled well pleased.

"I told you I hold many surprises." He smiled so sweetly.

"Now, my room is the last, so this first room is Cole's, these rooms are for family and friends. The more I like you, the closer I have you to me!" He looked at Cole and laughed. I looked at all the doors from here to William's room.

"Really, Brother!" He put the emphasis on 'brother'.

"I'm only jesting!" He roared a great laugh that echoed down the hall.

"I do hope it is alright with you Cole that I put you in the room on the left and Carla's across from you?" Cole smiled, nodding with a blush.

"Here you go then." He swung the door open for Cole and it was a beautiful room! A huge dark wooden four-poster bed, on the right with nightstands and lanterns a fireplace with hunting pictures that hung over the fireplace. Two blue chairs and small table sat in front of the fireplace with a bookshelf full of books, a desk and a door. Two large windows overlooked the front drive. Heavy curtains hung straight down that matched the bedclothes and chairs. The door led into a washroom.

"Will you be comfortable here, Cole?" William smiled at Cole.

"It will be dreadful to get use to, but I think I could tolerate it for a week." He laughed.

"Now, Carla, this is your room." He swung the door open to a beautiful room in soft green blue and pink floral wall paper with matching curtains hung by two windows and bedclothes to match. To the left was a fireplace with a mirror hanging above the thick dark wooden mantle and two white chairs that had small soft pink in the material and a small table with roses. Next to that was a door for the washroom and the other side of the fireplace was a tall wide bookshelf with an array of books from top to bottom. The four-poster canopy bed was a washed white trimmed in gold that had sheer curtains tied back with soft pink ties. Lovely, I thought. So simple yet so lovely!

"Carla... will this do for you as well?" He smiled sweetly at her.

"My...heavens yes! William, it is beautiful!" She covered her lips with her fingers taking in the room.

"Wonderful! Then I shall leave you two to freshen up and when you're ready, we will meet you downstairs and to your left through the center doorway in the sitting room." He smiled at me taking my hand in his.

"That will be fine... Let's say..." Cole looked at Carla.

"How about an hour?" The boy's carried our bags and took them into their rooms. Then I saw two maids coming down the hall. One smiled at Cole as she walked to William and the other looked down as she stood in front of William.

"Patty Smith, this is, Cole Glenn, you will be tending to his needs. Cole, this is, Patty, she is one of the best!" He smiled at Cole. She curtsied to Cole nodding and went into his room. Cole looked at Carla and shrugged his shoulders. Patty is short and thick with black hair and glasses about thirty-five I would guess. I'm sure Carla had no problem with her tending to Cole. He winked at Carla and made his eyebrows go up and down. She rolled her eyes at him and he laughed as we all did.

"Now, this is one of the newest to become a part of our family. This is Nancy Collins. She will be your personal attendant. Nancy, this is Carla

Taylor, you will see to her, whatever she needs." He smiled warmly at Nancy.

"Yes… Milord… Ma'am…" She curtsied to Carla.

"It's nice to meet you Nancy." She smiled and went into her room.

"And now… for my lady." We walked to the end of the hall where the last two doors were. This one will be your room Rebecca…for now." He grinned shyly causing my stomach to flutter and then swung the door open. The room was…unbelievable!

"I hope this pleases you." His tone was almost a whisper.

In the doorway, the first thing I saw was a huge dark wooden four-poster bed that reached almost to the ceilings. There were shear curtains that were pulled back on each poster, even at the foot of the bed. A shimmering white satin spread covered the bed and satin pillows at the headboard, lots of pillows. It was so elegant and looked too beautiful to sleep on or under. I swallowed hard and was almost afraid to look any further.

"What's the matter Rebecca? You don't like the room?" He tried to smile, but I could tell he didn't know what to think.

"William, it is too fancy to sleep in!" I looked up at him seriously.

"Rebecca..." He laughed.

"Well it is, William." I was serious!

"Rebecca, it's supposed to be. It's for my intended." He softly smiled and kissed my hand, his eyes looked at me tenderly.

As we entered the room, I could smell the light scent of roses. William placed his hand on the small of my back. I looked up at him and he motioned with his head to go ahead.

Lanterns softly lit the room with cozy warmth. William's hand gently gilded me towards the center of the room. As we approached the center of the room, I immediately noticed the enormous bed with shear curtains tied back in white bows. The beautiful white and gold canopy bed towered towards the ceiling vanishing into the darkness. The wall behind the bed was curved thinking this was one of the end rooms we saw as we came to the front of the estate. Two matching nightstands were on either side of the bed with lanterns and small bowls of rose buds on a lace doily that matched the bed.

The wall to my right had a beautiful white and gold vanity that matched the bed with three mirrors and a large crystal vase of red roses off to the left. Several crystal bottles of what I thought was perfume were grouped on the right of the vanity and a gold jewelry box opened with pearls and gems sat next to the small crystal bottles. In the center of the vanity laid a white lace like doily with a golden hairbrush, comb and hand mirror on top. Next to the vanity stood a tall dressing screen carved white wood with gold accents and white shear curtains with red roses and green leaves touched in gold brushed on the sheer material. It was thick enough that one could not see through.

A tall wardrobe with two doors stood next to the vanity that matched the bed, nightstands and vanity. To my left was an enormous fireplace with two chairs the material covering them matched the curtains and dressing screen. There was a small table between them with a vase of red roses in the middle. On the right of the fireplace was a door that I supposed was the bath and to the left of the fireplace was a bookshelf simply in white filled with books top to bottom.

"Come, I want to show you something." He took my hand leading me to the triple windows that were to the left of the canopy bed. He pulled a drape to one side revealing two French doors that led to an outside balcony and opened one door stepping out on to a very roomy balcony with a small iron table and two iron chairs, small tea roses and flowers were all over the balcony. It was simply beautiful! The balcony curved around the outside and vanished. I presumed it connected with William's balcony. I looked out to see so many trees and rolling hills. It seemed endless!

"The sun rises over the trees... just there..." He pointed straight out.

"It's beautiful, William!"

"Come..." He took my hand seeing that I was well pleased and led me back into the room leading me to the door across the huge room towards the door by the fireplace.

"You'll love this." He opened the door to a very large washroom complete with running water, a chair, vanity with a sink, huge bath, dressing screen, a full-length mirror and... another door? I looked at him and slight devilish grin slid across his lips.

"This is the best surprise!" He led me to the door never taking his eyes off of mine as he swung the door open. It was another room! Full sitting room complete with a sideboard, fireplace with a window on each side of it, a big over stuffed divan, wing back chairs, end tables with lanterns, books, a desk, chase lounge, blankets on the back of the divan and chase lounge, small what knots all over the room and roses in a tall crystal vase off center of the room on a small round table. It was a retreat!

"Oh, William, this is… wonderful!" I looked at him smiling up at him, and he was well pleased.

"Do you really like this room?" He took my hand.

"Yes! I think it's wonderful! It's so cozy and private!" I turned to look at the cozy room.

"It's my favorite of all rooms in this place. When I can't sleep, I come in here and read or write…yes and sleep." He was so excited to share everything with me. I looked around and saw another door.

"Where does that door lead?" I think I knew the answer to that.

"To my bath and bedroom… Would you care to see it?" He smiled and a small amount of color rose on his cheeks.

"Yes, I would." I smiled witnessing a moment of shyness in his handsome face. It was heart melting!

"Alright…" He took a deep breath as if he was nervous and led me to the door.

"This is my bath." It was almost like the one in my room, but much more masculine. I could smell his scent all over the room. Everything was so clean! His bathtub was much bigger than the one in my room, but then he was a very large man indeed! I thought there was room for two! Heavens! I was blushing and staring at the tub.

"It's big isn't it?" His voice was soft and husky. I was afraid to look into those eyes knowing that he would see much more than a yes in my eyes.

"I don't think I have ever seen one so large." I glanced at him.

"I am… a large man." He lowered his tone and my breath caught instantly. I swallowed hard and smiled a nervous smile biting my own lip now!

"This is my room." He swung the door open and my eyes went wide.

An even bigger bed was in the center of the room with black shears, but his bed was so enormous with a thousand pillows. His spread was black his floor was black as well. There was a fireplace with a golden-framed picture of angels in the clouds and someone on a horse coming in the very distance and on either side of the fireplace were bookshelves, two black leather chairs in front of the fireplace and a small table between them with deep red roses in a vase. His walls were stone like mine, white washed very tasteful and he too had a balcony. As I looked around, I could smell his scent everywhere! My head started to spin as I looked at his room. My thoughts were taking over and I knew I had to get out of his room fast!

"Do you not like this room?" He looked worried.

"It's wonderful! You have wonderful taste! It's so much like mine it's almost unbelievable!" I laughed. He suddenly pulled me to him.

"Rebecca... I want you to love this place. I want you to feel like this is your home already. If you do not care for something and I mean anything, please tell me and I'll have it changed right away."

"I wouldn't change a thing... its perfect!" I could see in this he meant every word.

"Well I'm quite comfortable with it and hoped that you would fall in love with it, as I am." His eyes softened.

"I do love it already. It's unbelievable William and so cozy and warm as you said." I smiled locked in the depths of his hazel eyes.

"Rebecca...I must talk to you tonight. It is very important." He was serious.

"Alright, whenever you would like." I nodded.

"I think first we eat dinner and relax with Cole and Carla, then after they retire, we'll talk." He smiled softly.

He took my very breath and the thought that this was his room and his room was connected to mine, was going to be very hard to deal with.

"Why don't you freshen up and I will do the same then we'll go down together. I'll knock on your door." He smiled tenderly at me.

"It won't take me long... Shall I change?"

"No... I think you look beautiful enough for the staff." He smiled widely.

I walked back through the washroom through the retreat and into my bath and a woman in the room startled me.

"Oh pardon me Miss. I was putting your things away." She stood in front of me.

"Oh! You scared the day light's out of me." I laughed.

"I'm so sorry Miss, my name is Betty Anne Maze. I'll be seeing to your needs."

"Well, Betty Anne, please call me Rebecca. I won't be called anything else!" I laughed. This was going to be hard to get use to I think!

"I..." She was about to refuse.

"I mean it!" I smiled at her and laughed.

"Alright Miss... I mean, Ms Rebecca. Now, what will you be needing?"

"I'm to freshen up and William will knock on the door shortly." I smiled at the middle-aged woman with salt and pepper hair rather plump with rosy cheeks and round glasses at the end of her nose. I liked her right away!

"If I may say so, Ms. Rebecca, you are lovelier than I thought you would be and so young!"

"Why thank you, Betty, and though I am young, I was married for eight years... I am a widow."

"You ARE?" She turned and looked at me in shock.

"Yes, my husband was killed in a storm." I looked down.

"But, I believe God sent William to me." I added.

"And he you!" She smiled sweetly nodding.

"I'm going into the bathroom and freshen up and I will be out in a minute. You can talk to me. I'll leave the door open. I went into the washroom and all my toiletries were already out. I washed my face and fixed my hair.

"How long have you worked here Betty?" I called out to her.

"Forever!" She softly laughed shaking her head.

"Do you like it here?"

"We all love Lord Andrews. He's a wonderful man and sometimes he comes to our side of the estate and plays cards or chess with us. He even eats in the kitchen with the head cook and the staff." She laughed.

"That's wonderful! I hear tales of many Lords that aren't so nice." I walked back into the bedroom.

"Oh our William is like one of us and we were all so pleased that God has finally sent him a bride. We were worried he may never find his true love." She smiled softly.

"Well I thank God for him every day!" I liked Betty already very much.

"I think you'll fit right in the family Ms. Rebecca." She laughed.

"I hope so!" I winked at her and then a soft tap in the door made Betty jump. William peeked his head through the door.

"Come in, William." He was smiling at Betty as he walked in the room.

"I see you've met Betty... She's a peach!" He hugged her around her shoulders.

"Now, William... you can't be loving on me in front of the bride to be...she may get jealous." She laughed as William and I did.

"Well she's just going to have to deal with it! You know very well I need a hug from my girl every day." He smiled at me and winked.

"I think I can share!" I laughed.

"Thank you, Ms. Rebecca, for he is like 'the son I never wanted'!" We all laughed.

"She's a hoot!' William took my hand and led me out the door.

"Betty loves you already." He kissed my hand leading me back down the hall.

"I've only been here for an hour and already love it here and Betty as well!" I smiled.

"I'm so pleased!" He let out a huge breath!

"I want to show you the rest of the estate before we eat dinner."

"Are we going to eat in the kitchen?" I looked up at him.

"That Betty! She told on me didn't she?" He teased.

"Yes, and I'm sure she will tell me a lot more." I teased.

"We'll see about that… I'll take her to the dungeon and have her put on the rack if she betrays me." He roared a great laugh that echoed through the hall!

"So you are the Ogre type of Lord I see." I looked up at him with a devilish grin on my lips.

"That I am, but you were not to find out till dark tonight when I turn into the beast." He laughed wickedly.

We went down the steps and to the left into the sitting room. Cole and Carla were sitting before the fire drinking coffee.

"Well it's about time!" Cole raised his brow with a grin and I blushed.

"Cole!" Heavens!

"Coffee?" Carla smiled.

"That sounds wonderful!" William fixed me a cup and handed it to me.

"Come…I want to show you the rest of our home. Take your coffees with you."

We followed William to the left and down the hall. He opened two large glass French doors that opened into a large library filled with old books, a very used fireplace with black scorch marks below the mantle. He used this room often I thought. There were several dark green overstuffed chairs, more works of art hanging in gold frames and a large dark wooden desk piled with papers and books. To the game room with a pool table and chessboard, his office was immaculate. His desk was huge dark wood and even more books on bookshelves. Thousands of books! He loved watching our reactions to what we were seeing and watching him so pleased!

He then took us to the sun room with light colored furniture and plants of all kinds and windows on all three sides. The door to the back led to a very large terrace. The room is very bright and warm. I liked this room! He swept us next to his weapon room that had all kinds of

swords, dagger's and guns. It was not one of my favorite rooms but Cole
liked it a lot! William promised to show Cole some of his favorite
weapons from his great, great, great, Grandfathers' collections. William's
weapon room made me realize the darkness that I see in William's eye
when he speaks of training corpsmen. So many swords and guns lined
the walls that it looked like he could arm the entire Territory!

The backside of the estate was the servant's area. We backed tracked
through the way we came not wanting to intrude on them. William said
they would most likely show us that when they were ready saying he
never intrudes on them.

We continued to the other wing, it only had two huge rooms. The
formal dining room and the ballroom, the ballroom had to wait till later
for the wax was not dry and they would have his hide if we were to walk
on it! The dining room was stunning with a huge crystal chandelier that
dripped from the ceiling. The walls glistened with white background
paper and gold leaf print on it. Beveled mirrors hung all around the hall
to help reflect the light and a beautiful fireplace was lit and showed off
the gleaming black, gray and white floor with hand painted design on it.
The design was so large I couldn't see what it was and would look at it
later, but it was absolutely beautiful! Wall sconces hung on the walls
dripping with crystal teardrop bobs and of course, a huge table went the
length of the room that sat fifty at least and was being prepared for
dinner at the moment.

William held his hand towards the doors again and led us to the back
of the entryway to a wall of French windows.

"Now, I want to show you this!" He pushed open the huge doors and
it opened up into the center court. It was absolutely beautiful! There
were at least five big trees and a pool with a grassy area that he said was
for sport.

"It's too cold to go for a swim right now, but this next summer it will
be wonderful on those hot sultry nights. I live in the pool then." We all
were in awe at his home.

"Like I told, Rebecca, the second floor right wings were bedrooms and
the third floor was almost the same. I would love to show you the
grounds next if you would like. I have had Jules to bring the surrey up to
the front of the house."

"William, I don't think any of us has ever seen such a place!" I smiled
up at him for it had already taken an hour to go through the house!

"Did your father build this?" Cole asked.

"No, my great-grandfather did eighteen generations ago. That was another reason why I had to buy it back. The roots run deep here. The estate is over four hundred and seventy five years old. The Great War took it all the way to the ground, but it was rebuilt to the best anyone could guess. There were plans of the estate found in the cellar. From what I know the only thing left was the bottom row of stones. My father always said that as long as the foundation was strong and still solid, it would last through anything." He winked at me and led us to the front entryway.

A small surrey was sitting out front with one horse to pull us. Cole helped Carla in and William helped me. William took the reins and we were off! There were small roads everywhere though you wouldn't have guessed them to be there. He next led us to the beautiful red with white trim and black roofed stables. There were so many stalls, but very few horses in them.

"Where are the horses?" Carla asked.

"I'll show you, but first I want you to see the newest addition to our family." We followed William.

"This is Tosca she just gave birth this morning to this little one." He smiled as he put his hand on my back and stepping behind me.

"Oh, William, he's beautiful! He's coal black!" I smiled at him. His eyes looked down into mine.

"Coal, that's his name then. We don't have a horse named Coal."

"Are you sure you want to do that to that poor creature?" I laughed and so did Carla.

"Cole isn't a bad name!" Cole huffed.

"I tell you what…we'll spell it C-o-a-l." William laughed.

"Thanks." Cole rolled his eyes and laughed.

"Your most welcome brother…" William laughed grinning at Cole.

He next took us back out to the surrey and the men helped us back in. William took us to a huge fenced in area. He hopped down and opened the gate.

"Hey, Will." This must be Lord York I thought.

"Vick, I was wondering where you were!" William smiled.

"My, my, Will, she is breathtaking!" Lord York's eyes took me in from head to toe.

"Vick, this is Ms. Grayson…Rebecca, this is, Lord Victor York."

"My lady, it is a great pleasure to meet the only woman in the world that felt sorry enough to say yes to this old bas...er...excuse me Ma'am, I mean old sway back." Cole laughed behind me and coughed.

"Victor, it is a pleasure, but I happen to love this old sway back." I smiled at the tall muscular man with brown sun tipped hair and mustache, not particularly that handsome, but clean and neat.

"I see you have found a woman not afraid to speak her mind." He smiled at me winking.

"Yes, and she probably can part your hair six ways to Sunday as well." He laughed and kissed my hand with thank you in his eyes.

"It is a pleasure." He laughed as he led the horse out to the pasture.

"The lot is by the creek Will." He tipped his head at me as William reined the horse to go.

"See you later, Vick." Vick smiled nodding and waved.

"I'm sorry about that. I think he relates to horses better than people." He laughed.

"He was fine." I assured William. I thought Vick was just being himself which I did like!

We took a short ride up to the top of the hill and looked down into a valley with trees and a creek. William whistled one long whistle and two short ones and suddenly the sound of thundering hooves echoed through the air and they came flying out of the trees.

"William... they're beautiful!" There were all colors of horses running towards us.

They all stopped short of us and I saw Diablo running and stepping in front of them.

"They are all his wives." He looked proud, then looked down at me and gave me a sensual grin.

"He has many females that he claims for his own and has sired many colts last year."

"I see." I was blushing and he saw it and softly laughed.

"Like horse, like master." I whispered softly as he laughed again grinning wickedly.

We rode all over the estate to one of the many ponds that he had and all so breathtakingly beautiful. He was indeed telling the truth at how big the place was. He has several barns and a herd of cattle that would envy any large rancher. There was one very well manicured road he did not take us down and didn't say anything about. I will ask him one day. I saw him look down the road as we passed it and he sighed softly. The last thing he showed us was the small pond that was landscaped by the side of the house. There was a small stone walkway into the woods.

"There were ducks that were here in the spring and through the summer, but they already flew south. I like to come here to think, watch the ducks and feed them." He nodded as if he missed them.

Once again I've seen something I didn't know about William. He is a very sensitive man and seems to care about everything. That was why his training of his men as he claims bothered me. It wasn't the William I was seeing, but the more I knew about him, the more I loved him, my heart pounded at the thought.

"Well, that's about all of the estate that we can reach from the surrey, thus ends the tour. You all may go wherever you'd like, for a surrey ride or have Vick find you a mount. It's up to you, but right now, I know that Libby Walters, my head cook, will have our heads if we're not ready for dinner. For now, we can go freshen up again and meet in the dining room?" William smiled at everyone. I noticed that Cole and Carla were very quiet when we went on the tour of the grounds and I think Cole was overwhelmed.

"I would like to freshen up before dinner." Carla smiled looking at Cole.

"William, I am speechless! This place is magnificent! All I could do was try to take it all in." Cole was still looking around.

"I'm glad you like it." He smiled down seeing in his eyes that he was hoping I loved it.

"I know I will enjoy this vacation so much." Carla smiled at William.

"Well then, let's head back to the house." William took us back.

When we arrived back at the estate, we all retired to our rooms. I smiled at Cole as he kissed Carla's cheek knowing he was in love for good this time! William looked at me smiling down with his eyes twinkling well pleased.

"I shall see you shortly. Would you like for me to come for you?" He leaned down holding me in his arms.

"Yes, I would." He leaned down and kissed me softly.

"William, I love your home." It was strange how I felt so comfortable in it already.

"I was hoping you would and soon it will be our home, very soon." He kissed me tenderly again. His lips brushed mine and then opened my door.

"An hour?" His eyes were full of desire.

242

"An... hour." The man had an effect on my thoughts and voice all the time that I had whispered. Betty was waiting sitting reading a book.

"Well, Ms Rebecca, glad your back. What did you think? Do you think you could stand living in this shack?" She smiled and sat the book down on the small table.

"Shack? Betty, I have never seen such a beautiful place! I feel like I'm in a different world." I laughed.

"I know what you mean... magical isn't it?" She smiled going into the bath and putting fresh water in the wash sink.

"Yes, and it reminds me of the place in a legend called 'Camelot', though they say that it really existed." I smiled back at her.

"Aye, it did, my mother, God rest her soul, use to tell me of the story and she said that her Great, Great, Grand Mother had the history book on it." She took out a dress for me and laid it on the bed.

"William reminds me of a noble knight." I smiled.

"That he is, Ms Rebecca. He is very noble indeed." She went into the washroom with me.

"Is there a bad side to William? If there is, I have not seen it yet." I looked at her and she smiled.

"Bad side? Heavens no! If there were, I have not seen it ever." She laughed.

"I can't believe how wonderful he is." I smiled taking a face cloth and wetting it.

"That he is Ms Rebecca and I dare say that you are the same way." She looked at me deep in thought and smiled.

"Me? I'm much the same way I suppose, except when my brothers Cole and Mike try to run my life. I can get a bit upset." I rolled my eyes.

"Well any young lady would not like that!" She laughed with her hands balled up in fists on her hips.

"I can't wait to take a bath tonight, but you don't have to stay. I will want to soak for a while and ready myself for bed." I smiled at her.

"As you wish. Again... welcome to your new home." She smiled so sweetly making me feel as if she was an Aunt.

"Thank you very much, Betty, you and William are making me feel so welcome." I felt as if I really did belong here.

After I washed up and fixed my face and dabbed a little perfume on, Betty insisted on fixing my hair for me and went to work brushing and smoothing.

"There, now that looks lovely on you Ms Rebecca." She brushed my hair out and put it into a clip at the top of the back of my hair and did a fancy braid.

"Betty, please call me Rebecca... I insist."

"I see I'm not going to win with the likes of you either! Very well, Rebecca it is!" She laughed shaking her head as she was braiding the bottom of my hair.

"Why I love this! What do you call it?"

"A French braid." She laughed.

"It does look like French braided bread!" I laughed and heard a tap on the door.

"Rebecca?" The door opened slowly.

"Come in, William." I smiled.

"Are you ready?" He looked at me wide eyed.

"Thank you, Betty." I smiled at her as she stood with her hands in front of her clasped and she was smiled ear to ear.

"Was my pleasure, Rebecca." Her face glowed.

"Your hair, Rebecca... it's beautiful and suites you well." He was well pleased.

"Well thank, Betty, the miracle worker." I laughed.

"Thank you my love." He winked at her.

"Shall we?" I took his arm and looked back at Betty once more and she winked at me smiling, nodding her head.

"Libby has prepared a special dinner for us in honor of you, Cole and Carla." We walked towards the stairs.

"She didn't have to do that!" I laughed not believing all the fuss over us.

"She insisted that I stay out of the kitchen, which I have not shown you yet... Libby is very funny about her kitchen." William sighed shaking his head.

"She only tolerates me in it when I want to cook something. I think if I wasn't Lord here she would throw me out on my ear!" He chuckled.

"When do we get to taste your Quiche?" I was watching where I stepped as we went down the steps.

"Monday morning." He looked forwards and smiled a devilish smile.

"William, what is happening tomorrow night?" I looked up into his face to watch his reaction.

"Well that is what I wanted to speak with you about later. I will tell you then. Is that alright?"

"Yes, and thank you, I only want to be prepared." I laughed but for some reason, there was a worried look in his eyes.

"Here we are. Good evening Ms. Grayson." Jules bowed as he opened the door entering the dining room. Cole stood by the fireplace with Carla.

"Come, sit everyone." William held my chair for me as he seated me to his right, which until we are married I would sit on his right.

"William, if I left today, I would have such memories! I would cherish them the rest of my life!" Carla smiled sweetly at William.

"Ah, but it's only just begun." He smiled and winked at Cole.

"Sir, wine?" Jules smiled at me with a nod.

"Would you all care for wine, tea, coffee, or something else?"

"I would love a glass of wine and some coffee after dinner if I may?" I smiled at Jules.

"Anything for the Lady?" He smiled sweetly.

"That goes for us as well." Cole smiled and William nodded to Jules and he bowed a slight bow and left the room. Just as he left two men came in with bottles wrapped in cloth, they poured all of us a glass and set the bottles in two trivets.

"A toast, to my bride to be, my brother in law to be and his bride to be as well." He winked at Carla and noticed she did not even try to protest. Did William know something I didn't?

"To my intended and her family, I pray that we all are blessed and I feel I could have never met a more suited bride than Rebecca. To my brother in law to be, take what God has given you and cherish it for the rest of your lives. Time is short brother do not waste a second you'll not get it back!" His words startled me, for those were Robert's own words. I smiled at to myself thinking that was another conformation that this was indeed the hand of God.

"Here, here!" We all said in unison. We all clanked glasses and drank the wine.

As William poured another glass for all of us our dinner arrived on three carts. The one I assumed William called his head cook, Libby was overseeing the young servants as they uncovered the platters of food one after the other.

"Libby dear, this is my intended, Ms. Rebecca Grayson. Rebecca, this is, Libby." She smiled softly. Her dark brown hair in a tight bun made her look stern and her blue eyes sharp. As she smiled, I noticed that she had happy wrinkles around her eyes and mouth, which to me means that she is happy naturally, but what surprised me the most was, she wasn't heavy, but rather small for a cook.

"It's a pleasure to meet you dear. William has told us all about you. I insisted that this meal be special for his long awaited bride to be and her brother."

"Cole, and this is Carla, Cole's intended." Cole must have asked her for she did not fight any of the assumptions that were being made, or perhaps she just gave up!

"I'm glad to be cooking for more than just William, Nick and Jon Luke!" She laughed.

"So tell us, Libby, what are you going to spoil us with tonight love?"

"Ah, roasted pheasant in a rich glaze with all the fixings, Paul got him late yesterday."

"Very good, Libby… it has been a while." As they served us our plates, William bowed his head.

"Father, I humbly come before you to thank you for many things this day. I first would thank you for this wonderful bounty and the loving hands that prepared it for us. Bless them and their families indeed for they are my family and I have been blessed with their kindness, support and love all of my life. Father, as your humble servant in your army of knights, I have believed and have waited as you commanded. As unworthy as I am, it was in your will that you chose this time in my life to bring me such a special gift as Rebecca. I knew from the moment I saw her on that dusty road and you whispered to me that she's the one, I knew your hand was on her and I. Thank you and thank you for this overwhelming feeling of love that beats in my heart every time I am with her. Thank you for her family for I love them already and bless them each one. And lastly…Father, please…let my words flow from my heart tonight and speak what is in my heart. Thank you, Father, for all that you have given me and all that you will…for it is only from Your hand that we are blessed. In Jesus' powerful and wonderful name we pray, amen."

"William… that was… beautiful!" Carla wiped tears as I did. Cole rolled his eyes. Then they laughed.

"Well it was!" I defended Carla.

"William…" I couldn't speak wiping my tears.

"You women! I just don't know!" Cole laughed.

"Let's eat before Libby here gets it all over us." William laughed and winked at Libby. She bowed, and then she and the rest left us to our dinner.

"Tell us William, where do you get your horses?" Cole took a bite of pheasant and so did I. I closed my eyes the taste was wonderful.

"I get them from Lord James Byron. He is known for them all over the world. James lives not too far, in Cherry Grove."

"Well I have never seen such powerful animals. Your horse Diablo, did he come from the Byron's stock?" Cole took another bite.

"Yes, he is the direct descendant of James's horse Dark Wind. It took a lot of doing to get him, but finally he agreed to let me purchase one." He smiled and took a bite.

We ate dinner talking about the horses and stables and learned that William has Vick take three of his finest horses to shows all over. One of the places he went himself for the shows was, 'The Port of Capri.'

"I wish to take you there soon." He smiled at me and winked.

"It sounds heavenly!" I smiled back at my husband to be. His hand covered mine.

"The sunsets there are unlike anything on earth. I stay at the Ocean Inn when I go down. One of my best friends in the world lives there. Lord Jonathan Lawrence. He runs everything." He squeezed my hand and finished his plate. The servants came back with dessert. I was so full from the pheasant and pearl onions, dressing and rolls I didn't think I could eat another bite. William saw my discomfort and everyone else's and suggested the dessert wait for an hour or so and it should be served in the sitting room. The servant nodded and left. After finishing our wine, William stood and escorted us to the sitting room where coffee was already waiting.

"Let's sit by the fire." I took Carla's hand and sat on the overstuffed divan sinking into it.

William and Cole were having Brandy and were deep into a discussion but they were speaking so softly I could only hear the rumbles of deep voices.

"Carla, has Cole asked you to marry him?"

"No, but everyone assumes that we are engaged." She stirred her cup of coffee and sat the spoon down on the napkin on the table.

"What will you say if he asks?" I sipped my coffee.

"I would say yes of course, but I don't think he is as serious as you think."

"I do. He never tried to correct anyone's assumption. Knowing my brother, he would if someone was assuming wrongly." I sipped my coffee and looked at her over my cup.

"I noticed that myself. Perhaps he did not want to embarrass me?" She looked down.

"I'm positive that Cole would have corrected them." I was sure of that!

"So what do you think of this place?" I smiled at her.

"It's unbelievable Rebecca! I would love to live here!" She laughed softly, then looked at the men still talking quietly and I turned to her.

"I wonder what they're talking about." They both were being strangely quiet.

"I don't know, but whatever it is they look rather serious." Carla looked at them again.

"Probably business… again!" Cole and William looked at us and both of them winked.

"I wonder what time it is." I covered a yawn. The servants brought in the dessert and plates.

"Oh, chocolate cake! I think I can stay up for that!" Carla licked her lips.

"I love chocolate cake too, but I'm afraid that I'm too full."

"You can take a piece to your room if you'd like." William stood next to me.

"I think I'm about ready for a bath." Carla yawned trying to cover it up.

"That sounds heavenly!"

"It's already nine o'clock! No wonder I'm tired." Cole winked at William.

"Well tomorrow is a very busy day and we should get some rest." William glanced at Cole.

"Yes, I think that is wise." He winked at William as if they were up to something.

"May I take a cup of coffee up to my room as well?" Carla asked.

"Carla, you may order an entire menu to be served in bed if you'd like!" William laughed as he looked at me.

"I'm having dessert and coffee sent up so we may have our talk." William took my hand in his and wrapped it around his arm.

"We shall see you for breakfast." William smiled and winked at Cole again.

"What's going on between you and Cole?" I hugged his big arm looking up at his handsome face. He bit his bottom lip and smiled showing his irresistible dimple.

248

"You'll find out soon my love, soon." He whispered softly. He took me to my bedroom door and stopped.

"Rebecca…I do have to talk to you tonight, but I would rather do it before you take your bath."

"Of course…" It would not be proper to be seen in my nightclothes.

The servant was coming with the coffee and dessert. William took the tray from her and I opened the door to my room, William followed me in.

"Let's go into the retreat." I opened the doors as we went through the washroom and into the retreat.

"Ah… Jules started the fire." He smiled and sat the tray on the table.

"Here… sit." He took my hand and eased me down into the overstuffed divan.

I watched him pour each of us a cup of coffee and hand one to me then placed a piece of cake next to the saucer. William looked so deep in thought.

"Are you having second thoughts?" My heart pounded in my chest.

"No Rebecca. I love you so much that I ache for you day and night." He knelt on one knee in front of me taking my hands in his looking down at them and the ring he gave me. I looked into his eyes and they were overwrought with worry.

"What is it William? You're so consumed about something that it's making your eyes dark and full of…" I lost my breath. I could see that they were full of… love!

"Rebecca, you know I want to marry you…" He began as he licked his dry lips.

"Yes, and I you." I smiled placing my hand on his cheek.

"As you know, I do not wish to wait." He looked into my eyes with worry still in his.

"I recall you saying that as well." I was searching his eyes.

"I know you love me." He was rubbing his thumbs on the back of my hands.

"Oh, yes William, I love you with all my heart."

"If I asked you to marry me next month… what would you say?" He was holding his breath searching my eyes in such a way that his eyes darted back and forth. They looked as if they were… changing colors!

"Well… I would say yes." I was searching his eyes thinking where was this going?

"Well then what about next week?" He looked at me biting his bottom lip.

"I... would say... yes. Yes I would." His lips covered mine in a deep kiss. His hair was falling out of his leather tie. Then slowly he pulled away resting his forehead on mine.

"Are you sure you would marry me next week Rebecca?" He whispered his eyes closed. My arms went around his neck.

"I would marry you tomorrow if you asked me William."

"You would?" He straightened and looked at me wide eyed.

"I... would yes..." He was looking at me as if I said the magic word!

"You would? You would marry me tomorrow... if I asked?" He was breathing heavy.

"William I would marry you right now if there was someone here to do it!" I looked in his eyes. This I was so sure of that!

"Rebecca...you are saying...that if I asked you to marry me tomorrow... you would." He bit his bottom lip.

"Yes, William I would... now what is all this..." His lips crushed mine in a deep passionate kiss searing mine to his instantly. He slowly pulled away and looked at me tenderly.

"Then... marry me Rebecca... marry me tomorrow." His fingers ran down my cheek. I looked into his eyes and I could see he was serious! He was truly asking me! I struggled to find my breath and searched his eyes again as tears welled in my eyes. He truly wanted to marry me tomorrow! He waited for me to say something.

"William, if what you're asking me to do is marry you tomorrow then... I will. I will marry you tomorrow." His face brightened and took a deep breath as if he couldn't breathe.

"Rebecca...I am so pleased! So very pleased! I doubt that I could wait a month, nor a week!" His lips burned as he kissed my face and down my neck. My whole body screamed as my legs weakened and my heart pounded so hard that I couldn't breathe. My hands dug at his shoulders and I had a fist full if his shirt. God help me. One more time! We must not! He pulled away slowly.

"Rebecca... I love you with all my heart and give you my word that I will be everything you've ever wanted in a husband and give all I have to you laying my very life at your feet." He panted, with his forehead against mine.

"Oh, William, I would you!" Tears streamed down my cheeks, as he looked into my eyes so deeply that he touched something inside me no other has ever touched. It was as if his eyes were telling my very soul something it could only understand.

He pulled me to his chest almost knocking out what breath I had left, covering my lips with his. I pulled away.

"William..." The words were like a betrayal to my body and mind... but my heart honored God and William.

"I know, one more night." His heart thundered under my hand as I trembled.

"Yes, only one..." I took a deep breath and tried to regain composure.

"One..." He smiled a half smile still trying to catch his breath.

He ran his fingers through his hair letting out a breath.

"Let's drink our coffee and you can tell me about tomorrow." I sipped my coffee and I really needed it!

"Right... about tomorrow..." He let me go and I almost fell on the divan, my legs were still weak!

"I know how you feel my love." He softly laughed.

"I was praying that I could convince you into marrying me tomorrow for many reasons. One is I knew I could not wait another night except this one. I knew if you said yes, I could fight one more time. One last battle, the hardest... The second reason is that I know you're a gift from God and do not want to risk betrayal. Thirdly, we would have married soon or I would have had to stay away because my desire for you is so immense that I would have failed.

On my word, I have given orders for Nick to bring your mother, Mike, Aunt Marie and Hannah here tomorrow, along with my cousin Clarissa and Uncle Clarence and Aunt Chloe. I had arranged for a friend of mine to marry us and Jon Luke is waiting on my word to send for him, which was if you said yes."

"So that is why you didn't let us see the ballroom! Depending on what my answer was..."

"Ah... you are so clever." He laughed softly shaking his head.

"And mother's coming?" I was trying to take all this in. Things were happening so fast! Yet there were no doubts that this was the right thing to do! I felt wonderful!

"Yes... but the wedding will only be family and friends as well as the reception. Seeing how things have come about so quickly, I felt it was best to be discrete."

"You are right again Lord Andrews. It amazes me to no end how well you know me." I sipped my coffee thinking that he really did know me well. It was as if he has read my thoughts at times.

"Well my love. I can't wait to know you even better." He leaned towards me and ran his finger down my cheek. His eyes full of desire and that look... I was learning very quickly!

"This is the most imminent reason." He grinned slightly.

"As I you, my Lord." I laughed and shook my head.

"Again, I want to warn you my love. I do not wish to wait to have children." He had a serious look on his face. I stopped sipping my coffee.

"You mean... you want to." My eyes widened.

"Yes..." A sensual grin played on his lips. My breath was gone again! I felt butterflies attack my stomach.

"Right away..." My cup still at my lips frozen in place as waves of heat flooded my body.

"Right away..." His voice was deep and husky and his eyes so dark!

I looked at him for a moment and suddenly felt afraid. I had not ever been with a man. Oh my! Of course he would want to...Heavens!

"William... I've..." He saw the worry in my eyes.

"Rebecca, I give you my word, I will not hurt you and there is nothing to fear." I stood and walked to the washroom door leading into my room.

"I need to take a bath William." He didn't want to wait! Why should I think he would wait? He wasn't like Robert in his beliefs about children. William was ready and nothing like Robert! I looked at William thinking this was meant to be! He was going to love me like I have only dreamed to be loved! My heart pounded with excitement!

"Rebecca, is there something wrong?" He came to my side.

"I think I have to stay away from you right now." I smiled a devilish grin and he knew why I got up.

"I see." He kissed me softly then opened the door.

"I shall see you in the morning." I smiled and turned to walk into the bath and he stopped me.

"And then after that you will awake with me every morning." He kissed me tenderly... then let me go. I closed the door and leaned against it thinking about what just happened, and then closed my eyes in disbelief. Cole knows! That would explain why Cole and William were acting the way they were from the time we left Hickory Hill until after dinner! I knew Carla didn't know, she would have found a way to warn me, I think?

"Lady William Andrews… Lady Rebecca Andrews." I said softly out loud. I started the water for my bath and poured oil in the hot water. I sat swirling the oil in the water thinking how mother would be tomorrow. Oh and Aunt Marie will cry for a week! I smiled and I knew that this was right… it felt right. Why prolong something that was going to happen in a matter of a month or a few weeks?

I went into my room and saw that my nightclothes were laid out… A dress! What about a dress! Oh no!

I ran through the bath, through the retreat and opened the door to William's washroom and slid to an abrupt stop! William was already in the tub full of bubbles! He laughed at my face for my mouth dropped to the floor! Oh my Heavens! My face was instantly warm and very red!

"Rebecca, what is it?" He was going to get out of the tub and I turned on my heel and started out the door with my head spinning! I never have even seen Robert in the bath before!

"Wait!" He called and I heard water splash! I stood froze and closed my eyes tightly. Oh Lord, help me! Oh Lord in heaven, help me!

"What is it my love?" He turned me to him and I knew he was… undressed! I kept my eyes shut tightly.

"What…" He laughed.

"I… well… I was wondering… about a dress… You know… a dress to wear tomorrow?" I stumbled with my words but wasn't going to open my eyes! I could hear him laughing softly and my heart beat in my ears as well!

"Rebecca, I have a towel around me. You may open your eyes, it's alright." His voice sounded amused.

"I think I shall leave them shut!" I nodded with certainty!

"Alright, but I'm not that horrible to look at, at least that is what I was told." He mused. Was he taunting me?

"By whom?" I wanted to raise my brow but couldn't!

"By you of course! Your eyes told me you were quite pleased at what you saw the other day." I felt his finger run down my cheek. Lord in heaven give me strength!

"William, please this is hard enough like it is!" I pleaded with him.

"Very well, but after tomorrow, you'll never want to close your eyes again, that I promise you!" He laughed softly still amused with me.

"William… about the dress, I have an off white one and it's…"

"I have one for you already. My mother's, I know it will fit you perfectly. It's in another bedroom. I hope you don't mind or does your mother have one you'd rather wear?"

"You were really sure of yourself?" I crossed my arms over my waist.

"No not at all, but I was sure of what God was telling me… and… a… I think your tub is full!" He chuckled.

"What?" My eyes flew open and I saw that he was wearing a towel and froze in that very spot. I slowly looked down and back up. My goodness he was huge and so muscular and he was wet! I swallowed hard and he laughed again. I realized that my mouth hung wide open just then and shut it quickly!

"It's alright my love. You've seen…" His face went blank as I looked into his eyes and I did not want to tell him the truth.

"Rebecca… have you ever seen a man… undressed?" He put his hand on my shoulders.

"Yes… or no… I mean yes and no." I bit my lip as he was finding out more than I wanted him to, but I would not lie to him if he asked.

"Rebecca, what does yes and no mean?" I couldn't look in his eyes now!

"Well the truth is, Robert said that nakedness was a sin before you are wed…as after Adam and Eve had sinned in the garden, God made them ashamed because of their sin and they covered up their bodies for the Lord showed them their nakedness." I looked down and tears filled my eyes. I just knew that Robert wasn't exactly right about that now…now that I've talked some with William.

"Rebecca, wait… stay here just a moment." He left the washroom and went into his room.

"I have to turn off the water." I went into the washroom and shut the door and leaned against it. I know Robert loved me! He may have not believed as other do, but he was a good man! William may not want such a naive woman!

"Rebecca, may I come in? I am decent now." His voice was soft and tender. He opened the door and I backed up.

"William, I'm sorry. If you do not wish to marry me now…" I felt my heart crying.

"Rebecca, I love you and a thousand angels could not stop me from marrying you. Please, may we speak?" I took a deep breath and opened the door. He was wearing his night pants and robe. I let out a sigh of relief.

"Rebecca, come... sit with me." He had his arm around me and led me to the divan.

We sat down and he was facing me holding my hands. I knew in my heart he would understand... he had to!

"Rebecca, what you tell me about you and Robert will not go beyond you and me. Do you trust me?" He took his finger and raised my face to look at him.

"Yes... I do trust you William." With my life!

"Then can you tell me what yes and no means? I do not wish to do anything that may cause you to fear me, upset you or embarrass you in any way, but I must know about your relationship with Robert." He took my hands in his rubbing his thumbs across the tops of them.

His eyes were tender, loving and he was not judging me or Robert. I knew it was right to tell him and I had to tell him everything.

"What do you want to know?" I looked at him not wanting him to feel sorry for me but knew what he wanted me to tell him. I knew what two people were supposed to do. It was just that Robert had his own ideas and beliefs about marriage and how he thought we were supposed to live until we were ready for children.

"I asked you if you ever seen a man undressed before and you said yes and no. What do you mean by that?" He furrowed his brows listening and waiting.

"Alright, I will tell you what I think you want to know, but please, be patient with me? This is not easy for me to speak about." I licked my dry lips and he saw my discomfort.

"Take as long as you wish." He sat back and poured another cup of coffee and one for me. I took a deep breath fearing that he would not love me as much as he thought he did after I told him about Robert and me. But he would find out soon enough anyway.

"As you know, Robert and I were childhood friends and grew up together. From the moment we met, we were never apart. When we were old enough, Robert told me it's time for us to get married and that was the way it was supposed to be. So, we married. On our wedding night, I was a bit afraid, but looking forward to whatever the night held. I loved and trusted Robert completely." I sipped my coffee and took a deep breath. William said not a word.

"Robert explained to me how he felt about being together and yes, I protested, but he promised I would not have long to wait. He only wanted to be a good husband and a father and that it was our responsibility to make sure we can provide for a child. So from that night on, I never saw him undressed. It was the only way to avoid temptation. I did see his chest and that was it and that was only because he was dressing and accidentally walked in on him. He never saw me undressed ever. Robert and I held each other at night but it was nothing like when you kissed me. We didn't kiss to often either in fear of the temptation." I looked down then back up.

"William, I am not ignorant and I do know what two people are supposed to do when they are married as strange as it may seem, he did make me happy in other ways. Robert says you have to love the person all day and not just at night, all day was more important. He was always in the fields or hunting and wasn't home much of the time. I begged him sometimes and it only led to him sleeping on the divan. So after a year of marriage, I stopped asking.

Sometimes he would let me touch his chest muscles and he would kiss me so hard that my lips felt bruised. Anything that would lead to us coming together was avoided.

Robert was almost ready to add on to the house too and then the storm took him…" I looked up at William and he had his knee bent and his foot under his left thigh. His elbow rested on the back of the divan and a hand over his mouth with his thumb on his right jaw and cheek his first two fingers held his lips shut… his eyes were as big as saucers.

"Oh William, I'm sorry I am not the woman you thought I was. I see in your eyes your… appalled!" I stood to leave and he caught my wrist.

"Rebecca… No! Please forgive me! I must look like a beast to you! Kissing you the way I do and touching you more than I should have." He looked away and let go of my wrist.

"William! I love the way you kiss me! I have never been kissed like that in all my life! You make me feel things I have never felt before my body feels things in places that I never knew existed! I feel alive and…and for the first time…loved completely!" I touched his face lightly and he looked at me.

"But I…" He was so afraid that I wouldn't love him and I was afraid he wouldn't love me!

"William, I can't wait to be loved the way I should be. I want you to love me… no one else… just you!"

"Then you still want to marry me tomorrow?" His words were soft.

"Do you still want to marry me William?" Mine as well.

"God in heaven… yes!" He pulled me to his lap as he sat down and looked into my eyes.

"Tomorrow night, I will show you love like you have never known. I will let you love me any way you wish, as long as you… just love me." He smiled softly and I put my arms around his neck and I kissed him deeply and tenderly then slowly pulled away feeling myself warm.

"I still need to take that bath…" I was smiling feeling so relieved now that William knew the entire truth now.

"Yes, Rebecca, you better have your bath or you'll not have to wait another night!" He grinned raising one brow of warning.

I stood and smiled going into the washroom leaving him sitting on the divan. I closed the door and he was smiling biting his lip. He still loves me and wants to marry me! Thank you God for him! I undressed and slid into the bathtub taking a quick bath feeling so tired and I was sleepy. Tomorrow I would know everything! I would be loved by William and I would love him. I would finally know what it was like to be held and loved and touched and kissed. I dressed and went to bed. I heard a door close in the hall. Tomorrow I was to marry William… Tomorrow…

《

13 》

"Rebecca... time to rise and shine... it's your wedding day!" I opened my eyes and became aware of where I was...William's!

"You have a late night?" I heard a female voice. Oh yes, Betty!

"Betty?" I sat up and yawned, stretching my arms out.

"Yes love." Betty was hurrying around the room all smiles.

"What time is it?" I yawned again.

"Almost ten o'clock... William said not to wake you too early." Betty smiled getting a day dress out.

"How did you know it's my wedding day?" I rubbed my eyes as I tried to get that fuzzy, I'm not awake, feeling out of my head.

"Rebecca dear, everyone knows. Remember the ballroom?"

"Of course... are Carla and Cole up?" I smiled to myself as I scooted to the edge of the huge bed.

"Heavens! Yes! William has them doing all sorts of things. Ms. Carla is handling all the deliveries and Cole is helping William. Now you get dressed, your mother and family should be here soon! I have to find William and tell him you're awake." Betty had everything out and was gone in a second! She amazed me!

I hopped out of bed and washed the sleep from my face and dressed hearing William call to me as I started brushing my hair.

"Rebecca?"

"In the washroom..." I called out as I stepped out dressed and my hair brushed. He walked towards me and put his arms around me.

"I love you, my lady and you look beautiful this morning!"

"And I you, my Lord..." He brushed his lips across mine.

"Today you will be my wife and mine forever." He brushed his lips across mine again.

"And today you will be my husband forever and I'll find if you've been nothing but a tease!" I laughed teasing him.

"Teasing? Ah, you think I jest?" His voice was deep and sultry and his eyes held a devilish look.

"We shall see my love… we shall see!" I laughed.

"I have brought some fruit, rolls and coffee… Come…sit!" He nodded.

"You are so good to me." I started to pull my hair back.

"No, leave it down for me… just for a little while?" I nodded and sipped my coffee.

"William, I feel much better telling you about Robert and I." I haven't slept better in weeks!

"I love you even more for telling me and tonight will be the first for you and for me as well."

"What do you mean?" For him as well?

"Well, I have never made love to a woman I was madly in love with." William smiled a sensual grin.

"I see! That is well, for I would not like it if I found you longing for another… as in a lost love." I laughed sounding so dramatic.

"One day, we will fill this house with many children showing our love in each one." William's eyes absolutely twinkled when he talked of children! I just had to tease him more. He was so excited!

"And how do you know that?" I raised my brow at him.

"Well, after tonight, I doubt that I will ever let you out of the bed!" He roared a great laugh. All I could do was shake my head. He stood pulling me to my feet.

"Honestly, William! You better not either!" I tried to be serious at first, but instead I laughed.

"You my love, have my word!" He brought my hand to his lips and tenderly kissed my palm, closing his eyes as if he was writing it on his heart. I stood in front of the powerful man thinking that he loves me and today he would forever be my husband. Tonight I will know what I have yearned for the last almost nine years. His eyes held promise and I had no doubt that he would indeed keep his word.

"William, you are not supposed to see me before the wedding!" I covered my lips with my fingers remembering the old saying.

"Ah, Rebecca, do you think God will have this day spoiled? I think that He is more powerful than any superstition!" His words tenderly relieved me of any other thought.

"I know that was silly… but… I…" My hand lay on his chest as he pulled me close, his lips only a breath away.

"You know, when you become my wife, it will forever change you and me." He brushed his lips across mine softly, taking my breath with it. He was so consuming with his passion, I had no doubt that he would not hold back this night!

"I know that when I first met you… I was already changing. I felt a bonding like I had never felt before. It was as if I had no control over it." My eyes searched his intensely.

"Ah, but my Lady, I want you to think about something… all day…" His lips lowered on mine slowly. He teased me softly with a brush of a kiss slowly pulling away, covering my lips tenderly and purposefully. The depth of this kiss was beyond all others. He breathed me in as he seared and melted his lips to mine. I could not think! His arms consumed my body engulfing me in his hold pressing me to him. He trailed kisses down my neck and nipped at my ear causing my body to weaken and I was at his mercy. Then his lips crushed mine in and intoxicating kiss that I will never forget. I felt as if I was someplace else! Being immersed in a kiss that had no words to describe it, it was beyond passion, desire, hunger, need, wants, urgency, consuming, breathless a claiming forever! I held on to his neck knowing if he let me go, I would surely fall. My body was screaming for his touch in the way's Robert had promised. I heard a soft rumble in his throat and escaped through his lips in a breathless plea. He pulled away so slowly.

"Rebecca…" His words were hoarse and at a whisper.

"William… I… my… can hardly…" My eyes were pleading with him to end my suffering, but we both knew we must wait.

"I know, but that is what I want you to think about that all day and know that is a promise of things to come on this night. You have my word." His eyes held no argument and I could not speak!

"And that my love, was only… your lips…" He added in a whisper as he kissed my cheek and went to the door grinning. I steadied myself holding on to the wing back chair.

"Now, enjoy your breakfast and coffee. I have things I must attend to. I will send your mother to you as soon as she arrives." He mouthed I love you as he softly closed the door.

Frozen, still in my place, his words, 'That was only your lips...' made my knees weak again! Oh My Goodness! Betty came back in as I was fanning my flushed and hot face.

"I see that William has seen to you personally!" She laughed in a teasingly way.

"Oh and, Rebecca?" William peeked back into the room.

"I'm sure you want to know what time you will be getting married."

"I... yes... Please... tell me." I still couldn't think!

"At four... when you're ready and it's time to leave your room, Betty will show you where to go. I'm sure you'll be surprised." He smiled and softly closed the door.

"Betty...he is..." I swallowed hard trying to be able to talk.

"Handsome, charming, sweet, loving, caring, full of surprises and unbelievably perfect?" She raised her brow at me.

"Yes!... That was exactly what I was thinking." I couldn't even look at her. His words were still swirling in my head...'and that was only your lips.'

"I know he is all that and more." I saw the love Betty held for William.

"Betty, what should we do for another...what... five to six hours?"

"Well... we must see that you're ready for your husband to be! Let's get you in a hot bath! Then when you're out, we'll tend to your nails, feet, your hair and beauty needs, your undergarments and perfume... and then the dress." I sipped my coffee and nibbled on a breakfast cake.

"My goodness! Are you sure we will have enough time?" I looked at her in earnest and sat in the chair.

"Yes, Ms. Carla wants to do your nails and if you would like, I could do your hair, I'm quite good or so I've been told." She smiled waiting for an answer.

"That sounds heavenly!" I felt like this was all a dream. Was it? Am I dreaming?

"Good! Then let's get you into the tub!" She nodded with a bright smile.

Betty shooed me to the washroom and started the tub of water. I stood in disbelief that I was getting married today... Today!

I watched her pour the most intoxicating scented oil in the water. It soon filled the room with light Lavender. She then closed the door and left me to my bath. As I undressed, my thoughts were about William. I do love him and he does have everything that Robert wanted me to have and he wants children right away. I'll not have to wait any longer for children and I know he will make a wonderful father and husband. I want to be a wonderful wife to him and will be! I slid into the tub and into the hot water that was so relaxing, and I needed to relax! I was so nervous!

"Rebecca?" Betty called.

"Come in..." I called after her.

"I forgot to give you the shampoo and rinse!" She smiled and set on the edge of the tub.

"Betty, am I really getting married today?" I had to hear someone else tell me that I was indeed getting married today to believe it!

"Yes my dear, you are indeed getting married today, this day, to Lord William Andrews. Child, are you feeling cold feet?" She sat in the chair next to the tub.

"No...not at all! It's just that I can't seem to make myself believe that William wants to marry me." I stared into the bubbles very worried.

"Now, let me tell you something that you must keep to yourself."

"Of course, Betty..." Keep to myself? It must be serious.

"William has been looking for you, waiting for you all his life! He has never given up hope on God sending him a wife who will honor him and be his helpmate in all matters. One who can make him smile and laugh and his heart thunder in his chest and one who can stir his blood. He spent many hours talking to me about such things and I assure you, my dear, you are the one if William says you are, he has never said that about anyone else. I have witnessed him on his knees to God in prayer, with tears streaming down his handsome cheeks, asking him how much longer shall he wait. It tore at my heart! He told me God spoke to him saying 'soon my son, but not yet.'

He has been to many balls where many swoon at the sight of him. Ladies have spared for his affections, but he found them lifeless and boring. He hated to go to most social events and he always hoped of meeting you at one of the affairs, but always came home heavyhearted. He would not do much of anything for a couple of days after his prayers went unanswered. Until you that is..." She laughed shaking her head.

"I wished you could have seen him flying into the house calling at the top of his lungs that he had found his love, that God finally answered his prayers! We all came running to see what in the world William was yelling about! William has never yelled at the top of his lungs, but that day he was. He was announcing his search was over to everyone and yelling your name out dancing with all the maids and cooks and even lifted me off the ground and swung me into a waltz, and that's no small task!" She laughed.

"I was flabbergasted with him and everyone thought he'd gone mad! He was so happy and full of joy and was singing at the top of his lungs that he wanted everyone to know that God had finally answered his prayers! He announced that he wanted to marry right away and we were to prepare for the wedding today. He prayed that you would say yes, if not, he was planning an announcement ball instead. I too, thought William finally had lost his mind! But when he told me about you, that you were the one and God whispered to him telling him so, he believed it. His eyes were so full of love and I could see life in him that had been too long absent." She started to wash my hair for me and I let her as I was intently listening to her.

"He told me that if God indeed put you into his life to be his bride, then when he did ask you to marry him, you would say yes no matter how long or short the wait was until the wedding day. He had everything planned in two days and it had to be perfect for your arrival! And we all love William so much that perfect was what he would get!" She laughed and tears fell down her sweet cheeks as she scrubbed my hair.

"And what about my mother, aunt and Hannah? He said that Jon Luke was waiting to go fetch them. What if mother doesn't believe him?" I worried that she might think it was an attempt to take her hostage, for money.

"William sent the proper announcement along with Jon Luke to insure that they will come. He had Cole sign it as well last night when you agreed to marry him. You will not find a better man Rebecca. He truly loves you!" She rinsed the soap out of my hair and then put the rinse on.

"But does he truly love me or is it that he thinks because God told him I am the one he sent to him that he should marry me?" I was deep I thought.

"Rebecca, if you had only been here to see the boy's face! He was so over full! So in love, so happy and the way he took control of the next days were as if he was commanding the tenth to go to battle! He was amazing! I knew it was real when he asked me to have his mother's wedding gown cleaned and taken in one and a half inches at the waist." She rinsed the wonderful smelling cream out of my hair.

"It's just so hard for me to believe that he wants to marry me, a commoner, and not even a real lady! I would think he would want someone more practiced in the area of entertaining and knowing the affairs of a Lord." I looked down into the clouds of bubbles.

"Ah now child, what he loves about you is that you are a natural lady. He told me you were one who can stop a man dead in his tracks and put him in his place with her words and on the other hand, dance in the fields barefooted with the butterflies." She smiled wrapping my head in a towel.

I thought about how boyish he appeared to me at first before I knew how old he was. He looked so impish in the carriage when we were going to the river.

"I find it hard to believe that he has never been in love." I looked at her for her reaction to my statement.

"As far back as I recall and I've been with the boy since he was three and when he was old enough, I have never seen him taken with a single lady and not because he didn't try. He would take one or two out from time to time, but always ended in the same way."

"How was that?" I gazed into the bubbles feeling so numb.

"He would say…no angels today and the poor dear would look so defeated." She sighed truly feeling William's pain.

"It had to be so terrible when his family died at sea." Tears welled in my heart.

"To be sure! I remember him running to find me crying into my neck. I cried as well for they were all as kind and sweet as William. We all mourned. When they took William to Wellington, I shall never forget his face! He was full of hate, anger and lost his faith. His eyes were dark as a storm! I just knew he would never be the same. He told me not to worry and he would be back that he loved me. Child, I cried for the boy, but I thank God for his Uncle Clarence and Aunt Chloe! They watched over him, though I knew in my heart he would not stay there. I knew he'd enlist in the guards." She gave out a sigh.

"I thought I would never see him again. I thought that he would be killed in the after wars, but God knew better. The day he returned is one that I shall never forget." Tears welled in her eyes and mine as I listened.

"He came to my home and called out the pet name he had for me through the screen door. I was sitting in my rocker and quilting a blanket. The sound of a deep thundering voice I had never heard before cracked through the silence like lightening. He yelled, 'Bee', a name he called me since he could speak, he could not say my name for the longest time." She shook her head laughing.

"What happened?" This was the best story I have heard!

"When I heard that strange voice, I shivered...I sat still listening afraid I had lost my mind! Then I heard it again, 'Bee!' I looked up not believing but hoping, thinking, could it be? Could it really be? I laid my quilt down and slowly went to the door. The boy was a man full grown! I kept looking up forever it seemed and finally found that little boy's face hiding in that handsome face of a man staring down at me with tears in those unforgettable blue hazel eyes. His bottom lip quivered as it did when his little heart was broken as a boy. I swung the door open and he lifted me into his arms and cried. He hugged the day lights out of me. I looked at him and he was smiling that devilish grin I knew so well!

Then he told me he bought back the estate and would move back in a few months and wanted to know if I wanted to go home? I cried and said, 'in a heartbeat!' He had rounded up all the ones he recalled and asked the ones who weren't too old if they wanted to come back and most said yes, all but a few of the old ones. The ones too old he saw to their financial needs and took care of all of them. Then when he did return, we expected him to have a wife or soon to, but he didn't. For three years we all waited with him...waiting for you!" She smiled and handed me a towel!

"You then believe I am the one as well?" I looked at her wrapping the towel around me getting out of the tub.

"Oh yes child, without a doubt! I knew the first time I laid eyes on you! He described you to me so many times I knew you before you even came here."

"What do you mean? You knew me?" Now I was really confused!

"He used to tell me of the woman who would be the only one he would ever marry. Why, he even knew you before he met you himself!" She winked at me.

"Well I hope I don't let him down." Dear Lord, help me! Now I was worried that I would not be all he dreamed about!

"Ah child, all you have to do is love the boy. God will take care of the rest... you do love him don't you?" She looked at me right in the eye.

"Yes... oh yes, he makes my legs weak, my head spin, my heart pound and my thoughts scatter." I sighed thinking he did even more than that!

"Well then child, what are you so concerned about?"

"It's all so fast!" Which, it was the truth.

"I know you haven't been a widow too long, but we can never doubt when God puts who he wants into your life and when he wants to do it!" She smiled a warm smile.

"I thought of that as well and heard it a few times recently too." I sighed, a deep breath.

"Well child what is it, I know there's something else?" It was as if she could read my thoughts.

"I…" I was at a loss for words.

"Not to worry… William is a very loving patient man. Just be you and things will take their course." She patted my hand.

"Thank you, Betty… I love you already!" I hugged her tightly.

"And I do you as well. You're as special as William said you are." I sat down on the stool and Betty took the wrappings from my hair.

"I feel so much better now. Thank you for telling me all this! I love him so much! Wild horses couldn't stop me from marrying him!"

"That is well for I think William is going out of his mind worrying that you'll change your mind."

"No, I wouldn't do that to William. I have no reason not to marry him!" I laughed softly.

"He told me just this morning that all his dreams were about to come true."

"What do you think he is doing now?" I smiled up at her. She knew him the best.

"He's probably on his knees thanking God for sending you to him and telling his mother, father, sister and brother about you." She smiled softly.

"Tell me, Betty, yesterday, we went on the tour of the grounds. William took us down all the roads except one." I just had a feeling it was something special. Betty laid her hand on my shoulder and gave me a serious look. It had to be.

"That road leads to his most sacred place." Tears welled in her eyes.

"What Betty?" I looked into her eyes.

"William, well it is a place he goes to talk to his family. There's a beautiful statue of a woman and child and four markers one for each of his family, a graveyard sort to speak. They never recovered the bodies.

He built a gazebo and planted all the flowers that his mother loved and his sister loved to honor their memory, for his father, he had a ship with sails encased in glass made for his father's stone and his little brother had a dog named Ralph, he had one carved out of stone for him. It's quite

266

beautiful. He and I took care of everything. He wants to be put there when he dies and anyone who he would call his family and now of course you as well. He was probably going to take you there next week." She nodded with certainty.

"It's a lovely thought for him to do that for his family. He is almost too good to be true!" I shook my head still not believing that he is so perfect! No one is! There must be another side to William.

"He says that about you as well!" She laughed and shook her head.

"Then that settles it once and for all…I am the one!" I laughed as she did keeping the thought that there had to be more to William than I've heard. There had to be, yet, no one talked bad about him in the least. I guess I was going to eventually find out, good or bad I would know sooner or later.

"Betty, do you know when Jon Luke was going after mother?" I looked at her reflection in the mirror.

"Let's see…" She took out a lovely timepiece and opened it.

"That's beautiful!" I turned to get a closer look at it.

"William gave it to me for Christmas one year. He said it was time and time is more precious than anything in the world." She smiled at me recalling that is what Robert use to say.

"What does it say?" I looked at Betty and tears welled in her eyes. She didn't say a word and handed it to me. I looked at the inside lid…

To my Bee
You are as precious to me as my own mother.
I love you,
You're William

"Oh, Betty… It's beautiful…" My heart pounded that William loved Betty like that! I knew why he loved her. She is so warm and sweet. She makes you feel welcome and she loves William like a son. My heart was so full. How could I ever think that there was another side to someone that so loved a woman that was not even his mother? That was very humbling to think about. I closed the lid and handed it back to her.

"Well enough of that! Now let's see to your hair." She wiped her nose with a handkerchief.

"So what time do you think mother will be here?" I smiled at her as we both were still tearing at how sweet William was. How blessed I was as well.

"Oh, I'm sorry dear. Your mother should be here any time, which is if she doesn't take long to pack." She rolled her eyes. I thought, just like one of us!

"Rebecca?" I heard Carla call.

"In the washroom…" I called to her.

"Why you little… please tell me you didn't know?" Carla looked at me with her arms crossed at her tiny waist.

"I didn't! Truly! William asked me last night and that is why he didn't want us to see the ballroom. It depended on what I said." That was the truth too!

"Well that is a relief! Cole knew about it last night and he told me after you went to bed. I couldn't come to you. William came out of his room and Cole and he met in the hall. I couldn't make out what he was saying, but Cole laughed and I heard William calling for a Jon Luke." She sucked in a big breath. I thought she would pass out for lack of air. I looked at Betty and we busted out in laughter.

"I hope you will stand with me?" I was still laughing.

"Well I should think so!" Then she laughed.

Betty soon had my hair in rag rolls and wrapped back in a towel and dressed in my underclothes and then my robe just as the door flew open.

"Rebecca?" Mother, Aunt Marie, and Hannah came running in with their arms opened wide with rivers of tears.

"Mother, Aunt Marie, Hannah!" I cried as well and we all hugged.

"Well, just what I thought!" Mike stood at the door shaking his head and behind him was Cole and William, mother, Aunt Marie, Hannah and I turned and at the same time shouted…

"Oh shut up, Mike!" Then we looked at each other and laughed hugging again.

"Rebecca, Jon Luke came to us the first thing this morning. I thought there was something wrong, but he gave me the letter. I am so pleased and this place is out of a fairy tale Rebecca!" Mother kissed my cheek again.

"I know it truly is! I can't believe how big it is and how beautiful all the rooms are." I smiled at mother feeling much more confidant that she was here and if she was here, that meant everything was in order and alright.

"Men, let's leave the ladies to their getting ready. We only have a few hours to go and the guests will arrive." William's deep voice made my stomach flutter. He mouthed I love you with a wink as he shut the door.

268

"Mother, I would like you to meet a new friend that I already have fallen in love with. This is Mrs. Betty Sue Maze, Betty. This is my mother, Martha Glenn, Aunt Marie and a dear friend of mine, and Robert's Aunt, Hannah Carson. Everyone, this is Betty." I knew they would be fast friends. Hannah smiled at Betty and asked her about my hair.

"Mother?" I wanted to ask her about how she felt about William and she read my mind.

"Rebecca dear, I think William will be a wonderful husband! You have no worries and think he will see too you're every need, and besides he loves you so much…and I can see you love him. It's all over you faces and has been for two weeks!" She had tears in her eyes already!

"Really?" I looked at her and wondered if she was just saying that?

"William put me next to Cole's room and Hannah next to me and across from me he put Aunt Marie."

"Carla dear, are you having fun?" Mother smiled at her.

"Oh yes, but this… this was a total surprise!" Carla shook her head still in disbelief.

"Well to be honest, I had a feeling this was going to happen. I saw it in William's eyes. He reminds me of Papa." Mother smiled looking down remembering a tender thought.

"Cole is just like Papa and I think William reminds me of Cole." That was true as well.

"I'm just glad you're not putting this off any longer than you have to!" Mother smiled.

"Why?" I looked at her not expecting the answer she was about to give.

"You know dear, it's too hard to wait…for the wedding night!" She whispered.

"Mother! I haven't…" I was shocked!

"I know… I can tell that as well… but that's mostly written all over William's face!" She laughed out!

"Mother!" I was shocked at her remarks.

"Well, it's true!" She laughed and looked at my nails.

"Carla love, will you see to Rebecca's nails?" Mother smiled at Carla.

We all sat and talked in a big circle for another two hours. Betty was enjoying Hannah and her secrets. Mother and Aunt Marie fussed over my makeup and when it came time for them to ready themselves, my stomach started to get nervous. I glanced at Betty.

"Oh my girl, are you getting a bit nervous?"

"Yes, I have to admit I am a bit." I took a deep breath in blowing it out.

"I know just the thing!" Betty ordered a small bite to eat and tea with a splash of brandy for the nerves.

The others left Betty and I alone to finish up. It was almost time, as I looked at Betty and she smiled. The tea arrived and teacakes. I took a sip of the special tea and was surprised!

"Betty… this is wonderful!" I took another sip.

"Ah, there's nothing like a splash of brandy for what ails you. If the men can have it, so can we! But be careful… not too much now." She warned.

"Thank you, Betty. I think this is the perfect remedy!" I took another sip.

"I think guests are now arriving. She looked out the window.

"There are quite a few here already."

"But I thought that William said that it would be small?" I was getting very nervous now!

"Not to worry my dear, the ones that are coming are family. All the workers and their families, a few from Winchester and your family I'd say." She looked up placing her finger on her cheek deep in thought.

"Probably close to a hundred or so." Betty smiled like that was nothing?

"A hundred or so! That's what you call small?" He said small!

"It's his family and I think you'll relax once you see them. They're not dressed in ball gowns, but only in their Sunday best. Not to worry my dear… Oh heavens! We must hurry!"

"What time is it?" I looked around.

"Three thirty! We have a half hour!" I enjoyed Betty's special tea and cakes as she performed her magic with my hair. Betty took the rolls out of my hair and helped me into the crinolines then carefully placed William's mother's dress in a small circle on the floor so that I could step into it. She helped me slide it up. The all-satin lace sleeves fit perfectly all the way to the small hoop that fit over my middle finger on the pointed sleeve. Betty started to button all the tiny pearl buttons in the back. I felt as if I had to hold in a breath as she buttoned higher, but it was not necessary, the dress was a perfect fit! I recalled William having the dress taken in one and a half inches. How did he know that?

The bodice of the gown was cut low and deep down the front and back and the neckline was low as well, showing an ample amount of my

270

breasts. Which I was not too comfortable with, but there was nothing I could do now! Betty took a small pearl necklace and ear bobs from the vanity jewelry box and put them on me. She finished up with my hair putting a small spray of white rose buds and baby's breath in my hair. Then lastly, she dabbed on some wonderful smelling perfume then stood back with tears in her eyes.

"Betty... what is it?" I looked and she said nothing and just nodded for me to turn to the mirror.

I gasped a breath as I looked at myself in the mirror! The dress looked like it was made for me! The white satin shimmered as I moved and the entire dress was covered with satin lace roses and tiny pearls. The train on the dress was about four feet long, but not too long. The dress was unlike any I have ever seen or dreamed of and the bodice made my waist look so small, trimmed in a satin cording making it firm to the touch.

As I looked up, I saw that the neckline I was worried about was really perfect for the dress and my figure. It too was trimmed in the satin cording. I turned sideways and saw my hair in ringlets falling from a cluster of curls gathered on the back of my head. The rose buds and baby's breath are so pretty! I could not believe it was me in the reflection of the mirror! I stood staring at my reflection and almost cried. William's mother must have looked beautiful in this dress, I thought. Betty wiped tears away and took me by the waist.

"It's almost time!" She whispered and then there was a soft tap on the door.

"Rebecca, are you ready?" Cole called.

"Come in." The door opened slowly and Cole stood frozen taking me in from head to toe. Saying not a word, he jutted his chin out with pride, smiling as he offered his arm. Cole covered my hand shaking his head.

"Beck, you look beautiful!"

"And you are so handsome! When are you going to marry Carla?"

"As soon as I ask her..." He smiled down and kissed my cheek patting my hand.

"Betty?" I motioned for her to come along. She followed me to the top of the stairs.

Patty came to get Betty. She looked confused as Patty insisted that she go with her. Betty shrugged her shoulders and went down the stairs. I took a deep breath and looked at my handsome brother dressed in a black suite that looked tailored to fit. He patted my hand and we walked down the steps and into the empty entryway

"Beck, I have no doubt that William loves you more than his own breath. You have chosen well Sister. I know he will make you happy." Cole nodded.

"Thank you, Cole, please don't say any more, I'm already fighting tears…and I love you too, Cole." I kissed his cheek as he kissed mine.

"Ready?" He took a deep breath as if he too was a bit nervous. I nodded taking one as well.

"Your next big brother!" I whispered as he opened the door shooting me a warning glance.

The dining room was breathtaking with roses everywhere! White table clothes and crystal vases and glasses and red bows. I looked at the doors going into the ballroom, then at Cole.

"Papa would have approved and loved William." He smiled down tears welled in his eyes. Papa...

"Cole! Don't you dare! I'll start to cry and…" An orchestra was playing! I looked up at Cole realizing my legs were weak.

"Well, this is it Sis." He patted my hand again and smiled. Mike was on the other side of the door smiling as he opened it.

The ballroom was overwhelming! White ribbons hung from chandelier to chandelier with bows in the middle floating down and there was an isle down the middle of a very full room with a hundred chairs on each side. The chairs had bows on them and roses and bows on the end of each row. The walls were breathtaking in gold with mirrors everywhere! Even the windows had tie backs with the white ribbon and red roses in the center.

I looked up the aisle and a white carpet with red rose pedals led me to the most handsome man I have ever seen in my life... William. Right then and there I was in complete awe. He was in full uniform with golden buttons shinning down his double breasted dark blue waist coat on both of his shoulders were gold braids handing down his shoulders with five braids on each shoulder. On his collar were stars and five on each side and across his chest was a white and gold sash, with a coat of arms on it in a gold medal rested on his hips. His pants were form fitting with gold cording down the sides tucked into shinny black boots. I couldn't breathe! Cole started to walk me up the isle to where William was standing.

"Attention!" One man stood and shouted.

I jumped and Cole patted my hand seeing about ten men dressed in uniform on each side stood and lifted their swords in the air and crossed tips over the isle as Cole and I approached them. They stood as statues, I took a deep breath this all felt like a dream! My eyes then locked on to William's. He stood entranced... so tall... his eyes tearing as mine were. He smiled a proud smile as his chest grew. A tall man in the center stood with full uniform on and holding a bible in his hand smiling as I came closer. I squeezed Cole's arm and he patted my hand again. Mother, Aunt Marie and Hannah were wiping tears as I smiled. Mother nodded mouthing 'I love you.'

"At ease" My attention was drawn back to the men as he shouted. Cole held my arm and I held his with a death grip!

"Who gives this woman Rebecca Ann Glenn Grayson?" The man's tone was serious and loud as he waited for Cole to answer.

"I do, her brother, Coleman Lee Glenn." He kissed my cheek and shook William's hand as he handed me to William.

I took another deep breath as I looked up into William's handsome face holding a slight grin off to one side and then looked into his eyes seeing them twinkle softly. He took in a deep breath as he covered my hand with his.

The man bowed his head for prayer.

"Father, we come today..." The preacher started the ceremony but my thought went to God. This is really happening God? Thank you... I'll never forget you Robert.

"Amen... and Amen." We looked at the man in front of us, then to each other.

"We are gathered here..." I glanced into William's eyes again finding him staring into mine. This felt so right! How I love him! My heart pounded like a hammer in my chest realizing that this man did all of this for me! Tears that threatened fell down my cheeks, as I could no longer contain them. A soft smile crept across his lips. We were speaking to each other without saying a word. It was magical! Tears welled into his eyes as he squeezed my hands gently.

"Do you, Rebecca, take this man, William Elijah Andrews, to be your lawfully wedded husband?" I looked at him knowing I could spend the rest of my life giving him everything I could.

"Till death do you part?" I looked at the man.

"I will." My voice was hoarse.

"And do you, William Elijah Andrews, take this woman..." He was staring so deep into my eyes it felt as if he were touching me. I smiled softly as a tear fell from the corner of his eyes down his cheek.

"Till death do you part?" He looked at the man.

"I will." He smiled at me as he nodded slightly.

"If there is anyone that has reason…" His eyes dropped to my lips as they were so dry and he a sensual grin crept across his lips.

"Then by the authority of God and these United Territories, I now pronounce you husband and wife. You may kiss your bride William." The man laughed.

William stood for a moment slightly smiling then leaned down kissing me tenderly.

"Let's bow our heads."

He prayed a breathtaking prayer for William and I, for health and children. I couldn't believe I was married now!

"Amen." We raised our heads.

"Now, I have the extreme pleasure to introduce you to Lord and Lady William Andrews!"

"Attention!" The uniformed men crossed tips as we walked under their swords. His eyes never left mine. He was my husband! Thank you God! We walked to the door of the ballroom and dining room and stood together.

"I love you, my wife." He smiled and kissed my hand tenderly.

"William… you hold my very breath, heart and soul… I love you… my husband." I kissed his hand and he smiled softly.

As we stood by the dining room doors, many of the women cried in his arms saying how happy they were for us. He held each one as if they were truly his own family. I could see that he cared for every one of them. Though I knew it would take a long time to learn all of them, I also knew I had all the time I needed and, that I would soon call them all my family as well.

The men moved all the chairs and put them around tables as we chatted with all his family. The men shook his hand and smiled well pleased and then they kissed my hand.

"Oh sweet heart you look beautiful! Where in the world did you get that dress? I have never seen one so beautiful and with golden strands running like roses all over it."

"It was my mothers." William smiled and hugged his new Mother to him.

"William, thank you for loving Rebecca…" Mother cried in his arms as well.

274

"What's there not to love and shouldn't I thank you in the first place?" He smiled laughing softly and kissed her cheek turning her bright red.

"Rebecca…" Aunt Marie sobbed. I hugged her and rolled my eyes at Mother.

"Now I have a new Aunt!" He took Aunt Marie in his arms and hugged her plopping a big kiss on her cheek. I thought she would swoon. William also hugged Hannah and thanked her for being so kind to us, considering she was Robert's Aunt.

"You two kids belong together." Hannah winked and followed Mother and Aunt Marie.

"I thank you for that, Hannah. She is a gift straight from heaven!" Hannah hugged him tightly and then me.

"Come… I need to speak to the maestro about playing a special request I have for you. Actually I have several." He winked at me as he nodded to the maestro and that meant the start of the reception. Everyone came into the ballroom and mingled with one another.

"Shall we?" He stood as the maestro started the lovers Waltz. He smiled staring into my eyes. With the next beat swung me into the waltz. I felt as if I was still in a dream and one I never wanted to wake up from. I closed my eyes and could feel my shelf relaxing and loved how it felt to be in his arms. He held me close to him and looked deep into my eyes. I searched his and smiled a devilish grin. His eyes opened wide and a devilish grin played on his lips.

"You know, we do not have to stay too long." He leaned down and whispered into my ear feeling his warm breath on my ear and neck.

"We should stay for a while… though it does sound tempting."

"I do know one thing…" He whispered.

"And what is that my lord?" He smiled biting his bottom lips, his dimple showing.

"Father, always said how beautiful his bride looked on their wedding day. Now I know why." His eyes followed the neckline of the dress.

"William! People are watching!"

"I care not. I want them to all know how much I love you!" He leaned down and kissed me softly. We heard clapping and William and I looked around realizing everyone was watching, but they were either smiling or crying. William and I looked at each other and laughed.

"You are breathtaking… my love… no one can keep their eyes off of you." He tenderly smiled.

"I can feel that there are some broken hearts here mourning over you as well, husband." His eyes lit when I called him husband and made him smile a devilish smile.

"I can't believe that I am anyone's husband, especially yours." He tightened his hold.

"Nor can I believe you are mine." I smiled up at him with my own devilish smile not being able to help but to think about tonight.

As the waltz ended some of the men in uniforms came up to us. The first man I recognized from the restaurant. He was very tall and very handsome and very muscular. He had dimples that hid beneath the well-trimmed black beard. His hair was long and a blue black. His eyes were a laminating blue and twinkled as he smiled. He was taller than William by a couple of inches.

"Congratulations, William, you my brother are a very blessed man, very indeed." He shook William's hand and took mine bowing deeply over it then placing a whisper of a kiss on it. My cheeks reddened for he did not take his eyes off mine. Were all these men like this?

"Milady... you are beautiful!" He smiled at William and I with a heart stopping smile and I had no doubt that he was one who left broken hearts in his wake as well!

"Thank you, Graham." William patted my hand as I held on to his arm.

"William, may I have your permission to dance with your bride?" Lord Graham kept his eyes on me as he asked William.

"That will be up to my Lady." William looked at me.

"It would be my pleasure, Lord Graham." He held out his arm for me to take and winked at William.

"Please, call me Lee." He led me out to the dance floor and swung me into a waltz.

"Only if you will call me Rebecca, Lee." I looked at William as he smiled.

"William is a wonderful choice for a husband. I think that there is no better of a man than he." He smiled holding me swinging me in a circle and dancing so well like William. Lee kept his eyes on mine the whole time we danced.

"One day, Rebecca, I hope to find a wife such as yourself...If I am blessed as William, that is...But I am still young and I have a few years to go before I would consider being serious about getting married." He was very charming as he spoke.

"Well thank you, Lee. I know you will find the perfect wife one day, when you least expect it."

"Like William found you?" He smiled so sweetly at me, I blushed.

"Yes!" I shook my head in disbelief that I was really married. As the waltz ended Lee led me back to William.

"William, she is delightful!" Lee slightly bowed.

"That she is, Lee..." William beamed.

"Thank you for allowing me to hold your bride in my arms." He bowed deeply to the both of us.

"Well Lee, I'll not let her dance with too many this night. I can see they are all curious about my wife... " William squeezed my waist.

"That is wise brother! They will want her in their arms, all of them!" Lee laughed and bowed, then looked towards Carla.

"I believe she is spoken for as well." William shook his head.

"I see no ring on her finger and besides, I can only help whoever is courting the beauty to realize that until there is a ring on her finger, his place is in jeopardy!" He smiled a devilish smile.

He bowed again and walked towards Carla. I watched her eyes grow huge as she looked up and up to Lee's handsome face. She was as red as an apple! Cole was dancing with mother and I saw Cole's eyes grow dark as Lee led Carla out to the dance floor.

"I think my brother in law sees that his position has just been challenged." William softly laughed, for he spotted him as well.

"Well, like you my love, Gabe helped your heart along." I smiled as he looked at me wide eyed.

"That is true!" William took me into his arms.

The servants are bringing the food in. He leaned down and softly placed a kiss on my lips.

"I'm starving!" I stared into his eyes not being able to look away.

"Ah, my lady, I too...am starving." His eyes held mine in a sultry gaze.

"Then you must eat my lord." I teased.

"But... food is not what I desire." His voice was deep, husky, sultry full of desire and want. His teeth held his bottom lip as he smiled. I could say not a word, as my thoughts seemed to read his.

"Soon, my love... soon." His eyes held promise.

Servers poured the champagne and filled our plates with prime rib, potatoes, rolls, onion soup and sautéed mushrooms. My eyes went wide at the size of the plates, or platters it seemed. I glanced at the table to see who was sitting with us.

I sat at William's left. Carla sat next to me on my left then mother, Aunt Marie, Mike, and Hannah. On William's right sat Cole, Betty, Jules, Aunt Chloe, Uncle Clarence and Clarissa.

After everyone was served, William stood waiting for the room to become silent. Not even the rustling of a skirt was heard. William did not speak for a moment.

"Heavenly Father, today you have given me the greatest gift you could ever give to such an undeserving man. Today you have granted all the desires of my heart and today I give you all the praise and glory and in front of these witnesses, they themselves have seen the power of your mighty hand and the love you have for each of us. Father, Rebecca is so beautiful and loving and I give you my word as your Knight that I will honor her for all my days and with my last breath and I know she was sent by you.

Bless us all today and as we walk through this life that you have given us and that we may stay in your will. Bless this bounty and the hands that worked and prepared this feast, for without your grace and mercy, there would be nothing. Lord, bless all those who are here and their families, without them, I wouldn't have had any family to call my own and now I have added more to my family. Thank you, Father. Bless our marriage and keep your hand on us as we spend our days together, that we may fill our home with the laughter and joy of children, to raise them knowing you and loving you in Jesus' name we all say Amen and Amen." William looked up and then to me and raised his glass.

"Now, I would like to toast my wife... Rebecca." He took my hand and pulled me to stand.

"Rebecca...Thank you for loving me. Thank you for becoming my wife even though we haven't known each other as long as most, but when God puts two people together, who would ever judge when it is the proper time. All that I am and all that I have is yours. To my wife Rebecca, I give you my solemn word that I will be the best husband and provide you all that you would ever want or need. I love you... and will for all my days, to Rebecca!"

"To Rebecca!" Everyone said out loud. He raised his glass to me, as did all the guests. He clanked his glass with mine and we drank the whole glass.

"Enjoy!" William smiled softly down at me and wiped the tears from my eyes.

"Thank you, William that was beautiful!" I was speechless!

278

"I meant every word." He held my chair as we sat.

"Now my love, after we eat, we'll dance and visit with our guests."

"You mean our huge family!" I laughed.

"Yes the family." He laughed.

We ate and talked with the rest of our table. William kept his eye on me most of the time. William's cousin Clarissa, Uncle Clarence and Aunt Chloe waited till after we ate to chat.

"Rebecca, I am so glad you are married to my cousin. He was so distraught with you the night of the dinner party. He didn't know he was truly in love with you till he saw you in Lord McCray's arms!" Clarissa hugged me tightly.

"Clarissa, I must admit when I saw him in your arms, I didn't know you were cousins and I too was very distraught with the whole thing!" I laughed and so did Clarissa.

"I wondered why you were staring at William and me the way you were. I mean we've known each other for years and it never dawned on me that you didn't know William was my cousin." She shook her head. Clarissa glanced around the room. William was talking to Cole and Uncle Clarence.

"My, there sure are a lot of men in uniforms here tonight." She was still looking around and then she looked at Nick.

"Um, Clarissa? Do any of the guards appeal to you?" I asked in a soft voice hoping she would say it was Nick!

"They're all so handsome." She sighed.

"Well, I've noticed that one in particular has been staring at you all evening." I smiled looking at her blue eyes light up.

"Me? Who? Which one?" She whispered. I looked at Nick and he turned away.

"Do you see any that you'd care to meet?" I smiled whispering to her.

"Well… I have noticed one of them that I think is so handsome, but I'm sure he would think me under his station." She looked down at her skirt and brushed it lightly.

"Which one?" Oh please say Nick.

"I know him and have for a long time, but that is just it. I know he still thinks of me a child! When I danced with him at your dinner party, he called me pumpkin. That's what he's called me for years."

"Who?" I held my breath.

"Nick Baptiest." She looked at him and he was in deep conversation with three other guards.

"Well, if he asks you to dance smile and say, 'It would be my pleasure, my love'... Then, watch his eyes. I bet they will get wide and then he will be speechless." I smiled waiting for her to ask why.

"Why?" And there it was.

"I know he thinks a great deal of you as well."

"He does? Well of course he does, he's known me for years!" She shook her head.

"Just trust me Clarissa, it's more than that...I know." I smiled and winked at her.

"Alright, but he'll only laugh." She was blushing slightly.

"No, he won't laugh, he'll be speechless and it looks like you're going to get your chance right now!" I smiled looking up at two very handsome men.

"Rebecca... Congratulations! I know you have made William the happiest man in the world." Nick took my hand and bowed over it.

"Thank you Nick and you look very handsome tonight...isn't that right Clarissa?"

"OH... a... yes... yes, Nick, you are quite handsome tonight." She smiled blushing lightly. He took her hand and bowed deeply over it and placed a feather soft kiss on it never taking his eyes from hers. Her cheeks reddened.

"Rebecca, this is, Lord Ashton Cross. Ashton, this is Lady Rebecca Andrews and, Miss Clarissa Nelson."

"It is a pleasure to meet you, Lady Rebecca." He bowed over my hand then Clarissa's she blushed.

"And you as well. Thank you for being here for William." I smiled at Lord Cross.

"I wouldn't have missed it for the world. I know why he got married now... for I am looking at an angel!" Lord Cross was so charming.

"Clarissa? May I have the honor to have the next dance?" Nick smiled nervously. He was adorable! I watched Clarissa take a deep breath and smile taking a quick glance at me and I slightly nodded.

"It would be my pleasure... my love." Nick's eye widened larger than I thought, and his mouth opened slightly as he offered his arm to her.

"Ha!" I knew it!

"Knew what, Milady?" A deep voice shook my thoughts and suddenly realizing that Lord Cross was still next to me.

"Oh, I just think they don't know it yet, but they have a lot in common." I laughed.

"Ah, a match maker I see." He raised his brow as I glanced at him then turning my attention back to Nick and Clarissa.

"No not really, but I am guilty of it from time to time!" I laughed.

"Guilty of what?" A very deep voice sounded from behind me that mad my stomach flip. I laughed nervously.

"Your new wife has an eye for match making." Ashton smiled with a nod.

"She does, does she?" He raised his brow higher.

"I have always found that most people waist so much time on being afraid to step out to tell one how they feel. I just give it a little shove." I smiled and watched Nick dancing with Clarissa.

"Ah, I see you two have made friends again. That is well!"

"I never was angry at her, just jealous a bit. Well, a bit more than a little, I suppose." I corrected as I looked into William's heart melting eyes.

William held his arm out for me to take and he swung me into a waltz holding me in his arms tightly.

"I could dance with you all night, my love!" He smiled down then at my lips as I licked them and gave him a devilish smile. Then he bit his bottom lip and smiled.

"And I would let you, my love. I love to be in your arms." I grinned slightly. He widened his smile well pleased at my forwardness.

"I hope you're pleased." He smiled so sweetly with a small light of doubt.

"William, ask me tomorrow for right now I'm too busy being in heaven." I closed my eyes and enjoyed being in his big arms, being swung in circles.

"Now…for my surprise!" He kissed my cheek and whispered something into Mike's ear, Mike who was headed for me and William went to whisper into the maestro's ear.

"For my new bride, Rebecca." He turned his head and cleared his throat. Betty appeared next to me and hung on to my arm whispering in my ear. Then he sat behind the grand piano.

"You knew he could sing didn't you?" I looked at her shocked and just shook my head no!

The room was as silent as when he prayed. Then the orchestra and William started to play a tune I didn't know. Then the most beautiful deep, but not baritone, voice filled the room. I stood frozen and listened to the words.

Heaven has sent me an Angel…with two arms that hold me tight
Ohooowoe Heaven has sent me an Angel…tonight.
I could never have found her, on my own…
One day our paths crossed on a dusty road…
The first time I look into to her eyes….
Her smile stole my heart by surprise…OhoooOh
Heaven has sent me an Angel…
And today I have made her my bride…
Heaven has sent me and Angel…
To love for the rest of my life Ohooowoe
Heaven has sent me an angel
To complete my life…to complete my life.
You're my Angel…and I'll love you for the rest of my life.

I stood in shock as the last note rang out. I noticed tears in every one's eyes. He thanked the maestro and walked towards me and I was speechless. I licked my lips and he stood in front of me as tears streamed down my face.

"I love you, Rebecca, and that is your song."

"You… you wrote that for… me?" His thumbs wiped my tears.

"For you…" He leaned down and kissed my lips and my arms were around his neck hugging him tightly.

"Oh, William… I love you… that was the most wonderful thing you could have ever done for me!" My feet were off the ground and he tightened his hold.

"Now, my Lady, will you dance with your husband?" All I could do was nod! He was amazing!

The orchestra played the musical version of his song as we danced around the room. I could not believe that he would do something like that! He has a deep beautiful voice and so smooth! I recalled Betty's story today about William never finding his angel and now he has!

We danced a few more dances and then danced with other people. By the time we danced and talked to so many people and were exhausted and the maestro finally announced the last waltz. William held out his arm for me to take and led me to the floor. We danced holding each other and staring into each other's eyes never wavering. He held me to the last note, then leaned down and kissed my lips softly and whispered I love you.

"Come…" He took me out of the ballroom and people stared as we left. I wasn't fast enough and he scooped me up into his arms and took the stairs two at a time, but he didn't stop at the second floor. He was going to the third floor!

"William? Where are we going?" I tightened my arms around his neck.

"You'll see my love… another surprise!" We reached the top floor and William wasn't even winded and then carried me to the left. William said that these rooms were for guests. He never said that there was anything but bedrooms up here. He carried me down the first corridor and turned left down another to the back of the hall there was a door that stopped right in the middle of the back corridor.

"What is this?" I smiled.

"You'll see." He swung the door open and it was another retreat! It was enormous! As big as four rooms put together!

"William!"

The walls were white washed stone with crystal sconces all around the room. Huge dark wooden beams ran across the ceiling. A massive stone fireplace on the back wall was already lit with a beautiful iron fire screen patterned with scrolls and roses to stop burning embers from falling out on to a plush white rug and pillows on the shiny polished black stone floor. There were windows on each side of a huge stone fireplace with a thick wood mantle. The windows are tall and big with heavy white curtains with sheer ones under them.

Directly across the room was a huge area covered with the same heavy white curtains and sheers hiding dark wood framed glass double doors that stepped out to a rather large balcony looking over the courtyard. In front of the fireplace sat a satin white divan with two chairs that matched and overstuffed with throw blankets over the back of them. They looked as if one would sink if they sat on them. A full sideboard with an icebox and sink had fruit in a bowel and chocolates in a dish. There was another door I supposed was the washroom.

Roses were on every table in crystal vases. Two huge wardrobes on each side of the door that we were standing in and bookshelves full of old books. Last but not least a massively enormous bed towered in the center of the room that ten people could sleep in and still get lost! The bedclothes matched the curtains, divan and chairs a dozen pillows across the headboard of the bed looked so welcoming and with a coverlet at the end of the bed lying across a chest was the perfect touch. I looked at him amazed and speechless.

"Do you approve?" His eyes excited.

"William… it's… it's beautiful!" He carried me in kicking the door shut with his foot.

"This is now our room." He smiled down covering my lips with his. He kissed me tenderly and pulled away slowly.

"Our room? But, I thought that the room on the second floor was ours?" I was confused.

"No, they're really for married people that don't sleep together due to snoring or health problems or people with children." He smiled a breath from my lips.

"William?"

"Hmm?" He was brushing his lips across mine.

"You can't hold me all night!"

"Oh yes I can!" He rumbled like a lion.

"But then I could not… take a bath!"

"Of course! You must want to relax! Forgive me, but I'm rather fond of holding you." He brushed his lips across mine again.

"I love you too, William." I ran my finger down his cheek slowly.

"I love you." His lips crushed mine and I felt weak instantly, then he pulled away.

"Do you wish to take a bath now?" He smiled softly and his cheeks turned red.

"Yes, I think it would feel wonderful… my feet hurt." I could not look away from him.

"Your wish is my command." He carried me to the door I guessed to be the washroom and swung it open to see that it too was huge! Black floor and black bathtub way too big for one per… Ah, I see! I was going to have to be brave now. No man has ever seen my body, let alone touch it the way that William was. The thought made my insides about flip completely over!

"I've had all of your thing's brought up here with mine and do not wish you to go to another room even a month or ten years after tonight like some do. I want you with me every night, till the nights are no more." His voice was soft and like music to my heart.

"William?" I smiled shyly.

"Hmm?" His lips were a breath from mine again.

"I can't take a bath in your arms!" I laughed softly.

"Oh… right… I'll let you have time." He smiled tenderly and whispered softly.

"Take all the time you need." He smiled sitting me on my feet slowly kissing my hand before he turned to go out.

"Thank you, William." I loved that he was so considerate about my nervousness. I started the water and saw that all my things were in the washroom with his. How strange it looked! I saw a box in the chair and a card on top. I picked up the card and opened the seal.

To Rebecca, my bride on her wedding night,
I know you did not expect to be married and realize that you would probably want something special to wear tonight, so I took it upon myself to buy you a gift for tonight. I love you with all my heart, and if all you want me to do is hold you all night, I will be honored to do just that. You have my word...

You're Knight,
William

Oh my! I lifted the lid on the box. I have never had a gift for nighttime, though I've seen some nightclothes in the ladies stores before and always wanted to wear such things. I wonder what kind of taste William has.

I pulled back the paper and a saw a plain off white satin and practical, but still pretty nightgown. It had long sleeves with a 'v' neck and a tie that went around the back, the gown would touch the floor. I thought how sweet, William was so considerate of my feelings. Then I looked down into the box and saw a lace covering the bottom of the box. I gently held it up and it was breathtaking! Long lacy sleeves and a bodice 'v' shaped with a low neckline and small pearl buttons that buttoned all the way from the floor to the neckline. The back was just as low as the front. The gown was soft satin lace with a shear lining and I knew this was the one William truly desired me to wear and for him and I would. On the very bottom of the box, a lace robe that was simple enough to match either nightgown. I wanted to please William. Sometimes I wondered if Robert didn't like how I looked. I knew that that was silly, but he knew me all his life and I his. It had occurred to me that possibly what had happened between Robert and I was that, I married my best friend and he, his. I loved him and he loved me as well, but we were friends and perhaps that we married because we were so use to each other. We were happy living that way to, but I longed for children and I was not getting any younger. William would make a wonderful father and husband and one I would want to spend the rest of my life with. I laid the beautiful gown on the chair and smiled at how wonderful William was to me. I smiled as I undressed, then carefully picking out light oil that had the scent of roses and slid into the water. I relaxed in the hot water and closed my eyes thinking about what William might think of me.

Then before I knew it, I found myself finishing up my bath and drying off. I stood in front of the mirror and looked at myself before I dressed and I knew one thing, I was nervous! I took the fine satin lace gown and put it on buttoning it up from the bottom to the top. I thought that if I were a man I would love this on my wife. I slipped the robe on and tied the ribbon tie at the waist and took my hair out of the clip letting the curls tumble down around my shoulders. I was surprised how I looked. I was really pretty. I smiled now more sure that William would approve. I powdered my nose and put a little more rouge on my lips and cheeks and dabbed a little perfume on that matched the oil I put into the water. I took one last look in the mirror as I took a deep breath and slipped the soft slippers on my feet then slowly opening the door.

I saw that William was not in the room. Where was he? I looked around to the bed and fireplace. He must have gone for something. With another deep breath, I walked around my new bedroom and looked out the window down to the back of the estate. The balcony was empty and I stood taking in the view. It was so majestic with trees, hills and valleys as far as one could see. I sighed thinking how beautiful this view would be in the morning.

Then I walked to the fireplace and to the bookshelves seeing some really old books from the late nineteen hundreds about history and who was who. Then looked at a different shelf containing Legends and Myths type of books and old Fairy Tales and laughed thinking William read these books. On a different shelf there were nature books and carpentry books. Another shelf had current history about the recent Great War and the horror of it. I recalled once reading some of it. After the Great War, there was nothing left and it was a miracle that anyone survived! Then I thought about even as recent as when William was thirteen to have a remnant of the Great War takes his family. My heart welled with tears thinking how brave he was to enlist at fourteen. How he survived and grew into a God fearing man that was now my husband. I felt so proud to be his wife. I smiled to myself thinking that soon I would be in his arms and he would be loving me, a Colonel, knight and a man who honored and revered the Lord. I hugged my waist and went back to the fire looking at the small framed painted pictures of people on the mantle. I picked the one of the man up. It was his father! He looked just like him!

Then I picked up the woman's picture thinking this must be his mother. I covered my lips with my fingers in awe thinking she was so beautiful! Her hair was dark brown and she had blue eyes and a straight nose like William's. Her lips were full and she had high cheekbones making her look Spanish even with her having blue eyes. Then I picked up the picture of the little girl. Oh my, what a pretty little girl. She looked to be ten with dark hair in ringlets, big blue eyes and chubby cheeks. Tears welled in my eyes realizing this was his sister. How he must miss them!

I picked up the last picture and saw it was a boy about seven. I could see William and his father in him making my heartache. I picked up his father's picture again and held it to the light and looked to be about William's age in the picture. His hair was short but light in color and his eyes were hazel. He was smiling in the picture with a dimple in his right cheek just like William!

"I see you've found the pictures of my family. William stood staring at me taking me in from head to toe with a slight smile across his lips. His hair was wet so he must have gone to another room to take a bath and was already dressed for bed. I saw no shirt on under his robe, but could see silky dark hair peeking out. My heart pounded feeling myself getting even more nervous.

"I'm sorry, William… I…" He stepped to me putting his finger on my lips.

"Rebecca, it's alright. I wanted you to see them. I had them painted when I bought the place back. My mother was beautiful and about your age in this portrait. I know, I look just like my father and everyone who knew him said I was his very image. He was about my age in this portrait and as for my brother Lucas and my pretty sister Ellen, they too were beautiful. This was my family and next week I want to show you a very special place. He smiled down at me raising his hand to my cheek wiping the tears with his thumb.

"You must miss them so…" More tears fell.

"Rebecca, thank you." He pulled me to his chest.

"It's so very sad, William." How hard it must have been!

"It is, and it touches my heart that you are so moved by my loss, but I know that they're all together and the reason why I am still here." He hugged me tightly.

"William, I will try to be the best wife you could have ever prayed for."

"You already are my love, you already are." He released me and went to the sideboard pouring two glasses of wine and walked back to me handing me a glass. He sat on the divan and held out his arm and motioned for me to come join him.

"I'm pleased you chose the lace gown." He softly whispered in a deep husky tone.

"I've always dreamed about one day wearing one."

"Well now, you will have as many as you wish. I think I have never seen such a beautiful sight as I saw when I came back into the room, as you sat my mother's picture down." He was smiling so sweetly.

The fire was making his tan skin look so warm and golden. His hair was not tied back and hung down around his shoulders and down his back making him look so incredibly handsome. This way he looked so relaxed.

"William?"

"Hmm?"

"I want to give you your own family."

"Rebecca, that would be another great gift from God."

"I want to, I want as many as we can afford."

"What? Afford?" He roared out in a thunderous laugh.

"What? Did I say something wrong?" I looked up at him confused.

"Well, frankly yes."

"William... I'm..."

"If you could ever possibly have all the children we can afford my love..." He laughed again shaking his head.

"What?" Now I was really confused.

"Well, we would have our own territory! You would have a couple hundred." He hugged me to his chest laughing.

"Are you saying I could never have enough?" I looked up at him in disbelief.

"I'm saying that we could afford a couple hundred children." He laughed again.

"I think it will take me a while to get use to all this." I shook my head still not believing that he could afford that many children.

"In more ways than one my love..." He took my hands in his.

288

"But, if you really want to have as many children as we can afford…"
He smiled softly and ran his finger down my cheek then across my lips.
My heart pounded at his slightest touch. He bit his bottom lip smiling,
making his dimple appear.

"William?" I barely got his name out and saw the overwhelming look in
his eyes.

"Hmm?" He was not smiling yet his eyes were soft and warm, very
tender.

"I'm a bit…" I took a deep breath for the reality of knowing I was
about to be made love to for the first time, made me rather
apprehensive.

"I know my love. Just let things take their course. I would never do
anything that would hurt you or go farther than you want me to. I have
waited all my life for this moment and do not wish it to be anything but
beautiful." His words melted my heart and made me feel safe.

"William, I trust you." I whispered, as I searched his eyes and raised my
hand to his cheek feeling it shake a little.

"And I… trust you." He raised my chin with his finger and looked into
my eyes. I knew he would never do anything to hurt me.

"I am so happy William." Tears started to threaten at the
overwhelming feelings that were taking over. He slowly brought me to
his lips and gently kissed me. He pulled away from my lips and backing
up a little he looked into my eyes searchingly.

"Rebecca, I have no words to tell you how I feel right at this very
moment. This is the first time I have ever felt these feelings." He gently
pulled me into his arms. My hand lay on his satin robe and my thumb
was touching the warm silky hair on his chest. I could feel his heart
beating softly under the palm of my hand.

"You know you are more beautiful than I ever dreamed and you smell
wonderful." He raised his hand to my hair and picked up a curl wrapping
it around his finger.

"And I love your hair down." He took in a breath and slowly let it out.

"I'm sorry that I am so nervous." I looked down feeling rather naive.
His hand held mine.

"To be honest, I am as well." His lips brushed mine.

"William, I have waited for this moment as well. I too want it to be
wonderful. I haven't… I mean… I don't know…" It was the ultimate
admission for me.

"Ah, please don't worry about that. We have the rest of our lives." His eyes were telling me the truth and in them I could see his true concern for my feelings and me. No one has ever talked to me the way William does. He is so kind and gentle and reassuring with his warm words.

I reached up and brushed his long hair away from his handsome face. His eyes were full of love and I was fast drowning in the depths of the fire that smoldered in them. I struggled for calm resting my hand back on his chest as I breathed slowly wanting to run my hand across the vastness of his chest, but I didn't dare to move. I really didn't know what I should do!

"My heart is so full it is overflowing. I can't believe that for the first time, I am overwhelmed." He leaned down and kissed me tenderly, then deeper. His arms pulled me to his lap. My heart pounded a little faster. He pulled away slowly.

"You know when I saw you on the road, when we rode out of your sight. I was taken with your dusty face and a dog that sat next to you with his tail wagging and an old horse pulling your entire world behind you. I wanted to protect you then and there." He spoke softly then bit his lip.

"I thought you were the sweeter one, and when you smiled.... Nick scared me though. He was so dark and looked rather threatening." I laughed thinking what a big softy he truly was. I had no doubt he could be very ominous when warranted.

"He is that way for my protection and it's his duty to protect me at all costs." He said very seriously.

"Even... die for you?" I swallowed hard thinking how important William must be if Nick would die for William.

"Yes." William looked down at his hands holding mine with me cradled in his arms.

"Why would anyone want to hurt you?" I looked into his eyes now worried about his safety.

"Rebecca, not tonight, just believe me when I say that I am safe. I will tell you what I can tomorrow, but tonight 'We' are safe and when I officially retire, we will never worry again." He hugged me to his chest sighing deeply.

"Tell me, has anyone tried to kill you?" I felt a sob in my chest.

"Yes, many times... but please... not tonight." He sighed.

"You're safe right now?" I turned his face to mine searching his eyes.

"I give you my word… we are safe." He lowered his lips over mine brushing a kiss across them.

"I would give my life for you, Rebecca." William whispered softly into my ear and his hot breath seduced my thoughts.

"And I would for you my love." I whispered back in his ear my lips brushing his ear.

His lips covered mine in a passionate kiss sending waves of heat flooding throughout my body taking away all my nervousness. He trailed hot kisses down my neck slowly as if he was consuming me and I felt my heart pounding harder. His arms tightened around me as I moved my hand across his chest hearing a soft rumble escape his lips. His kiss deepened as I matched the depths of his passion, I was lost in the feeling of being in his arms. I felt his body tense and pulled away slowly.

"William…" I whispered as he kissed my neck his lips covered mine as if he knew what I needed.

I did not want him to stop as a great need was building inside me that I had never felt before and realized there would be a release and an end to this suffering. That thought alone made me want him even more.

I covered his lips passionately feeling so free to love him and then kissed him deeply, deeper than I had ever been allowed before. I felt his arms tense around me accepting my response. I pulled back from him and looked into his eyes. He was not pushing me away as Robert had.

My eyes begged him to satisfy these feelings. He closed his eyes putting his forehead on mine.

"I trust you, William." I licked my dry lips.

He gathered me into his arms and stood breathing differently than before.

"You are mine…" He whispered over my lips searching my eyes as if to say are you ready?

I gazed into deep depths of my husband's eyes and pulled him to my yearning lips wrapping my arms around his neck to let him know I was ready. A soft growl escaped his lips as he carried me to the bed placing me on my feet. His arms still around me, he reached up and gently took my hair that was in my face and moved it over my shoulder. I strangely was not nervous any longer. William had taken my worries away with his loving words.

My eyes never left his as he softly ran his warm hands down my arms. He lifted my hands to his lips softly kissing them and then holding them to his chest as if to say, trust me.

"I love you." His deep husky voice called to my very soul.

He said not a word and raised his hand to my chin and slowly lowered to my lips and softly kissed me. My hands slid on the satin robe around to his broad back fanning my fingers out over his shoulder blades feeling his muscles jerk at my touch and his body tense pulling me to his chest.

I was ready to feel the warmth of his skin against mine. I slowly pulled away and gazed into his eyes as my hands found the tie to his robe. Slowly I worked it loose and the satin belt fell down. Tonight he looked even more than what I remembered, so much more. My fingers slowly took in his massive chest, taking time to feel the sculpturing of his magnificent build, feeling the silky dark hair running between my fingers and feeling his heart was pounding faster. Then I ran my hands under his robe to his shoulders making his robe fall at his bent elbows. No words were needed as he dropped his arms letting his robe fall to the floor.

"Wait right here…" He took a regretful breath and went to the fireplace throwing another log on and around the room blowing out all the candles and lanterns leaving the one on the nightstand next to the bed lit, but turned it down to a soft glow.

I stood silent staring into his eyes, I slowly let my eyes travel down his chest taking him in again. His muscles are so powerful and strong and with his every move, they jump at his command.

The soft light was welcome as it hid my shyness knowing my cheeks were sure to be blushing as my robe dropped to the floor around my feet. I looked into his eyes as he took me in from head to toe and then he closed them tightly, then taking in an endless breath. Was he not pleased?

His eyes slowly came back to mine and he leaned down kissing my lips softly and in one gentle movement lifted me into his arms and placed me on the bed. I sank deep into the feather mattress and pillows. He slowly lay at my side and gathered my hair fanning it out across the pillows, then running the back of his fingers down my cheek still looking into my eyes. What was he thinking? My heart was pounding against my lungs pushing all the air out of my body.

"I never dreamed that you were so beautiful, Rebecca. I want to savor this moment and remember you just like this, so beautiful and innocent. The way your eyes look when I touch you and the way you make me feel when I touch you is almost more… than I can bear." He bit his bottom lip.

His eyes went to my bodice. His fingers barely touched a button, and caused me to shiver. His gaze darted back to my eyes.

"Are you afraid? Would you rather wait?" His eyes told me he would.

"No, William." I felt as if I was going to scream if he didn't touch me.

He kissed me softly and gently resting his chest on mine and his elbows on either side of me. My arms went around his neck pulling him closer to me. I deepened my kiss letting him know that I was not afraid, that I wanted him. He ran his hands through my hair, down to the buttons of my gown again. His hair fell all around my face.

All my fears were fading by the moment and it felt so natural, so right. I could feel his fingers skillfully unbuttoned each button slowly, as he freed me from the shear shroud. His hand came back up to my face and rested on my cheek as his kiss deepened with so much passion and desire that I heard a small moan escape my own lips.

Slowly, he kissed my chin and neck pushing my gown off my shoulders. Hands that were so strong, yet so incredibly gentle, I was aware of his every touch. My fingers ran through his hair, as my body seemed to be taking over without any control of my own, naturally responding. He gazed into my eyes.

"Rebecca… If you want me to stop, just say so." His voice was breathless.

"William... no...don't stop." I needed him more than I could have ever imagined. I need to know what my body has yearned for all these years.

His eyes took me in and his brows furrowed with an intense look.

Oh God, Please no! He is not pleased! I felt tears threaten.

"William… I… I know I'm not… what you expected… I…" I took a deep breath and closed my eyes turning my face away from his so I would not see the disappointment in his eyes. Then gently he turned my face back towards him.

"NO! God no! You are much more than I ever expected… I am so… Overwhelmed! You are so beautiful! My God Rebecca! I am so blessed to have you as my wife and I am at a loss for words, thought or breath." Tears welled into his eyes and I felt his heart thunder against my chest. He was pleased!

I shivered with want, need and desire as his lips trailed down my neck, as he slowly and gently kissed and nibbled, consuming me entirely. His fingers burned my skin as he slowly moved touching me gently. I tensed and arched as he found my most secret of places. My breath caught in my throat as he kissed my body gently sending waves of heat rushing through my veins. He looked up into my eyes as he disrobed and moved over the top of me, but still, I was not being crushed under his weight. His eyes held something I've never seen. I begged for something from him, yet did not know what it was…but he knew.

"I must make you ready for me my love." He whispered, as his eyes said trust me. My heart was about to explode.

He had to satisfy this, whatever it was soon or I would soon go mad. I kissed him deeply and thoroughly searching him. He groaned as my hands touched the rippling muscles of his broad back then to his hair filling my fists with the soft silk. I moaned as his lips went to my neck, and slowly lower. His hands slid down to my knees as he kissed lower. I tried to relax, as I took in all the things I was feeling and what William was doing felt wonderful!

My emotions and body were at the brink of exploding the more he kissed and touched. William, please! My thoughts begged as my body couldn't relax any longer. I grabbed the bedclothes as he moved lower. He kissed my thighs and then like a crack of thunder, everything went white throwing me into wave after wave of surging energy. My body shivered and trembled as my breath seized.

"William!" I cried out to him as he reached my lips crushing them. My fingers dug into his back and he lay fully on top of me feeling my body aggressive and demanding as I felt him pervade my body slightly. I gasped again as this feeling was wonderful! Then he stopped rising up on his hands.

"Rebecca… Do you wish me to stop? I do not wish to go any further if you do not want me to." His hair was in disarray around his face falling into mine.

I could do nothing but shake my head no! My emotions were running like mad and strangely enough, I wanted to cry with this overwhelming bliss. I was feeling so much all at once in such a release as if a floodgate had been opened.

"Trust me." He whispered kissing my lips tenderly and moved slowly and gently. Then with one firm move, I gasped in pain at the same time his lips covered mine muffling my outcry. The pain was stinging and sharp, but slowly started to subside with his movements. Soon I felt as if I was floating high in the clouds moving and drifting in and out of thought and feeling. He started to move with greater need as his breath puffed hard and fast. His eyes closed his lips pulled away from mine. I looked up through the dense fog I was floating in seeing his brow furrowed and was intensely looking into my eyes with his head bent down.

His head went back as I kissed his neck feeling his pulse pounding, kissing his chin then covered his lips with mine as he moved me.

"William!" Suddenly I cried out feeling something more build. His movements became more unyielding and suddenly he pulled me to his chest holding me tight almost squeezing the air out of me. He let out a roar as I called out his name.

"Rebecca!" He roared out.

His jaw flexed and rippled as his teeth clenched and his eyes shut tight and then slowly his movements slowed down to a rocking motion as my body still floated. Then slowly, he became still.

Sweat ran down his face and body feeling my body was drenched. He held me to his chest for the longest time not moving but breathing so hard.

"I love you." He whispered breathlessly almost void of a voice.

"I feel wonderful, William." I shyly smiled.

"Are you pleased?" He looked into my eyes searching.

"William... I'm so overwhelmed that I all I want to do is cry, I am so full of love for you!" I laughed feeling silly. He smiled and reached for the glass of water on the nightstand. He offered it to me first.

"Thank you." I smiled then took a long needed drink. Water dripped down the side of my mouth and he leaned to my lips and kissed it off. I handed the glass to him and he finished the rest.

"I don't want to move yet." He pulled me to him again as we stayed as one.

"Can you do it again?" I shyly smiled.

He laughed and winked at me still holding me. His lips covered mine softly. His hands slipped off my gown and he laid it behind him. I felt passion growing the deeper his kiss went. He gently laid me back down on the bed and kissed me, moving slowly.

This time he loved me slow and without such urgency. His kisses were deep and full of passion. I wanted our joining as one to have me with child as soon as possible. The thought of having his child and the joy it would bring him was almost more than I could bear. My heart ached to give him everything I could to complete his hearts desires and I knew he wanted children right away.

His tender movements rocked me into a soft warm loving place. I was finding out there was more than one way to make love. I softly called out his name as I felt his body tense and slow to a very comfortable movement. Then he stopped and looked down into my eyes just staring and smiling for a little while. We said nothing, nor did he move, we laid still feeling so complete.

I felt his deep breathing raising me up and down and could hear his heart slow it's pounding to a soft drum making me sleepy. His scent was intoxicating as I breathed it in. I looked up and saw his eyes closed I felt his arms tighten around, holding me. I leaned over to the lamp and turned it down till it went out. The soft glow of the fire danced across the walls and softly illuminated his peaceful face. I lay still just looking at my husband's face thinking this still felt like a dream, and if it was, I did not want to ever wake up. I was lost in the depths of his love. Lost in the desire and passion we had for each other... lost forever in him.

~ Chapter 13 ~

A warm glow of light shinned in my eyes, stirring me awake. Yawning, I felt my husband's soft silky chest hair and smiled to myself as I listened to his strong heartbeat. I sleepily looked up seeing him so peaceful with his brow relaxed and his lips slightly parted. His hair was fanned out over the pillows making him look like a warrior and I couldn't wait to know even more about him and all his ways... he is MY husband!

This was a new life for me and now I am married to Lord William Elijah Andrews! That... would take some time to get use to! Lady Rebecca Ann Andrews!

I took a deep breath and felt William stirring beneath me. I watched and waited quietly for his eyes to open. His hands ran up and down my bare back as a deep rumble escaped his lips, feeling the vibrations. His eyes did not open, but a slight smile appeared on his lips. Was he awake? I lay quietly waiting, then suddenly feeling him awake in a different place. My eyes widened! I felt him stirring and propped myself up looking into his face. With one eye, he peeked and laughed out loud! He was laughing!

"Well... good morning wife!" He laughed.

"Husband... good... morning." He awoke that way? Good heavens!

"Sleep well?" He smiled and pulled pillows under his head.

"I had never slept better in my life and don't think I ever moved!" I laughed.

"I know and felt you sliding off several times and put you back." He sleepily smiled. His eyes were so blue green this morning, not light green like last night.

"Your eyes... they change colors..." I stared into them.

"They do. You can tell what mood I am in by them as well."

"You can?" This amazed me!

"If there more green than blue, I'm most likely working and if they're more blue than green, I'm very happy and at peace. Now, if they're dark blue green, I'm usually angry or in battle. And if they're really light green... then I'm making love to you." He smiled as his eyes were turning lighter green.

"I see... like now... you're..." I shyly smiled realizing his eyes were light green. Heavens!

"You have no idea how I dreamed of this." His arms surrounded me in a warm embrace.

"Well, I know for a fact that a certain knight gave me his word that he would."

"Then he must! For a true knight never goes back on his word." He smiled a devilish smile.

I felt his hands run down my back and he pulled me up to him. He grabbed my legs and pulled them close to him one on each side of him. He smiled a devilish grin then he sat up a little more and I knew what he wanted, just as he spoke last night, I did know!

Soon, we lay feeling complete bliss as his arms tightened and I snuggled close, feeling totally safe, warm and loved. I was never so happy in all my life.

We lay quietly enjoying just being together in the moment. His hands rubbed my back as mine rubbed his chest playing with the silky soft hair. I stared out the window wondering what it was going to be like being his wife and wondering what he would expect of me. All I knew was how wonderful he is and how much I loved him. If William was right about God sending me to him, then I would be with child soon. I smiled to myself thinking that carrying his child and then once born, to hold it and see the intense pride in having his children would be truly a blessing indeed.

"Are you?" He laughed.

"Oh, I'm sorry, William, what did you say?" I looked up at him with a start.

"I asked you if you were hungry..." He laughed.

"Yes... I am... I'm sorry, William, my mind was drifting off."

"And what took you away from me?" He smiled tenderly at me.

"Children..."

"Children?" He looked down at me.

"Yes, I can't wait to be with child."

"Rebecca, if you don't conceive right away, I'm sure you will soon enough. We DO have the rest of our lives..." He brushed the hair away from my face.

"But you don't understand William."

"What don't I understand?" He looked concerned.

"If we are to have our own territory..." I raised my brow and laughed.

"Oh yes, right... I forgot." He laughed and gently rolled me off his chest and onto his side.

"William, I've been waiting to see that other side of you. Most people have another side, a side that most don't know about or see. You're just almost too good to be true!"

"Rebecca, I do have another side, but... I will tell you about it later."

"Is it bad?" I looked at him thinking that it could be.

"No, let's just say it rather has an... appetite." He smiled a sensual grin.

"Interesting..." I wonder what he could mean.

"You could say that, but let's get washed up and be ready for our breakfast. I wouldn't want for the staff to see you or me still in bed, though that is where I plan on spending a lot of time." He grinned wickedly.

"I believe, my husband that you are right when you warned, 'be ready for our breakfast'. We'll need it!" I laughed a devilish laugh back at him.

"Ah, a Lady after my own heart." He softly laughed.

"How did you ever guess?" I laughed and he pulled me close.

"I knew..." A tap on the door interrupted a tender kiss.

"I'll get it, though we didn't make it out of the bed." He laughed and rolled his eyes, giving me a quick kiss and hopped out of the bed.

For the first time I saw his magnificent form. I watched him stand turning and smiling at me, and winked, and I couldn't help but blush. He walked to the end of the bed seeking his robe and watched his muscles flex and jump at his command. His skin was so smooth and tan like satin with his hair tapering down his back almost to the middle, accenting those shoulders so wide and powerful looking and giving way to his lean waist. His legs were very muscular, bulging out at the sides as he leaned over the bed reaching for his robe. He glanced at me as he stood. I almost bit my lip too hard at all I saw

"Like what you see?" He softly whispered in a low voice grinning.

"Oh heavens! Yes I do my husband!" I blushed as he softly laughed and winked and slid his robe on, tying it at the waist. I saw the muscles in his calves and there wasn't an ounce of fat anywhere! It was hard to believe he was thirty-seven. William was in such magnificent shape! I was blessed indeed!

He opened the door a crack and I couldn't hear what was said but he laughed and pulled a large cart in the room pushing it in front of the divan.

"Smells wonderful! I'm ready for coffee, aren't you my love?"

"Yes, and a lot of it too!" I laughed out.

He reached for my robe at the end of the bed and my hand, to assist me out of the bed. I slid to his side of the bed trying to hold on to the sheet, but it slipped away.

"Please, don't be shy, Rebecca, I love every inch of you!" His words were so tender and sweet. I stood and turned for him to help me into it and his arms wrapped around me tying my robe for me.

"You really don't know just how lovely you are, do you?" His breath caressed my neck and ear sending shivers of delight down to my toes. He turned me around to face him and he looked down at me.

"You know, I plan on having you without clothing as much as possible. I think I enjoy looking at you more than I do anything." He smiled brushing his lips across mine.

"And I enjoy the sight of you as well my husband, you are magnificent!" I kissed him tenderly taking him into my arms and then slowly pulled away.

"I was hoping you would be pleased." He smiled leading me to the divan.

"And you as well." I smiled up at him as he helped me to sit.

"This smells wonderful." I watched as he opened the cover of the first tray. Waffles, strawberries topped with whip cream and they smelled heavenly. Then he raised the second lid, bacon sausage and toast. There were two glasses of juice and a pot of coffee, cream and a bowl of sugar. William poured us a cup, sat down and then bowed his head.

"Father, thank you for this food and bless the hands that worked to grow it and prepare it. Father, I have no words to express the happiness that I feel this day for your gift of sending Rebecca to me. She is perfect! Thank you, Father, and bless our marriage and in your time allow us to have many children and bless us with healthy children…Keep your hand on us every day and keep us from harm, in the name of our Lord and Savior Jesus… Amen."

"I love how you pray, William. You have a way of praying that makes my heart feel your words."

"I owe him everything. He has watched over me and protected me all my life. He is the real First Knight. Now, let's eat for I am famished." He smiled cutting his waffle. I fixed my coffee and stirred watching him eat. His jaw flexed as he chewed. He was all muscle from head to toe! I could watch him eat all day. He motioned to my plate and winked. He was so handsome with his hair in disarray. He licked his lips and my eyes went to them.

"You know, the thoughts you are having right now isn't conducive to our appetite, though... I'm sure I could easily rectify that." He put his fork down smiling a devilish grin.

"William, it's just to me, you are so incredible, that I have a hard time concentrating on much of anything!" I admitted and blushed.

"Well, I'm glad you think so my love, for that is exactly how I feel about you. But, I have to eat... so must you!" He shook his head and laughed.

"I'm sorry..." I sipped my coffee then cut into the strawberry covered waffles. He stopped putting his fork down and taking my chin on his finger.

"Don't ever be sorry for that. I love to see you look at me that way." He winked and I nodded knowing exactly what he meant.

We finished breakfast and dressed for the day. But in all honesty, I could have hid in here all day. As I dressed, I had wondered if Cole proposed to her already. I hope so!

"William, I'm a little nervous about seeing everyone this morning. I'm afraid my cheeks will blush so much, they will never be the same!" I nervously smiled.

"Rebecca... everyone knows what people do on their wedding night." He smiled covering my hand with his as we walked out of the room.

"I know." He stopped and looked down at me.

"Rebecca, it doesn't matter what anyone thinks. People have been having wedding nights for centuries!" He kissed me softly and then turned and we started down the hall.

"I know that it is silly, but I will still feel nervous!" I sighed, feeling my stomach fluttering about.

"It will be over before you know it. Just think if we didn't come out for days! Then what would they think?" He gave me a small sensual grin.

"I see your point." I laughed knowing William could have arranged that as well!

We walked down the stairs and heard voices coming from the dining room. He smiled and nodded to me patting the back of my hand. I took a deep breath as we entered the dining room. We found everyone having just finished breakfast and sipping coffee.

"Well, well the love birds are here!" Cole smiled. I looked at Carla and smiled blushing even more. How was I ever going to relax?

"Good morning everyone!" William helped me to sit. I knew my cheeks were flushed.

"You two look wonderful this morning!" Mother winked at me, feeling my cheeks get even warmer!

"We thought we wouldn't see you two for days!" Mike laughed.

"Mike!" Mother scolded with a brow raised.

"What? I was just…" He laughed out knowing well what he was doing!

"We know what you were 'Just' saying, but that's not the point. Rebecca… you look beautiful." Cole smiled and looked at Carla.

"Are you alright?" Carla leaned to whisper.

"Simply wonderful!" I whispered back.

"So, what is on the agenda for today?" William looked at everyone. One of the servants poured William and me a cup of coffee.

"We thought we'd like to go into Winchester for a little shopping." Mother smiled.

"Yes, and lunch at the Palace Hotel." Carla smiled.

"That sounds wonderful." I agreed.

"What do you two have planned for today?" Cole raised his eyebrow up and down winking at me.

"Whatever my wife would like to do…" William smiled at me squeezing my hand.

"It's up to you, William."

"I think I would like to take my new bride along with you fine people to Winchester. I want to show her a few things that just might please her." He smiled with one brow up as if it were another surprise. I was getting to like all these surprises that William had!

"Oh could we, William?" I smiled and touched his arm.

"Of course my love, anything you want." He covered my hand with his.

"Aren't they so adorable?" Hannah smiled and took a deep breath letting it out in a sigh.

"Women!" Mike huffed.

When we finished our coffee, William had Jules ready the carriage for us all as we grabbed our warm shawls. The air was cooler than it had been for a while. William had his arm around me all the way to Winchester and Cole held Carla's hand. It was a bit cramped, but we all fit.

When the carriage stopped, we women decided to go in some of the more feminine shops and the men decided it would be best we go our own way for a bit.

"Rebecca, look at this!" Her cheeks were as red as fire as she held a lacy gown up.

"That's beautiful Carla! Are you going to wear it soon?"

"Would you wear such a thing? Me? What did you say?" She looked at me shocked.

"Yes, you and yes I would!" I whispered laughing softly.

"OH!" Carla laid it back down.

I held up a lovely white satin sleeveless lace gown with a low neckline.

"It's beautiful…" Carla had the same one in her hands.

"Now I would wear this… and this… and this!" I found three very scant nightgowns. I saw mother talking to the woman that ran the store and the woman smiled and started towards Carla and me.

"Lady Andrews?" She smiled with her big painted red lips and blue on her eyelids. She looked like a festival clown with a slight French accent.

"Yes?"

"May I be of assistance to you? I understand you have just married Lord Andrews?"

"Yes that is true! I am looking for something very special for tonight. Lord William had gotten me a gown like this one and I wore it last night, but I want something even more…" I shyly smiled. Carla was about to fall on the floor.

"My name is Brenda Harper and I will be happy to show you the newest from France, if you would like? Oui?" We nodded to her as she motioned us to follow her to a back room.

"I must say that knowing Lord William as I do, he must be an overwhelming man and lover!" She spoke so frankly with her French accent, but I had heard that Europeans were very forward.

"Well, yes he is… and I want to surprise him." I felt I could speak just as frankly with her as she was with me.

"I have the perfect thing, I want to show you." She opened a garment bag and held up a very, very scant whatever you called it.

"OH MY!" Carla about fell over, putting her hand on her chest.

"These are the latest from France. No one but me has seen them. These are underclothes of a different sort and a lot of women use them to sleep in now. They revised them with lace and less material. I'm sure they won't last long, but they are beautiful, No?" She held the two pieces up to her showing how you would wear them.

The small white straps looked more like ribbon than material and lace flowed down the front over the satin white material, what little of it there was. It just met the pants that matched. There was hardly anything to them. The legs were high to the hip and the only material was in the front and back in pieces. I had to have that! Then she showed me another one that was shear. It was light blue. Then she showed me a yellow one that tied up the front with ribbon and the panties as she called them, were even less. I blushed thinking how pleased William would be, I took it as well. Carla, I think was shocked!

"I have several more, but am saving the best for last!" She smiled as she showed me three more than the one she saved for last.

I gasped! It was a robe, all lace and long to the floor, black! Then under it was another scant outfit, but it was like a one piece that slid on. She showed us the hidden feature and I blushed horribly! William would just have a fit! I would fashion that one for him tonight! I also found some bath oils and perfume form across the ocean. I picked out some hair what knots and combs. I loved this shop and would come here again soon!

"Would you like to set up an account?" She smiled.

"No, I want to see if these please my husband first, which I have no doubt they will."

"Alright then, if you do later, I'm sure that I can accommodate you in any way Lady Andrews." She added the total up and I paid her.

"Did you find anything dear?" I forgot mother was even here! Heavens! Thank goodness Brenda had all the things wrapped in boxes already.

"Thank you, Mrs. Harper."

"Please call me Brenda and thank you!"

"Well, I'm sure you'll be seeing a lot of me so you best call me Rebecca as well." I laughed and winked at her as she nodded in a knowing way.

"Ready?" I asked everyone and they all nodded.

We left the store and placed our purchases in the carriage baggage area and walked down towards the Palace Hotel. We had all worked up an appetite.

"I wonder where those men are." Carla looked up and down the street.

"They'll show up." We wandered down the busy streets looking in the windows at different things.

There were so many people walking up and down the street and carriages flying past. The dust was bad, it hadn't rained in a few days. I saw a children's clothing shop and my heart ached to go in, but I had no reason… yet!

"Look!" Carla saw a dress shop and boutique all in one.

"I'll be…" Hannah smiled and raised her brow at Carla and Carla raised hers at Hannah, I could tell where this was going. Then they looked at mother and mother smiled.

"Are you gal's thinking what I'm thinking?" Hannah smiled and they all nodded.

"I think it will work." Carla smiled.

"So do I." Hannah agreed.

"Well, I do own the buildings. If I can get the store next to me to agree to swap with your store then we can open three places up by knocking down a wall or two." Mother smiled loving the idea more and more.

"I think you should call it 'La Palais'… French for 'The Palace'. The women could have tea or coffee while they pick out material or dresses and nail colors having their hair done. It would be wonderful… an all in one place!"

"You mean all in one 'Palais'." Mother laughed. Aunt Marie loved the idea so much that she said she would help with anything they needed.

"Thank you so much, Marie." Mother smiled hugging her.

"Well, I think every woman in town would love to save time." She smiled looking excited.

We still had not sighted the men and decided to go to the hotel anyway.

The hotel was five stories tall and was a light tan in color and constructed with big blocks. There were beautiful golden lamps on each side of the door. A man stood just to open the door for us as we walked through a huge glass door. Inside, the man pointed us to the direction of the restaurant and we headed for it.

The hotel was beautiful! Red carpeting and golden walls and plants everywhere, chandeliers hung from the ceiling. Chairs and divans sat scattered about down the lobby, and on the walls hung huge paintings in heavy gold frames. It was breathtaking!

As we approached the restaurant, a tall man in his early sixties with white hair and mustache...bowed and smiled at mother.

"May I be of assistance to you Ladies?" He smiled at mother so sweetly. She blushed as he took her hand and bowed again over it.

"Yes we are having lunch here. Has Lord Andrews arrived yet?" I asked him smiling knowing he was being fresh with mother and I hid a laugh.

"Lord Andrews? My Lady?" He looked surprised.

"Yes... I'm his wife." I smiled proudly.

"You are, are you?" He acted like he didn't believe me.

"Yes... I am. Has he arrived?"

"No, milady, he has not." He threw his nose into the air in a snobbish way.

"Then you may show us to a table that will seat at least eight." I ignored his snobbish attitude.

"Very well milady... if you will follow me." He smiled at mother again and offered her his arm. I was in shock for mother took it smiling!

"Here you are ladies, my name is Charles. What may I have the waiter bring you while you wait for... Lord Andrews?" He cleared his throat before saying, Lord Andrews. I don't think he believes me! Well when William shows up, he will then!

"Coffee" We all chimed then laughed.

"Very good, your waiter will be Harry. He will be here momentarily." He bowed again looking at mother and he winked at her! She blushed so much she had to fan her cheeks.

"Mother! I think he was taken with you!" I laughed as soon as he was out of earshot.

"Oh don't you be silly. He was only being nice to an old woman." She tried to disregard the thought.

"So tell me then, Mother, what made you blush?" I tried to interrogate her as she has done me in the past so many times!

"Blush... Me? Why, I think you're seeing things." She denied blushing.

"Well, I saw it too!" Hannah came to my defense.

"So did I, and you are a lovely woman with a wonderful figure. Why shouldn't he notice your beauty?" Carla defended.

"Well... I..." Her cheeks reddened.

"Mother, look, he's still looking at you!" I smiled and winked at her.

"I will not give into this!" She fluttered the menu up to her face, but I caught a glimpse of a smile before she completely hid behind the menu.

"I wonder what has the men so tied up." I looked at Carla.

"I thought I heard Cole say something about... getting his watch fixed."

"He had complained that the wind up was getting worn out." I smiled to her thinking, aha! The jewelers! You may be too slick for Carla, but not for me brother!

"Are you enjoying yourselves?" I looked at everyone especially Carla.

"Cole and I took a long walk after the wedding reception. William's place is so lovely... I love the pond area." She looked down.

"I can't believe that beautiful place is now my home." I shook my head in disbelief.

"Well my dear, you deserve a beautiful place like that!" Mother patted my hand.

"There are the men." Carla smiled and sat straighter in her chair.

"Please forgive us for being late. We had to um... wait on the man to fix my watch... It's perfect now... see?" Cole nervously held it up and I saw no difference in the windup part.

"Did you have a good time shopping?" William kissed my cheek as he sat next to me.

"Yes." I smiled as he took my hand raising it to his lips.

"Wonderful!" William raised his hand to Charles and he came rushing over.

"Yes, Milord... how may I be of service to you?" He smiled bowing slightly and giving mother a glance.

"I would like Marcel's special lunch and dessert for all and I would like a bottle of your best wine, if you would please. Would you care for anything special, my bride?"

I looked up at Charles and he tilted his head in an apologetic way. I nodded back.

"Very good, would any of you like anything special?" Charles smiled and looked at mother again.

"I would love a glass of water."

"What is the Chef's special?" Cole smiled at William.

"Ah, I hope you like variety." William laughed and held my hand.

"Another surprise?" I smiled at William.

"Why yes, my love." He nodded winking.

"So, what did you ladies find?" Mike smiled looking at me as if he knew something.

"This and that, bath oil, perfume, you know, women things." I smiled.

"I see." Mike's eyebrows went up and down teasing Carla and me.

"Did you set up an account there? At…" He wanted to know the name of the shop.

"The Lady's Boutique? And no I did not. I wanted you…" I smiled stopped myself from saying any more forgetting that there table was full of people! Good heavens! Whenever my eyes are locked onto his, I forget about everything else it seems. He just smiled realizing what I was about to say and his eyes went wide.

"I had several accounts set up while you were shopping at several stores in town that I knew you would eventually go to, including Madam Adams a local dress maker." William looked at Hannah with a plea of forgiveness in his eyes.

"Not to worry, that was a wise decision. I won't have any extra time in the near future." The men looked at her lost.

"What do you mean, Hannah?" Mike looked confused as well.

Mother, Carla and Hannah told them all about their idea as lunch was served. They stopped talking and were in awe of what was sitting in front of them, three platters of seafood of all kinds and pasta, rolls, prime rib and potatoes. Everyone's eyes were wide.

"This looks wonderful!" Cole said placing his napkin in his lap looking at the lobster.

"There's a bit of everything on these platters. This is my most favorite lunch." William smiled and looked at Mike and Mike bowed his head.

"Father, we thank you for this food and hope that we may put the proper dent into it. Thank you for my family and the ones to come and bless Rebecca and William for I pray that you fill their house to over flowing… Amen. Let's eat!" Mike laughed.

"My goodness! Look at all this food!" Mother was in awe.

"Enjoy!" The waiter brought over the wine and poured everyone a glass.

"To family and love." William held his glass up.

"To family and love" We all chimed in unison.

By the time we filled our plates with a little of everything, they were over flowing. William asked about the rest of their ideas on their business adventures. Hannah, mother and Carla were more than willing to talk about it.

William paid close attention to the details and nodded at the ideas and the potential for a larger chance of more customers, Mike rolled his eyes.

"I know what you're thinking about, Mike, all we will need you for, is to help renovate the building and that will be under Cole's instruction. After we open, we won't need you so you'll be free to do whatever you wish, yes and to work with Cole again if you'd like." Mother smiled at Mike.

"Thank God, for another miracle! I needed to hear that." Mike laughed and Cole nodded at Mike.

Mother, Carla and Hannah sorted out the details of their joint venture and William, Cole and Mike nodded their heads at what they discussed. I was pleased that the men did not laugh at them. Some still believe that a woman's place is in the kitchen, but not the Glenn men! William offered his services and several men when they were ready to renovate or move.

"Thank you, William. You've won my heart forever." Hannah smiled tenderly at William.

"How could you resist him... he's just wonderful!" Aunt Marie cried.

We finished lunch and Mike told us that he was leaving today to head back to Hickory Hill to check on things and would be waiting on mother's return. I hugged him and kissed him telling him that he needs to marry that Gail Cropper before someone else does.

"Now, Rebecca, she is my business and I'm not ready to answer to ANY woman yet, but I love you anyway...Thank you William, it was really a nice vacation and I love the shack!" We all laughed as everyone said goodbye to Mike.

"Oh yes and, William... I'll expect a niece or nephew soon!" He laughed and blew me a kiss. We all waved at him and couldn't help but to miss the rogue already.

We shopped in town together after Mike left and then went our own ways again. William and I walked down the street arm in arm and he nodded to people he knew and told me a little about each one he ran across.

We ended up at the park in the town square with children, mothers, lovers and loner alike. A small band was playing in a gazebo as people listened and enjoyed their lunch on a blanket and children playing tag or with a ball. William led me to a nice bench off to the side and we sat down.

"Aren't they wonderful?" He was laughing.

"What is wonderful?"

"The children…" He smiled tenderly. I could see the longing in his eyes.

"Yes, I think that we should have at least twenty." I nodded looking at the children playing.

"A huh."

Just as William stretched his long legs out in front of him, a red ball was kicked to his feet and he leaned over and picked the red ball up. As a little girl of maybe six or seven came running up and handed it to her. His eyes glowed and his smile went all the way to his eyes!

"Here you go." He handed the ball to the little girl smiling a heartbreaking smile.

"Thank you, Sir!" She curtsied and was about to turn, but she stopped turning back to us again and tilted her head.

"Are you going to have a baby?" Her question caught me off guard.

"I would love to… soon." I smiled down at her beautiful face.

"Well…my mother won't sit on that bench your sitting on anymore! She says that every time she does she finds out she's going to have a baby." Her long blond braids fell down her back. The blue in her calico play dress was precious and matched her bright blue eyes.

"How many brother's and sister's do you have?" William leaned forward clasping his hands together resting his elbows on his knees listening intently.

"Well…" She counted on her two hands.

"I have four brothers and six sisters and me. That makes seven girls and mother is going to have one more, she calls it an even dozen." She giggled rolling her eyes.

"Well, you, Milady, may tell your mother that we will take over her bench for a while."

"Oh she will be so glad of that! She wanted father to buy it and burn it in a bonfire." She giggled and so did we. She was adorable!

"No, he couldn't do that! What would we do then? We wouldn't be able to sit here."

"Well, I'll tell her!" She giggled and ran to her mother.

"If we sit here and you become pregnant, I'll buy the bench and put it on our balcony!" William kissed my cheek and the little girl's mother shook her head, waving with the back of her hand motioning for us to take it away! William and I looked at each other and laughed.

"William? Did Cole buy Carla something at the jewelry store?" He looked at me surprised.

310

"How… did you know?" William was shocked.

"I know my brother and he's a horrible liar." I laughed. I just knew it!

"Yes, he bought Carla something." He took a deep breath.

"Oh…" I looked at him from the corner of my eyes and saw him wrestling with not telling me. I just waited.

"Alright, yes, he bought her the loveliest ring and yes it's an engagement ring." He blew out a big breath.

"I knew it!" I was so good at match making.

"Did he say when he planned on asking her?" I smiled trying to keep myself calm.

"He said that he would sometime while he was here, back at the shack." He laughed.

"Soon then?"

"He's got the ring, so I'd say so." William stood and took my hand.

"Did you see the way Charles looked at mother?"

"Yes and I thought he was going to ask her if she would dine with him!" He laughed.

"He was so obvious!" I laughed thinking about her blushing.

"I bet that is where she goes for lunch tomorrow with Hannah and your Aunt Marie." William laughed as we started to walk back to the carriage.

"William?" I looked up into his handsome face.

"Yes, my love." He walked me across the street.

"Are you enjoying this day and my family being here, truly?"

"Yes I am. I love your family and feel like I have a real family again." He truly looked happy that he really felt he had a family to call his. Now all I need is to be with child.

"So… a… did you find anything… interesting at the Ladies Boutique?" He gave me a sensual smile.

"You'll just have to wait and see." My tone was rather teasing.

"That implies that you did and I can hardly wait to see what you have bought for me."

"For you? Oh yes, I see what you mean." I gave him a devilish look.

"So you did?" He was like a little boy at the candy counter.

"Yes, several things that may pique your interest." I gave him a sultry look with a raised brow.

"Let's go home!" He smiled and tried to pull me, teasing me.

"Oh, William… I love you…" I hugged his arm.

"And I do you, with all my heart." He leaned down and spoke in a deep soft voice.

We found mother, Aunt Marie, and Hannah coming out of the general store with several huge bags.

"What in the world?" William went to assist them taking the huge bags.

"You could have had this sent to the estate." William's eyes went up.

"Now he tells us!" Mother laughed grateful of William taking the bag from her.

"Are you two about shopped out?" I laughed at Aunt Marie rolling her eyes.

"Yes, I think I am. I did get some lovely material that I can't find anywhere." Hannah smiled.

"Well then, let's look for Carla and Cole and then we can head back. I'm sure dinner will be wonderful tonight." William smiled and hauled the great bags to the carriage putting them into the baggage space. Carla and Cole walked up behind William.

"Mike just left for Hickory Hill. He said to thank you and will see you two Monday." Cole smiled at us.

"Well then, are we ready to go back? I'd like to see your ledgers this afternoon after dinner so that I may study them." Cole nodded at William.

"That would be fine with me! I intend to spoil your sister tonight." William winked at Cole.

"Well, let's be off then!" William took mother's hand and helped her into the carriage, then Aunt Marie, Hannah, and me. Cole helped Carla in and sat holding her hand. I couldn't help but think Cole was going to purpose to her tonight. That would make mother's year and that would only leave Mike to deal with, who knows what he will do or not do!

We all were worn out from walking and shopping and I was looking forwards to a rest. The ride back was quiet. William held my hand kissing it several times. We were going home... Home! The thought was completely strange to me. My new home was huge! A castle! I still couldn't believe it!

When we pulled up to the front of the estate, rain started to come down with a cold wind.

"I think winter is on the threshold." William wrapped his arm around me after he helped mother, Aunt Marie and Hannah out. We hurried into the hall, Jules took our shawls and told one of the servants to retrieve the packages from the carriage and put them in the proper rooms. William slapped Jules on the shoulder and smiled at him.

"It's always good to get back home." William laughed.

We retired to our rooms to freshen up and rest a spell. William had coffee or tea sent to all their rooms. When we reached our room, we went to the fireplace to take the chill off, taking in the warmth. Jules must have seen to it being lit. William stood behind me wrapping his arms around me, burying his cold nose in my neck, sending shivers of goose bumps down my arms.

"I had a nice time today." William spoke softly. I covered his hands with mine. He gently swayed me back and forth.

"So did I." I turned within his arms.

"This is how it will be from now on my love." His eyes were so full of love.

"It's all like a dream come true to me." I shook my head. A tap on the door made William release me.

"Coffee?" He smiled walking towards the door. William returned with the tray of coffee and sat it on the table in front of the divan and motioned for me to sit with him. Coffee sounded and smelled wonderful.

"Like a dream come true you said? Like how?" He sat as I did, pouring us both a cup.

"I just feel like a princess. How you love me, how you treat me, the wedding, this place. I could have never dreamed I would ever be happy again." I put sugar and cream in my coffee and stirred it and then took a well deserved sip.

"To me you are. You're not just my princess, you are my Queen and I am your King for this my love, is a castle." He laughed softly.

"Well... I never thought of it that way." Another tap on the door startled me.

"Your purchases..." His eyebrows went up and down.

"Honestly, William." I laughed shaking my head. Betty smiled at me as she brought in the things I bought today.

"Hello, Betty."

"Hello, milady." She winked.

"I want to put those away if you don't mind." I winked at her.

"If you are sure..."

"I am, but thank you anyway." I smiled and William grabbed her on the way out.

"William!" She laughed.

"You did not give me a hug or a kiss today Bee." He spoke in a musical tone. She smiled up at him with love in her eyes.

"Oh you!" She hugged him plopping a big kiss on his cheek.

"Ah... much better! Now I shall survive the rest of the day." He kissed her cheek.

"Dinner will be in a half hour." She winked at me and rubbed his cheek. William closed the door after her.

"I know you won't show me what you bought, so I won't ask to see it, but what color is it?"

"Well, what is your favorite color?" I smiled sipping the wonderful coffee.

"It depends what it is. Now if it is a nightgown, I would say white, black or deep green or even red." He gave me a sultry smile.

"Alright... then you will be very pleased tonight." I'm not giving away the color.

"You my love... do not play fair." William smiled a sensual smile.

"I want to surprise you." I gave him a sultry smile myself.

He leaned forward and gently kissed my lips so softly and tenderly and then leaned back and sipped his coffee. He smiled over his cup at me and was deep in thought.

"What are you thinking about?"

"Well... tomorrow I would like to take you to my special place, but I would like it to be just you and me."

"I don't see that that would be any problem. I would love to go there with you."

"I like going in the morning. The sun shines so brightly and everything is still damp with the night dew, but since it's raining and cold, I think we'll go before dinner sometime... that is if it's not still cold in the morning." He smiled at me. This was his most favorite place? I recalled what Betty had told me.

"I know I will." I sipped my coffee thinking that it was his favorite place. Of course it was, it was where he would like to think his family was. Now he has me and I will give him his own family I pray soon. We finished our coffees and went into the bath to wash up.

"Should I change?" I looked at my dress.

"No... I'm not going to, besides you are beautiful just the way you are."

"Do you think Cole really wants to see your ledgers or is he going to propose to Carla?"

"Your guess is as good as mine. I will get the ledgers out for him and he can choose for himself, that is. After we have dinner, you can take your bath while I talk to Cole, after that, I shall be up." He smiled and winked at me.

"That sounds good to me." And it did. Last night and today simply wore me out!

We went down for dinner and everyone was tired. Mother and Hannah talked about their new business plans and Cole and Carla listened and Carla agreed with them. She wanted mother to work out the details and let her know the bottom line. Cole thought that the coffee shop should be in the back of the store and all three businesses in the front. He said then everyone would win. I never doubted that mother was capable of planning and making decisions about business. William was very interested in their plans and decided that he wanted to go back to Hickory Hill a day or two after they left so that he could help. Cole welcomed it and knew he too was pleased.

After dinner, William took Cole into his office and was showing him where his ledgers were. They went over them. I excused myself and went up to our room. I started a bath and looked into all the packages. I poured some new oil into the tub and placed the rest next to my husband's on the small shelf. I couldn't help but take one of his oils, breathe in, and then took all the nightwear or whatever she called them and put them in the top drawer of the wardrobe, which was full of my crinolines and stockings. William insisted that I have the top drawer.

I undressed and hung my dress up and took the nightwear into the washroom with three bottles of perfume I also purchased. I slid into the hot water and let out a breath and just relaxed. The scent of wildflowers fell all around the room.

Out of the tub, I dried and stood with a towel wrapped around me brushing my hair out. I dabbed on perfume, but just a small amount as the oil was rather strong. I took the top of the black nightwear and put it on lacing up the front loosely the slipped the bottoms on. I looked into the mirror and smiled thinking I even liked how this looked with the black satin lace and it was solid enough to be mysterious. I was pleased, even at myself! I finished brushing my hair till it was smooth then allowed it to curl on its own. I put on the matching robe that went to the floor and tied the black velvet ribbon and fluffed my hair. Then went into the bedroom to the sideboard and got a glass of ice water and sat on the divan and waited. William finally came through the door.

"I think I shall go take a bath now my love, I won't be long." He unbuttoned his shirt by the bed and taking it off, I couldn't help but watch over the back of the divan. His muscles rippled as he laid his shirt across the chest at the foot of the bed and then took off his boots and unbuckled his pants and slid them off. He looked up at me and winked laying them across the trunk as well.

As he walked into the washroom I wondered about the scars? What happened to him? He would tell me soon, or I would just have to ask him soon. I'm sure it wouldn't surprise him if I did. The idea that someone would do such a thing to a person was contemptible!

"Rebecca?" He called out to me

"Yes, do you need something?" I started to get up.

"No, but I just wanted to hear your voice. I am finding it hard to believe that you are my wife." His laugh echoed in the bath.

"Well, you're stuck with me, Lord Andrews." I smiled, thinking that any woman would desire to be 'stuck' with him for the rest of her life.

"We should have bathed together." I heard the water splashing.

I remembered when I saw him in the tub last and to think, I was worried about a wedding dress.

"Next time…" I called out hoarsely.

"I'm going to hold you to that." He laughed.

"And I believe you." I knew he would, I thought, shaking my head. I heard water running in the basin and I was getting a little nervous at the idea he would soon see my new gown and nightwear. I went back to the sideboard to get another glass of ice water.

"Rebecca?" I heard his feet pad across the floor, but didn't turn. Then he stood behind me but not touching me. I could feel the heat from his body being so close to mine and feeling his breath softly puffing in my hair. I looked over my shoulder seeing he was only a breath away from me. A sensual grin crept across my lips as I saw he was only wearing a white towel neatly tucked around his waist.

His hair was wet and hanging down and he wasn't wearing any cologne tonight, just his natural scent. I slowly turned towards him holding the glass of water. He towered over me staring down into my eyes, not moving a muscle. His eyes burned with passion like I have never seen before! They darted down to my lips.

316

Then slowly, he took me in from head to toe as he reached for my hand, raising it to his lips. I dare not say a word noticing his chest rising and falling, breathing faster than normal. His other hand went to my cheek and his thumb ran it over my lips. I looked back into his eyes now filled with a look that made me shiver. What was that look? It was full of desire, passion, love, and something very different! His eyes were more light green than I've ever seen before. They looked almost…wild! His eyes darted back to my lips again as I licked them again. He was still silent holding my hand.

He took the glass out of my hand and sat it back on the sideboard, then scooped me into his arms not taking his eyes off of mine. He covered the area between the divan and the bed in a few steps. He then laid me gently down on the bed staring at me for the longest time, but when I was about to say something, I stopped. His eyes squinted slightly. I didn't know what to do! I couldn't move, nor did I dare to! I had never seen him this way!

He blew out all the lanterns and allowed the moon light to seep through the shear curtains casting its light on the bed. He slowly sat on the bed, seeing his body, golden brown in the moonlight as his face was partly shadowed with his hair hanging down. But his eyes! His eyes seemed to be illuminated! The way he looked at me, it was as if he was touching me, feeling my entire body. I could barely stand this much longer. This was almost torture!

He finally blinked as his nostrils flared and reached for the velvet ribbon tied around my waist. His hands trembled as I felt the pull of the ribbon, he slipped the satin robe off my shoulders. I shuttered as I felt his warm fingers graze the skin on my shoulders then going under the thin straps. He put a hand behind my neck and pulled me to his lips.

His kiss was so deep and consuming, that he bit my bottom lip as he slowly pulled away. I closed my eyes as a wave of heat rushed through my body. As I close my eyes, he moved on top of me covering my lips with a deep passionate kiss breathing me in with every breath. My arms went around him grabbing his back as he trailed burning kisses across my chin and down to my neck and shoulders. I heard a groan escape his lips as he covered mine again. He rose up and touched my cheek as if he wanted me to see what he was doing. A hint of a sensual grin played on his lips as I took a deep breath and watched. He took my hand and kissed each finger and felt his tongue on the pad of my fingers as he put one in his mouth. I closed my eyes.

"Look at me…" His voice was at a whisper, but a command. I opened them to find him loosening the laces of my camisole, pulling them one at a time.

He untied them all and the camisole fell away like silk on silk. His eyes grew wider as he took me in. Going lower, he held my knee and kissing it slowly and then my thigh. I closed my eyes again.

"Look at me…" He commanded. I felt extreme heat rise to my face. His eyes were so different!

His hand softly ran over my stomach and then, he closed his eyes kissing my ankle, knee and to my thigh. When he opened his eyes, he stopped. A very sensual smile crept across his lips. Suddenly he ripped the towel away from his waist and his head went back flipping his wet hair back.

When he looked back to me, the look in his eyes changed again! They were glowing! A deep growl came from him as his hands seized and touched every part of my body, as if he needed to take me all in, to consume and claim what was his. His lips found mine taking them in harder, he left them bruised.

I couldn't hear a thing but could feel myself cry out. He suddenly pulled me to him, crushing his lips on mine and entered me with one fierce move, sending me higher than I ever had been before. My body moved to his command, as if I had no control. I ran my hands across his shoulders and dug my fingers into them holding on. I heard him cry out as he moved me, his hands seizing me. I had no strength to move and was at his mercy as he moved me where he wanted me with such control. I put my hands on his chest, wet with sweat. This passion was almost too much for my body to endure. My fingers felt as if they sunk into the skin on his chest.

I looked deep into his eyes as he stared into mine and thought I saw something strange. It was as if it was not William looking at me. I closed my eyes knowing I was seeing things. He pulled me to his chest and his arms wrapped around me holding me tightly pushing me down. He growled out in a strange tone. His lips crushed mine and he tensed once again in a violent way and a thunderous roar filled the night. He held me so tightly that I thought he would crush me.

"I… can't breathe…" I panted.

"Oh, Rebecca… I'm … sorry." He shook his head and loosened his hold more. I took a deep breath and kissed his lips.

"William…" I panted catching my breath more and more.

"I'm sorry…" He hugged me gently.

"Sorry?" My arms were weak barely able to hug him back as I trembled.

"I wanted to tell you about… this." He whispered in a hoarse voice as he was trying to breathe.

"This?" I panted trying to catch my breath.

"Yes…" He eased me back to the bed and lay next to me.

"What do you mean?" I knew there was a different look in his eyes. He bit his bottom lip with worry on his furrowed brow.

"This is… what I was going to tell you about, but tonight when I saw you in that lace robe, I felt like something snapped inside of me. It was as if I had lost all control." He let out a huge breath.

"I… I don't understand, snapped?" It was different. He was very aggressive and forceful at times to the point of it hurting. His hands are so strong!

"When I am full of desire… It seems like something else takes over."

"I saw that in your eyes!" I knew I saw that!

"You did?" He looked intently into mine.

"Yes… they were… it was as if they glowed and they looked wild!" I thought I was seeing things.

"Yes! That's how it feels." He ran his fingers through his hair.

"Then… you have… felt this… before?" I bit my bottom lip.

"Yes…" He looked into my eyes.

"What happened?"

"I'm not sure, that is the problem… I could hardly remember, that is another reason I never got too close to anyone."

"Do you remember tonight?"

"Yes, but I still held back." He looked down.

"Held back?" What was he telling me? Was there more?

"I'm not too sure exactly what I would do or if I would hurt you. I can't take the chance."

"Then what you're telling me is that you're not sure what it is and what would happen if you let go and just let whatever it is, take control?"

"Yes." His voice was soft and he took a deep breath.

"Then, with the woman… it came out the first time and you didn't remember? Did you hurt her?"

"Not that I know of, but I never saw her again." He rubbed the back of my hand with his thumb.

"Did you ask her?"

"Yes, she said it was the Ale I drank and not to worry. She wasn't bruised."

"Then you must not have hurt her." I was relieved. He is so strong after all.

"No, but remember, I wasn't in love with her, and I am you. Tonight it just came out all by itself. I didn't expect it. It happened on its own." He looked into my eyes and searched them.

"But you were with her more than once you said... so that means you must have been attracted to her in some way?" He had to at least like her.

"Her name was, Rosa, she was my age. We talked a lot, but she wasn't like the rest. Yes, she was a whore, but she was different. She liked to know her clients." He frowned.

"Then you thought of her more as a friend?"

"In a way, but I was not in love with her. I tried to tell her that she wasn't living the life she ought to be living. She agreed, but she said she was saving her money up for a better life. She had mentioned there was one man that she fancied and the last I heard she is with him now and married happily."

"It's alright, William... it was long ago and you said it never happened since? I mean whatever takes over?" I tried to ease his fears.

"No... this is the first time in years and years. I didn't want that to happen again."

"So she said you did not hurt her?"

"I saw how red her skin was and I could see my hand prints on her body. I asked if I slapped her... she said I didn't, just held her very tight." I saw fear in his eyes for the first time ever.

"You're afraid that you'll do that to me?"

"Yes, if not worse." He looked into my eyes hoping I'd understand.

"I don't think you would ever hurt me William. In your heart, you know you love me. I think that somewhere you would see me."

"I don't know. I just want you to know that if it happens again, try to remember that I love you and I would never hurt you on purpose. I would rather die than to hurt you." Tears welled into his eyes.

"William, you know it will happen sooner or later and when it does and if you get too rough, just know I'll understand and that I love you too."

"I want to let go... but just when I think I can, a fear creeps throughout my body telling me 'No don't', and I find myself like tonight."

320

"So, do you want to let go?"

"Yes."

"Then we will live with it and we will deal with it until it does come out." I touched his worried brow. He must feel frustrated and incomplete.

"I just don't know what will happen. I never allowed myself to get like this since Rosa." Fear filled his eyes.

"Well, you didn't hurt me. It was rather wonderful... I liked it if the truth be known... I felt myself let go as well."

"You did? You liked it?" He looked surprised.

"I did... though I really have nothing to compare it to, except you." I blushed. And I truly did. If he can't trust me and feel safe, then when could he?

"I'll be damned!" Though he looked relieved shaking his head and softly laughed.

"William!" I was shocked at his choice of words.

"Forgive me, but you are right! You would tell me if I hurt you though... wouldn't you?"

"I would and you, my Lord, have my word." I smiled and ran my fingers across his lips.

He pulled me into his arms and kissed me deeply and tenderly. I could tell he was more relaxed than ever before. How this secret must have been a burden all these years! To be afraid to love and to hurt someone, that was why he never let himself get to close to any one person. Then the thought occurred to me, why me? Why was he able to allow himself to fall in love with me?

"William..."

"Hmm?" He rumbled.

"What made you fall in love with me? You said that you never let anyone get close, but you did with me. Why?"

"That's something I cannot explain. That is another reason why I think that God put you in my life. It just happened and I didn't plan on it." His voice had a serious tone.

"Then did you try to fight your feelings toward me?"

"I did, but I couldn't get you out of my thoughts and every time I closed my eyes you were there!" He turned pulling me to him.

"You do have a big appetite!" I laughed and pulled away from his heated lips.

"That I do… that I do!" With his deep voice, he laughed softly and crushed his lips over mine and I was instantly lost in the depths of his arms. We made love so deep and profound, that it was like a dream. I was never so much in love and so happy in all my life. Robert's memory was fading so fast that it was hard to picture him the way I use to. In a way I was glad. Now, I felt like William's wife in every way. He wrapped his arms around me and I laid my cheek on his chest listening to his heart slowing...

~ Chapter 14 ~

I opened my eyes to a well-lit room thinking it must be late. I reached over to touch my handsome husband, but he was not in the bed!

"William?" I softly called, then calling louder.

"William?" I heard a strange noise. I slid out of bed and listened quietly as I put my heavy robe on.

It was coming from the windows from the center court area and sounded like William yelling! I went to look out tying my robe slipping into my slippers. Gasping as I looked out the window, it was William and someone else. They were fighting! I didn't know the man, William was fighting! Then the man sliced into William's shirt! GOD NO! William was bleeding! I screamed and ran out of the room and down the hall and stairs and then out to the courtyard. My heart pounded like it was going to beat through my chest.

"My God! William!" I ran across the open area and across the wet grass almost slipping.

"William!" Oh God, please don't let him get hurt. My mind was racing.

"William!" I screamed as the other man attacked him with such a great blow that sparks of white rain showered down from the air. This was real!

"Stop!" I cried as tears fell down my cheeks. I felt darkness trying to overcome me. William swung his sword and attacked back. PLEASE STOP! My mind screamed.

"William!" I felt myself fade away into an abyss of darkness.

I could hear William's voice in the dark. 'I'm here.'

"God Please… Wake up, Rebecca. It's alright!" His voice sounded like it was so far away. I'm here, but I can't wake up.

"Here… put this under her nose… it will wake her…" I heard Betty's voice sounding worried.

"Rebecca, my love… its William, I'm right here." He patted my hand. I could hear him clearly and blinked open my eyes. Everything was fuzzy as I blinked to try to clear my vision.

"There, that's my girl." William's voice was so soft and soothing.

"William?" I whispered.

"Water! Get her some water!" He roared at someone.

"Rebecca, my love, can you hear me?" His voice was so sweet. I nodded.

"Can you see me?" He had a smile on his face and raised my hand kissing it softly.

"William… what happened?" I squeezed my eyes shut and opened them looking around. Betty and Jules and another maid stood around me. Where was I?

"You passed out on the grass in the courtyard." He kissed my hand again.

I started to recall… A MAN! Fighting William! I looked above me and that man that William was fighting stood looking down at me.

"William!" I sat up and turned to the man. Fear washed over my entire body, but I had moved to quickly and felt dizzy and sick to my stomach.

"Shhh… it's alright… I'm fine." William leaned down and kissed my forehead.

"William, that man…. He… he… was attacking you!" Tears fell.

"No, Rebecca, No…He was not attacking me, we were sparing." He brushed the hair out of my face.

"No, William! His sword cut you! I saw it!" My heart pounded against my ribs so hard.

"Rebecca, my love…" He sat behind me and pulled me to his chest and wrapped his arms around me.

"William… he's behind you!" I cried out. The man stood and looked at Betty.

"Listen to me my love… I was practicing at wielding my sword with Jon Luke. This is Jon Luke, Nick's brother." His tone was soft and calming. Suddenly a flood of relief washed over me and I felt light headed.

"Nick's brother… Jon Luke… Nick works for you?" I remembered now.

"Yes, that's right. Jon Luke. He and I were exercising." He hugged me to his chest.

"Here, drink this." Betty held out the glass with a worried look still on her face. My hands shook as I took it from her shaking so hard that I was spilling it.

"Here, let me help you." He covered my hand with his and guided it to my lips.

"That's my girl." He rumbled.

"Rebecca, this is Jon Luke Baptiest, Jon Luke, this is my bride, Rebecca…"

"Forgive me milady, I never would ever hurt William. I'm sorry to have frightened you." He bowed slightly.

His black hair was like Nicholas's, blue-black and very long. His eyes were a light blue and had a day's growth on his face and he looked younger by a couple of years than Nick.

"At your service…" He smiled.

"Jon Luke, please forgive me for assuming the worst." I was embarrassed, to say the least.

"Jon Luke just got back. I know that you have never met him." William laughed softly. Betty smiled softly and Jules stood stiffly smiling.

"I'm so sorry everyone." I looked back at William.

"I should have told you that I like to have a little sport in the morning and when I found out Jon Luke was back I couldn't resist. Please forgive me."

"I thought you were going to get killed!" I let a frightened breath out.

"I am terribly sorry, my love." He kissed my temple and slid out from behind me lifting me into his arms. His eyes pleaded for me to forgive him.

"Thank you everyone." He smiled to Betty and Jules, then to Jon Luke.

William carried me all the way back to our bedroom and then gently sat me on the divan.

"Rebecca, I am so sorry. You must have been scared to death." He pulled me to him.

"I was and all I saw was a man coming at you with a look of murder in his eyes! I heard no laughing or friendly jesting!" I was angry at him for scaring me like this.

"Rebecca, please forgive me. I'll try to warn if I ever do something you know nothing about. I had forgotten that you have never seen 'sport' before." His eyes begged me to forgive him. How could I not forgive him? His face was like a little boy.

"I do forgive you, William. I love you so much. I was afraid you would be taken from me…" I wrapped my arms around him tightly and cried thinking about Robert and how it felt when the storm took him.

"I love you so much, Rebecca… I would never scare you on purpose…"

"Now I know that I would surly die if something was to ever happen to you." I cried.

"Nothing will ever happen to me my love and you have my word on that." He hugged me tight then kissed me tenderly and then he slowly pulled away.

"I am in need of a bath!" He smiled sweetly.

"Me too…" I laughed.

"Well you go ahead… I need to inform everyone that you have exonerated me. I shall return shortly." He gave me a quick kiss and left me in the room. I never thought that he was doing his sport the way Jon Luke looked at William. It appeared that Jon Luke's intent was to indeed kill him. I took a deep breath and went to the wardrobe.

"Rebecca?" Betty called through the cracked door.

"Come in, Betty." I called to her.

"Are you alright?" She walked towards me.

"Yes, though I was truly afraid for William's life! I had never met Jon Luke before or saw a sword fight before." I smiled slightly, still thinking how I must have looked.

"Now don't you fret my girl, I would have done the same thing if I didn't know." She took out my yellow checked dress. It was heavier and warmer than the rest of my dresses. She went into the washroom and started the water.

"Thank you… Betty." I took a deep breath.

"For what?" Betty as stripping the bed.

"For making me feel so well loved and taking me with a grain of salt. It's just going to take me some time to get use to all of this." I shook my head as I went to the bath.

The water felt heavenly. I sank down in the warmth of the heat and warmed my bones. The way Jon Luke was leaping at William looked so real and I thought what if that was truly a real fight? Has William fought like this before? Was this normal? He looked so powerful with his sword, the way he swung it and his legs heaved muscles as he leaped forward. His arms rippled as the swords rang out in a thunderous clash. His hair was flying about his shoulders as his body spun in circles to deflect his opponent! Lord almighty, he was beautiful now that I had time to reflect on it. I took another deep breath thinking I would need to watch one of these exercises so that I knew what to expect from now on!

"Betty, would you know where my family is this morning?" I called out to her.

"Yes, they all went to town to pick some more fabric and some more oils and different teas and coffees. I heard them speaking of their business venture this morning and wanted to purchase some things they can't get elsewhere. I think they wanted to check out several stores and how they run their businesses."

"Well that is a very good idea." I let out a deep breath.

"I know Cole wanted to take Carla to one of the ponds this evening." Betty's voice sounded rather musical.

"Really?" I washed my hair and heard the crisp snap of a top sheet being put on the bed.

"I think your brother has indeed fallen in love with his lady. It's in his eyes, like William's."

"Well, the way he acted the first time he laid eyes on her, I knew she was perfect for him."

"Well, it would seem like you have the gift for such things. You knew about William as well I gather."

"I did and it was in his smile when he looked at me. I could never get that smile out of my thoughts."

"He has a way about him." Betty grinned.

"That he does… that he does."

As I finished up my bath and dried off, I heard Betty humming a beautiful melody that I recognized and I started to sing with her humming. I heard her hum louder as I dressed and sung. I walked out brushing my hair and sung to the tune.

"For I will always love you… with all my heart." I sung out and wrapped my arm around Betty.

Clapping came from behind us and startled both of us. We swung around not expecting anyone to be in the room, but finding William leaning against the door frame smiling and clapping softly.

"That was beautiful ladies!" He walked to us and took both of us in his arms hugging us tightly.

"Thank you… We do try to please!" I laughed.

"It was more than pleasing, I told you Betty, she sings like an angel!" He kissed my forehead and Betty's.

"She has a beautiful voice and you as well, so don't hide your light under a barrel! Either of you!" She winked at William.

"Betty, when he sang that song at the reception! I was in complete awe!" William blushed.

"Jon Luke plays the piano. Maybe he would play and you two sing some time?" Betty smiled and added.

"Milord, you play as well, you should play for her…that is unless you do my dear?"

"Me? No! I don't, though I always wanted to." I admitted.

"I shall show you the scales and teach you how to read music if you would like?" William smiled so tenderly.

"I would love that… soon?" I was excited.

"Yes, soon." His eyes grew sultry.

"A hmm, I think I shall go down with the linen and see to it getting washed." Betty hurried out of the bedroom.

"Now, I am taking a bath and I shall meet you downstairs for breakfast. I want to take you to my favorite place today."

"Alright then…" I gave him a kiss and walked towards the door not really wanting to leave.

"I'll see you in a little while." He winked as I walked out the door.

The hallway was dark this morning. It looked like it would rain anytime, though it was not raining earlier. I made my way to the stairs and took my time getting to the dining room. I did not want to drink coffee in this huge room that looked so empty. I went to the kitchen and found everyone so busy.

"Good morning everyone…" I smiled at all the busy faces.

"Milady, can we help you with anything?" Libby smiled with her rosy cheeks. I sat at the small table by the window and looked out.

"I would love a cup of your coffee if you don't mind and I would like to have it in here. The hall was so empty this morning."

"Of course milady." Libby nodded.

"Libby, please call me Rebecca… it is not easy to get use to all this. It doesn't sound like me." I frowned.

"But milady it would not be proper!"

"Do you call William Milord?"

"No… but…" She stuttered.

"Alright then it's settled… you will call me Rebecca." I laughed.

"Very well… but I must insist on calling you milady in front company."

"Agreed..." She brought over a cup of coffee.

"Come join me, Libby." I waved my hand to the seat across from me.

"No Ma'am, I couldn't..." Her mouth was wide open.

"Oh Phooey! Come on." I laughed.

"Alright." She smiled weakly. She brought over a cup of coffee and sat down hesitantly. I smiled at her softly.

"If I may, Lady Rebecca?" She smiled at me softly with her deep brown eyes.

"Yes, Libby?" I haven't really gotten a chance to talk with Libby and it was time to get to know her.

"I... Well... 'We' have never seen Lord William so happy. It is so good to see him smile.." She sipped her coffee.

"Libby, is he truly happy?" I looked into her eyes and waited.

"Oh yes, Mi... I mean, Rebecca. Why he was always nice and smiled treating us with kindness and respect but there was always something missing in his life and you were it."

"It's so hard to believe he had never married, until now." I looked at her over my cup deep in thought.

"Well, we were beginning to think he would never get married to someone he loved. We thought he would end up having to marry one for an heir only that would have been sad. William is so loved by everyone. The thought of him marrying that Lady Dawson was unthinkable to everyone. She is beautiful, but she doesn't have any thought deeper than her forehead!" She shook her head and laughed.

"Lady Dawson? I hadn't heard of her." Who was this? William never spoke of her.

"Oh dear, I thought you knew about her." She looked guilty that she had betrayed William.

"Tell me about her and how he knows her." Libby suddenly got nervous.

"Lady Rebecca, I shouldn't..." She looked so guilty as if she committed treason!

"Oh, not to worry! I'm his wife now and there will be no threats, so tell me about this woman." I smiled and winked at her. Ah, this was going to be good!

"Well Ma'am, her name is Lady Denise Dawson. She lives in Madison and is the daughter of Lord Kelvin Dawson whom is a very wealthy man that owns everything in Madison. He knows William through the purchases of William's horses. His daughter is not what you call bright, but she is beautiful. They were to wed in the spring if Lord William had not taken on a bride by then." She sipped her coffee.

"I see, go on." Hmmm, so he married me to prevent another marriage?

"Well, William has known her for many years and has spent time with her from time to time. I knew his heart wasn't in it from the get go. He never was happy when he returned. He would wield his sword with Jon Luke for hours after returning."

"Was there a contract?"

"No, not that I know of. William did not want to marry her. He claimed that it would be an arranged marriage and that after they would marry, he wanted to have his children right away so that he would be sure to have his heir." She sipped her coffee again.

"So, he wanted to start right away?" Just like me. My heart sank to my feet. I was feeling rather sick to my stomach at the thoughts I was having and feeling.

"Yes, he said that he wasn't getting any younger and it was time to have his children."

"Then he wanted to marry for children?"

"Yes, but we all wanted more for him. Then you came into his life and suddenly he was a changed man. When he came to the estate and announced that he was bringing the woman he would marry to his home, we all thought it was Lady Dawson. I was sad until he told us your name."

"So, you saw he was happy?" My heart lifted a little.

"Oh yes! In love to be more exact."

"You think he truly loves me?"

"I do and from what I gather. He planned on marrying you the first time he laid eyes on you." She shook her head and laughed.

"I see. He wanted to start having children right away with me as well Libby. I do hope he didn't marry me out of lack of choices." I was holding back tears. Was I right in thinking that he was too good to be true?

"He truly is in love with you. He wanted us to have everything perfect when he brought you back. He was as nervous as a cat!" She laughed and sat back.

"You think he truly loves me?" I doubted it now.

"I do... Now see... I didn't want to tell you in fear that you would doubt his love for you. I'm telling you he does love you Lady Rebecca." She smiled tenderly.

"Here you are my love." William stood holding the door open and was dressed in his dark blue work jeans and white shirt. He looked so handsome.

"How about one for me love?" He bent down and whispered into Libby's ear.

"Of course William, right away." Libby popped up and went for a cup of coffee for him.

"I looked all over for you!" He took my hand in his and kissed it tenderly not taking his eyes off of mine. I looked at him searching his eyes. Was he fooling my heart into believing that he really loved me? He did tell me that he did not want to wait to have children? It was as if he chose me for lack of choice? My heart ached at the thought and if that were true then everything would be a lie...everything!

"What is wrong?" His eyes searched mine.

"I was just thinking about the rain and if it would hold off for us to go." Now that was a white lie.

"I could have the surrey ready then we could go no matter what." He smiled so sincerely. How could he be lying? I fought back tears that welled from the depth of my soul... Please God... Don't let him be lying!

"I would enjoy that..." I smiled looking at him and he sat back staring at me knowing that there was something not quite right.

"Have I told you how beautiful you look this morning?" His eyes looked tenderly into mine, but now I couldn't decide if he was telling the truth or not. I wanted to cry, but fought back the tears.

"What's wrong my love?" He held my hand tighter. I couldn't even speak.

"Rebecca, are you not well?" His look was truly convincing.

"Not really, I feel rather sick to my stomach." And I was, but more like sick hearted.

"Maybe we should put our ride off..."

"No... A little fresh air will probably do me good." I watched him sip his coffee. I wanted to know, but I need to be careful for Libby's sake. That would solve the mystery of why he wanted to marry me so fast.

"If you are sure?" He kissed my hand not taking his eyes off of me.

"I am." I glanced at Libby and she was frowning knowing the thoughts that were going through my mind. I just couldn't help it! What woman wouldn't be suspicious? I smiled at her and winked trying to ease her.

"If you will excuse me I shall see to the surrey then." He leaned down and kissed my lips tenderly but quickly and searched my eyes suspecting something was wrong. I could see it on his face.

"Don't be too long now." I smiled at him as best as I could. William strode out of the kitchen and Libby came to sit back down.

"Lady Rebecca, please… don't let what I've told you hinder you in how William feels about you. I know he truly loves you."

"Then why didn't he tell me about Lady Dawson?"

"I don't know, maybe he thought it was not important any more after he found you!" Her face was worried and her eyes looked so concerned.

"Libby, I shall not tell him anything about this. I give you my word, but the second I have the opportunity to ask him, I shall. You know he would have to be talking about it already."

"You wouldn't say anything?" Her face was full of worry. I laid my hand on hers and squeezed it.

"No, not a word." I smiled.

"I just love him and I would hate to see him hurting for something I couldn't hold my tongue about." I could see she was truly now regretting telling me anything. She shook her head and tears welled in her eyes.

"This is between you and me."

"I hope you don't let this eat you up." She wrung her hands.

"It won't. I do love him truly." The words on my lips were true, though I could not say his were.

I sat waiting for William to return thinking of what Libby had told me. I wished I had never heard of the name Lady Dawson. She did say that he did not want to marry her, so I do believe there is no love lost on his part there, but had he really felt God sent me to him? Was that a lie? I would have to chance asking him, providing there was an opportunity too ask him.

"Are you ready?" William broke my thoughts. I smiled into his handsome face. Now I planned on being who he knew me to be, he was my husband now and that would not change no matter what! He held up my coat.

"Yes… Let's go." William took my hand as I stood.

"Ladies…" He smiled at the staff in the kitchen and I winked at Libby as we went out the back kitchen door.

"Are you sure you feel up to this?" He lifted me up into the carriage without missing a breath.

"Yes…I feel much better already." I softly smiled as I settled in the soft leather seat.

"Thank goodness! I wasn't sure I was going to agree on this if you still felt the same." He walked to his side and sat next to me taking the reins in his hands. He clicked his tongue and the horses started a slow walk.

"This is really nice." I smiled and wrapped my arms around his big arm. I smiled up into his handsome face and he looked down with a soft look in his eyes.

"Ah, I love the way you look at me, Mrs. Andrews." He winked and kissed me.

"And I love to look at you, my love." I hugged his arm laying my head against his arm.

"You know, maybe it's too cold this morning for you?"

"No, I love how the cool air feels on my skin." I laughed.

"I do too." He slapped the reins for the horses to go faster.

To look at, William, and the way he treated me, it would appear that he did truly love me. I wished to myself again that Libby had never told me about Lady Dawson. I looked up from under my eyelashes to study him and he looked so happy. Was he? Does he really love me? Or was I just the next best choice or the only choice? I know it isn't fair to think this without him being able to defend himself, but if I said anything, he would ask who told me and I would not do that to Libby.

The small road went into an opening in the fields and then down a small hill back into the tree lined road. Most of the leaves were off the trees and the evergreens were about the only thing that had green left in them. I looked ahead up the road and saw a wild turkey running across. William laughed and looked down.

"Well, I see the one that got away from Vick!" He laughed again shaking his head as we turned down the small road to the right past a small gate that hung open, like it was expecting us today. My heartbeat was a little faster as we approached a small clearing. In front of us was a large gazebo painted white with lattice and vines growing up them holding on for the last of the good weather. He pulled the horse to a stop and leapt down walking to my side. He held out his hands as I turned to let them surround my waist. I put my hands on his shoulders and he gently lifted me down, my hands slid down his chest slowly, his eyes never wavered from mine.

"You know Lady Andrews… you shouldn't look at me that way."

"And you as well!" I laughed.

"Come… let me show you this wonderful spot!" He took my hand and wrapped it around his arm covering it with his hand.

"This is beautiful William!" I looked at the gazebo and then to my left. I saw a statue of an angel and a child. I looked to my right as saw a statue of a woman and a man…

"It's beautiful William!" There were white marble benches in front of each one.

"Come…" He led me to the Angel and child statue. They were playing together then child was laughing up at the angel. On the bench there were the names of his sister and brother.…

In Loving Memory of
My Beautiful Sister- Rachael Anne Andrews
And
My Brave Brother- Kyle Lee Andrews

"William, this is beautiful! Do the angel and the child look like your brother and sister?" I felt tears well in my heart at this act of utter respect, devotion and love.

"No, not really, but I wanted them to look happy and hope that they are playing with the angels and the small dog statue on the ground is for my brother, his dog." He bit his bottom lip and pulled me towards the other statue.

"This is for my parents." He stood and looked at the huge statue of two people, a man and woman, holding each other in an embrace staring into each other's eyes with love and a glass case with a ship in it with billowing sails was at the base of the statue.

In Loving Memory…
A true knight and my hero and father- William Elijah Andrews
My beautiful and loving mother- Annabelle Kay Andrews

In the middle of the two statues was a fountain with a smaller statue in the middle. We stepped up to them. There was a nest with a mother bird and father bird feeding three baby birds and another plaque reading a small verse.

In your arms they safely rest
While I go through this life and live my best

They wait for me as time passes by
Forever in my heart and forever by my side

"Oh, William..." I could not help what I was feeling and tears fell.

I cannot imagine all he must have gone through! I looked up into his face and saw tears welling in his eyes and could not help but to hold him in my arms.

"This is the most wonderful place!" I hugged him then looked up.

"I feel close to them here." He spoke softly in a whisper.

"What you must have endured!" I hugged him tightly and laid my head on his chest.

"Now you are my family, Rebecca, along with Cole, Mike, Aunt Marie and your mother. I love them already and you and, we will one day, Lord willing, have children to love and take care of adding to our family." He held me tightly.

"I do love you, William, and the more I find out about you the deeper I fall in love with you."

"Come…" His arm was still around me as we walked up the three steps of the gazebo feeling this was truly a place of love, it was everywhere!

"William, I can't believe that a man would do this for his family!" I was almost speechless.

"It was my way to grieve over the loss. I had to do something to honor them. Their bodies may not be here, but they are here every time I am here. Sometimes in the summer when everything is in bloom, I come here to feel close to them and always feel much better after I do. Now I have you to love and talk to, sharing everything with you. When we have our own children, my heart will be full and my life complete." He looked at me so full of love I thought I was going to burst.

"Oh, William… I hope I am with child now. I think that you will make a wonderful father and know why it's so important for you now."

"I could have married a woman from Madison this spring, but I didn't love her. I've known her forever and she, to me, is like a child still. When I met you, I knew you were the one to make all my hopes and dreams come true."

"You were going to marry this spring?" I looked up at him astonished at the fact that he admitted this to me so freely. Now I didn't have to wait! Thank you God!

"Yes, I didn't want to do it, but I needed someone to have my children. People have arranged marriages and do it all the time. For me, it was not something I was looking forwards too. Lady Dawson is her name. She is a beautiful woman and sweet, but not very intelligent, rather simple. I didn't have a thing in common with her and she was more worried about her dress and hair than anything, not that she is vain, but she likes to dress up all the time as if she was at a ball."

"Why would you consider marrying her then?"

"To be honest, and I do not mean this in a cruel way, but I could control her and she would only require a small amount of my time." He looked down and I could see the obvious agony of this confession.

"That doesn't sound like you at all William." I frowned.

"It's not me at all, but the other choices were not going to do me any good either"

"And what were they?" He had other options?

"There was a woman from Wellington, Susan Nash, and she is spoiled, another one of my Brother Knight's daughters from Port Christi. She is a beauty, but not very nice and very demanding." He looked down at my hands as he took them.

"So you found me and married me to avoid…"

"NO! Rebecca… I fell in love with you and that is why I know God sent you to me. I don't think I could have gone through with any of them… I would have probably died a lonely old man."

"Really, William?" My heart leapt for joy.

"Yes, my love. Like I said, I fell in love with you right away and knew I had to make you mine." His hand went to my cheek as he leaned down kissing my lips tenderly. Thank you God, I thought!

"Rebecca… I do want children and to spend the rest of my life raising them and loving you. I hope that you are with child now as well, but if you are not, it will be such a traumatic and insufferable job seeing that you do become with child…" He smiled a sensual grin and winked as a deep rumbling laugh came from his lips.

"I love you, William." I pulled his lips to mine as the rain started to come down again.

"Hurry!" He took my hand and we ran to the surrey. William lifted me up.

"It's too cold to get wet and stay out here." He laughed and it was colder.

"Will it snow soon?"

336

"It usually doesn't before the first of the year." He smiled and took the reins heading back to the estate house.

While we warmed up in front of the fire and had a cup of coffee, we heard mother's voice. They were back from town and most likely because of the rain. They had a lot of packages and boxes delivered.

"What in the world?" I laughed at Aunt Marie. Her hat drooped over her face dripping and her dress was wet. Hannah covered her mouth with her fingers hiding a laugh as well.

"A carriage splashed her as we went for the carriage." Carla laughed.

"Are you alright?" William took her cold hand.

"Yes... I am fine, just damp. And on that I think I shall go take a warm bath and rest a bit." She smiled walking up the stairs.

"Rebecca, we bought a bunch of things for our business endeavor. I know this is a wonderful idea." Carla smiled and looked into Cole's eyes.

"I will feel a lot better when this is all settled. Having all my favorite ladies in one place will be less taxing. Frankly, I'm worn out!" Cole laughed. I could tell he had had his fill with shopping. Cole shook his coat and gave it to Jules. Jules smiled at William knowing he wanted to laugh at Aunt Marie at least she was not crying.

"Coffee will be sent to the parlor." Jules winked at William.

"Thank you, Jules." He offered his arm to mother and I, Cole and Carla followed.

"Rebecca and I got caught in the rain a little while ago as well. I took her to the memorial for my family." William smiled down at mother.

"Memorial?" Mother looked at me then William.

"Oh, Mother, he has statues, a gazebo, a water fountain and so many flowers in memory of his family. I have never seen such a wonderful thing in all my life!" I smiled at mother.

"I knew you would make a fine son William." Mother patted his hand.

"Well, since there was no recovery of any of my family, I had to do something for them... for myself... for closure." William handed mother and me a cup of coffee.

"William dear, I don't think you could have done any more." Her eyes welled in tears. William looked down at her and stared.

"Mother Glenn, you are more than I could ever hope for in a mother."

"Mother Glenn? Why my boy! You make me sound like an old duck! Please for mercy's sake, just call me Mother. Heavens!" She laughed as we all did, though it's proper to call her Mother Glenn.

"I... well thank you, Mother." He leaned down and kissed her cheek.

"That's better." Mother sipped her coffee.

"Cole, did you buy anything?" I smiled at him with a knowing look.

"No." He was so quiet. I wonder what was wrong with him.

"Cole is tired of shopping I think." Carla laughed.

"That I am and I hope you ladies are too. I think your town will have to restock." Cole laughed.

"Cole we weren't that bad! Honestly!" Mother scolded.

"I will have to rent a wagon from my brother-in-law to get all your purchases back home." Cole laughed a thunderous laugh.

"Really, Cole!" Carla laughed.

"I think your business endeavor is quite a brilliant idea and you will be very successful." William winked at mother.

We all relaxed as we all listened to what they purchased and their ideas about the merger. We spent most of the morning and through lunch planning on how to put their plans into action.

Jon Luke entered the parlor with a solemn look on his face.

"A word, William..." He barely smiled and looked at all of us. He was dressed in uniform. William stepped out of the parlor and came back in with a solemn look on his face as well. I knew this wasn't good.

"Rebecca?" He held his hand out and I went with him out into the corridor.

"I have to leave. A situation has transpired and demands my immediate attention, but I will return as soon as the situation is under control." He took my hands in his raising them to his lips kissing them. I did not like the look in his eyes at all. My heart started to race.

"Leave? But where?" I tried to swallow but could not, for my heart was now in my throat.

"I cannot tell you. You must trust me." His words were absolute.

"Are... you... in danger?" Tears welled in my eyes.

"Rebecca, I will return soon, you have my word." He held the look of a warrior as if he was going to battle.

"How long will you be gone?" I pursed my lips together knowing I had to be brave for him.

"Two days, three at the most. Come! I must hurry." He led me up to our room walking fast!

"William, I'm frightened." I admitted that, but I was more than just frightened.

338

"Rebecca, I will be alright." He kept up his pace as we entered our room closing the door behind us. He walked to his wardrobe and took out his uniform.

"William…" I covered my lips with my fingertips just watching him ready himself.

"Rebecca…" He stopped, as he was about to shuck his pants off and took me into his arms.

"Everything will be fine… you have my word." He softly and tenderly kissed my lips. Tears fell down my cheeks.

"Then do what you must." I took a deep breath mustering up all the courage I had.

"That's my girl!" He smiled with a proud nod.

He kissed my forehead and finished undressing pulling on tight black pants that were form fitting and a black tight shirt that hugged his upper body like a glove, then a black tunic. I had never seen this uniform before. The tunic had a crest on it in gold and the trim was gold as well. He girded his waist with a black thick leather belt that had a scabbard attached for a sword and a sheath for a knife. My heart was hammering so hard at my ribs that I could not breathe. He slid on tall black boots, then a dark cloak which he did not put on but just draped over his arm and grabbed black gloves and tucked them into his belt. He held out his hand to me and I took it trembling.

"I'll be fine, Rebecca, I love you." His lips covered mine and he pulled away.

"I know… God is with you." I felt the over whelming need to pray.

"Come… I must go." He grabbed my hand firmly.

We went down to the main floor and into his weapons room and I watched him take his sword and put it into the scabbard and a dagger in the sheath. He took out another dagger and slipped it into a pocket in his boot. I nervously licked my dry lips watching and trying to stay calm. This is what he did, who he was and I have to believe in him!

He went to the desk and took out an envelope, with a deep breath he looked at me and walked slowly to me handing me the sealed envelope.

"Rebecca, if something should go wrong…" He stared deeply into my eyes.

"No! Don't even say that William!" I cried.

"Rebecca, you have to listen to me, this is very important!" He put his hands on my shoulders and the look on his face very serious!

"Oh, William, I don't like this." Tears fell down my cheeks unceasingly.

"I know, but you must be brave and listen to me." His eyes were dark.

"Alright." I tried to calm myself knowing that he wouldn't be doing this if it wasn't! My insides were sick with my stomach rolling.

"Now… if something should go wrong… I know it won't, but if it does… Take this envelope to a man in Madison… to a Lord James Byron. He will know what to do. You must trust me and him if it comes to that. Do not open it, if you do, it won't be worth anything and be void."

"William, I love you… and will do whatever you ask of me." Tears flowed and he wiped my cheeks with his thumb.

"I love you with all my heart and soul. You are the reason I will be back, you have my word." He kissed me tenderly and held me in his arms.

"William… we must leave now." Jon Luke appeared in the door breathless.

"Rebecca, I love you." He stared into my eyes deeply not taking them off of mine. They were talking to my heart, my soul and saying things that only my heart could understand. He was etching my face in his memory and on his heart, as I was his. He closed his eyes and took a deep breath then kissed me deeply.

"I love you and will be waiting for you my love." Tears still flowed down my cheeks.

He kissed me again and took my hand in his as we quickly walked to the door. My hands were moist and shaking and felt William squeeze it gently looking down at me with a slight smile. His eyes were saying I love you and trust in me. Jon Luke walked out in front of us. Their black horses stood ready and waiting. I saw Diablo and trembled as he stood raking his foot on the ground and snorting like a bull as if he could sense the seriousness of the matter at hand.

"I will be back in two days… two days. Victor and Nick are here and close by. Try not to worry." He kissed my lips once more and in one powerful move he swung upon his horse. He pulled the leather tie out of his hair and tossed it to me. I ran up to him putting my hands on his tense thighs and handed him my handkerchief. I wanted him to take something of mine with him. He held it to his nose and breathed in. William bent down and wrapped his arm around my waist kissing me hard and deep, then released me shouting to Diablo.

"Caballo a todo correr!" Jon Luke and William rode out not looking back. The horses' feet sounded like thunder as they raced off into the night. I stood on the threshold and watched my love disappear into the dark... and my heart.

"Rebecca, was that William?" Carla came to my side taking my arm.

"Yes." I whispered.

"Where are they going?" I stood staring at the road with tears running down my face.

"Rebecca?" I heard Cole's voice rumble behind me as I felt his hands on my shoulders.

"Sweetheart?" Mother took my other arm.

"William had to leave." It was all I could get out with this numbness I felt.

"Rebecca, where did he go?" Cole turned me towards him. I looked up batting tears away.

"I... don't know!"

"What did he say? What is that?" Cole looked down at the envelope in my hand.

"Rebecca, let's go into the house." Carla took the lead and walked me to the parlor. We sat on the divan and Cole handed me a glass of water.

"What's in the envelope?" Cole knelt in front of me. I took a deep breath and a sip of water.

"William was called out on some sort of mission and he couldn't tell me anything, but he gave me this envelope and said not to open it." My words were nothing but a whisper.

"That doesn't make any sense!" Mother's face was washed with worry.

"It's.... it's..." Tears streamed from my eyes.

"It's what?" Cole tilted my face to his.

"It's in case something... goes wrong." I didn't even want to speak the words.

"What?!!!" Mother gasped.

"If something should happen to William, I'm to take this to Madison, to Lord Byron's." I held the envelope to my chest and sobbed.

"Nothing's going to happen to William..." Cole sat next to me and put his arms around me hugging me to his chest.

"How long will he be gone? Did he say?" Carla still had my hand I hers.

"Two days... two days." That seemed so long.

"Then whatever it is, it must be close." Cole stood looking deep in thought.

"Not to worry, Rebecca. He knows what he is doing and he is strong and experienced with whatever it is or they wouldn't have called for his services." Cole nodded.

"Rebecca... William knows what he's doing and I'm sure he expects you to believe in him as well." Mother smiled softly.

"You're right. I do believe in him and I know he will be home in two days just like he said. I must trust him and believe in him!" I sat up taller believing in William.

I asked for everyone to be in prayer tonight for William, Jon Luke and whoever was involved with the mission, God was with them.

"Milady, dinner is served." Jules smiled and winked at me.

"Thank you, Jules... Shall we?" I stood and straightened my skirts and went to dinner just as if William would want me to.

Though I wasn't very hungry, I ate a little to show them I was confident in William. No one talked too much, though they tried to talk about 'other' things. However, they didn't see what I saw in William's eyes and they didn't feel his heart thunder under my hand. They didn't feel the last kiss he gave me.

I fought my fear throughout dinner and the tears threatened with every thought. It was a battle of another kind tonight and I'm going to pray my heart out for him and whoever was involved, that they all returned unharmed, safe and without delay. I took another deep breath and tried to enjoy the conversation. I tried to contribute to it as best as I could, but all I could do is think about William and fear crept through my body like the plague.

I hope William wasn't worrying about me and distracted. All I wanted to do was take a long bath and go to bed. The faster I do, the sooner it will be tomorrow.

Cole and Carla went for a walk after dinner. Mother and Aunt Marie went to the library to read and I finally excused myself and went to my room, starting the bath water, undressing and then sliding into the hot water. I poured some of William's oil in the water and breathed him in. I know it was silly, but I needed to feel close to him.

Please Lord in Heaven, keep him safe. All of them! What if he is worried about me? What if he was worried about me being here without anyone else here watching over the place? Well, there's Victor and Nicholas. They are close by. William would not leave this place unprotected or us for that matter. I trust him and if there was real danger to his home, he would not leave at all. He looked so deeply at me and his

342

eyes said to trust him and believe. So I am and that's all there is to that! Yes, he will return back to me safe and sound. I took another deep breath and blew it out.

"Rebecca dear..." Betty called through the door.

"I'm soaking..." I called back to her.

"I brought up some tea and cookies for you. I thought you could use some company." She called out and I could tell she knew I was afraid.

"Yes... I would love to have a nice chat. I'll only be another moment." I called to Betty as I hurried to finish my bath. I did need to talk to Betty. She knows William so well and I'm sure she would be able to settle my nerves or answer my questions. I dried off and dressed for bed wrapping my robe around me I walked out to see her smiling reassuring face.

"Oh, Betty... I..." Tears began to fall as I walked to her. She stood and gathered me into her arms.

"Shhh, it's alright now... He'll be just fine. William has done this many, many, many times." Betty whispered in my ear. I was so glad she of all people was here. I needed her.

"Betty, I'm frightened." It felt good to admit that.

"I know my dear, but you also must know that William loves you more than life itself and will do whatever he has to do to get home to you. You are his reason to survive now." She uttered softly.

"Is he in danger?" I whispered as we sat on the divan.

"William is in danger every time he leaves the estate for any reason, but try not to worry, he is doing his job and he does it well. He is the best of the best." She smiled in confidence.

"But, Betty... what if something happens to him?" I cried.

"Now see here! William would want you to believe in him and believe that you will be here waiting for him with a strong resolve." Betty patted my hand and then handed me a cup of tea.

"I know, but I have never been through something like this before." I wiped my cheeks.

"I know, but I'm sure this, whatever it is, requires his personal attention. He has an entire legion of guards to protect him."

"Do you know what kind of mission he is on? I mean you have been with him so long, you know how serious it is by the way he acts or dresses?" I was still shaking, but feeling a little calmer.

"Well, what did Jon Luke say? Did you hear?" Betty sipped her tea.

"Jon Luke came in the parlor and called out William and then he called me out. We hurried up to our bedchambers for him to change."

"What did Jon Luke have on?"

"He was wearing a dark blue uniform and had a sword and dagger in his scabbard." I watched her reaction, but she didn't show too much concern.

"And William?" Betty sipped her tea again.

"He changed into a black uniform, a tunic with a crest on it and got his sword and dagger as well."

"Oh…I see." Her look was concerned this time as her brows furrowed. She sat deep in thought for a few minutes before saying anything.

"When William and Jon Luke wear their uniforms, it's important. When William wears his black tunic, there is reason to believe that he must be unseen, so to me that means that he has a very important job to do." She sipped her tea not looking into my eyes.

"Betty, he is in danger isn't he?" I stared into her eyes.

"Yes." She looked down deep in thought.

"We must pray for his and the other's safety with all our hearts." Betty smiled softly as not to show her own fear for William, but I knew she was just as afraid as I was.

"Yes, I'll agree with that." She looked heart filled at me.

"What is it, Betty? What aren't you telling me?" I felt there was something she wasn't saying.

"Well… did he give you and envelope?" She hesitated in asking.

"Yes…" I pulled it out from my dress pocket holding it to my heart. Now my heart started pounding harder and I felt fear flood my entire being.

"Then my dear, it is a dangerous mission and he'll need all the prayers you can muster up!" Tears welled into her eyes now and worry washed over her face like a veil.

"Oh, Betty! I'm so afraid for him." Tears fell from my eyes.

"I know how you feel. Every time he leaves, I too, am afraid." She admitted finally.

"Do you know what is in this? He told me not to open it, but to take it to Lord Byron."

"No I don't, but Jules and I have held that damn thing more times than I care to." She looked angry.

"What do you suppose it reads?" Tears fell down my cheek harder and my heart ached like it never has before.

"I believe it is his Last Will and Testament." She took my hand in hers.
"No!" I laid it on the table as if it burned my fingers.

"Rebecca, he loves you and because he does, he will fight his best battle to get back to you. I think that is his best weapon, his love for you... something to fight for." She sat her cup down and hugged me.

"We must believe that God is with him and that God wouldn't have given you each other to just take one away." She was crying as well.

"Betty, stay with me tonight."

"Of course my dear..." She held me close. Betty loves William as much as I do.

"Here let's have a little more tea." She refreshed our cups. I felt the urge to pray and slid off the divan sinking to my knees and prayed soon feeling Betty next to me.

I don't know how long we both prayed, but I was going to pray until he walked through the door. My heart cried out to the Father for William's protection and for the other's. I prayed that he would give me the strength and courage for whatever was ahead. I prayed for that peace beyond understanding that would tell me William and the others were safe. When I said Amen, I opened my eyes and found mother, Hannah, Aunt Marie and Carla with us praying. I sat back on the divan and stared into the fire. Soon all of us embraced each other, feeling their strength. Soon we agreed to be strong and believe, we went back to the sitting room to wait with renewed faith.

"Rebecca, I know William will return unharmed." Mother hugged me tightly.

"Thank you everyone." I wiped my tears and took a deep breath deciding that now. I must be strong for William.

"I'll have more tea made up." Betty stood smiling a soft loving smile.

"Thank you, Betty. I don't know what I would have done without you." I hugged her.

"I love you too, Rebecca." She kissed my cheek and left the room.

"Oh, Rebecca!" Aunt Marie cried out.

"It's alright Aunt Marie. I know William and the others will be fine." I hugged Aunt Marie tightly.

"Now we must believe and wait for them to return. Where's Cole?" I looked at Carla then mother.

"Cole? He's... I don't know where Cole is... Carla?" Mother looked at Carla.

"He went for a walk saying he wanted to talk to Victor about some horses for a ride tomorrow, then went out to the stables." Carla softly smiled wiping her tears.

"You don't think he…" Mother gasped and covered her lips with her fingers.

"No, I don't think he would do anything foolish…would he?" I looked at mother.

"Sweet Jesus…" Mother gasped.

I stood up and knowing the look on mother's face, Aunt Marie's, Hannah's and Carla's and my thought's. Grabbing my coat, mother called after me as I ran down the hall. I had to talk to Victor myself!

I ran out into the dark toward the stables and down the dark path until I saw a faint light. At the stable, I swung open the door and could hear the horses' soft whinnies and shuffling of the hay. I lit a lantern and found my way to the stairs that lead to the upper part of the stables.

"Don't move!" A deep voice ordered a warning from behind me, but I knew it was Victor's.

"It's me…Rebecca." I breathlessly spoke as my heart pounded out the air from my lungs.

"Rebecca… Lady Rebecca?" Victor walked around facing me. His white shirt was unbuttoned hanging down untucked from his pants he was pointing a gun at me with a look of shock on his face. He lowered the rifle.

"What in the hell are you doing sneaking around here at this hour? I could have killed you! Don't you know this hour is serious and we are all on alert?" He grabbed my arm.

"Stop that! Yes, I'm very aware of the seriousness of this!" I pulled away from his grip. He took the lantern and turned it up for more light.

"What are you doing here?" His eyes were dark under his furrowed brow.

"Have you seen my brother Cole?" I tried to catch my breath.

"Yes, he was here about an hour ago asking about the horses and which was the fastest and the slowest."

"Dear God!"

"What?" Victor demanded.

"Are any of them missing?" I tried to remain calm.

"Not that I know of…" He glanced up and down the aisle.

"No they're all here, why?"

"Are there any horses out in the corral that are fast?"

346

"Sure… But… Damn! You don't think he…" Victor eyes went wide as he turned towards the tack room.

Victor had turned wide eyed looking like he'd seen a ghost.

"A saddle is missing." He frowned turning quickly running out the door to the corral and I followed him.

"Damn it! Talon is gone! Damn it to hell!" He stormed back into the stable.

"He went to find William?"

"No, he went to find Lord McCray." Victor's face was full of anger.

"Why?" My heart pounded.

"Lord McCray ordered this mission, William's last mission." He spit on the ground.

"But, why would Cole go to find Gabe?"

"I told him that Gabe knew where and what William had to do. Gabe always gave the missions out to the commanders and if there was a problem with a mission, he'd call for William to make sure it was carried out so that the mission would be successful. Damn it! I should have never said anything and I should have known that he was one of those men to think they're the answer to all the problems." Victor yelled pacing back and forth raking his hand through his hair.

"Cole would never interfere…He would…" I tried to explain but Victor spun around and grabbed my shoulders and was hurting me.

"Listen! Gabe McCray won't tell Cole anything. He's probably trying to protect you!" Victor shouted. His eyes were dark.

"By going to Gabe? I…I don't understand!" I pulled away from him.

"Just pray that Cole doesn't go borrowing any trouble trying to be a hero. That is a good way to get you killed." His eyes were even darker and full of anger.

"What are you saying?" My heart was about to leap out of my chest, Cole in trouble?

"I'm saying that Cole best not try to find William… William could end up killing the wrong man."

"WHAT!" I gasped. My heart was in my throat choking me.

"William isn't far away and there are men all over the area looking for those infiltrators that were spotted in the area. If Cole is headed to find McCray for answers, well he could be mistaken for the man they're looking for or the other men may mistake him for William or one of his men. The orders were to shoot first and ask questions later." Victor raked his hand through his hair again.

"It's only an hour away to McCray... Cole could be..." I couldn't even say the words.

"Yeah, there or dead!" He suddenly looked directly into my face full of rage.

Dead? Please Dear God NO!

"Now, please... get back to the house. I'll have Nick watch over the place and go find your damn brother, but for God's sake, do me a favor please?" He was being downright nasty.

"Yes?" Tears rolled down my cheeks now afraid for Cole.

"Don't leave the damn house again! You almost got yourself killed as well!" He rolled his eyes cursing under his breath and then abruptly pivoted on his heels storming up the stairs, I ran back to the house. The nerve of that man! Who does he think he is? 'My damn brother' indeed! Lord, please protect my brother! William would never let harm come to Cole's mother, Aunt Marie, Hannah, Carla and Betty stood in the entry as I ran up the steps.

"Good heavens, Rebecca! What is it?" Mother put her arm around me.

"Victor thinks Cole went to find McCray. He is going to have Nick watch over the place while he tries to find Cole. Oh God, Carla!" I looked at her and she was standing so still and so pale.

"Cole...Gone?" She whispered.

"Victor will find him." I looked at Betty and gave her a grave look.

"Oh No! Not Cole too!" Mother grabbed the back of the divan and Jules came to the rescue and helped her to the parlor.

"Mother, it will be alright. It won't take too long to reach Oak Grove and I'm sure Cole is there."

"Rebecca?" A deep voice boomed across the room startling me.

"Rebecca, are you and your family alright?" Nick was dressed in his uniform and his eyes dark with worry. He stepped closer.

"Yes, Mother just felt faint but we're all fine." I was trying to be brave for William.

"Rebecca, stay inside. I'll have the staff check all the doors and answer for no one. I mean no one!" He was serious seeing warning in his eyes. This was worse than Betty ever thought. She tried to cover a gasp.

"Alright... have you heard anything?"

"No, it's too soon, but I will inform you as soon as I know." He tried to smile.

"Thank you, Nick." He nodded then shut the parlor door.

348

I knew there wasn't going to be any sleep for anyone, this promised to be a very long night.

"Now, let's try to calm down and trust William and his men. For now, I think I shall go to the kitchen and see if Libby has anything that might suit everyone, tea or coffee anyone?" What did Cole think he was going to do?

There was another knock on the parlor door.

"Rebecca, its Nick…"

"Come in." I called to him taking a glass of water to mother.

"This is Bethany De Spain. Her brother was called to serve tonight and William sent her to come here." She stood with huge blue eyes that looked so afraid. Her auburn hair was in disarray and her dress was dirty.

"Of course, come in." I held out my arms to the young woman.

"Was there any other word?" I looked with hope at Nick.

"No, I'm sorry."

"Thank you, Nick." I smiled softly at him and he closed the door as he left.

"Bethany, was it? Come and sit." I gilded her to the divan.

"My name is Bethany De Spain and you must be William's new bride?"

"Yes, I am and this is my mother, Martha Glenn, My Aunt Marie Brice and my dear friend Carla Taylor, Hannah Carson and Betty Maze."

"It's a pleasure to meet you all and I'm sorry for the intrusion. My brother and I were on our way to Winchester for a holiday and we ran into William." Her eyes welled with tears.

"Here, here. Everything will be alright." I put my arm around her as Betty poured a cup of tea for her.

"Thank you for allowing me to stay here with all of you. You must be use to all this?"

"No, not really… This is the first time this has happened to me. William and I were just married."

"Yes, I heard he swept you off your feet." Her eyes held a small glimmer of sadness.

"That he did and before I even realized what had happened!" I smiled.

"I heard that the guards were like that." She sipped her tea and looked down at her ruined dress.

"Bethany, you look about my size, would you care to take a bath and borrow one of my dresses?"

"That would be wonderful! I'm afraid that my dress is beyond repair." She sighed.

"What happened that you got this way?" I looked at the torn ruffle on the bottom of her dress.

"My brother and I were heading towards Winchester and some men flew in front of us and down the road spooking our horses. I was thrown and my brother's horse reared up almost throwing him. That's when we saw William and one of his men. William told one of his men to escort me to his estate and took my brother with him. Everything happened so fast! On the way here William's man saw another rider and hurried me to the estate for my safety and pursued the man on the horse. The ride here was so fast!" Bethany sipped her tea.

"The man on the horse must have been Cole!" I knew I was right.

"Well we are all safe and warm! God willing, so is William and your brother. What is your brother's name?"

"Daniel... Daniel De Spain." She sat up taller and proud. Her chin had a darling cleft in it.

"I'm sure he is a brave man if he is in the guard." Mother smiled.

"Thank you for saying that. I'm his youngest sister. We hale from Ida Grove. You see, my birthday was last week and my brother offered to take me with him to Winchester. I wanted a couple of new dresses and some bath oil. Ida Grove doesn't have much." She frowned.

"Well it sounds like you have a wonderful brother." Hannah smiled.

"I do and he treats me well. He even spoils me with things he brings from all over. He calls me his Beth." Bethany said that as if that was the last time her brother Daniel would call her Beth.

"It will be an honor to meet him when he returns." I smiled as she sipped her tea.

"Do you think he will be alright?" She looked down into her cup.

"Of course! He's with William isn't he?" I tried to be positive with her.

"Yes and I know William! You're a blessed woman for capturing his heart! I have been in love with him since I was a small girl." She shyly smiled.

"I'm sure he adored you as well."

"He brought me a horse for my sixteenth birthday and honestly, I thought one day I would marry him." She frowned and added,

"But I'm pleased to see he married someone such as you." She smiled.

"Well thank you, Bethany."

"If you don't mind Carla, I would love that bath and to borrow a dress?" She smiled at Carla and stood.

350

"Alright, let's get you in a room close to us and you can stay there until your brother comes back. After that, we'll all sit and chat some more. I myself could use a change of nightgowns." I looked at my own soiled robe and gown.

"That sounds wonderful. I don't think I could ever sleep tonight." She smiled wearily.

"I know our men will be just fine and I plan on getting a few winks, but call me if you need me. I think you younger gals can stand less sleep." Aunt Marie and Hannah stood next to mother.

"We'll be fine, Mother. I will call if I hear any news, get some rest." She yawned and checked her timepiece.

"No wonder I am tired... it's three in the morning! Where did the time go?" She shook her head and walked arm in arm with Hannah and Aunt Marie. Carla and Bethany went up to the spare room. Betty and I followed.

"Betty, I'm going to freshen up and then make more coffee, why don't you try to rest?"

"I think I will do just that, though my boy is out there I will try, but don't be surprised to see me in a little while. We'll make some breakfast." She smiled walking out of the room with me on her skirts.

I went to my room and washed up and changed into a reserved blue day dress and then returned back down stairs and to the kitchen. I had coffee and found Libby's dough for rolls and popped them into the oven. I wasn't the least tired. Soon Bethany and Carla came down.

"Oh it smells heavenly! I'm famished!" Bethany smiled licking her lips.

"Libby's rolls are the best!" Carla laughed.

"Coffee?" I smiled feeling better about having Bethany here too. She took my mind off of William and was trying to be so brave in fear for her brother, who I knew was her entire world.

"What's going on in here at this hour?" Libby wiped the sleep out of her eyes.

"William went on a mission and Cole is somewhere, God only knows. This is Bethany, her brother is with William. We can't sleep." I tried to sum it all up.

"I understand and I smell my rolls and fresh coffee. May I join you?" Libby gave her a heart filled look and softly smiled.

"Of course Libby... I suspect Betty won't be able to sleep and will be down shortly." Knowing it probably was the truth.

"Rebecca, try not to worry about William. He will be just fine. He's a fine warrior." She poured herself a cup of coffee and sat at the table with us.

"Libby, William said two days, would it be just two days?"

"If he said two days, then two days it will be." She softly smiled, but her eyes said more than her words. I could see concern in them.

"I believe in him and know he will be back soon and so will the rest of the men safe and sound." I nodded my head. I was trying to be just as strong as Libby's convictions.

"That they will and we will make a special dinner of it!" She smiled at me nodding.

"I'm worried about Cole." Carla stood by the door looking down.

"Oh, Carla, of course you are. William will not let any harm come to him. Victor will see to that as well. I'm sure he is safe as we speak." He was not just my brother, but Carla's everything. I knew Cole had bought her a ring and so far has not given it to her. I could only wonder what was keeping him.

"Carla, how are you and Cole?" I smiled trying not to look too concerned.

"Wonderful!" She tried to smile but I could tell there was something else bothering her as well. She looked down into her cup.

"What's wrong then?" I took her hand.

"I think he is going to ask me to marry him soon."

"That's wonderful, Carla... right?" I looked into her eyes.

"Yes, but I think he is afraid." She looked up at me hoping that I could help her with the reasons why it was taking him so long.

"Cole has been very careful not to let his heart go to anyone. He just wants to be sure. I know he's in love with you Carla. It's in his eyes every time he looks at you." I took her hand.

"He has told me that he loves me... but..." Tears welled in her eyes.

"But what?" I could feel her heart crying.

"Well, honestly? I think he's afraid I'll say no." She took a deep breath.

"Why would he think that?" I was shocked and did not expect her to say that!

"I told him that I was planning never to marry, but that was when we first met." Tears fell from her cheeks.

"No, I'm sure that he wants to ask you and he knows you love him doesn't he? I mean when he says he loves you, you tell him you love him?"

"Yes, every time, I just wished he'd hurry up!" She looked at Libby and blushed.

Betty did come down as expected and we all poured our energy into cooking breakfast for everyone. I did find out Bethany was my age, twenty six, and ready to meet someone before it was too late as she said she would be dubbed an old maid. Which she thought she was already! I tried to tell her there was hope for us old maids and I was a good example that even old maids got married. We all laughed about that. Carla was even older than I so Bethany said there was truly hope for her yet and she was not giving up! The look on Carla's face was priceless and then we all really laughed.

The day wore on at a snail's pace. There was no word from anyone, but we did notice that there were more guards on the grounds than I had thought. We'd offer coffee and cake and sandwiches with soup to them for it was cold today and a thick blanket of gray clouds that threatened rain blocked the sun. If it got any colder it could snow I heard one guard say.

Mother, Hannah and Aunt Marie fussed over them as if they were family and that kept them busy. I knew mother and Carla were just as worried about Cole as I was and about William.

We had not heard from Victor yet and Carla was starting to really worry as I was. I didn't let on to her that I too, was very worried. I wished Mike had not gone back to the lumberyard wishing he were here with us.

We ate dinner in silence. No one ate much of anything and just picked at our food. I had taken a long hot bath and dressed for bed after we heard, from Nick, that there was still no word.

One of the guards thought he heard gunfire but wasn't sure for a thunderstorm was on the way. That thought alone was enough to set me on edge and everyone for that matter. I needed to feel William's arms around me, to see his face, to hear his deep voice say my name, I needed him home! Tears fell as I threw another log on the fire and sat on the divan sipping a brandy and tea. I was so tired but still could not sleep, besides I knew I couldn't. I was waiting for him to walk through the door any minute, with his hair in disarray, falling across his broad shoulders and taking me into his arms.

Please hurry home with Cole and Daniel! I laid my head back on the divan and stared into the fire. I could almost feel him. I closed my eyes and could smell his scent. I took a deep breath in, Oh, William... Come home… Please hurry… I love you! I need you so much! I floated off thinking of William and his smile. It seems almost real that I had to open my eyes.

"WILLIAM!!!" I cried out blinking my eyes to make sure he was real!

"Rebecca, my love!" He picked me up in his arms hugging me so tightly. I pulled away and put my hands on each side of his face.

"You're home! You're home!" I pulled him to my lips kissing him.

"Rebecca." He uttered as he kissed me tenderly.

"Oh, William, I was so worried!" He pulled me down on the divan keeping me in his lap.

"I know you were, but I had no time to prepare you."

"I was fine, what about Cole and Daniel?"

"I shall tell you about Cole first. He was heading to Oak Grove and I saw him and stopped him. He was half way there and he said he was going to see McCray to get some answers. He and I got into an argument…" He looked down at my hands.

"He was trying to help and almost got himself killed! If he had gone another mile up the road, Hesston would have taken him. He did however help in the capture…"

"How?" I looked into his eyes that looked blue green now.

"He rode ahead of us and five men tried to ambush him. We surrounded them and took them all. Cole lay on the ground and we attacked, but he stood just as one of Hesston's men was about to put a sword in my back and your brother hit him like I never seen anyone hit another man before! His fists were like iron!" He shook his head and laughed.

"Then what happened?" Cole saved William?

"After Cole hit him, he was on the ground unconscious and Cole tied him up while we took the others down, but not before…" He furrowed his brows and frowned and his eyes went instantly dark.

"Before what?" I held my breath.

"Daniel was injured with a sword and… I'm afraid it's pretty bad."

"Oh No! Bethany! Does she know?" My heart hammered against my ribs.

"No, she's still asleep, I'll tell her when she awakes."

"Where is he now?" Tears welled in my eyes.

"We took him to Winchester. He's at the doc's. We stayed with him till the Doc said that there was nothing else he could do and that Daniel was in God's hands." I saw pain in his eyes.

"Was anyone else hurt?" I wiped my tears.

"No, not that I'm aware of, but there were other guards in different places under Colonel McInnis' command. I haven't gotten a report from him yet. We'll go to Winchester and take Bethany to see Daniel... Cole's with Carla now." I wasn't surprised.

"I think she will have the news you have been waiting to hear when you see her." He smiled a breath from my lips.

"He's going to ask her tonight?" I whispered lost in his eyes and drowning fast.

"No, this morning, it's six o'clock in the morning." He stared into my eyes for a long time.

"I'm so happy your safe my husband! You must be exhausted!"

"Yes, I'm very tired, but I must take Bethany to Daniel. I need to bathe first."

He stood taking me with him to the washroom, starting the water. I helped him undress and get into the bath. He took a scrub brush and soaped it up and then scrubbed his hands. I saw blood on them and did not want to know whose it was. I stepped over to him and took the sponge and wet his hair and washed it for him.

"That feels... wonderful." He relaxed as I scrubbed, then rinsed his hair off. He relaxed for a bit while I got his clothes out as he asked me to. I laid them on the bed and went back to find him asleep. I took the sponge and washed the blood off his chest and he opened his eyes smiling.

"You know you could... join me." He grinned.

"I think another time." He saw the blood on the sponge.

"I'm sorry... of course." He frowned.

"Next time..." I kissed his wet lips.

"Yes, next time." He stood in the tub as I took fresh water to rinse him off. I saw his ribs were bruised and he had cuts on his arms and legs.

"William, your arms and legs!"

"Oh, they're mere scratches, but you can take care of them if you'd like." His smile was sultry and his voice was full of desire.

"Oh you!" I laughed.

"Yes... me." He laughed as well.

I threw him the towel and he dried wrapping it around himself and went out to dress, then we made our way to the dining room. Mother, Hannah and Aunt Marie were already there drinking coffee. When they saw William they about spilled their coffee getting to him and hugging him, tears fell from their eyes.

"William, you're home!" Mother cried.

"I'm fine and so is Cole."

"What about Bethany's brother?"

We all sat down and the servants served us more coffee and breakfast while William told what had happened. They were hanging on his every word and as he finished up the story, Carla and Cole walked in arm and arm. Yes, by the glow radiating from her face, she had something to announce. Something she could not ever admit, she was glowing and so was Cole.

"Good morning everyone." Cole smiled looking at William, then mother.

"Oh son, I am so glad to see your handsome face." She hurried to him and hugged him as well.

"Yes and so was my fiancé." He waited for mother's reaction and then it hit.

"YOUR WHAT?" She said as if she heard wrong.

"I said so did my fiancé." He laughed and hugged her again.

"Congratulations, Cole." William stood and shook his hand and then kissed Carla on the cheek. Hannah did the same and Aunt Marie, of course, cried.

"When's the big day?"

"We haven't decided."

"If you'd like to do it today…" William teased.

"No!" Carla spoke up.

"We have to marry in Oak Grove." Carla looked at Cole then me.

"Why?"

"Because we do! I want the whole town to know that you chose to marry me."

"Whatever you wish. As soon as we get back you ladies may plan the wedding." He smiled and kissed her tenderly.

"I knew you were perfect for each other!" I had an 'I told you' look on my face as I looked at Cole.

"You were right, she is perfect."

"Let's sit and have breakfast and we'll discuss your wedding plans."

"I'm afraid I can stay but to only eat. Rebecca and I have to take Bethany to Winchester to see Daniel." William smiled slightly and held out his hands as we all took each other's.

William said grace thanking God for the battle, coming home safely, and to heal Daniel.

As we ate, Bethany walked in the dining room and then she stood still noticing her brother wasn't there. Her face said it all...

William instantly stood and walked to her, putting his arm around her, walking her away from us. I went to her knowing that she would need me. She covered her face with her hands leaning into William's chest she cried.

"We'll return later." William kept his arm around her and took my hand in his as we went to the door. A carriage was waiting for us as he had arranged early this morning. He helped her into the carriage and I sat across from them as he held her, comforting her.

"William, did he say anything?"

"Yes, he told me to take you home."

"What else?"

"Nothing." He kissed her forehead. She wrapped her arms around his neck and cried hard.

"Shhh he's not dead." William whispered.

"But you said it was bad."

"It is, but he's not dead. I had a guard stay with him and he was told to come at once if he..."

"No guard came, he's alive!" She batted those big blue eyes at him with tears filling them fast.

"Yes, my Beth, he's still alive." William tilted her chin up.

Bethany rested on William's chest the whole way to Winchester crying several times. She had said that Daniel was the only one she could really count on in her family. Her parents love her to pieces, but Daniel was her friend as well as her brother. He was the only one she could talk to, besides William...

~ Chapter 15 ~

We arrived at the Doc's seeing there were six beds and five of them taken. William talked to the Doc as I took Bethany to her brother. He looked so pale lying there so still with his chest bandaged up. I looked at the other beds as William talked to one of the other men across the way. I looked back at Bethany as she picked up Daniel's hand.

"Oh Daniel, fight, I need you." She brushed the hair off his forehead.

"I need you to fight and you must meet Rebecca! William's new wife, she's wonderful Daniel." She whispered to Daniel.

"Beth..." A faint whisper came from his lips. His eyes tried to open.

"Daniel..." She kissed his forehead. He heard her!

"I'm... sorry." He breathlessly whispered.

"Don't you give up on me! I need you damn it!" She ordered. His eyes opened wide.

"Don't swear! You're... a lady." He licked his parched lips.

"I'll swear till you get well enough to do something about it... damn it!!!"

"You're not too old... to be thrashed." He whispered and pain hit. My heart cried for Daniel as he struggled to make Bethany feel better.

"Shhh... don't talk... rest now... I'm not going to leave you." She wiped his forehead as he slipped back to sleep.

We sat for a couple hours by Daniel's bedside. Bethany's eyes never left him as she watched for anything, and held his hand and rubbed it. He opened his eyes a few times but went back to sleep. Then she sat foreword.

"I'm dead." He sighed.

"No, your quite alive brother."

"No, I'm dead or... soon will be. I see an angel... in front of me." He smiled a beautiful sleepy smile.

"No you're not! This is Rebecca, William's new wife." She smiled at me.

"Damn!" He closed his eyes squeezing them and opening them trying to stay awake.

"Daniel... please." She leaned down and whispered in his ear.

"She's an angel!" A grin appeared across his lips.

"This is Rebecca." She furrowed her brows.

"I can... dream... can't I?" He whispered to Bethany.

"Now, Daniel..." She frowned.

"It's a pleasure, Daniel." I walked to his bedside touching his hand. It was hot, too hot!

"It's all mine... Angel." He smiled like he had too much to drink, but I knew it was fever.

"I need to speak to William, please excuse me for a moment. I'll be right back." I nodded and quickly walked to William whispering in his ear. He walked back to Daniel and shook Daniel's hand.

"Damn glad to see you, Daniel." He smiled at William.

"Your wife... she's an angel." Daniel took in a deep breath and winked.

"That she is." William patted Daniel's shoulder.

"I..." Daniel coughed and groaned.

"I'll be right back." William looked at me and went to get the Doc.

"Would you like a sip of water?" I smiled down.

"Please..." He whispered. I took the cup and held it to his lips and as he took a sip, it was as if the water evaporated instantly on his lips! He was so hot!

"Let's have a look at you." The Doc pulled the curtain as he ushered us out.

"What's wrong?" Bethany's face washed over in fear.

"We think he's running a fever." I took her hand. I couldn't lie to her.

"No! That... I know is bad!" Tears welled in her huge blue eyes.

"He's in the best place to have a fever if he does have one." William put his arms around her. The doctor came from behind the curtain.

"I gave him something to make him sleep and an antibiotic for infection." The doctor frowned.

"Will he make it?" Bethany grabbed the Doc's coat.

"If he makes it through this fever and the night, I think he has a good chance, but recovery may be slow." He patted her hand.

"I'm staying." She held her chin up, as the doctor was about to refuse her, he looked at William. William nodded to the doctor knowing well that even William couldn't get her to leave him now.

"Very well." He shook his head as two men carried an enormous man into the room and put him on the bed next to Daniel's.

"Doc!" The guard called out.

"McInnis!" William whispered.

"Who?" I looked up at William.

"McInnis." William whispered down as he looked at the man's still body.

The Doc pulled the curtain and heard material ripping.

"He'll need surgery, help me with him to the operating room."

"Hurry! He's losing a lot of blood!" One of the guards called.

The curtains flew open and I saw a badly injured leg. His thigh was slashed deeply and you could see inside and something hanging out of the wound. I felt faint and leaned into William. That could have been William!

"Rebecca..." He caught me as was about to fall.

"I need to get you home. This is too much for you." William looked down at me concerned.

"Bethany..." My heart was crying for her.

"She's staying with Daniel." He searched my eyes knowing I was not leaving either.

"William, please. I don't want Bethany to be alone... in case..." I swallowed hard.

"Alright, alright, I tell you what, I have to wire Colonel McInnis's company and let them know he's here and check on other things. I'll be back in a couple of hours."

"Thank you, William. It's just that I know how she feels and I wouldn't want to be alone." He hugged me as I thanked God for his safe return.

"If you are sure..." He looked into my eyes so tenderly with understanding.

"If you should need me, the wire office is right down the street, on this side."

"Alright..." He winked at me and walked out. I took a deep breath and went to Bethany. She was wiping Daniel's forehead.

"I'm staying with you." I smiled and took the water bowl to get fresh cold water.

"I think whatever the doctor gave him, is already working." She smiled whispering.

"Good." I felt his chest and it was still warm. I pulled back the blanket.

"What are you doing?" She looked at me shocked.

"We need to get him cooled down. The doctor is busy with the Colonel, so we have to help him and now! I know that he needs to be almost cold. Hand me a wash cloth and wet it." She did as I told her to do.

"What do you plan on doing?" She looked at me still in shock.

"I know he's your brother, but in order to get him cold. We need to pull back all the covers..." She knew he was probably bare under the covers.

"Would you do it while I go to the powder room?" She blushed.

"Yes, it may take some time and after you get back, if I'm not through, why don't you check on the others and see if any of them need anything like perhaps a drink of water." I smiled I understood her shyness, after all it was her brother.

"Yes... I... I could do that!" She smiled pulled the curtain and left pulling it closed again.

I felt his head and it was too hot, so was his chest and took the cloth wiping his face neck and any chest area that wasn't bandaged. I wiped his stomach and huge arms that were so heavy and then took a deep breath and pulled the sheets back. I tried not to look, but I had to cool his legs down, they too were burning up. I draped the sheet so it covered most of him up allowing his legs to be exposed. I knew he wouldn't make it if he didn't cool down a bit.

After wiping and cooling the wash cloth off for the hundredth time, I was wiping his flat hard stomach off and heard him rumble a deep rumble in his chest. I looked into his face and his eyes were opened.

"That feels... wonderful..." He took a deep breath.

"Daniel, are you awake? How do you feel?" My heart pounded.

"I feel like I have had... an angel... wash my body... right to my soul... I'm in heaven." He whispered.

"Would you like a drink of water?" I smiled.

"Yes." He coughed slightly.

"Rebecca... I'm back." Bethany whispered. I looked back down and he was blatantly smiling at me.

"Is everything alright?"

"I'll be only a moment longer."

"Alright…" He tried to grin.

"Now, Mr. De Spain, you will behave yourself or your Sister can do this!"

"Alright Angel…" He laughed and winced as he dropped his hand on the bed.

"I hope that hurt." I softly laughed shaking my head.

"It did." He closed his eyes and licked his lips.

"I see." I wiped his legs and feet. Then took another cloth and wiped his face off. He was cooling down by the minute. He sighed softly.

"Are you feeling better?" I felt his head and it was cool and then covered him back up.

"Yes, much and hungry!" He opened his eyes a little wider. Bethany came through the curtains.

"Daniel, you look much better!" She smiled and kissed his forehead.

"I believe his fever broke." I crossed my arms at my waist.

"That's wonderful!"

"Thank you." He smiled a 'forgive me' smile. He must be something else with the ladies!

"You, Daniel De Spain, are welcome."

Bethany fluffed his pillows as he tried to stay awake.

"Now, where were you stabbed?"

"Right here… Doc said the knife missed my vital… organs." He closed his eyes.

"How old are you, Mr. De Spain?"

"Thirty… one." He sleepily smiled.

"Are you married?"

"No…" Daniel sighed.

"Here, let's wipe your arms." Bethany took the washcloth.

Bethany and I talked for the better part of two hours with Daniel as he floated in and out of sleep. William wasn't back and the Doc hadn't come in the room since they brought in McInnis. Bethany and I heard the door open and a squeak of a cart and footsteps.

"So how is the patient?" Doc opened the curtains and was wiping his hands.

"His fever has broken…" Bethany smiled at me brightly.

"Very good! How long ago did it break?" He felt Daniel's head nodding.

"About an hour and a half ago… how's Colonel McInnis?" I looked into his eyes and could see worry.

"We repaired his thigh and did the best we could. The man who did that to him should have been shot! Why, it wasn't just a slash or puncture. Someone turned and twisted the blade up, down and sideways insides his leg chopping muscles up: but I managed to fix most of it. He will never walk with a normal gate anymore and most likely have a limp." He shook his head clearly saddened.

"Oh my!" Bethany gasped.

"How old of a man is he?" I felt sorry for his wife.

"He's forty three, a widower with two small children. He was retired, but the men they were after, were in his area and they called him. There wasn't anyone in the area with his experience." The doctor shook his head with a frown.

"Can they do that?" I was shocked that they would do that! Could they with William as well? I thought about William having to leave.

"Yes, if there isn't anyone in the area that can handle the mission. They will call on one of the experts in retirement." The Doc was softly smiling.

"He is a widower?" Bethany frowned looking at me.

"It's a sad thing... he was so in love with his wife. If it weren't for his children, I believe he wouldn't be here." The doctor frowned himself and shook his head slowly.

"Will it take long for his recovery?" Bethany looked up at the Doctor.

"It will take some time and he has a good chance of making it, but it will be hard on him. Logan is a proud man and doesn't take kindly to people feeling sorry for him. When his wife died, he never shed a tear in front of anyone and he stood by her grave side holding both children not allowing anyone to hold them."

"How... how did she die?" Bethany glanced at me.

"She had a blood disorder, a Leukemia type of disorder or a sort of blood poison." He frowned.

"Will the children get sick?" I looked at the Doctor.

"No, it wasn't contagious." He pushed the curtain back all the way.

"That poor man!" Bethany frowned deeply as tears welled in her eyes.

"He will need therapy, a lot of it, but I'm afraid it won't be his leg that gets him, it will be the lack of ability to take care of his children. I've known him all his life. He's always been independent."

"Are you a nurse?" He looked at both of us.

"No, I'm not. I'm a school teacher." Bethany smiled at me then the Doctor.

"I'm William's wife, Rebecca." I nodded.

"The way you took care of Daniel, I thought you were a nurse."

"I have two brothers and they are in the lumber business. They have gotten hurt several times. I've also tended to them when they were sick with the fever once." I nodded to the doctor.

"I've not been sick a day in my life, but we had the fever and other small emergency's." Bethany smiled.

"Since you're staying Bethany, I was hoping that you might give me a hand with the patients for a couple of weeks. I seem to be pretty busy with the emergency calls and right now. I have no one to help me, my nurse just had a baby and she'll return in a few weeks. I sure wasn't expecting this to happen, as you never do." He held his hand out to all the full beds.

"Yes, I will help you. With my brother here, I would be here anyway." Bethany smiled up at the doctor and then to me.

"I have a room upstairs and it wouldn't cost you a thing. I need someone to help get water and food, maybe help change bandages and beds from time to time. You know nothing too much, and if I have an emergency, I won't have to leave them alone. I could pay you…"

"I think I would enjoy it very much! How long will Daniel be here?"

"Perhaps three weeks. He was cut all the way through." He looked at Bethany with hope in his eyes.

"Yes, I will help you as long as you call me Bethany." She laughed.

"Thank you! You are an angel. When can you start?" He smiled widely.

"I already have." She smiled at the Doc and he shook his head nodding.

"I'll get you a key." He chuckled and went out of the room.

"Why, Bethany, you are an angel for doing this!" I smiled at her very proud.

"What else would I do? I won't leave Daniel, I don't have anywhere else to go and I don't know anyone here, so it's perfect!" Bethany smiled looking at her sleeping brother

"Yes it does and you'll get some good experience." I was proud of her.

"I think so." She smiled so big.

"Well, you two about ready to head back?" William walked in and put his hands on my shoulders.

"I am, but Bethany is staying. The Doc needs her help. So while his nurse is off on maternity leave, Bethany is taking her place for a few weeks." I smiled at her as she wiped Daniel's face.

"That's wonderful!" He smiled at Bethany proudly.

"Yes, I even have a room to stay in free of charge upstairs." She smiled at William so proudly.

"If you are sure that is what you want to do…" William smiled.

"It is and you two may go home and rest. I know Rebecca is very tired. Thank you both so much." She hugged William and then me.

"We'll come back in a few days to check on you and Daniel. If you should need me…" William smiled tenderly down at her glowing face.

"I know William… you're only a moment away!" He kissed her forehead like she was his little sister.

"Watch out for McInnis, he can be rather…" Bethany cut William off.

"I know, I was warned!" She laughed.

"Alright, Rebecca…" He held out his hand for me to take.

"Thank you again you two and by the way William?"

"Yes, my Beth?" He looked at her tenderly.

"You chose the perfect wife. I love her already." She kissed William's cheek.

"I know… how I know!" He smiled and kissed her forehead again and we walked out as the Doc was coming back in with the key.

"See you in a few days, Doc."

"Get some rest, especially you, William." He shook William's hand and then walked back into the room and turned.

"Rebecca thanks for the help!" Doc patted my hand.

"You are welcome." I smiled and William's brows went up.

"What was that about?"

"I helped Doc with Daniel when they brought McInnis in. He had to do surgery on the Colonel's leg."

"Did he say what the outcome would be?" William opened the carriage and helped me in.

"He said he would recover slowly, but would walk with a limp."

"Now I really feel sorry for Bethany. He'll not be an easy patient." William shook his head frowning.

"I think she will do just fine." I smiled laying my head on William's chest thanking God he came home unharmed.

William and I fell asleep on the way home so it seemed like we just left Winchester when the carriage stopped.

"We're home, Rebecca." William whispered.

"What are you doing? I can walk!"

"I know... Shhh..." He walked into the house and up the three flights of stairs to our room. We did not see anyone. I was rather relieved about that. I was so tired!

He gently sat me on the bed sitting next to me taking his boots off.

"William?" I softly and lazily spoke.

"Hmm?"

"Will you be doing more missions?" I softly spoke.

"I hope not. I sent my letter to Byron two weeks ago and I know he sent off the proper paper work to Washington this week. I should receive word next week from Colonel McCray accepting my retirement. Why?" His voice was soft and deep sounding sleepy.

"Colonel McCray? You mean Gabe?" Surly not Gabe!

"No, his brother... Lord Craig McCray. He is in the council in Washington. I may have to go there, but I doubt it and if I do, you will go with me." I felt his arms tighten around me.

"I've never been to Washington."

"I wished I would have had the time to tell you about my job and to prepare you for things like the mission I was just on... but to reassure you, I was safe."

"Your men would have died for you before they got to you, wouldn't they?" I took a deep breath.

"Yes." His voice was very low.

"When you retire, who will take your place?"

"That depends, if there is someone here that can take over then they will. If not, one may be sent from someplace else... transferred."

"I see. Do you want to retire, because I don't want you to quit because of me."

"What are you saying?" He turned me towards his face.

"Well, I know you were worried about me and couldn't live with myself if I knew it wasn't what you really wanted to do." I saw the look in his eyes and he closed them taking a deep breath. I waited for him to continue.

"Rebecca, I'm tired. I need to retire. I'm not as fast as I used to be. This time, I was almost the one in the Doc's office, if not dead. If it were not for your brother I probably would be dead."

The thought made my breath disappear.

"But, your brother saved my life and I owe him mine. Things happen for reasons Rebecca and I think that this was a sign. I was right in knowing that it's time to retire. I'll miss it of course, but I plan on being on a new mission." A sensual grin played on his lips.

"And what might that be?" I raised my brow at him.

"Making babies with the most beautiful wife a man could ever ask for."

"Then you must! You wouldn't want to disappoint her."

"No, I wouldn't now, would I?" He grinned...

After a short rest, we went down and joined the others as dinner was being served.

"Hello you two! We thought you wouldn't be joining us."

"We couldn't do that now could we?" I laughed at mother.

"Where's Bethany?" Carla smiled and I took her hand admiring her new ring.

As William and I took our seats, William and I told them about Daniel and his injuries and Bethany's new job.

"That's wonderful." Carla smiled.

"We will check on them before heading to Oak Grove on Monday." William took a sip of wine.

"I can't wait to get back to Oak Grove tomorrow. I want to get started on our endeavor as soon as possible!" Mother smiled looking at Hannah and Carla.

"I have enjoyed the company and I am sorry about the trouble that has happened."

"That is alright, now we have a wonderful tale to tell, and my son is a hero."

"No Mother, I am not. It was war and in war, there is no hero, just men doing what they have to do." Cole frowned.

"No Cole... your mother's right, you really are a hero and I owe you my life." William held his cup up to Cole.

"You would have done it for me..." Cole nodded.

"To Cole..." William called out to honor him.

"To Cole!" Every one stood raising their glasses.

"My brother may you be blessed in everything you do. Thank you for saving my life." William raised his glass higher and we all said here, here.

"Now let's say grace and eat! I'm famished!"

With that we bowed our heads William said grace thanking God for Cole and the rest of us and remembering Colonel McInnis and Daniel.

We ate and talked about the infiltrators, how Cole saved William, about Cole and Carla's wedding, and of course the business adventure. After dinner we retired to the parlor, the men had brandy while we women had coffee.

"When are you planning on leaving tomorrow?" I asked mother and Hannah. Aunt Marie and Carla were talking about the wedding.

"In the morning after breakfast... William is sending a wagon with us so we can get everything back home all at once." She laughed shaking her head.

"I just got you home and now you won't be there." Mother had tears in her eyes.

"Pardon me for interrupting, but the thought occurred to me that it might be a good idea to have Cole build us a small place to come for a visit. When we have children, I know she'll want to be close to you." William leaned down and kissed mother's cheek.

"Rebecca dear, I think you have the most understanding husband in the world! That would be wonderful! You can build it by the pond!"

"Can we, William?" My heart fluttered at the thought.

"Anything you want, remember you are a very rich woman, very rich indeed!" He roared a thunderous laugh.

"Oh, William!" I blushed still trying to get use to the idea.

"I hope you two are busy trying to have a grandchild!" Mother smiled and winked at William.

"Mother!" I whispered blushing red.

"Oh we are... we are." William winked at her and she chuckled nodding.

"Honestly you two!" I blushed even more.

We talked about what kind of place we wanted, we both agreed that we wanted it to be cozy, like a cottage blending in with the scenery. After an hour or so William yawned and I realized that he hadn't been to sleep, or had gotten very little sleep in the last few days. I stood and gave him a nod, we excused ourselves and retired to our room. It seemed so far to walk to tonight!

"Here..." William scooped me up into his arms and carried me the rest of the way.

"I promise when your family leaves, we will get a lot more rest and it won't seem so far to walk.

"Why is it so far away?" I yawned again.

"It's secluded." His brows went up and down.

"Ah... I see!" I laughed putting my arms around his neck and kissing his cheek.

368

"I was hoping you would." He laughed softly as he took the stairs two at a time.

~ Chapter 16 ~

The sun was out when William woke this morning. We dressed and went down stairs. Everyone was leaving this morning.

"Everything packed?" William smiled as we entered the dining room table.

"Yes, just about. Your staff is loading everything up in the wagon." Cole smiled.

"Consider the wagon as a gift for your new business." William smiled at mother, Aunt Marie, Carla and Hannah.

"No, William, we couldn't!" Mother frowned slightly.

"I insist! You are my mother-in-law now. It's well within my rights to give you such a gift." He smiled and put his hands on her shoulders.

"Well, I don't know what to say." She blushed.

"Just say, I love you son." He smiled and hugged her and I do think he loves her. Tears filled Aunt Marie's eyes.

"How could I not love you, William… you big bear!" Mother hugged him again and kissed his cheek.

After we ate breakfast, I helped mother, Hannah, Aunt Marie and Carla making sure they had all their things. I could tell mother was sad that I wasn't returning with her, but she also loved my new home and knew William would well take care of me. She kept looking at me and trying to give her best smile.

"Mother, I will visit often and you may come here. It will be fun, like a mini holiday. Please don't worry."

"Rebecca, I'm not in the least worried. William will be the most wonderful husband and you have a beautiful home. I could not want any more for you, but I do want those grandchildren soon." She winked at me.

"We're working hard on that I promise you. But…"

"I have no doubt that you are, but I know sometimes it takes a little time." She smiled picking up her handbag taking my arm as we walked out of her room.

"I know, but I want William's children so much."

"I'll tell you a little secret."

"What's that?" I looked at her as if she couldn't possibly know any secrets.

"Have a glass or two of wine… it relaxes the body. You'll conceive faster. Make a night out of it. You know with candles and wear something pretty." Her brows went up and down.

"Mother!" I laughed.

"It's true! It does help. Your father and I were married a year before I found out the secret from a friend."

"Alright, Mother, I'll try." I didn't want her to go on with the subject in detail.

"Don't be too disappointed if you're not with child right away. It takes time to relax and for your nerves to settle." She patted my hand as we walked down the steps.

I thought about it and she was right, I was nervous. I would probably get this month's cycle, but hopefully not next. I still will be a bit disappointed anyway.

We saw everyone waiting by the door as we reached the bottom of the staircase.

"Ready? We have lots to do when we return!" Cole smiled and then hugged me tight.

"I love you, Cole." I hugged and kissed him and he smiled saying he loved me too and shook William's hand then hugged him as well.

"Thanks for everything… and the excitement." Cole smiled at William with a look of 'you better take care of my Sister' and then William nodded.

"You are welcome anytime! We shall see you on Monday." William smiled warmly at Cole.

"I had the most interesting time William and I'll miss you Rebecca." Carla had tears in her eyes.

"Don't worry, I'll be there Monday and I'm sure that you'll all see us frequently, Sis." I smiled and hugged her and kissed her cheek.

We hugged Aunt Marie and Hannah and said our goodbye's watching them drive away. I couldn't help but feel a bit lonesome. It was true, I had just returned home, to only leave again. This time it was different. I was married to William and knew I would be seeing them often.

"Now my love, it's just you and me." His eyes were warm and tender.

"Whatever shall we do?" I smiled and his arm went around me and mine, him.

"I have a few ideas." He smiled a devilish smile that I recognized right away and I smiled one back at him. We went up the stairs together.

~ Chapter 17 ~

We spent the rest of that day and the next being together, enjoying not having to entertain anyone. Just sharing and loving, eating and sleeping in each other's arms feeling truly loved. I still couldn't believe that he was my husband! I was never this happy in my entire life! I finally felt complete!

We agreed that all we wanted to do was stay in our bedroom until Monday, but he also wanted me to get to know the estate and the grounds better. William promised to take me on a honeymoon soon, but only after he was officially retired, I agreed.

We walked out to the courtyard, sat by the pool of water, and soaked up the sunshine. The walls that surrounded the courtyard blocked a lot of the wind and felt warmer. William and I also spent a little time in the library. He showed me some of his favorite books and some history books of the Great War, stories of how it was in the old days, back to the early two thousands. I was amazed that they had not only wagons, but also self moving wagons, they called cars. Lights that when you pushed up a button they came on, even things that flew in the air carrying people!

"I'd always wondered why we couldn't have some of these things." I smiled at William.

His face darkened and I didn't like this look! What was it?

"If we allowed these kinds of technologies back into our lives, there would eventually be another war like this..." He looked down deeply into my eyes.

"But, now that we know what happens if you abuse things, why can't it be regulated?" I truly didn't understand.

"That's what I do. I prevent information from getting back to the territories. Mankind then was careless and men were power mongers.

They abused it alright, tried it again about four hundred years ago, and once again. Someone got greedy and tried to start an uprising. Before it all got out of hand, that is when the council decided to take all precautions against technologies and science, never allowing it back in this world again. That... is how Special Forces came to be.

Because of this, it resulted in almost total annihilation. Nuclear power was what it was called, it was the downfall of man, along with greed and power. God became almost a fairytale, like this book of Cinderella. The thought of that makes my blood boil.

That is why it is so important not to allow anything that leads anyone to build or recreate anything that leads to this nuclear power. We have oil lamps and candles, crop farms, and livestock farms and we heat with wood or coal.

They say history repeats itself and we live like they did back in the eighteen hundreds. It has to stay that way... it must." His eyes were so dark, so very dark.

"So, your job was to intercept people trying to infiltrate and corrupt what has taken hundreds of years to get back."

"Here, let me show you something." He looked at me with a warning in his eyes. William walked to a painting and lifted it off the wall. Under the painting was a small silver box with a dial on it. He moved it one way then the other and back again.

"This is called a safe... it is fire proof and only I can open it. It contains my important papers, documents, and a book, for my eyes only and now you... But I must warn you, the book that is in here is very old and it contains images taken by a small light trapping box they called a camera.

It held images of whatever you pointed it at. The pictures are about four hundred and eighty years old, this is but a copy. It was reproduced overseas for the Special Forces. A reminder of why we do what we do at all costs. They're horrible images, beyond any nightmare you could ever have, right from the bowels of hell. They might be too much for you and I won't be upset if you care not to look at them, but once you do, you'll know why I am who I am." He reached into the silver box and pulled out a large book and took it to the divan sitting down.

My heart pounded knowing this must be very important. I didn't know if I wanted to see. He fluttered the book open to the first page. 'The End of Man Kind' then turned the page to how we used to live. I saw what they called cars and planes and how people dressed. Women wore pants and their underwear to the beaches. I was appalled that women would walk around naked by all practical purposes. I saw children abused and children that looked like slaves. People had green markings all over their bodies. They were of lions, women, and other things that people worshiped. I saw images of huge buildings that appeared to be in the clouds. Then I saw starving people, dead animals, tortured people that wouldn't do as they were told. Many were murdered for their faith or steeling for food because their children were starving. Some were children they killed. I was horrified! Tears welled in my eyes when I saw pictures of thousands of men, women and children and being put in one great hole and buried. The caption said 'and some were still alive. . . .' I was sick to my stomach. I thought I would wretch, but couldn't look away or even blink.

I saw images of great long things flying through the air and what happened to an entire city after it crashed into the earth. I turned away tears streaming down my cheeks.

"Oh, William! My God in Heaven! People did that to themselves?" I didn't want to believe it.

"Yes." He closed the book even though there was a lot more to look at.

"William, my God!" I wrapped my arms around his neck and cried.

"I shouldn't have shown it to you, but you must know why."

"I understand." I wept.

"I'm sorry." He whispered.

"No, I'm glad to know and I do understand why you do what you do and why." I was never so proud of who William was and why.

"One man's life is not worth millions of lives. We have to choose our battles. We have to make sure this never happens again. . . ever! But you must never speak of this outside the Brotherhood. You are now privileged to know why, but I cannot share details with you about missions. You alone now have the power to undo all we have worked so hard to preserve. So you must never speak of what you've seen from the past." He stared deeply into my eyes and through my tears I nodded.

He looked down and then into my eyes and I looked up into his thanking God that we were not born in that time. What a horrible existence for children. I was taught only about the war in school. I never saw pictures of this magnitude before. They would stay with me for the rest of my life. I have no need to see the rest of the book.

"Please, forgive me." Tears well into his eyes. . .

"William, there is nothing to forgive. I am glad that you shared that with me and I am proud to be the wife of a great knight who is committed to do what he must. I shall never speak of what I've just seen. I give you my word!" I tiptoed up to his lips and he bent down and kissed me softly. His arms went around me as he deepened his kiss. My heart was so full of love for this man that I would never be able to thank God enough for him. William pulled away slowly and replaced the book in the safe covering it up with the painting, then we sat silently for a while.

Now I knew what this was all about! The rumors of the old timers were true and not legend! The vagueness of the teachings in school now made sense. It's all controlled by the government. I thank God for the wise men that run our Territory! I now understand William's devout commitment to God and the Union.

"I think it's about dinner time, let's go check. After diner, I want to go to the stables. I have a surprise for you." He smiled like a little boy biting his bottom lip showing that dimple.

"Can you tell me, or give me a hint?" I looked up at him as I took his arm. He covered my hand with his. His smile was still that of a boy. My insides jumped for he was so handsome the way his eyes twinkled.

"You'll just have to wait and see." He chuckled. He bit his bottom lip and kissed me tenderly.

"William, I don't want you to think that you have to surprise me or buy me things. I have all I ever need with you just holding me in your arms." I tiptoed, he met me half of the way down, I kissed him back tenderly. Then I pulled away slowly as my head was spinning just from his lips.

Actually a surprise is what I needed to get my thoughts off what I had just seen. It was going to take a while for those images to fade from my memory, if ever.

"Let's go before…" He rolled his eyes and I smiled a knowing smile.

Dinner was wonderful and fun! We ate in the kitchen with the rest of the staff. I noticed that he was more relaxed in the kitchen. We should do this more often. I liked being his wife already.

Libby made a delicious pot of vegetable soup, and corn bread. We all ate until we were about to explode. Then to top it off, Libby brought out the most wonderful surprise. It was chocolate with whipped topping and nuts with a drizzle of chocolate on top. I don't know what it was called and neither did she, saying that she had got the recipe from one of her friends in Clifford Valley.

376

After dinner, William and I strolled to the stables. The night air was cold and crisp, not a cloud in the night sky, with a billion stars twinkling in the heavens. The moon was so bright that we needed no lantern to find our way.

I glanced up at him several times noticing that he smiled the entire time we were walking. Inside the stable was warm and his horses were in the stalls fed and happy.

"Hello, William." Victor smiled at William and me. I looked at him dryly not forgetting about the 'damn brother' incident, but that was water under the bridge now and no point in bringing it up. Everyone was safe and sound… well except Daniel.

"Good evening, Vick, where are the others?" William shook Victor's hand.

"Aww… in town… you know" He winked at William. William just smiled and nodded which meant they were out at the brothels.

"And how are you, Lady Andrews?" He took my hand bowing slightly over it.

"Well, and you?" I smiled and slightly nodded.

"Thankful." He smiled a soft smile. I thought I saw regret in his eyes.

"As we are all…" William smiled a huge smile.

"I want to show her the special surprise that I have for her." He winked at Victor and he stepped aside. William took my hand and led me to a stall on the other side of the stable.

"This side is what I like to think of as a nursery." His eyes danced with joy.

"A nursery, for mothers and mothers to be?"

"Yes, come." He pulled me walking so fast I was winded. He looked at me as I tried to keep up with his large gated walk.

"I'm sorry, Rebecca, I'll slow down." He laughed so excited.

"Thank you." I slowed down to catch my breath as we finally came to the end stall.

"Here, stand on this." He took a small barrel and placed it in front of the stall and lifted me up on the barrel.

"This is Diablo's mate, one of many, but this one seems to be his favorite…She is about to give birth." A regal chestnut horse with black socks, black mane and tail stood grunting before us.

"Why is she grunting?" I looked eye to eye at William. The barrel was the perfect height.

"She is in labor and will have the colt soon. This is your surprise."

"I don't understand." I looked at the horse and then back to William.

"The colt she gives birth to... is yours." His smile was so bright.

"Mine?" I was speechless.

"All yours and you can name him or her, whatever you wish." He smiled and looked at the terribly stressed horse. She puffed out and cried out a great noise!

"She's ready! I only hope it is not breach, which would be hard on her." He whistled up into the air without using his fingers. I saw all the horse's heads lift up and heard whinnies from all directions.

"It's time is it?" Victor was running down the aisle smiling.

"Let's get the straps and bails ready in case she has trouble." William clapped his hands together and rubbed them fast. Then he and Victor went to a large cabinet, a way down, and brought back all kinds of things. It looked like torture equipment!

"What... what's all that for?" I was feeling so sorry for the mother.

"The straps help to keep her up and steady and these bails we put along the walls so she does not hurt herself or the colt. We have had no trouble from her yet and hope this will go smoothly." He kissed my cheek and the entered the stall.

"Aww, come on now Missy, it's alright. You've done this many times before and you can do it again. This will be the last colt for you girl." He stroked her neck cooing to her.

I watched as her ears fluttered at the sound of his voice. His hands rubbed and soothed her as he talked so quietly to her. He gently felt her belly as his other hand patted her. Victor was busy building the walls. Missy grunted again and puffed some more, but they were getting closer and closer together.

"Now, Missy, sweet Missy." He cooed to her again. He started to hum a tune and then looked at me with his eyes wide open.

"Rebecca... would you mind singing?" His eyes were so wide.

"Sing? Here?!!" For the horse?

"Yes please! We hum to help calm the horses when their in labor. It seems to relax them." I looked at him and then Victor.

"It would help believe it or not, besides if you sing better than William or I, I bet Missy here would appreciate it, but not as much as I would." Victor laughed and William shot him a warning glance.

"Well alright...what would you like me to sing?" I looked at William and then Victor.

"How about that song you sang at your mother's dinner party? It's soothing and soft." William nodded very sure.

He was checking under her tail. I closed my eyes and started to sing 'A Rose' I was lost in the song and heard Missy grunting and quiet back down. I opened my eyes and saw Victor staring at me and nodded. Then he turned back to William as he worked on Missy. One would talk while the other checked on her progress. They both were sweating. William smiled at me as I finished and nodded to me knowing he wanted me to keep singing. I sang the other song I had sung. The 'Rain comes and Goes". Victor shook his head and listened to the old tunes and then I sang anything that popped into my mind. I closed my eyes and sang a favorite song of mine. 'Loving you'. I heard Missy make a loud grunt and William and Victor laughed out.

"It's a girl!" Victor, William and I watched the mother nose the baby. My heart was so full at the sight, tears welled in my eyes and William's eyes were full of pure joy.

"She's beautiful!" I said breathless.

"That she is... that she is."

We watched the newborn wobble and work its way to stand on its trembling legs.

"Look!" Victor smiled pointing that the baby was going to be alright. She went right to nursing on her mother.

"William..." I whispered and was speechless.

"She's all yours. You choose the name and every colt that this colt has, is yours as well." He softly laughed.

"Oh, William. I've never had a colt, but Fella, and he was already pretty big when we got him." I missed them.

"We need to get them here as well."

"I think I would like to leave Fella for Mike, but would like Jack to live here with me."

"When we come back from Oak Grove, we'll bring Jack." William wiped his hands on a towel and opened the gate walking out.

"You got thing's Victor?" William looked at Victor.

"Sure thing." Victor smiled and cleaned the stall out and placed fresh hay around.

"We're headed back to the shack." William smiled and held out his arm for me to take.

"By the way, Lady Andrews..."

"Rebecca." I smiled at Victor knowing that we started anew tonight.

"Rebecca. I have never heard such a beautiful voice before. I think you'll come in handy a lot more." Victor smiled nodding.

"Thank you, I think." I laughed and looked at William.

We walked back to the shack as he called it.

"Sir?" Jules was at the kitchen door.

"Yes?" William took my coat and his and gave them to Jules…

"A letter just arrived." Jules smiled at me, then back to William.

"Let's have a look shall we?" Jules handed the letter to William and Libby poured William and me a fresh cup of coffee. William sat down.

"Ah!" He smiled.

"Is it good news?"

"Yes… Very."

"Can you tell us?" Libby handed William a cup of coffee.

"Well… it looks like McCray got the letter to Washington sooner than I thought."

"You're retired?" I looked at William and he nodded.

"Yes, and now…I can officially start my new life. There will be a letter to follow that completes everything, but for now, they won't call on me for anything other than a dire emergency."

"Oh, William, that's wonderful!" I smiled and took his hand in mine.

"Well frankly, I am tired of worrying about you, William. Have some children and fill this house!" Libby laughed.

"I'm working on it… I'm working on it." William laughed and lifted my hand to his lips.

~ Chapter 18 ~

We set out for mothers on Monday. We had everything packed and were on our way early, both excited to see what mother had accomplished. He wanted to talk to Cole about our cottage as soon as possible, knowing that it wouldn't be until spring that the construction would get under way. William and I wanted to stay in the hotel in his old room and I agreed. The thought of staying there where it all began, it was a sweet sentiment.

We stopped in Winchester to check on Bethany and Daniel. Daniel was going to be fine. He was past any danger now and Bethany said that Lord McInnis was still in and out, but he was awake at times. She said the Colonel was feverish and talked nonsense. She had to tell him to hush up a couple of times, he was yelling at her about getting out of his room. William was tickled and told her she should write it all down to use against him when he was in his right mind. Then he wouldn't give her any more grief.

We left her and Daniel and said we would visit them in Ida Grove soon. She made William promise and give her his word, he did. We were soon on our way, William soon dozed off.

"We're here, William." I gently shook his chest. He breathed in deep and smiled.

"I'm sorry for falling asleep, but ever since I married you, all the extra activities have made me so relaxed. Unlike I have ever felt before." He smiled and kissed my lips.

"I know what you mean." The porter opened the carriage door for us and William stepped out taking my hand and helping me down.

"Let's get our room and then we'll go see your mother." I agreed, William and I went into the hotel. We were able to get William's old room and wanted to settle in and freshen up.

"Here we are." The bellboy smiled opening the door. We stepped in and the boy took our valise to the wardrobes.

"Here you go." William gave him a tip and the boy's mouth dropped open.

"Thank you Sir, if you should need anything else. Please do not hesitate to ask." He smiled as William nodded.

"I will… thank you son." Those words made me think of that boy, Joey and small girl in the alley. I would tell William about them tonight, and what I saw.

"Ah he went to the bed and flopped down.

"Are you tired, William?"

"No, but it feels so good not to be bumped and jostled."

"It doesn't matter how nice the carriage is, if the roads are bad." I smiled sitting next to him on the bed.

"Well, let's freshen up before I change my mind and take you right now." He laughed and growled and looked like he was about to pounce.

He held out his hand for me to pull him up and I took it and he pulled me down to him.

"You know, I always wanted you in this bed." He smiled a sultry smile, then bit his lip showing that dimple.

"Is that right?" I smirked.

"Yes, and tonight I will have you in this bed… right here!"

"You will, will you?" I laughed as he pulled me to his lips.

"William?" He kissed me again. I pulled away from him and laughed.

"What?" He smiled a seductive smile.

"Is this what you call freshening up?"

"For me, yes. It takes all my tension out and I always feel better." He gave me a delicious seductive grin.

"You fall asleep…after." I laughed.

"Me?" His brows rose.

"It amazes me that I can conquer a huge knight and completely incapacitate him without weapons!" I laughed teasing him terribly.

"Well you're right about conquering me, but I don't agree that you don't use a weapon." He pulled me on top of him.

"I don't!" I tried not to laugh.

"Ah but you do." He laughed a thunderous laugh, as I knew what he was referring to.

"Well then I guess you are my only threat."

"And now that I think about it… I wonder if I didn't use 'my weapon' would it break your will into doing what I want you to do." I gave him a sultry smile.

"That is not fair play." He frowned.

"No?"

"NO!" He almost pouted!

"And why not?" I wanted to laugh.

"Because… well because… it's just not." His brow furrowed.

"Ah I see." I brushed the hair off of his face and ran my finger over his lips.

"Rebecca…" His tone was low.

"You're the one who pulled me on top of you!" I was about to laugh.

"Yes but…"

"So the tables have turned?"

"No…They…" He stopped and stared into my eyes and looked into my hair.

"What?"

"…A…" His eyes were big and looking at my hair.

"What! What is it?" I straightened up.

"Well… do you like spiders?"

"NO! WHY?" I straightened my arms and holding my body up and off of William.

"Well there's a…" He pointed to my hair and I screamed and jumped up.

"GET IT OFF! GET IT OFF!" I waved my hands jumping up and down.

"Here…" He stood and raised his hand to my hair.

"WHAT!" I looked at him wide eyed as my heart pounded in my chest.

"Oh, it was only this…" He showed me a piece of fuzz from my shawl.

"William… that wasn't fair!"

"Well, neither were you, my love." He laughed softly.

"Truce?" I smiled.

"Yes, truce" He laughed and hugged me tight.

"Now let's freshen up and we'll take care of this matter later." He gave me a warning smile as he walked into the washroom.

"I can't wait."

We freshened up and hung our clothes in the wardrobe and then walked to mothers.

As we passed Hannah's store a sign hung reading, 'Closed for relocation' I smiled at William and we went on our way.

"Carla's place reads the same I bet." We looked across the street and saw her shades pulled and a sign in the window as well.

"They have to be at mothers." William nodded and continued down the walkway. We reached the Tea Shop and a sign was on her door as well, but we heard Cole's voice.

"Hello?" William called out as we went through the door.

"Rebecca, William, Come in!" I walked into a huge mess! Workers were tearing down walls and piles of rubble were all over the place.

"I'm glad you made it!" Mother hugged me then William.

"Mother." William kissed her cheek and she blushed. He still could make her blush!

"Well it looks...." Terrible!

"Wonderful!" Mother laughed.

"Well those weren't my exact words... but..." It was a mess with plaster and wires hanging everywhere and so much dust!

"Ah brother!" Cole and Mike walked up.

"Hello, Rebecca." Cole kissed my cheek and took William away. William looked back and shrugged at me.

"Cole is so excited! He wants to show William the blue prints."

"Where is Carla?"

"She is in her old shop packing up the rest of her things with Hannah. We have to move her out and the other store in so that they don't lose business, but I had to agree to pay the rent on their store for two months or until business gets back to normal." Mother wasn't pleased about that one bit, but could see their point.

"So how long will this all take?" I looked around at the mess and thought a year or two.

"Cole says it's not going to take as long as we thought. I'll show you what colors and paper we have picked out and I have the wall sconces and well a lot of things already ordered." She took my arm and we went into the back room where there was no dust.

She showed me the sconces, which were crystal and were lit by oil and she chose beautiful soft yellow wallpaper with dogwoods on them and olive green leaves. The ceiling was white with white trim and the curtains, an even paler green, were double hung drapes with white shears under them. It was going to be very elegant and comfortable.

She showed me her sketches of the floor plan and it would have a center, almost parlor, in the middle of the entire building where you can wait or relax in soft comfortable wing back chairs with small tables between them. By her Tea Shop, were small tables around a center open type counter where the coffee and tea were brewed, with small stools in front of the counter and the kitchen would still be in the back. It was perfect!

On one side of mother's business was Carla's shop, with new counters and chairs, and she was hiring a woman to do women's hair and nails. She wanted to run the place and have someone do the work, smart girl I thought. On the other side of mother were Hannah's sections. Her floor plan was very nice with chairs and tables. The walls were going to be lined with readymade dresses in all sizes and everything to go with them, or that a woman could want. Even those scant underclothes Carla had told them about.

"Well Mother, does Cole think it will prosper?"

"He does and Mike thinks he just might stay on here."

"I know… to meet women." I laughed.

"I think you're right. He and Gail had a falling out when he returned, she wanted to go along with all of us and he said no."

"I see, maybe that is for the best."

"I don't know. She kept Mike in line." She shook her head and laughed.

"I think Mike will be just fine." I laughed.

"I think you're right!" She took my arm and we went back out.

"There you are my love."

"What have you been doing William?" He was covered in white plaster dust.

"Working." He kissed my cheeks.

"I can see that!"

"Cole wanted me to ask you two if you would go help Carla for a while, he said we're just about to burst through a wall and it will get rather dusty in here." He smiled ushering us out the door.

"Alright, but be careful!" I smiled and kissed his white cheek.

"Tell you what, let's say at four I shall meet you back at the hotel and we'll clean up and eat in the restaurant tonight, I'm sure your mother is tired."

"That sounds wonderful. We shall" Mother smiled.

"Until four then…" He winked at us and I nodded. He went back into the shop and we went to Carla's.

"Yoo hoo!" Mother sang out as we walked in.

"Back here." Carla called out.

"Well hello, Rebecca." Carla hugged Hannah and me.

"You are simply glowing." Hannah smiled at me.

"No it's plaster dust!" Mother laughed.

"Oh you!" Hannah laughed.

"We're here to help you two, they're about to go through the last wall. I hope Mr. Crane has his entire things out." Mother laughed.

"Me too…" Carla laughed.

"Now what needs to be done?" I smiled grabbing a crate.

Carla showed us what to do, and to pack, we started in. We packed and wrapped all afternoon and by four we were almost done and so surprised! We had boxed everything we could box and stacked it all up on one side of the room… it looked so bare. I had told them about our dinner plans and that we should meet in the restaurant at six. Hannah and Carla agreed and we all went to take baths and change. I walked with Hannah to her shop as she lived above it.

"I take it you and William are still honeymooning?"

"We will be for the rest of our lives." I smiled and kissed her cheek.

"Ah young love is so sweet." She smiled.

"Hannah, does Mother Grayson know I got remarried?" I looked at her worried.

"Yes she does, she is very happy about it, and so are her children." She smiled.

"I was hoping that she wouldn't be upset."

"She was as happy for you as she could be…truly."

"I'm glad." I smiled and hugged Hannah again.

"Now go get cleaned up." Hannah smiled.

"You'll be there by six?" I smiled and backed up.

"I will love." She went inside and I went to the Hotel.

My back ached from bending over boxes all afternoon and was glad that it was almost finished. Though mother said we had to help with the Crane's store next. I wasn't pleased about that at all. I started the water as soon as I got into the room and took out my robe taking it to the washroom with me. I was soon undressed and slid into the very hot water, steam filled the room.

I put some oil in the water that William liked and sunk all the way under and out. I soon washed my hair and rinsed it and started to just relax when I heard the door open and close.

"Rebecca?" The sound of William's voice was wonderful.

"I'm in the tub." I called out to him.

"I'll be right in." He was coming in the water with me?

"William!" He was so dirty!

"What?"

"Have you looked in the mirror lately?"

"No, but I'm sure I am a sight." He laughed for his hair, face, and clothes were all white.

"You are indeed. Let me finish my bath, you'll need two!' I laughed at him.

"Well don't let your water out then, I'll get the worst off with it then take a fresh one."

"That will work." I stood and looked at William and he was standing just smiling at me.

"Would you hand me a towel?"

"No." He smiled a devilish smile.

"Please?" I begged.

"No." He still stood there.

"William...I'm cold."

"I see that." He smiled biting his bottom lip.

"Oh you!" I started to get out but he handed me a towel.

"Yes me!" He laughed out.

"Thank you." I laughed shaking my head wrapping the towel around me.

"Now undress and I shall help you."

"Yes, my love anything you wish." He was undressed and in the tub and I was scrubbing his hair.

"I'll need to do this twice." He sighed as I rinsed his hair.

"It feels wonderful."

"Here, you wash while I get your clothes out. What would you like to wear to the restaurant?"

"I think my gray suit with the black trim." He smiled up at me as I washed his back.

"I love you, William."

"And I, you." I kissed his lips softly.

I finished his back and went to take his clothes out. I heard the new bath water running and smiled.

I loved being his wife I thought as I hummed a tune laying his clothes on the bed. I thought about Bethany and Daniel. Daniel was about as big as Lord McInnis, I know as big as William. At least Bethany was a strong woman. I think she will have no problem handling him. Her brother was enough for anyone.

"Ready?"

"For you? Always..." I pushed on his head and made him go under the water. He came up smiling.

"Why you're stronger than I thought my love. His hair was all in his face. He took one hand and wiped it all back.

"Don't ever underestimate me, my Lord." I gave him a warning look teasing him.

"You know if you don't stop looking at me that way..." He smiled as I started in on his hair again.

"Why, I thought you liked it when I looked at you this way?"

"Oh but I do, but you are teasing me right now...and I may call your bluff."

"I'll be ready... I'll be ready." I laughed as I washed his hair and rinsed it then his back and chest.

"If it's alright with you, I need to do my hair."

"Go ahead, I'm about through, but can you wear it down and just pull it back?

"Anything for you..."

I brushed out my hair until it was almost dry and then dressed. William was through with his bath as well and was dressing.

"You look beautiful." He smiled as he buttoned his coat.

"And you my husband are too handsome for your own good."

"I see you have my mother's necklace on."

"I thought you would like it with this dress."

"It's perfect as are you." He kissed me softly and pulled away.

"Are you ready?"

"Yes."

We went to the restaurant and everyone was already there. They went ahead and ordered. It was a wonderful time! Cole was well pleased at the progress of the work and thought that it would be done soon.

"It's nice to have your help. You took that wall out like you were in battle." Cole laughed.

"It was like wielding a sword." William nodded.

"I've never seen anyone so strong." Cole smiled and sipped his wine.

"I'm just glad to help." William smiled at me.

We ordered our dinner as Hannah and Aunt Marie sat chatting about Cole and Carla's wedding.

"When is the day?" I smiled at Carla and Cole.

"Well we decided that it should be sooner." Cole cheeks turned a little red.

"I think a Christmas wedding would be wonderful." Mother smiled.

"With all that I'm doing. I think we may have to wait." Carla looked at Cole.

"No, I think mother's right. We should be done with everything in three weeks and you'll have two weeks to plan."

"But, Cole, that will be hard to do…" Carla protested.

"Some of my men will arrive the day after tomorrow to help with the renovations and the moving. I don't see it will even be three weeks Cole." William winked at him.

"How many men are coming?"

"Five of the best damn carpenters I know." He smiled sipping his wine.

"William, you didn't have…"

"Now, Mother, I do it for my own and you are my family now." William smiled softly and winked at her.

"You…" She blushed.

"Yes… me." He laughed and glanced at me. I shook my head… oh yes you William!

Dinner was served and we said grace and then ate laughing and talking about Cole and Carla's big day.

I could help her out and so could mother, Hannah and Aunt Marie, we could have everything ready by then.

"But it will be so cold. Where should we have the reception?" She looked at Cole and he was lost for words.

"I…"

"How about here, in the hotel?" William smiled.

"But they have customers." Carla sighed out.

"Let me look into it and I shall find out what I can, alright?"

"Alright…" Carla smiled at William.

We finished dinner and everyone agreed to turn in early for an early start. Cole said that if we could get everything packed and out of Cranes in two days, they could start on the carpentry work and then it would go fast. But us women, needed to stay out of harm's way. The next few days were going to be rather messy with things everywhere that we could injure ourselves on. We women decided to take care of the stores and in the moving of them.

After we bid each other good night, William and I retired to our room and dressed for bed. I took my simple gown out the one that was my second choice in the box that William had given me. I took down my hair and crawled into the bed. William took me into his arms.

"I've waited all day for this." He kissed me tenderly and made love to me slow and gentle. He was in a quiet and tender mood tonight. He made me feel like I was floating on air. He was so gentle and loving. His touch was like a feather. He held me in his arms afterwards, content.

~ Chapter 19 ~

We both woke at the same time and lay in bed enjoying each other and just being together, close.

After a little while, we gave in and dressed heading down to the restaurant, sitting by the window. We ordered our breakfast. I sipped my coffee glancing out the window.

"Rebecca, what's wrong? You're too quiet." William took my hand.

"I am looking for that boy Joey."

"Why?" He looked at me not understanding.

"Well, before we left for the estate, I had breakfast here. I watched that boy Joey, the one who you thought homeless?"

"Yes."

"Well, I saw him talking to a very tiny little girl pointing her back down the alley, like he was telling her to go back. Then he tried to talk to a couple of men and one walked away and the other pushed him down." I saw William's eyes go dark.

"So what happened?" His tone was cool.

"When I saw the man push him down, I ran out and crossed the street to see if I could find him and could not."

"Where did he go?" William's eyes were truly concerned.

"I don't know, but I walked down the alley to see if I could see him or the little girl."

"You did?" He sat forwards.

"No, I called out to them but didn't hear or see anything, so I came back here. I think he is homeless and has a little sister. William she had to have been no older than four." I sighed.

"We need to watch out for Joey."

"What will you do, William?" I held my breath.

"First we need to talk to Joey…" He stared out the window.

"What if they are homeless? It's so cold now…" He didn't say anything at first.

"The only thing I do know is, no child should be homeless!" His words were angry. He stared out the window watching. He didn't speak for the longest time. He pursed his lips deep in thought.

"You said there was a little girl as well?" I could see hurt in his eyes.

"Yes… she was so small and she looked so thin." Tears welled in my eyes when I thought about them and the possibly of being homeless and homeless in the cold!

"And you say that you went down the alley and called to them?" He looked back out the window. He closed his eyes and opened them still looking.

"Yes, maybe they went in one of the alley doors?"

"I tell you what… we will watch out for them and when Joey appears I will talk to him. He already knows me." I could tell this really bothered him.

"Thank you William." He squeezed my hand.

"If we didn't do something, then we would be just as guilty as if we put them on the streets, if they are homeless. I'll check around, maybe someone took them in?" His eyes were saying he didn't think it was true.

"You're right."

"I don't want you to go down the alley alone anymore. There may be a drifter in there." His words frightened me.

"All the more reason to find out about the children…" I shook my head now afraid for them even more.

"Yes." Our breakfast came and neither of us was very hungry. All I could do was think about Joey and his Sister and I knew William wasn't eating for the same reason. He kept looking out the window then at me. I knew he liked Joey the first time he saw him.

We both gave up on eating and decided to go on to mother's.

"Maybe we will see him as we walk." I nodded but could see the pain in his eyes. He really wanted to talk to the boy now.

"I have to admit, that I thought about Joey ever since I saw him." I looked up at him and he rubbed the back of my hand.

"I'm afraid that I am guilty of that as well. " He looked down at me giving me a slight smile.

"We're sure to find out about him or see him again." I smiled back at him.

We were in front of mother's shop and William stopped me and looked into my eyes.

"Go ahead in…I have to go check on something."

"Alright, William, how long will you be?"

"Not long, tell Cole I will be back in no more than an hour."

"But are you alright?"

"Yes my love, I couldn't be happier." He kissed me softly and his eyes looked into mine tenderly.

"Then go on do what you must." I knew what he was going to do and he knew I did, but there was no sense talking about it. He gave me a quick kiss and smiled wide as I nodded. I went into the store and smiled to myself. I bet he finds out something or has two children with him when he returns.

"Mother" I called out as I shut the door.

"Yes, are you ready to go to Carla's?" I called.

"Yes, one minute." She called back.

"Why are you yelling?" Cole laughed wiping his hands.

"I was calling for mother. William had to do something, and said to tell you he will be here within an hour." I wiped his face with the rag he had in his hand.

"I'll be glad for the strength he has. He sure can swing a sledge hammer." Cole shook his head.

"Alrighty, let's go." Mother smiled and pulled her shawl around her tight.

"See you later, Cole." Mother kissed his cheek and we walked across the street.

We entered Carla's and she was behind the boxes wiping the shelves off.

"How long have you been here?" Mother asked.

"Since five… I couldn't sleep."

"Why?" I looked at her concerned.

"Well…" She blushed and looked down.

"Where is Hannah?" Mother asked.

"She is in the back room cleaning." Carla's face was so red.

"I'll just go help her. I think you could use a sister." She winked as she turned to leave us.

"Thank you, Mother." I called after her.

"Now, what's this all about?" I took her hand to sit in the settee.

"Well last night… Cole…"

"What, Carla… Did he say or do something to you?"

"Yes and no." She had tears in her eyes.

"What, Carla?" I was worried now.

"Well, last night Cole and I went for a walk down to the pond, it was so cold we didn't stay too long. We ended up in the barn."

"Yes." I was listening.

"We sat in the tack room and warmed up. He made coffee on the burner and we stayed in there talking for the longest time.

"So what did he say or do, that has you so troubled?"

"He told me he didn't want to wait to get married to be together… and I…"

"You what?"

"Slapped his face…" She looked down

"You what?" I wanted to laugh.

"Well, I slapped his face! He was so angry and I didn't expect that reaction from myself, but there it was! I couldn't stop it."

"What did he do?" Her face told me this was serious.

"He grabbed me and shook me. He was mad…so mad."

"He didn't hurt you, did he?" I was in shock.

"No, but he looked at me and yelled at me for slapping him, then kissed the daylights out of me."

"He did?"

"Yes! Oh Rebecca, don't think less of me."

"I would never!"

"Well, he and I got caught up in the moment and we… we…" She looked at my shocked face.

"You and Cole… you…"

"Yes, it just happened. I wasn't aware of what was happening, it was way too late." She hung her head.

"Now look here, Carla Taylor. You're marrying him right?"

"Yes… but…"

"You love him and he loves you right?"

"Yes… but…"

"No buts about it, Carla. I don't think you did anything wrong. I would never think less of you or Cole. It is so hard not to when you're in love."

"Really?" Her eyes stopped tearing.

"Yes, really!"

"Honest?" She looked at me in disbelief.

"Yes!" I hugged her.

"Well, that's not all."

"What there's more?"

"Yes, I stayed in Cole's room all night, but I don't think your mother knows, but if she did, she would look less at me."

"No she wouldn't, but she would surely have had you two married by now though." I laughed.

"I'm glad you understand." She hugged me back.

"So you and he are getting married Christmas eve?"

"Yes." I hugged her again nodding in understanding.

We dove into work and had everything ready for the move and afterward we all headed over to Crane's store to help them, finding that they were finished as well. We decided to put everything in mother's barn and move Crane's store right away. William had not returned yet and it had been four hours since I saw him last. I was so busy thinking about Carla's predicament and the moving that time slipped by without notice. I went to mother's shop and one of Cole's men said Cole went to look for William. I went back to Carla's and started to load the wagon. We had it almost full when William showed up smiling.

"Here let me help you."

"Where have you been husband?"

"Ah, you missed me?"

"Yes!" I waited as he stood in front of me.

"Well, I've had to take care of a couple of things and I'll tell you about it when we get back to the room." He nodded.

"Well, everyone was worried sick about you. Cole went looking for you."

"Yes, I know. I just saw him. He's back at your mother's."

"Did you find Joey?" I searched his eyes.

"Yes." His eyes were twinkling.

"What happened?"

"That's what I want to talk to you about." He furrowed his eyes and looked down.

"Alright, William, we'll talk about this later." He smiled and kissed me.

"Thank you. I'll see you at dinner?" I smiled at him knowing whatever he did was the right thing to do.

"But, come for me before you go, I'll walk back with you to the room." He raised his brow.

"Alright…" I smiled nodding.

"Thank you, I'll be waiting." He kissed me quick and went to mother's shop.

"What was that about?" Carla smiled.

"I think William has done a wonderful thing."

"What?" She looked at me smiling.

"I'm not sure, but if I know my husband, he did." I smiled to myself know I would be very proud of him tonight.

"I don't understand." She looked confused.

"I do." I smiled and went back into the store.

We filled the wagon to the brim and drove it to mother's house and unloaded it and came back.

It took three trips and we were totally exhausted. Mother called it a day and we all chimed AMEN! It was close enough to four o'clock to call it a day. We went to mother's shop and sat in the back room, until the men were ready to leave we had a cup of coffee and relaxed.

"Alright ladies, are you already to leave?"

"Yes!" More than ready!

"Well, let's go!" Cole took Carla's hand and she glanced at me and smiled.

"I'll see you tomorrow." I nodded to Carla and Cole as William put his coat on.

"Come." He smiled as we all left and went our way. I was exhausted!

We went to the hotel tired and William ordered dinner in tonight. I didn't care what he ordered as long as it was food and it was hot! In the room, I turned on the bath right away. I went to the wardrobe and took my nightgown out and trudged back to the washroom.

"William...? Where are you?"

"I'm here." He came into the washroom.

"Where were you a moment ago?"

"Well I..."

"Oh yes, was there something you wanted to talk to me about?"

"Well yes... but it can wait until you've had your bath."

"If you are sure?"

"I am." He smiled and kissed my forehead.

I was so tired, I undressed and slid into the bath water. I washed my hair and rinsed for I knew if I relaxed too much I would fall asleep and I was hungry. Soon I was out and dried off dressed in my nightgown and robe.

"William?" I called for I had not seen him since he left the washroom.

"William..." I called out again. Hum, he must have fallen asleep.

I heard a tap on the door and went out to find William not in the room at all.

"Who is it?" I called when I reached the door.

"Room service..." Ah dinner! I opened the door and let the man come in with a large cart.

"This is too much food!" I looked up at the porter.

"No miss... dinner for four?"

"Four?" William appeared behind the porter with a 'please forgive me look' on his face.

"Come in." I knew what he had done...that...that angel! I wanted to smile.

"Here you go." William handed him a tip and shut the door and turned on his heel to me.

"Rebecca, we have guests for dinner tonight!" He grinned like a little boy, or little boy and girl!

"We do, do we?" I wanted to hug him and kiss his wonderful face, but I held back.

"Then, I best change." I turned to walk away and he stopped me by taking my arm.

"Wait!"

"William, what is it?" I searched his eyes seeing he was about ready to bust.

"The guests won't care what you're wearing."

"I don't understand..." I pretended even though I did.

"Wait here!" He was so excited. It was all over his glowing face.

I pushed the cart to the wing back chairs and took two pillows off the bed placing them on the floor next to my chair.

"Rebecca, I'd like you to meet two special friends of mine."

I turned around to see a small boy and William holding a very small little girl.

"Well, well who do we have here?" I walked over to William and his little guests.

"It's me! Joey!" He had on new clothes, new shoes his reddish dark hair was cut and shiny brushed to one side and clean from top to bottom. His nose was even shinny and his teeth were brushed white as he smiled a big smile with bright blue eyes and oh no! He had dimples! He looked very different than when we saw him in the street! I held out my hand and he shook it.

"My! What a handsome man you are, Mr...."

"Mr. McKinney, Joey McKinney, but I think it will be alright for you to call me Joey. This here is my little sister, Megan. She don't talk, but she understands everything you say."

Megan rested her head on Williams shoulder as she sucked on her two middle fingers. She moved to hide in William's neck but stopped as I spoke to her softly. Slowly William stepped into the room closing the door behind him.

"Well aren't you a beautiful little girl." Her reddish dark hair hung in natural ringlets and had at least one bow in her hair that I could see. She was so pretty but so small, it was pitiful. I knew she wasn't eating daily, maybe every other day if not worse.

"She's smart too and she is only four, we just had her birthday."

"And when was that?" I smiled down at Joey.

"Yesterday, I got her a brush and a sucker." I wanted to cry for I saw tears in William's eyes as Joey spoke proudly.

"Well, are you two hungry?" I cleared my throat.

"Yes Ma'am, though William here fed us lunch and bought us new clothes... and had a woman to stay with us all day. She scrubbed the daylights out of my hair. I thought I was gonna go bald!" He shook his head and I had to laugh.

"That was real nice of William." William and I sat down in the chair and Joey stood with his hands in his pocket.

"Here Joey, would you mind sitting on this pillow, just for tonight?" I handed him the pillow.

"No Ma'am! It will do." He took the pillow and sat down licking his lips. William tried to move Megan, but she held tightly on to him. He smiled and left her clinging to his neck.

"Megan." William spoke softly.

"I'll let you sit on my lap if you want, but we both can't eat this wonderful smelling food if you don't sit on my leg." He smiled at me as I wiped tears.

"Do you think that would be alright?" He tried to look at her face.

"She nodded slowly and let go sliding down his chest and onto his lap, her little dress was so pretty, light green with dark green bows and she had on ankle socks with black shoes.

"There... that's better now isn't it?" William looked into her little face waiting for her to do something and finally, she nodded with a sigh.

"Now, let's see what's under the covers." Her eyes went big watching William's every move.

"Joey, will you help me uncover our plates?" William asked him.

"Yes Sir." He stood back up and his eyes were as big as bug's eyes when he saw the steaming pot roast, potatoes, carrots and rolls… four tall glasses of milk and a pot of coffee.

"Lordy, Ma'am! This is enough to last me and Megan two weeks!" His face told me, he was serious.

I sucked in a shocked breath and William closed his eyes. Joey thought it was enough for the two for them for two weeks!

"So, Joey, tell me about yourself." I looked at William and he closed his eyes and took a deep breath. I knew it was going to be a hard story to hear. William cut up pieces of meat for Megan and I gave Joey his plate after he sat back down.

"Well, Ma'am, I'll just start back to the beginning. My Ma, Pa and me and Megan and our three other brothers and Sister lived in Clay, which is about three hours from here. Well, that's what William said anyway. We had a nice house and Pa worked the farm every day. We were really happy, you know a family.

Well one day, these men came to the house and we heard Pa yelling at them to leave. Me and Megan was playing in the barn up in the hayloft, you know catching mice. Well, I looked out the loft door and there was four men standing pointing guns at Pa. I told Megan to stay still and not say a word. Then they shot Pa dead and Ma ran out and they shot her dead and then they took my sister and my brothers with them.

I don't know what happened to them, I never seen them again. They burned our house down and started the barn on fire with us in it, but I knew that there was a tree out the other side of the barn and we crawled over to it as quietly as we could. We could hear them say that they would take my sister to their house and my brothers to a place called Link. I don't know what that was. Me and Megan waited till the fire was almost to us and had to climb down the tree. We stayed in the woods and watched everything burn to the ground. Megan cried calling for ma and pa, but there was nothing I could do. I looked for Ma and Pa and couldn't find them. I guess they drug them into the house.

We went to town and told people what happened, but no one would listen. They said Pa got what he deserved, but I never believed them. That's when I stopped asking for help. I had to take care of Megan and me.

I was born at that house, and I never met any of my Uncles or Aunts. Shoot, I don't even know their names. So, as I saw it, it was up to me. I didn't cry in front of Megan, she was scared like a rabbit, shoot, she was only two." He bit into his roast beef and took too big of a bite. His cheek was puffed out.

"So, you don't know who your family is?" I looked down at his sweet face.

"Nope, this one family took Megan and me for a while, a good Christian home, but they was mean and we left. There's no way I was going to let Megan get a whipping for something she didn't do. The people tried to find our family, but no one answered their letters. So one night Megan and I left and we walked and walked and ended up here. I guess we've been here since. Me and Megan stayed in a barn loft most of the time. I would have to steal food from time to time and take it to her. She's not doing so well though… she's getting skinny, but I'm trying. Most folks here are nice… at least they don't make us leave. I make Megan hide from everyone, cause they'll steal her away, then I won't be able to take care of her."

"No one's tried to help you here?"

"Nope, they turn their heads, but this nice lady leaves milk and rolls out every day in the morning and night for me. She doesn't think I know she does it, but I do."

"Is her name Mrs. Glenn?"

"Yep!" She smiles at me when she sees me, I like her. She tried to get me to go with her, but I had Megan here, so I couldn't."

"I see... So you didn't tell her about Megan?"

"Nope, but I think she would have been nice to her." He took a deep breath.

"And why did you let William know about Megan." I looked up at William and he winked as Megan chewed on a carrot.

"William here is a nice man. He was looking for me to help him do some work. He found me by the alley as I was trying to get Megan here to go back to our place."

"Which is where?"

"Oh, this great big wood box, it's warm and I have blankets and our things in there. You'd be proud of me. It's under lots of boxes and when it rains, we hardly get wet."

"So, William saw Megan?"

"Yes, but I wasn't afraid of him even though he is as big as a giant! I knew he was one of the nice ones. He asked me to come with him and if Megan could come too. He said he would take care of us."

"He did, did he?" I was so proud of William!

"Yep… I like him and so does Megan." I looked at her and she nodded.

"He's a good man." I looked at him chewing on a carrot that Megan was trying to get out of his mouth and I laughed at them.

"So, what do you think you would like to do?" I looked at William and his eyes pleaded with me.

"Who me?" Joey smiled.

"Yes."

"I asked William if he had a barn or a shack me and Megan could stay in and I would work for him for food and a place for us to live."

"Well, what did he say?"

"He said it was up to you." He looked down and then back up.

"Up to me huh?" I looked at William and he was biting his bottom lip and smiling. Hmm, he remembered to use that against me.

"Well, I think that William has the perfect place for you and yes, there is a shack…" I laughed.

"Yeppie Megan! I found us a home!" He smiled at her and she clapped her hands Joey laughed and almost falling off the pillow.

"But Joey, did William tell you that we wouldn't leave here for a little while?"

"Yes, but that's alright, he has a nice lady staying with us and all in the room next to this one. I never stayed in this place before, but I really like it, except the baths."

"Megan, would you like to go with us?" I smiled at her wanting to hold her in my arms, but knew to take my time. She nodded and hugged William.

"Well then, we have some things to take care of!" I nodded to Joey.

"Like what?" He turned his head sideways and looked at me squinting one eye.

"Well, don't you worry about that, William and I will see to everything. All you have to worry about is eating and sleeping for now." I smiled and he stood and wrapped his arms around my neck. I was startled. He whispered in my ear.

"Megan wouldn't have made it much longer. Thank you Ma'am." He kissed my cheek and sat back down. Tears welled in my eyes, those poor little children!

"Well, won't it be nice not to have to worry about Megan anymore or food or clothes and being warm?" I smiled at Joey.

"Yes it will. William says there are plenty of rooms in the shack and lots of food too."

"That there is!" I gave William an I love you smile.

I watched Megan and Joey eat, noticing that they were both full only after a few bites. My heart ached seeing now that they weren't used to eating. Joey had taken care of Megan for almost two years. Two years!

"How old are you Joey and when is your birthday?" I smiled down at him as he yawned.

"Me? My birthday is May twenty first and I'm nine."

"So your sister was older and brothers?"

"Yes, my sister was sixteen and my brother Henry was twelve and Paul was fourteen. I think their dead."

"Why do you think that?" I tried to stay calm.

"Well, I heard someone in the town say that they found three bodies in a gully on the outskirts of town. They were teenagers, shot."

"You are so brave to not cry, don't you miss them?"

"Aww Ma'am, men don't cry, babies do and yeah I miss them, but there with the Lord and Ma and Pa." He took my very breath. How brave indeed!

"Well, I already like you and your sister and think we can work something out." I just couldn't believe this brave little boy and all he's had to go through.

"Well, I'll make one thing clear."

"And what is that?" I smiled holding my breath.

"I want to work for William…for the shack and food. I'm not lazy and want to pay for my keep."

"Well, it's a deal then." I held out my hand and he shook it.

We finished our dinner and William uncovered the last dish, apple pie! He sliced them each apiece and Megan tried to feed William. I laughed as she stuck a huge piece in his mouth. Joey laughed as well. William rolled his eyes and chewed it up… He was in love with the children already.

I sat and watched William and Megan eat and if you didn't know better, you'd think she was his own. I looked down at Joey and he was asleep.

"William." I motioned towards Joey and he still had the fork in his hand. William looked down and looked at Megan and she smiled and nodded. William looked up at me and smiled.

"Megan, are you tired?" She nodded.

"Would you mind sitting on Rebecca's lap while I carry your brother next door? He's worked so hard today." She nodded.

"That's my girl." He stood and sat her down in my lap and she looked into my face and smiled. My heart pounded in my chest! She didn't weigh more than my handbag!

"Now, I'll be right back, unless you want for Rebecca to carry you over with us?" She nodded.

"Let's get you two tucked in bed." Megan wrapped her arms around my neck and we took them next door.

"We're back, Mrs. Bennett. This is my wife, Rebecca." She nodded and smiled. She had their bedclothes out and ready for them. I dressed Megan and wiped her hands and William took care of Joey. He wiped his hands and face off and he never stirred.

"Here you go sweetie." I tucked her in and William tucked Joey in and Megan smiled and turned wrapping around Joey. She closed her eyes and I leaned over and kissed her cheek. She never moved. William and I stood for a while at the foot of the bed just watching them sleep.

"I can't believe they were here all the time and no one saw them and no one cared when they saw Joey!" Mrs. Bennett was almost in tears.

"I think their lives have just been made much better." I looked up at William and he smiled tenderly with tears in his eyes.

"They'll never want for anything again." William took a deep breath.

"Let's get some rest. I think we have our hands full now." William smiled.

"Yes, and it's all your fault." I looked up to him and he looked at me with surprise.

"What?"

"Yes, your fault and you are an angel and I love you." Tears fell down my cheeks and William and I said good night to Mrs. Bennett and went back to our room. Once inside I went to the chair and sat down and cried.

"Rebecca... what is wrong?"

"Oh, William, those poor children!" He knelt in front of me and took my hands.

"Rebecca, we will take care of them now. We have to, they need us."

"We need them too." I cried in his arms and he did as well.

"I love them already!"

"So do I" William wiped my tears and I wiped his.

"We're parents!" I laughed.

"We are!" He laughed as well.

"Now, I know what took you so long, you bought them clothes, shoes and everything they needed. Hired a governess and fed them as well. You're wonderful William and I love you even more." I kissed him tenderly as he wrapped his arms around me. He stretched smiling with elation in his eyes and such joy.

"I still need to take a bath." He smiled.

"Go ahead and I'll put the cart outside the door."

"… save the pie!" Smiling he stood and went to the washroom.

I cleaned up our dinner and crawled into the bed. I have two children! Not just one, but two beautiful children! I was so happy and they were so beautiful! The thought of no one noticing Joey made me angry. I couldn't wait to tell everyone about them, especially mother. I know she had helped them more than she knew. I wonder if she ever saw Megan. The poor thing was so tiny. I wonder why she couldn't speak. Joey was so strong willed, it reminded me of William so much and maybe that was another reason he had to go after them, though he didn't know about Megan. I recalled the way William looked at Megan and how he was already so attached to her. She too took to him the way she nuzzled into his neck. It was so sweet.

"Good, you're still awake." William came out in a towel wrapped around his waist and hopped on to the bed.

"Do you think we should check on the children?" I looked up into his handsome face.

"No, I think they are sleeping soundly. Remember, they haven't slept in a bed in a long time and I think when Megan laid down, she was asleep by the time you kissed her cheek." He smiled tenderly.

"Joey is quite the brave boy… He reminds me of you." I smiled thinking about his 'matter of fact' ways.

"You know, that's what I thought when I first looked into that little fella's eyes. He was so brave and so willing to do my bidding. It reminded me of when I did the same thing he was doing when I was homeless." He looked down and then reached for the tin of pie and took a bite.

"What are you going to do now?" He held out a bite for me.

"What do you mean?" He took another bite of pie.

"Well, we have to insure their well-being legally, don't we?"

"Yes, I suppose you're right, Lady Andrews, and I want to thank you."

"For what?"

"For being the angel I know you are."

"What do you mean?"

"You were thinking the same thing concerning the children."

"I was, and to me it doesn't matter if I gave birth to them or not. They are children and it takes more than just two people making a baby to be real parents. I know it will take time for them to get use to 'The Shack'." I laughed.

"Ah, the shack...yes, can you believe that he wants to live on his own taking care of his sister by himself...and then work for his housing and food?" William shook his head in disbelief.

"He's so brave..." Tears filled eyes...

"You do realize that you are a Mother."

"I know and you are now a father."

"I know." William looked at me, love overfilling his eyes with tears.

"I love you, wife." His lips were a breath away.

"And you are a true knight in shining armor and I love you husband." He kissed me tenderly and deeply.

His lips covered mine with love and passion that soon grew to desire. We both loved each other with boundless passion and energy and are truly evenly yoked. My heart raced, as he called out my name in a thunderous roar. His lips crushed mine as the moment came to the pinnacle. We lay lost in the moment and in each other's arms. He was truly the most magnificent and loving man I could have ever hoped for. Tears fell down my cheek thinking how blessed I was that God brought us together.

"Rebecca, are you alright?"

"Yes." William wiped the tears from my eyes.

"Then why are you crying?" His voice was soft and tender.

"I'm just so happy and was thinking how blessed we are to have had God bring us together. My heart gets so full of love for you at how you love me that there is no place for it to go, so I can't help but to cry." He pulled me to his chest.

"Rebecca... That's the most beautiful thing you could tell me. I know how you feel. I feel like that too sometimes." He brushed his lips across mine and held me to his chest. I was so relaxed just listening to his heart softly beating.

~ Chapter 20 ~

"Rebecca?" William called my name.

"Rebecca, wake up my love. We have children." His tone was so full of joy.

I blinked open my eyes remembering that we indeed do have children!

"William, what time is it?" I sat up yawning, it wasn't very bright out.

"It's early, but I thought that we needed to be up before they are so we can enjoy a cup of coffee, want some?"

"You're dressed! How long have you been up?" He had his denim jeans on and work shirt.

"About an hour. It's six thirty, sun's coming up."

"Alright..." I sleepily sat up then realized,

"William, we have CHILDREN!" I jumped out of bed and hugged his neck as he held me in his arms.

"Why don't you get dressed and I'll fix you a cup of coffee and we can relax until Mrs. Bennett knocks on the door. Then we'll know then the children are awake." I nodded and rushed into the washroom, washing then dressing and pulling my hair into a loose braid. Then I powdered my nose. I was done in no time! Children! We have two children!

"Was that fast enough?" I smiled as I walked back into the room.

"Very and here is your coffee my love, come sit and wake up. It's going to be fun telling everyone about the children."

"That it will! William?"

"Hmm?" He sipped his coffee.

"Do you think we should adopt them right away?"

"Yes, I was thinking about that as I woke up this morning. We'll do that in Winchester. My lawyer will check into the children's family and do a wire search, and if there are no family members, we will petition for adoption"

"But what if they find someone who wants them?"

"Well that's a risk we'll have to take. You and I wouldn't be able to love those two if it wasn't right from the start." He smiled and sipped his coffee.

"You're right, William."

"Mr. Lawrence is mother's attorney. Maybe you and I can start it this afternoon."

"How about before we go to your mother's? Mr. Lawrence can then put out the wire to Clay and the sheriff's office. We should know something by this afternoon." He was right and his face was glowing with excitement.

"I know someone could claim them, and if they are good people, then we still helped them."

"That's right." William smiled softly and we drank our coffee waiting to hear for the knock on the door.

"Lord Andrews!" We heard a woman's plea.

"Lord Andrews! Please..." William and I raced to the door. It was Mrs. Bennett. She was wringing her hands.

"What is it, what's wrong?" William voice was panicked.

"The boy, he was gone when I woke up."

"And Megan?"

"She's still asleep, but the boy, Joey was gone. I didn't hear him leave!" She wrung her hands with worry.

"Alright, calm down... I'll go look for him." I had gotten William's coat before he even asked and he looked at me and kissed me a quick kiss and squeezed my hand and then he said not a word and ran down the hall and stairs.

"Don't worry Mrs. Bennett, William will find him and find out why he left." I walked with her to Megan's room and took the coffee with us. We waited for William to return with Joey.

"Mrs. Bennett, how long have you been watching children?" I sipped my coffee.

"Oh, since I was about twenty five. I was never married and never wanted to."

"I'm from here originally but I don't recall ever seeing you."

"And you wouldn't, I'm from Winchester. Lord Andrews sent for me right away."

"I see, you mean yesterday?"

"Yes. I used to work for his father. I used to watch them from time to time. Pity what happened to his family, they were such lovely people." She sighed and shook her head frowning.

"So you know William?" I was surprised!

"Yes, I remembered the name right away. His mother usually had Ms. Maze watch them, but when she couldn't, it was me their father sent for." She said rather proudly.

"Well, this is wonderful! No wonder William was not worried about you, he knew you already!" I laughed and shook my head.

"That he did Ma'am, you know if I recall right, that Joey was a lot like Lord Andrews when he was a tyke." She smiled softly chuckled looking down.

"That's just what I told him last night!" I thought that it must be true. He was a lot like William.

"Well I bet there is a good reason why Joey slipped off this morning, if he's a lot like William that is." I smiled and shook my head as well.

"I hope so! It scares the daylights out of me."

"I know Joey won't leave Megan or go far from her. He's been watching her for almost two years all by himself! I still can't believe it." And I couldn't!

"I know, the lad told me the whole story yesterday. I think they did drag his Ma and Pa into the house and burned it all down so there was no evidence." She nodded in a sure way with her lips pursed and her brow furrowed.

"I can't imagine them going through all that and coming out so strong." Joey was very brave and very different than most boys his age.

"I do know that Joey likes Lord Andrews and that angel sleeping in the bed over there cried when Lord Andrews left yesterday. You should have seen Lord Andrews face, why if I didn't know better, I could feel the man's heart break." William was such a loving man and the more I found out about him, the more I loved him, was there no end to his love?

"I know he was so full of joy last night that he had tears in his eyes."

"I think it was because of his own loss that he takes the children to heart." I nodded in agreement with her and we fixed another cup of coffee.

"I really didn't mean to scare you."

"I know son, but I would have gone with you." William and Joey walked through the door.

"Joey!" I couldn't help but to run to hug Joey.

"He's alright Rebecca."

"Joey, I was so worried!" I was so relieved to see him.

"I just went to get the brush and sucker I got for Megan and the rest of our things. William explained that if we were going to live on in the same place, we had to tell you if we wanted to do something and you would tell us if you were going to do something. We made a deal." He smiled.

"I think that is a good idea." I looked up at William and smiled.

"He promised to never scare us again and we would never scare him either, we're partners."

"Is that so?" I looked into Joey's sweet face smiling.

"Yep!" He hugged my neck and kissed my cheek.

"Well I'm glad for that!" I smiled and tapped his nose.

"You sure do smell good, Miss Rebecca." He smiled big.

"Why thank you." We heard the bedclothes rustle and Megan was holding her arms out looking at William. William's eyes softened and he went to her.

"Well, good morning my princess, did you sleep well?" She nodded and yawned scooting towards William.

"Are you hungry?" He brushed a curl away from her face. She nodded then pointed to the washroom.

"We'll get you two dressed, and then we will go down to the restaurant. Suddenly Megan took a hold of William's face with her tiny hands, one on each of William's cheek. She was shaking her head no, her curls flying outwards.

"You don't want to eat down stairs?" She shook her head No again.

"She's a bit shy of people." Joey looked up at me smiling.

"It's alright honey. We'll order it to be sent up here, alright?" Tears were in her bright blue eyes as she nodded and wrapped her arms around William's neck... then she pointed to the washroom.

"You want to take a bath?" She nodded scooting off his lap, jumping to the floor and took William's first finger wrapping her entire hand around it, pulling him to the washroom. He followed her laughing softly. He looked at me and Joey, smiling loving every moment of this.

"I bet you're hungry Joey?" I smiled down at him as he looked up at me.

"Yes Ma'am." He licked his lips.

"And what sounds good to you this morning?" I laughed for his face was so angelic.

"I think I would love some pancakes! I haven't had them in forever." He smiled and shook his head.

"I think that sounds wonderful! Does your sister like them too?"

"Well to be honest, she's never had pancakes." He looked down and frowned. I realized that she probably never had much of anything before.

"Well she will today!" I smiled wanting to cry.

"Rebecca!" William called out to me and we all raced into the washroom.

"What's wrong?" We stood in the door way, Megan had a hold of William's shirt.

"I think she wants me to take a bath with her." His eyes pleaded HELP!

"Oh... OH! A... Megan, William has already had a bath this morning, but I'm sure Joey here would love another bath." I looked down at him and he was about to say no, but I added...

"This bath will be fun, I have bubbles." I said in a bribing tone. Joey scrunched his face in thought.

"Alright, if Mrs. Bennett doesn't scrub the hide off of me." We laughed and agreed.

"I will get the bubbles while William orders room service." We all agreed and I set out for our room. William went down to the restaurant leaving Mrs. Bennett to tend to the children. When I returned, I found Mrs. Bennett in control. I poured a small amount of bubbles into the water and Megan's eyes went as wide as Joey's as the bubbles grew.

I stood in the doorway and just watched them playing with the bubbles. The thought occurred to me that they probably never had a bubble bath, from the look on their faces, I was probably right. I heard William coming back into the room, his arms surrounded my waist as we watched them having a time in the tub. Mrs. Bennett was covered with bubbles and Joey took a whole hand full of bubbles and blew them into her face.

"Now, now, I think I have enough bubbles on me and you and the floor." She was trying to calm them down, but when Megan blew some into Mrs. Bennett's face they laughed out so hard that they slipped under the water. It scared William so much that he ran to the tub and plunged both arms into the water and pulled up two sputtering children. Joey was laughing, but Megan threw her arms around William's neck mortified.

"Shhh, I've got you honey. It's alright now." Mrs. Bennett wrapped Megan and William in a towel and then got Joey out, though he protested a little, but got out. I took care of dressing Megan and William helped Joey. Megan pointed to my hair wanting it done like mine, so I braided it just like mine and put a bow at the top and bottom of her braid. Her dress was a blue long sleeved calico with white eyelet lace for ties. William had done a wonderful job at buying clothes for the children. Joey was dressed like William in denim jeans and a work shirt and was adorable. Just as we finished with the children, breakfast arrived.

We ate without incident and during breakfast, William and I explained that we had been working at mothers and had to help them today. I suggested that Mrs. Bennett could take the children to the park that was if Megan wanted to.

The children ate up the pancakes smothered in syrup. It tickled William to no end how Megan wanted to feed him. He was covered in syrup and butter by the time breakfast was over. He was going to have to change clothes, as he was wet from the bath anyway. William promised that if they were good, he would bring them back a surprise tonight and they crossed their hearts and sat like angels. After William was sure Megan was alright with him leaving, we were on our way to mother's.

"I can't wait to tell everyone about the children!" I hugged his arm as we walked towards mothers.

"I know what you mean, but I wish there was a way to introduce them and tell about them at the same time. With Megan being so shy, we couldn't take her into the restaurant." He took a deep breath.

"How about 'a get together' at mother's tonight?" I suggested.

"Do you think she will agree?" He looked down with his brows raised not sure.

"Well, if I tell her there is something I want to tell them about, or should I say that 'We' want to tell them all." I smiled know that would work for sure.

"But won't she think..." He was thinking what I was.

"Yes, but it is true anyway...we do have an announcement to make and we do have two new children." Which was the truth.

"You're right. I hate to mislead her though."

"But we're not, I don't care if I gave birth to them or not... as soon as they're officially ours, then we will be parents."

"Can you leave early?" He smiled down at me.

"I think I can get Carla to help me prepare dinner."

"Alright, then we'll do it."

"Mother loves to have all of us there at home anyway."

"Then it's settled. When you leave, I'll get the children and bring them to your mother's after I have the chance to get cleaned up. I'll give you time to clean up and get to your mother's and start dinner. I'll bring Mrs. Bennett if she wants to join us, she just may want the night off." He looked so excited.

"I'll find you and tell you that I'm leaving so you'll have an idea of how long you have. But knowing mother, she'll want to help right away. She won't be able to wait!"

"I bet that's right."

We got to mother's shop and went in. Mother was surprised to see us so early and was still drinking coffee with all the workers. The place was coming along so well, though it looked like a tornado hit still, but you could see the changes.

"My men should be arriving today, most likely on the morning train." William poured him and me a cup of coffee and sat in one of the dusty chairs. He gave me a smile and a wink.

"Great, then well make good time." Cole was pleased.

"I'll check the train and bring them here when they arrive." William kept smiling.

"What's going on with you two this morning?" Mother raised an eyebrow.

"We have an announcement to make but, well we were wondering if we could do it at your house tonight?" I smiled at mother and her eyes lit up brightly.

"Of course! Tonight?" William had guessed right, she was all too willing to grant our request.

"Thank you, Mother... you won't be sorry." I smiled at William and he winked smiling as he sipped his coffee.

"I tell you what. I think we will get done moving Crane's today early, if we work hard. Then we'll freshen up and go to the house." She was smiling so brightly.

"Thank you, Mother." I smiled knowing that she wanted to ask me so badly.

"Well then, I think we ought to get to work then. Carla will be here shortly. She went to the post office."

Carla soon arrived and we women headed for Crane's and jumped into to boxing and moving boxes across the street. I saw William heading towards the train station at nine this morning and a half hour later he came back with five medium built men with tools in a wagon. Mother kept asking me if I needed to rest and I assured her that I didn't. I felt bad that she was thinking I was expecting, but then again, I didn't, she knew of Joey and would be surprised to find out about Megan.

We had finished early as mother said we would and went next door to tell William we were leaving. They were going to continue to work for a couple of hours before quitting, so that was perfect. Mother, Hannah and Aunt Marie were covered with dust and dirt form Crane's for today they too would need time to get cleaned up.

We all needed a bath badly. None of us would even consider cooking without one first! I headed to the hotel and mother, Hannah, Carla and Aunt Marie went to get cleaned up. As soon as I was cleaned up, I was to head right to mothers.

When I reached my room, I took my bath, dressed and checked in on the children. I filled Mrs. Bennett in on what was going on tonight and invited her to come along. She refused, she said she wanted to rest tonight, go to the general store to get a few things, then take a long soaking and read a good book. I thanked her, being grateful for her helping so much and soon was on my way to mothers.

By the time I got to mothers and started to help, everyone, at one time or another, tried to ask me for a hint.

I wouldn't let a peep of a clue out. So finally they all quit asking and concentrated on making dinner. We cooked pork roast drowned in sauce, mashed potatoes, beans, corn bread, gravy, rolls, corn and I made a couple of apple pies to be put in the oven as soon as the pork was done.

"Sure does smell wonderful in here." Cole walked into the kitchen still dirty.

"Heaven's sake, Cole… you need to take a bath." Mother scolded.

"Mike's in the tub as we speak." He kissed Carla's cheek.

"Well you need to get out of here, Cole. I don't want that dust in the food!" Mother scolded.

"Alright! I'll wait outside!"

"Is William here yet?" I smiled at Cole.

"No, he went to the hotel to get the workers settled in and take a bath. I tell you those men are fine carpenters. I've learned so much today. They know all kinds of tricks of the trade." He laughed.

"So they are as good as William claimed?" Aunt Marie stirred the gravy.

"Yes, and with their help. I wouldn't doubt if by the end of two weeks that we're not through and ready to put the finishing touches on the place, if not sooner..." He shook his head.

"That's wonderful! We got Crane's moved in to Carla's today and they're on their own, so we will be free to help."

"No... we don't need your help... yet, besides it's still not safe for you ladies." Cole started out the door.

"We'll let you know when we're ready for you. I guess you can make sure that you have all the things you'll need to open for your grand opening. Have you had a sign ordered?"

"No!" Mother looked at Cole as if she had never thought of that.

"Well think about what you want and go to Hardy's and have one made up for the front. I'll measure the area tomorrow." Cole smiled as Mike walked in the kitchen going for a glass of ice tea.

"Lord... I'm starved." Hannah smacked Mike's hand as it went for one of the baked carrots.

"Ouch!" He cried.

"Go set the table. We're covered up in here." Mother shooed Mike and Cole out of the kitchen.

We soon had everything ready for dinner and were bringing the food into the dining room. We all sat waiting for William. What could be taking him so long? He's had a couple of hours to bathe and get the children ready, unless he had problems with Megan, I hope not. Mother gave in and let Mike have a roll to tied him over for he was drinking too much brandy, and on an empty stomach.

"Hello everyone!" William appeared in the dining room doorway and he winked at me so I knew everything went well. I stood and went to him.

"Before we eat we would like to tell you all something that we are very excited about." William took my hand and entwined his fingers with mine and kissed them.

"Well... come on... we've waited all day!" Mother cried out.

"First off... I want to say that this is something we both have wanted and we feel you'll all be pleased. So we won't keep you in suspense any longer." William looked down at me and squeezed my hand.

414

"Mother... William and I are... well we..."

"Oh, you're going to have a baby!" Mother stood.

"No, Mother." I smiled. Her smile faded as did the others.

"Then what, Rebecca?"

"Well, we are new parents." William smiled and looked at everyone.

"What are you talking about? Tell us already!" Cole was getting more confused by the second.

"There's only one way to tell you and that is to show you. May I introduce you all to the newest additions to our family?" William guided Joey from behind the door, he was a bit shy.

"This is, Joey... Joey McKinney... and ..." William bent down and picked up Megan.

"And this is my little princess, Megan." She held him as tight as she could, and hid her face in his neck. Everyone was speechless and their mouths hung wide open. Mother walked over to Joey and bent over.

"Hello Joey, I'm Rebecca's Mother. I'm so very glad to meet you and your sister."

"I'm glad to meet you too Ma'am." Joey smiled up at her relaxing a little. I heard an 'Aww' coming from the women. Then mother looked at Megan and her eyes softened tenderly.

"Well hello, aren't you a pretty little lady. I like your new shoes." Mother didn't touch her, but Megan peeked at her and tried her best not to smile.

"Let's sit down." I smiled at mother and took Joey's hand, Cole pushed two chairs up to the table. Carla went into the parlor and got two pillows to make the children be able to reach the table.

"I think Megan will want to eat on William's lap, she's very attached to him." I winked at Carla and mother.

"Megan, Joey, I'd like you to meet Rebecca's brothers. This is Mike and Cole, and these are Rebecca's Aunts, Marie and Hannah, and this is Cole's wife to be Carla. Everyone this is Megan and Joey." They all said nothing but smiled and nodded to them. Megan didn't let go of William for one moment.

"Shall we?" William smiled at Joey and tried to look at Megan's face, but she nuzzled into William's neck even more.

"Miss Rebecca?" Joey held out my chair and William looked at me prideful as I sat. William sat next to me with Joey on the corner of the table next to mother and me. Megan had a death grip on William.

"Shall we say grace?" Mother smiled.

"Rebecca's Mother, could I say grace." We all were about to bow our heads, but looked at Joey.

"Of course Joey...it would be an honor." Mother's eye lit up with joy.

"Alright then... everybody." He bowed his head.

"Dear God, Megan and I, well, God, you know I'm speaking for Megan too cause she can't talk. Maybe you'll see to that one day when you're not so busy, but God, me and Megan want to thank you for William coming to find us. We know you love us because that's what my Ma always said the bible said. Megan's too young to know that, but we want you to tell Ma and Pa that we have a home now with Rebecca and William. They have a shack for us and I can work for our keep and if our brothers and sister are there with you God, tell them we are alright now. And God, maybe, just maybe if you think it's right...Well, maybe William and Rebecca will want us to stay. I'm pretty tired of worrying about Megan. She wasn't doing so good, but now Rebecca and William will see to her when I can't. So, God...Thank you and thank you for this food, Amen. Oh Wait I almost forgot! God? Do you think you could see to it that me and Megan could have maybe some new parents one day. Not for me of course, I'm a man after all, but Megan needs a momma, that's all, Amen.

No one said a word and we all slowly lifted our heads. Even Mike was wiping tears away. Joey had prayed with all his heart and I could feel his strength in his words. I looked at William and he had tears streaming down his cheeks.

"What's every one crying for? I was just talking to God." Joey slightly smiled looking at everyone squinting one eye at me.

"Well Joey, I think that was the best prayer anyone of has heard, ever." I leaned over and kissed his cheek.

"Gosh, Rebecca..." His cheeks turned red.

"Let's eat!" Mother was still teary eyed.

We passed the food around the table and Megan still had a hold of William's neck. As we ate William couldn't get Megan to eat a bite.

"Mmm... this is so good." He whispered. Megan lifted her head a little. I knew she was hungry.

"Hey, Megan, it is really good!" Joey had mashed potatoes all over his face.

"Here... would you please try a little of these mashed potatoes. I think Rebecca made them especially for you." William spoke softly as everyone kept their eyes on their plates. Megan looked around the table and saw no one watching and took a fast bite and nodded her head. William was delighted and started to give her bites.

"So, Joey, William agreed to let you work for your keep?" Cole knew better, but went along with what Joey thought.

"Yep! And I'll prove to him that I can do most anything." He smiled.

"I bet you can!" Cole laughed.

"William said the shack was full of food and has everything we needed in it!"

"Oh the shack does, I can promise you that. I've seen it and stayed there myself!" Cole laughed.

"So, it's a good place?" Joey smiled and filled his mouth with a carrot. Megan was eating as well now, but still clinging to William's neck.

"Yes, the best!" Cole smiled.

"Say, we could use a helper at the shop...can you carry hammers and get water for the workers Joey? I'd pay you real good."

"Sure, I need something to do. I don't like having to sit in the hotel room all day." Joey smiled.

"Are you able to start tomorrow?" Cole looked at William and me, then back to William and he nodded.

"Sure, I can come with William... that is if it's alright with William." Joey then looked at William and William winked and nodded.

"This will be my first real job!" Joey smiled and ate the rest of his plate. He was eating much better in just two days I was well pleased. Megan was a bit slower, but she was eating more as well.

"Guess what, Joey?"

"What, Miss Rebecca?"

"We have a special dessert tonight."

"You do?" Joey and Megan looked at me.

"Would you help me?" I asked Joey and he stood and held my chair for me.

"Show me what to do." I took his hand and he followed me into the kitchen.

"Joey, can I ask you something important?" I looked into his bright blue eyes.

"Sure..." He smiled.

"Do you like William and me?" I held my breath.

"Yep! You're the first people that didn't push me down or look at me funny."

"Do you like the thought of going to our home in Winchester?"

"Well, at first I was a little scarred of the idea, but when that Mr. Cole said he even stayed at the shack, I wasn't worried anymore." He looked at me in a serious way.

"Well, after you and Megan see our home, do you think, if you like it, that William and I might have a chance of being those parents you need…I mean Megan does need a mother like you said to God."

"Well… if I like the place and Megan does. I'll talk to her about it, but I can't promise you anything. I do know Megan likes William and you."

"She likes me too?" I smiled brightly, I didn't know if she really did or not.

"Yep, she said you are like her Ma and William is like a Pa, but she's little yet." He looked deep in thought.

"Well, I'm glad to hear that, I like both of you too… a lot!" I laughed.

"Aw… well I like you too, Miss Rebecca, you're pretty and smell really good and you're really nice." He smiled up at me. I wanted to hug the daylights out of him!

"Well, thank you and now let's get dessert!" I smiled thanking God for his answer.

"What is it?" He stood waiting.

"Here, carry this whipped topping in and I'll carry the Apple Pie in." I smiled down handing the bowl to Joey.

"Apple Pie! Wow! We love apple pie! That's Megan's favorite!" He took the bowel and I followed him in carrying two apple pies.

"Look Megan, Rebecca made us apple pie!" Megan finally let go of William enough to clap her hands.

"You like apple pie, Megan?" William smiled at Megan tenderly.

Megan nodded and took William's cheeks in her tiny hands and made him look at her, then she pointed to the whipped topping.

"You want that too?" She nodded.

"Me too… and a lot of it!" William laughed.

Everyone was so taken by the children that they didn't talk through dinner very much. Mike cut the pie up and gave everyone a big piece. Megan fed William as usual. We all watched her stuff a huge piece in his mouth full of whipped topping… we all laughed and so did Megan, though we couldn't hear her. She was starting to relax as we finished dessert. Joey was so full!

"Did you get enough to eat, Joey?" Hannah smiled at him tenderly.

"Yes Ma'am, I can't even move!" He laughed.

418

"We know what you mean! They sure can cook can't they?" Cole laughed.

"Yes Sir!" Joey rolled his eyes! Then we all laughed.

William went into the parlor with Megan still attached to his neck and took Joey with him. Mike and Cole went with him while we women cleaned up the dishes.

"My goodness, Rebecca, I never dreamed that those children were here and I didn't know he was homeless. I thought that he was just poor and then to find out he had a sister!" She shook her head and tears filled her eyes.

"It's alright, Mother. We didn't know for sure he was homeless and didn't know about Megan till the other day, though I did see her before we went to Winchester. I thought I was seeing things. I even went in the alley to look for them but couldn't find either one of them." I hugged mother and told them their story. They all were crying and couldn't believe they survived all winter.

"So, are you two going to make it all legal?"

"William said when we get back to Winchester. He's going to do whatever it takes."

"I think it's funny that William refers to the estate as a shack and so does Joey." Carla laughed.

"All I know is William and I couldn't be more happy or excited!" I smiled and dried the last of the dishes.

"Well I can't wait until the children are all yours!" Mother smiled, Aunt Marie was all teary eyed.

"I just hope no one claims them. William said his lawyer will put out a search. He went to your lawyer and got it going from this end already."

"Good...but what if someone does?" Hannah took my hand.

"Well, we'll deal with that if it comes." I took a deep breath.

After putting everything up and putting the kitchen back to rights, we joined the men in the parlor spending the rest of the evening letting everyone get to know Joey and Joey them. He was bright and answered all their questions. I enjoyed watching William with Megan. I could tell there was no getting the two apart now. After a couple of hours, William saw Joey yawn.

"Everyone, I think it's time to head back and get these two in bed." He stood and Joey laid his head against my hip with his arm around my waist.

"I'm tired as well. Let's meet in the restaurant tomorrow morning."
Megan started to say no.

"Megan is a little shy of people, but maybe if I promise her that she can
sit on my lap just like tonight, she'll go?" She just looked at William with
a scrunched nose as if she was saying she'd think about it.

"Alright, I'm sure I speak for all of us when I say that it was nice to
meet you and come back soon, you welcome here any time." Mother
smiled and patted his arm.

"Thank you for dinner, it was the best!" Joey smiled and yawned again.

We climbed into the wagon and were headed back to town. In no time
the Joey and Megan were fast asleep. I had wondered why William had
not taken the carriage.

"It's so cold tonight William."

"I know, but that is one reason why it took so long to get here. Megan
was afraid of the carriage."

"And the other?"

"I stopped in at the lawyers to see if there was any news and there
wasn't" He smiled softly at me as I ran my fingers through Joey's dark
hair. William wrapped Megan up in his coat. I covered Joey up with the
blanket from under the seat.

"I love them, William." I smiled and looked into William's eyes and
knew his reply. He simply nodded and slapped the reins to go faster.

We soon had the children dressed and in bed not disturbing Mrs.
Bennett... she slept through it all and so did the children. We kissed
them and tucked them in, then went to our room.

"Ah, that little lady sure has you wrapped around her finger Lord
Andrews." I laughed.

"That she does." He pulled me to his chest and kissed me deeply, then
pulled away slowly.

"Should I be worried?" I teased.

"That depends." He spoke in a sultry tone.

"Depends? Depends on what?" I mused.

"Well it depends if you have me wrapped around your little finger as
well."

"And how would I know if I did or not?" I spoke in a soft seductive
way.

"Well, that's the beauty of it all, you don't know."

"Ah I see. Well I'm going to get ready for bed now and we shall see, we
shall see."

420

"I'll be waiting." He kissed me softly and went to his wardrobe and I went to mine, then to the washroom.

I chose one of my new nightwear, that I know he has never seen and it was the two-piece white laced one with the satin ribbon tie. I let my hair down and put a little perfume on. I fluffed my hair put on my robe and went out to find him waiting in the bed covered only to his waist. He had stoked the fire and turned the lamp down.

"Rebecca, you are breathtaking!" He smiled as I stood next to the bed on his side. He reached for the tie on the robe and undid it. His eyes took my outfit in and he was well pleased.

"Come…" He took my hand and pulled me to his chest.

"You smell so good!" He lifted my hair to his nose.

"As you do my Lord…" I rubbed across the hard plain of his chest feeling the silky soft hair between my fingers.

"I love you." He whispered tilting my face to his with one finger.

"And I, you…" His lips covered mine in a passionate kiss and it grew deeper sending warmth throughout my body. His natural sent was all around me like a drug, making my head spin. He slowly loosened the ties on my camisole with his fingers and was soon consuming me with his lips. He made me arch to his every touch as he devoured every inch of my body, I was thrown into rapturous waves of blissfulness. He moved on top of me covering me as he made love to me fulfilling both of our needs. We lay breathing softly, him holding me in his arms well satisfied.

"You are amazing." He whispered softly.

"And you my lord are magnificent." I kissed his chest.

"I could spend the rest of my life making love to you." He whispered.

"Ah, then I do have you wrapped around my finger." I teased.

"And then some." He reached over and turned the lantern off and covered us up holding me in his arms. I heard him rumble a deep rumble and soon was drifting off to sleep.

~ Chapter 21 ~

Once again, William and I woke up at the same time. We washed up and dressed for the day.

"I hope Megan will go down to the restaurant." William sighed.

Quietly we entered their room. Mrs. Bennett was getting the children dressed to our surprise.

"What's this?" William smiled at Joey and then Megan.

"Well, I had a talk with Megan and she said she wants to go to the restaurant this morning."

"She does?" William smiled.

"Yep! She said you said she could sit on your lap."

"I did... and she may." William held out his hand and Joey shook it.

"We're partners and I figured I had to help you with Megan too." Joey smiled at William proud.

"You're right, son." William smiled and winked at him. Joey had his denim jeans on and new work shirt ready for William's approval.

"I look just like you, William." He laughed.

"That you do son... that you do." William smiled just as proud.

"And as handsome as well, you smell so good too, just like William." I laughed knowing William had bought him some cologne as well as everything else he needed.

"I know." He laughed.

Megan was getting the finishing touches on her hair and was wearing a light pink long sleeved smocked dress with white trim. She looked like a china doll. When Mrs. Bennett finished, Megan ran to William and he squatted down and scooped her up into his arms. She kissed his cheek and hid her face in his neck.

"Megan, may I kiss your cheek too?" William chuckled as she nodded and held her little cheek out for him to kiss. When he plopped one on her cheek she giggled and squirmed in his arms so happy.

"Are we all ready, I sure wouldn't want anyone to eat all the pancakes or French toast or eggs? I'm pretty hungry!" William smiled down at Joey and laid his hand like a man on Joey's shoulder.

"Yes, we better hurry Mrs. Bennett." He took her hand and mine and pulled us to the door. We all went down to the restaurant and got the biggest table in the place and ordered coffee and orange juice for Joey and Megan.

"What's finch toast?" Joey asked me tucking his napkin into the collar of his shirt.

"It's wonderful, like pancakes with syrup, but made with bread. Have you ever had a waffle with strawberries?"

"No Ma'am, but finch sounds good!" He licked his lips.

"Well I'm having that, and Joey? It's called French toast." He nodded at William and winked! They were alike!

"And what about you, princess? Would you like a waffle too?" She nodded and kissed his cheek again.

"Well, well! What was that for?" He smiled at her full of love. She pointed to herself and hugged herself then pointed to William. William looked at Joey and he was blushing.

"What? What does she mean?" William leaned to him and Joey whispered in his ear.

"She said, I love you. " He sat up with a blank look on his face and tears filled his eyes, he hugged her. I heard him whisper to her softly.

"I love you too, Megan, and I promise that I will never let anything happen to you. I will love you for the rest of your life." Tears ran down William's cheeks. She wiped his face with her dress and shook her finger at him, for him not to cry, she put her tiny fingers at the corner of each side of his mouth and made them go up. He smiled and hugged her again and kissed her forehead.

"I'm sorry, Rebecca."

"For what?"

"Megan just gets to me." He looked back at her tiny face and kissed her cheek again then attacked her neck munching it and growling. Joey and I laughed. William was complete.

"Look Carla, what a picture." Cole smiled and held a chair for Carla.

"Good morning!" Carla smiled brightly.

"She's as small as Megan!" Joey leaned over and whispered to Cole.

"I know, I can hardly tell them apart!" Cole teased as we all laughed.

"Where's mother?" I smiled as Cole kissed my cheek.

"She's coming. She was waiting for Aunt Marie."

Mother and Aunt Marie came in and last Hannah and Mike. We all ordered and I watched William and Megan and knew he wasn't even here. He and Megan were in their own world. Joey and Cole talked about what job Joey was going to do today and that we girls were going to pack up Hannah's shop today. We told Mrs. Bennett we would take Megan with us today. Hannah thought she had some unclaimed dresses for Megan and wanted to see if they'd fit.

After breakfast we all went our ways, Joey was off with the men and we took Megan. She fussed a little about William not staying with her, but on the way to the shop William pulled out from his coat a toy yo-yo for Joey and a small baby doll for Megan and promised that if they were good they could check his coat tonight for more surprises. I knew William would spoil them rotten. They both nodded and were all too happy to do as he asked.

When we got to Hannah's we saw that Hannah had the whole store almost packed, except for what she was working on. It took us no time to finish. We all scolded Hannah for not letting us help, but she said that it was easier for her to do it, for there were some things she needed to store away like out of date material. We talked about Carla's wedding coming up and Carla asked Hannah if she would make her a wedding gown. What she wanted was so simple that it would only take Hannah a week to make.

After we finished with the last of the packing, we sat in the back room and made lists for the wedding. With us having everything done, we had time to send out invitations and plan the whole thing. Cole would be really surprised at Carla's wishes. Everything was simple and not over done. We watched Megan play with her baby doll and laughed at her as she rocked it. We heard the bell in the front ring. Hannah went to see who it was.

"Rebecca?" Hannah called her tone wasn't normal.

"Yes?" I walked out to find mother's lawyer by the front counter.

"Morning, Rebecca."

"Good morning, Mr. Lawrence." He was a handsome man in his early forties with a touch of distinguishing gray at the temples and a handlebar mustache, tall and lean with nice brown eyes.

"What can I do for you, Mr. Lawrence?"

"Well, I have some news, but it's not good."

"What?" My heart stopped.

"We've found some family of the children's and they're coming here today."

"Why?" I was so afraid to ask.

"They want to see the children. They want to claim them I believe."

"NO! They can't!" Hannah wrapped her arm around my shoulders.

"They can, if they can prove themselves relatives…"

"They can take the children?" Hannah asked worried to death.

"Yes, but I think they're only interested in the little girl."

"Why they can't split them up! Not to mention William. Oh God…William!" My heart was breaking.

"Is there anything we can do?" Hannah was hugging my shoulders.

"Not until I talk with them. They should be here on the next train due in two hours. I suggest you telling William, right away." Mr. Lawrence looked down and frowning.

"There must be something we can do?"

"Pray and I will do everything I can." His voice held conviction.

"I shall go to William at once." Tears filled my heart and eyes.

"Where are the children now?" He asked.

"Megan is in the back with mother and Carla and William has Joey." I wiped the tears from my cheeks and drew courage from the very depth of my soul. I had to do this!

"Good, go then and let him know, a man like William always has a plan." Mr. Lawrence smiled slightly.

"I will." I looked at Hannah and she nodded wiping her own tears.

I grabbed my shawl and ran to mother's shop and went inside. I saw William sawing wood and it was as if he felt my presence. He looked up the second I found him. I motioned for him to come to me. He dusted his hands off and his smiled faded as he saw mine.

"What is it my love?" He took my hands in his.

"Where is Joey?" My voice was shaky.

"With Cole at the lumber yard bringing more two by fours, why? What's the matter?"

"William, Mr. Lawrence came by Hannah's and he…" Tears filled my eyes.

"He had news?" William's face was blank.

"Yes, and I'm afraid it's… it's not good William." I didn't want to tell him this!

"Come…" He took me to the back room and poured us a cup of stout coffee.

"Tell me, Rebecca." He ran his hand through his hair and blew out a breath of air.

"Well Mr. Lawrence said there are supposed relatives coming for the children." My heart ached as I saw the pain rip across his face.

"Wha… what did you say?" His voice was hoarse.

"They'll be on the next train, Mr. Lawrence said it was relatives, he was not sure how they were even related, but he thought they were only interested in… Megan." My heart ached for William for he loved her so much. He ran his hand through his hair and paced back and forth very deep in thought.

"What about Joey?" He didn't look at me as I saw tears running down his cheeks.

"Mr. Lawrence didn't really know much, but he said he would as soon as he talked with them. He was to meet them at the station. What will we do William?" I went to him and he wrapped his arms around me tightly.

"I don't know. If they are their family… we can't deny them." I could tell he didn't want to even speak the words.

"I know that, but what if they're not good people? What if they only want the land that their parents had?" I was so afraid.

"You know, we can assume everything and not know anything, but everyone has a price." I had never heard the tone Williams had in his voice as I was hearing right at this moment. He was cold and calculating.

"Mr. Lawrence said you may have a plan. I hope you do." I hugged him tight.

"We'll see, they'll not take the children away unless they can prove who they are and why they want them… and they'll not split them up! I can't imagine why it took so long for them to step forward… and why now?" He was deep in thought and I was going to let him think.

"When were they to arrive?" He looked into my eyes deeply.

"On the next train due in two hours."

"I want you to take the children to the hotel and keep them busy. I will take care of everything. If they are family, there isn't much we can do, but if they're not close relatives, then we might have a chance. I need to find out from Mr. Lawrence where the wire came from and find out as much as I can about them. Then I will be able to ascertain the situation.

I'll get Joey, I'll just tell him that you want lunch in the hotel and I will be there later." I nodded tears streaming down my cheeks.

"Oh, William!" I cried as my heart was breaking.

"Be strong, Rebecca... be strong... for them... and... me." He kissed me firmly and went to find Joey. I waited by the door and soon saw William and Joey coming across the street.

"Hello, Miss Rebecca, I hear we're to have lunch in the hotel and I'm pretty hungry." Joey laughed.

"Well good, we need to get Megan." I smiled down at his bright face and couldn't even imagine anyone taking them away from us now. Now that we loved them... and they trusted us.

"I'll see you in a while and you too partner." William smiled and shook Joey's hand.

We went into to Hannah's and I picked up Megan and told Hannah to explain to everyone what was going on and then went to the hotel. Mrs. Bennett wasn't there and I told the children that we could go to William's and my room for a while so they could see it. We planned to have lunch there.

"What would you two like for lunch?" I smiled and couldn't help but to think what William was going through or what he was doing.

"Do they have veggie soup and corn bread?" Joey was deep in thought.

"Does Megan like veggie soup?" She wasn't listening to us for she was busy with her baby doll.

"Sure." He smiled brightly.

"I tell you what, I'll go down and order lunch, can you watch Megan? Of course you can! How silly of me!" I shook my head and laughed.

"Nah... it's not silly... besides, I like for you to look after her. It's nice not to worry about her all the time." He gave me a smirk as if admitting that was not a nice thing for him to think like that.

"Well thank you, Joey, I'm glad you trust William and me with her."

"Shoot! I trust you with me!" He laughed and hugged me tightly as my heart pounded at the thought of someone taking them away.

"I'll be right back." I smiled and went down to the service desk and ordered lunch. On the way back up, I was deep in thought. I almost ran into Lord McCray.

"Oh I'm, Oh, Gabe! I'm terribly sorry. I was deep in thought."

"What has you in such deep thoughts?"

"Well, William, and I have taken on two small orphaned children..." I explained the situation to him and asked for his council.

"Well, it's going to be a hard one, but if they're not next of kin. You might have a chance, if the judge will listen to Joey." He was deep in thought.

"You know two heads are better than one Gabe."

"I'm on it and you need not ask. Where is William now?" He smiled with such kindness in his eyes it almost made me want to hug him! I told him where William might be and he was off. I went back to the room to find Joey and Megan sitting on the floor. He was trying to put a diaper on the baby. What a picture. They were as close as two could be.

"Lunch will be here soon, you two need to get washed up. I ordered a treat as well." They both smiled and jumped up and down and then ran into the washroom to wash.

Maybe William and Gabe could figure this out. I hope William won't be upset that I told Gabe. He shouldn't be, Gabe had so many contacts.

"All clean… see?" Joey and Megan came out showing me their hands and face. I nodded and approved after a close inspection. They laughed at me checking behind their ears.

"Very good, now you'll be ready for lunch when it gets here!" They sat down and Joey went back to putting the diaper on the baby doll. Please God… Please don't take them away from us… from William!

I closed my eyes and prayed a silent prayer. When I was finished I noticed that the children were getting antsy. Just then a tap on the door sounded.

"Lunch!" Joey shouted! He was really hungry! Megan was even smiling.

I went to the door and wheeled in a cart. Joey and Megan's eyes were huge and sat wiggling on a pillow. We enjoyed our lunch, Joey was telling Megan and I all that he had done and was about to do when I came. He was so proud. To my great surprise, Megan ate all by herself for the first time! I had wondered if William were here, would she have.

I looked at my timepiece. One more hour and they'll be here. As I watched the children, my heart pounded. I hope William was finding out what he needed to know, if not, we would have no choice but to let them go, but how? How could we do that? How was William going to deal with this if we have no choice?

After they ate all their soup, I uncovered their surprise.

"What is that?" Joey's nose scrunched up.

"Chocolate pudding!" I looked at him realizing once again, they probably never had pudding before.

"Oh, it's heavenly, like you're eating a chocolate cloud!" I saw Joey thinking about it, but Megan took her cup and dove into it, smiling and elbowing Joey. She nodded licking her lips getting a huge chocolate mustache! I laughed at the two of them. They were so darling!

They gobbled the pudding up and I gave them mine too. They were so surprised that I would do such a thing.

As they ate my pudding I tried to stay as relaxed as possible. The children laid down by the fire as I read to them. I chose a book of knights in shining armor and dragons. Megan wasn't interested in the least. She lay down with her baby doll and fell asleep and I covered her with a blanket. I continued to read until Joey himself was sleeping. I closed the book staring down at the two angels sleeping at my feet. I watched as the fire cast deep rich red off their hair and made their skin glow softly. I reached out to touch Joey's soft cheek.

"Rebecca..." William whispered startling me.

I went to him right away and we went into the washroom and closed the door. The grim look on his face told me that it was not good news. I held my breath watching him pace back and fourth.

"William...what is it." I finally had to ask.

"Their relatives arrived." He blew out breath from his cheeks.

"And... what? Are they close?"

"Yes." My heart broke for his tone was cracking.

"Oh, William, what do they want?"

"They want only Megan."

"What?" No! My heart cried!

"They can't afford Joey too. Just... Megan!" William flopped down in the chair and with his elbows on his knees and his face in his hands I knew he was crying... GOD WHY! What do I do?

"Oh Rebecca!" His arms went around my waist, hugging me, I held him and cried with him.

"They want to see the children this afternoon in the restaurant. We have to take them." He looked up into my eyes and I saw all the pain and felt his heart breaking...I was overwhelmed.

"I'm so sorry. Isn't there anything we can do?"

"The woman is Joey and Megan's mother's sister from Lawrence she wants Megan. They're not wealthy, but they can afford her. They're trying to get a hold of her brother-in-law for Joey." He sounded like it was all hopeless.

We sat holding each other crying, I know William was asking God why as well as I was.

After a little while, William looked up at me and took a big breath of air.

"We have to be strong for Megan. She will be so afraid and Joey will think I had something to do with splitting them up."

"No, William, he won't! Joey knows you love Megan and Megan loves you." I hugged him again.

"Still, we have to pull ourselves together and be strong and act like this is the best thing in the world to find out they have real family. We have no choice. Gabe is still checking into things still, there's a chance that he may come up with something, we can only pray." William stood and kissed my forehead. Then he went to wash his face, as I did the same.

"We must be strong!" William looked into to my eyes for strength.

"We will, for both of them." We went back out and they were still asleep.

William took the seat that I had and stared at them till Megan stirred. She sat up and rubbed her blue eyes and saw William. She jumped up and leapt on his lap kissing his face. He took a ragged breath. He just hugged her and hugged her. It was breaking my heart.

"Have you been my good girl?" He whispered and she nodded.

"You know I love you don't you Megan." He whispered and kissed her little cheek and she nodded again, pointed to herself, hugged herself then pointed to William. I could see he was about to break down again and he looked at me and I held my chin square.

"Well, I have something wonderful to tell you when your brother wakes up." William smiled as best as he could. This was killing him.

"Something wonderful to tell us?" Joey sat up yawning.

"Are we going home?" He added.

"No, that's what I want to tell you."

"What is it, William." Joey sat on the floor and smiled at William with trusting eyes.

"Remember you told us that you didn't know who you're Uncle's or Aunt's were?" Joey and Megan nodded.

"What would you say if I told you I know who they are?" Joey instantly frowned and Megan wrapped her arms around William's neck.

"I don't care who they are. No one came for us all this time, so the way I see it, it don't count!" Joey's eyes filled with tears instantly.

"Joey, I know you don't know them, but they are real true family."

"No, you are!" He got up and ran into the washroom.

"Oh, William! What shall we do?"

"Megan, Megan honey…" William tried to pry her from his neck but she had her face buried so deep and hard into his neck he was afraid of hurting her.

"I'll try to talk to Joey." Tears welled in my eyes as William nodded and hugged Megan.

"Joey, may I come in, I need to talk with you, just you and not in front of Megan." I waited for a moment and the door slowly opened. I stepped in to find his little face tear streaked. I sat down in the chair and sat Joey next to me.

"Joey, why aren't you happy that we know who your family is?"

"Because, Megan and I have found the family that wants both of us…" He dropped his head.

"You know we feel the same don't you?"

"Well can't you make it right or something?"

"The law says that if they are the next of kin, we have no rights."

"It ain't fair!" He cried and threw himself in my lap.

"We don't think so either, but that is how they found you."

"What do you mean, Miss Rebecca?" Tears streamed down his cheeks as he snuffed his nose.

"In order to make it legal, we had to make sure that no one had claim to you. It's the law." His eyes searched mine for something, anything!

"But, Megan and I don't want anyone but you and William… we… we… love you!" His arms wrapped around my neck and he hugged me tightly, I busted out in tears as he did.

"Are you two alright?" William opened the door with Megan still hanging onto his neck.

"Oh, William, both of them don't want any of this!" I stood picking Joey up in my arms and we all hugged each other and after a minute.

"NO!!! I won't allow them to take you Megan or you Joey!" William had battle in his eyes.

"I need to go to Gabe to see what he has found out." William pulled Megan away from his neck.

"Megan, I have to do something. Stay here with Rebecca. I'll return shortly." He turned on his heel and hurried out.

He or I couldn't even tell Joey that they only wanted Megan. The thought alone was horrifying! How could anyone not want both of them? We went back in and all sat in the same chair and waited for William to return.

"Miss Rebecca…" Joey had calmed down. It had been close to an hour and a half since anyone had said a word.

"Do you believe in God?" He looked at me with all his heart.

"Yes, I know there is a God." I smiled into his sweet tear stained face.

"Do you think if I prayed hard he would answer my prayer?"

"Well that is a hard one, sometimes, he does and sometimes he doesn't. But there are reasons why he doesn't and why he does, but praying wouldn't hurt." We all prayed in silence and hard!

"Rebecca." William's face was grim, Oh God NO!

"We have to take the children to the restaurant, now." He looked as if he had been whipped!

"I ain't going!" Joey shouted.

"You have to or they'll come and get you."

"But… I don't want to!" He cried out running to William hugging his waist.

"I know son, but we have to obey the law." William turned his face up to his.

"But… you're… my… Pa!" It was more than William could stand and he plummeted to his knees hugging Joey. He rocked the small boy and whispered to him something I couldn't hear. Joey just nodded and William stood. Joey wiped his tears away and took a deep breath.

"Let's get this over with." Joey frowned.

I nodded and Megan held her arms out to William. He took her and I took Joey's hand.

We slowly went to the restaurant and saw Mr. Lawrence and the couple. I took a deep breath and smiled slightly as we went to their table.

"William, Rebecca, this is Mr. and Mrs. Walters. Mrs. Walters is the children's mother's sister."

"Pleased to meet you…" They nodded not saying a word.

"They have proof that they are in fact directly related, I'm sorry."

"This is Megan." William tried to pull her away from his neck, but she wouldn't let go.

"And this young man is her brother Joey." He smiled a quick smirk and looked down.

"Joey, say something to your Aunt and Uncle." I whispered to him.

"Hello." He peeked up at them.

"Megan, wouldn't you want to meet you Mother's sister?" William softly spoke. Megan shook her head no.

"Me and the Mrs. have two youngin's back home. Won't it be nice to have them to play with? One's about your age, Charlie, he's ten and Molly she's eight." He smiled friendly enough, but we thought they didn't want Joey.

"Megan, I'm your Aunt, don't you want to see me?" She touched Megan's leg and she jumped and choked William.

"I'm sorry, but when we found these two and they had been on their own for almost two years. Joey took care of her all this time, by himself." William's tone was cold.

"W... where were you when Ma and Pa were murdered? How's come you didn't come for us right away? The sheriff said he sent a wire out." Joey accused. His brow was furrowed as he frowned.

"We... well the truth is... we did get the wire."

"Sue Ellen!" The man tried to stop her.

"No, I think we need to tell them." She gave him a cold look.

"Please... continue." William sat up a little higher.

"We got the wire and we couldn't afford them. Charlie here didn't want them, but I do. They're my sister's kids! We tried to find them in Clay, but no one knew where they went, as soon as we got the wire form the sheriff we came right away. My husband could use the help."

"What?" William shouted.

"I said, my husband needs help on the farm. You know with all the boulders and rocks." She smiled as if it were some special thing.

"We gots us a farm and the crops are pretty good, but I decided that I need Joey here to help his cousin. Sue Ellen can't have any more children and at first we was only going to take Megan, see'ins how she is so young and all, she could help with the wash." He smiled at Joey.

"But surely you don't expect children to..." I couldn't even say the words! I was appalled!

"What's the harm in a little work?" Mr. Walters admitted that he intended to work Joey to death!

"So if you'll just give us our niece and nephew, we'll head back to..."

"To HELL if you're lucky!" William shouted and was at the breaking point.

"Excuse me?" Sue Ellen was shocked.

"What's your price?" William leaned forward with his brows furrowed deeply.

"Price? Why that's awful!?" Sue Ellen scoffed.

"What's your price, surely you need something? Some new plow horses, seed, wagon, and a new house? You name it and I'll see that it is yours." William stared Mr. Walters in the eyes.

"William… I don't think…" William shot Mr. Lawrence a warning glare.

"Now see here, them's our kids now. Besides we already own their Ma and Pa's land. Got the deed two days ago." He smiled looking at Sue Ellen.

"Mr. Lawrence, you heard them. You know what they plan on doing! Isn't there anything you can do?" I pleaded with him.

"I'm truly sorry, blood's thicker than water. However, they do have to stay here for however long it takes to make it all legal. Maybe the children will get used to them and you'll rest more easily."

"I'll never rest!" William looked at Joey and his eyes screamed out for help.

"William, I'll talk to the judge." Mr. Lawrence was saying more than his words were.

"Do they… have to go with them now?" I looked at William and back to Mr. Byron.

"I'm sorry, but yes." He frowned.

"The laws on our side now…" Mr. Walters sneered.

"Very well, at least let us talk to Joey and Megan… alone." He glared at Mr. Walters.

"We'll wait outside." They stood and left the hotel.

"William, Rebecca… I am truly sorry." Mr. Lawrence truly was.

"I know, Lawrence, but Damn it! There's got to be something we can do! Rebecca and I love these children! They're going to be free labor to them!" William was beyond reason! I gasped at the thought and felt faint.

"Rebecca! Get her some water!" He roared.

"The children!" I held Joey and cried.

"Miss Rebecca…" Joey whispered.

"I love you, Joey." I whispered to him.

"And I do you too, but you can't help this." I looked into the brave boy's face and was once again amazed by his strength.

"Oh, Joey!" I wanted to run with them!

"Miss Rebecca, it breaks my heart to see you crying. I'll look after Megan. I promise and William, when I'm old enough, I'll find you." He held out his small hand and William grabbed it pulling Joey to his chest Megan still hanging on to William with all she had.

"You'll always be my first son Joey and I won't stop trying to find a way to get you and Megan back. You have my word on that son." William hugged him and then stood, turning to Mr. Lawrence.

"William, I swear, if there was any way to stop this, I would! Even I can see where these children belong." Mr. Lawrence's batted his eyes and he cleared his throat.

"Where are the Walters staying?" I asked softly.

"At the motel down from your mother's shop..."

"That rat hole?" William was angry like I never seen him before.

"We'll send their things there tomorrow morning." I could hardly speak.

"Megan, we got to go." She shook her head no.

"Megan, you're gonna make William cry." She pulled back and put her hands on William's cheeks shaking her head no.

"Megan, I love you too and you'll always be my first daughter and I give you my word, I shall not stop trying to get you back." She nodded and reached for Joey. He took her hand and she frowned as tears like rain poured down her cheeks.

"Rebecca..." William took Megan's tiny hand and I took Joey's and we went outside.

"Bout time!" Mr. Walters laughed.

"Please, for God's sake, be good to them. They've been through hell!" William glared at Mr. Walters.

"We will." Sue Ellen lifted Megan and she looked into William's eyes.

"Remember, William, I promised you." Joey shook William's hand and hugged him one more time as I did. I couldn't speak. Joey was the bravest child I had ever met. William touched Megan's cheek. She blinked tears from her eyes and pointed to herself then hugged herself and pointed to William and then to me and William and I did the same back to her.

"Enough of this, let's get back to the motel. I need a drink." Mr. Walters huffed and pulled Joey along with Sue Ellen. Sue Ellen looked rather sad. Megan waved good-bye to us and we watched them disappear down into the crowd. We stood numb for a long time.

"William, I give you my word. I'll not rest till I find a way." Mr. Lawrence growled through clenched teeth.

"And you have my word. If that... that Mr. Walters so much as touches a hair on their heads. I'll hunt him down and kill him with my bare hands." His eyes held a storm like I've never seen before.

"There's got to be a loop hole somewhere." Mr. Lawrence was deep in thought.

"Come, Rebecca, and thank you, Lawrence. I realize your hands were tied." William shook his hand.

"I only wish there was something I could do." He frowned

I could see he truly meant every word.

"Just keep digging. I don't care about the cost." William tone was cold.

"You have my word." Mr. Lawrence nodded to me then to William and hurried down the street.

"We should have just kept them. We should have never gone to the Lawyers." He stood with his fists clenched. Suddenly I felt faint again and this time I fell into darkness.

~ Chapter 22 ~

"Rebecca..." I heard William's sweet voice.

"My love... Rebecca..." His voice sounded so wonderful.

"Here my love..." I blinked my eyes.

"What happened?"

"The Doc... said it was just nerves."

"What? Doc? William the children!" My heart wrenched.

"Shhh...it's alright now."

"Here my love, drink some water." I felt his hand on my back lifting me up.

"That's my girl." The water was so good and cool. I opened my eyes and they were so blurry.

"William..." I whispered.

"Oh, Rebecca, I'm so glad you're awake. Thank you God!" I felt his lips on my forehead.

"What happened?" I sipped more water. I was really waking up.

"We don't exactly know, but Doc thinks it was your nerves." I focused on my handsome husband's face.

"William, I feel sick, I'm going to..." I leaned over the bed and wretched into the basket next to the bed.

"You've done that a couple of times." William whispered.

"I have?" I drank more water.

"Well let's have a look." The doc looked into the basket.

"What's wrong with her?"

"William, will you go to my wagon and get my coat? I forgot something in it." William nodded and flew out the door.

"Doc?" He wiped my face. I've known him since I was a child.

"Well, my little, Rebecca."

"How are you doc?" I smiled and licked my lips.

"You gave us a scare, Beck... and I'm fine." He laughed.

"What's wrong with me?"

"Oh, nothing but a little less than eight months won't take care of." I shot him a wide look.

"What?" I held my breath.

"Beck... you're with child!"

"I... a... I'm with child?" He nodded.

"But why did I black out...how long?" I sipped a little water.

"Well, let's see... three days!"

"Three day's... Doc... the children."

"Shhh I know... William told me about them too."

"Does he know about... this?"

"No, I think you should tell him. I told him it was your nerves." He laughed.

"I'm going to have a baby!" William will be so complete.

"Your nerves and with you with child has set your world off kilter. I told William only that you needed rest and no lifting boxes or moving anything. He told me about that too."

"A baby! William's child! He will be so happy!" I hugged the Doctor.

"I know that he wants those little ones back as well. I thought about checking on them."

"Oh, Doc...would you? But don't tell William."

"Anything for you, Rebecca..." He patted my leg as William came back in.

"Here you go Doc... How is she?"

"Healthy as a horse, always has been. All she needs is rest." He reached into his pocket and took out his thermometer, then stuck it into my mouth and winked.

"What a relief!"

"How long before you go back to Winchester?" The Doc cleaned his glasses on a cloth.

"About a week I guess. They almost got the shop done."

"Good, I don't want her to do anything strenuous. She needs to build her strength back up."

"Why did she get so weak?" He looked into the Doc's eyes.

"She was worried about you... the children." He laughed.

"God! It's all my fault!" William hung his head.

"Don't be ridicules, William. With all she's been through, you're the best thing that has happened to Beck." He laughed and packed up his case. I'll see you in a couple of days. In bed for the next two days at least! Sleep, eat and sleep some more. He laughed.

"Rebecca… I was so afraid!" He laid his head on my chest.

"Has mother been here?"

"Everyone has been here." He laughed.

"What about Megan and Joey?" I had to know.

"Nothing, there still here but only for two more days." He frowned.

"Have… have you seen them?"

"No." He kissed forehead.

"I miss them…"

"Me too…" His voice was so soft.

William had ordered us dinner and vegetable soup for me. He also told me he let Mrs. Bennett go home. Mother came to visit and so did Carla and Hannah, Aunt Marie came later. I was feeling on top of the world, except for Megan and Joey. Then thought I would wait till Christmas it was only a few weeks away and then if something doesn't happen with Joey and Megan, then I will have a real gift to give him.

Mother was putting the finishing touches on the business as was Aunt Marie, Hannah and Carla. Hannah said she got Carla's dress done, but her parents couldn't make the wedding until almost New Year's Day, so they postpone the wedding till then. She had so much to do and I was no help. They all concentrated on getting ready for their grand opening and everyone was so excited. We were only a week from Christmas day. William and I decided that if there was no word from the lawyers about the children then we would go home to be there with his family. Mother wanted us to stay, but we had to at least check on William's estate. I was well enough to ride home and promised that we would come back two days before the wedding.

The grand opening was a smash and everyone was so excited about the all in one concept, though the men knew it would cost them. The store was spectacular, even nicer than the one in Winchester.

With everyone wanting to rest, the rest of the week, now that all the work was done, and just two days before Christmas, William and I decided to go home.

We were so sad that there was nothing we could do. Tomorrow we would leave and so would Megan and Joey and we probably would never see them again. The judge made them stay till the last of the searches came up empty, even Lord McCray came up empty handed.

"I'm sorry, William... truly I am. It would seem that they are truly family and there's nothing on either of them." He hung his head. I know Gabe tried his best.

"We're going home tomorrow. We'll be back for the wedding." William shook Gabe's hand and I kissed his cheek.

"That my lady, I shall forever cherish in my heart for always." He smiled and hugged me.

We went up to the room and I took a long hot bath. William slipped down behind me as he did so many times. He wrapped his arms around me and kissed my neck.

"I love you, Rebecca."

"And I love you..."

"I'm glad to see you're eating well"

"Why do you say that?"

"Well... you look better fuller, I like it." I felt a smile on his lips as his mouth tickled my ear.

"I just wished there was still a way to..."

"Me too, I miss them with all my heart." He took a deep breath.

"Me too..."

We sat quietly in the tub and after we bathed we dressed for bed. He wrapped me in his arms tightly and told me he loved me.

"William!" We heard banging on the door.

"Rebecca!" Joey!

We both bolted from the bed and went to the door. It was Joey!

"Joey... what is it?" William and I knelt down.

"Megan..." He puffed.

"They took her to the Doc! She's bad.... won't eat... hasn't..." He puffed.

"Hang on!"

Joey stepped inside, William and I rushed to dress, then William scooped Joey up in his arms and we ran to the Doc's.

"You look good son." William smiled and kissed Joey's cheek.

"You too, William..." Joey hugged and kissed him.

"Hurry... Doc says she's about..."

"Oh God, Joey! Why didn't you come for me?" William frowned. I barely could keep up.

"I couldn't! They kept the doors locked!" William cursed out loud and ran into the Doc's office.

"Doc!" William shouted.

"You ain't got no…" William looked at Mr. Walters with such rage in his eyes, unlike any I've ever seen and without a word, punched him right in the face. He walked right over his unconscious body. I had to admit I wanted to do the same.

"Sue Ellen… where is she?" William demanded.

"In there… I'm sorry." She cried. For some reason I went to her.

"We still want them… do you?" I looked into her eyes knowing there was something in them… fear!

"Take them! He's no good to them. I wanted to tell you, I was afraid." I nodded and went through the doors.

I gasped at the tiny pale little body with dark rings under her eyes lying in the small bed that looked huge. William was holding her hand and softly talking to her.

"Megan honey, its William and Rebecca. We're here." He whispered.

"Her lips twitched!" William looked up at the Doc. His face was grim. "Doc…"

"Beck… she's in God's hands. All we can do is wait…"

"They starved her?" William looked pale himself.

"Not exactly, she just wouldn't eat. She kept calling out for you. Keep talking to her." He patted William's shoulder. William whispered to Megan and I held Joey.

"Joey… whatever happens, you're staying with us. No Judge in the world would deny you now."

"William, I need to check her." The Doc had a hold of the curtain.

"I'll be only one moment." We stepped out and the Doc swung the curtain closed.

"I'll be right back." William's eyes were black. I've never seen them this color! I followed him but stayed behind the door and listened.

"Now see here, Lord Fauntleroy or whatever you call yourself. She's ours and so is the boy. You can have the girl, she ain't of no use, but we's keeping the boy." Mr. Walters huffed.

"If you and your wife know what's good for you…you'll leave town right now before charges of neglect are pressed on the both of you. I know the whole story and no Judge in the world would let you have these children! I may even see to it that your own are taken as well! I have no doubt in the world that they are in just as bad of shape as these children are!"

"Alright… we'll leave… but you ain't getting my children."

"Well then, I suggest that on your way home, something happens to you, that you change or I will see to it that someone will see to your children before you even get home! Mark my words! If this child dies because of your abuse and neglect...you WILL be hunted down by me and will have you hung for murder! And THAT you have my word on Mr. Walters. Now go before I take things into my own hands right now and have you charged...and I CAN do that! I am a Colonel Mr. Walters and you have met with the wrong man! I never want to see you again! You Mr. Walters are a sorry excuse for a man and your poor wife is afraid of you. For that alone I should kill you with my own two hands!" I heard the door shut and Joey looked up at me with shock in his eyes.

"You can come back in." Doc patted my shoulder and his eyes asked if I was alright. I nodded and he smiled. We all hurried back in as if we all knew she wouldn't be with us much longer.

"Megan, its Rebecca and Joey, William is here too." I softly spoke to her brushing her once beautiful hair that was now matted, out of her pale face.

"Megan, please, Megan, hear me. It's your William, I'm here...you and Joey are with Rebecca and me forever! Your Aunt and Uncle are gone and they gave you to us now." He whispered softly with tears streaming down his face.

Suddenly Megan shuttered a strange breath.

"Oh God, Rebecca... she's..." Her breathing had changed.

"Megan, fight! I need my girl... Please fight! I don't have anyone to hug me like you do..." William kissed her tiny lifeless hand. Joey hugged me tightly weeping.

"Megan, you must fight! Joey needs you... he's crying... and so is William." I touched her pale cheek.

"She licked her lips." William looked at me.

"Please, Megan... who's gonna feed me breakfast?" My heart ached and tears streamed down my cheeks.

"I love you... Megan... I need... you." William softly laid his head down next to her ear on her pillow and spoke, his hand still holding hers.

"I want to be your Pa, but I can't unless you tell me you want me to be your Pa." He sat up and took her hands into his and kissed them. Then he made her finger point to her then hugging herself and then to William and I couldn't bare watch any more, she was fading fast. I rocked Joey in my arms and sung amazing grace softly.

"Please, my Megan… I give you my word. You are my daughter Megan and I love you and I need you, your Papa needs you." He laid his head back down next to her ear. William was quiet for a little bit and then I heard him softly speak.

"Megan… it's William. I don't know if you can hear me, but I know you can feel my heart... and it's breaking. I love you Megan and I want you to be with me forever, but you must fight if you want me to be your Pa. I need to hear you say it, but if there are angel's…" He took a deep breath and my head screamed NO!

"Megan, if there are angels that want you to fly away with them and you have to go…" My head was screaming NO… Don't Say it William!

"Megan, I love you enough to let you fly away with them, but please don't. Tell the angels first that I need you…that I want you and that I love you…that I give them my word to take care of you and love you and will always be there for you no matter what! Please Megan tell them….tell them that you need to take care of me…because…because I just…I just won't be able to…" William laid his head back down on her pillow and Joey and I prayed.

"P… Pa… Pa… Wi… William…" I froze thinking I heard her.

"Pa…PA…" I looked up and William was praying. He didn't hear her. I shook him hard.

"Pa… pa." William slowly raised his head in disbelief.

"Megan?" He barely whispered.

"Papa… William." Her blue eyes blinked.

"Megan… oh, Megan!" He kissed her forehead and looked at me and Joey as tears poured down his cheeks.

"Megan, you have to fight for your Papa William and your new Mother, Rebecca…we need you as much as Joey does."

"I told them, Papa…" He suddenly realized that not only did she hear him… she was talking!

"Doc!" William yelled.

"Doc!"

"Well I'll be, why hello young lady. I thought you had blue eyes." He patted William's shoulder.

"Hungry, Papa… eat!" She looked at William and he looked at me and laughed out with tears.

"Whatever you want… princess." William kissed her cheek.

"Pancakes…" Joey smiled.

"I'll go right now!" Joey ran out of the room and then back in. I need money Pa!"

"Here... take it all!" He laughed pulling out bundle of bills.

"I'll be right back!" Joey was going to run all the way there and back.

"It's alright if she eats?"

"Of course!" The Doc was amazed as all of us were.

"When did she start to talk?"

"I told you she was calling out for you, guess you didn't hear me." He laughed.

"Megan... are you fighting?" William smiled speaking to her softly. She nodded.

"That's my girl! I love you, Megan." He smiled and kissed her on her cheek.

"I told them, Papa... I told them!" She smiled a slight smile for she was so weak.

"Told who, Megan?" He looked at her then at me confused.

"I told the angels, Papa." She furrowed her tiny brow licking her dry lips.

"What angels?" His face went pale.

"The angels that fly... I said Papa needs to eat... I need to feed Papa." William cried out and took a ragged breath in and out, tears fell unceasingly.

"Oh, Megan... Thank you!" He kissed her cheek. She was quiet for a bit she just looked at William.

"Papa... Love Megan?" Her voice was so weak and so small.

"Yes... he does, more than anything." He whispered softly for his voice was cracking and my heart was over flowing as she looked at me and held out her tiny hand to me.

"Mama loves Megan." I cried so hard I couldn't even see through all the tears!

"Yes... Megan Mama loves Megan so much, so very much!" I tried to breathe just one breath.

"I told them no! I can't fly... Papa and Mama needs Megan. I told them no..." Her eyes closed. Then she opened them slowly.

"Megan... did they let you go or are they still waiting for you?" William held his breath.

"They flew away... all gone." She tried to raise her hands but was so weak. William let out an endless breath.

"Here… I ran!" Joey came back into the room with a plate of pancakes.

"Megan, are you still hungry?" She nodded. William took the fork with shaking hand and cut her a small piece and fed it to her and she nodded.

"Papa…" She wanted to feed William. He helped her with the fork and he took a bite.

Though she didn't eat much and the Doc was well pleased. He nodded as he checked her out. He didn't make us leave for now, Megan was ours.

"She should get better by the day now. I don't believe that I've ever seen such a miracle in all my days! And this…was truly a miracle." Doc shook his head.

"How long before we can take her home?" William was so relieved.

"We'll have to see how fast she gains weight, if she gains on a steady rate… then in a few days."

"She can't gain pounds in a few days!" William protested!

"Ounces son… ounces and by the way, I'll tell the judge myself about all this, so don't worry. You just tend to your daughter. You're the best medicine I have ever seen." He laughed and went about his way.

"Did you hear that Megan? A few days and you'll be all ours, a family, you me Mama and Joey."

"Joey's asleep. I think he was worn out. I don't think we could have asked for two more perfect children." I smiled and William kissed me tenderly.

"Papa loves Mama…" She tried to laugh but it was only a sound.

"That he does…that he does!" William laughed.

William stayed with Megan every moment until the day she was released.

We decided to stay at mothers for Christmas day, but were leaving to go home that afternoon. William had always spent Christmas with his 'family' and he was so anxious to bring home the best gifts.

Cole and Carla did shopping for the children, for William and I, knowing we were caring for Megan. Megan was much stronger and now that she was talking! She was nothing but a chatterbox and it was wonderful!

On Christmas morning we all went to mothers and she was so glad we stayed. The tree was beautiful. William showed Megan everything on it there was to see. Joey looked at all the presents and there were a lot of them!

"Now everyone, I want to eat breakfast before we open the gifts. I bet our Megan here wants some pancakes!" She held her arms out to Megan and Megan went to her.

"Pancakes Gamma!" Everyone laughed.

"Cole would you do the honors?" Mother smiled and Cole nodded.

"Father, in heaven, this Christmas day is the most blessed day of the year and on this day, we all want to thank you for the miracles that have happened and for William and Rebecca so deserving. Thank you for the children and all, we love them already. Thank you for you own son whom you gave for us all. Father, bless this family as we try to live in your will the best we can and that you see to it that this year and the ones to follow are just as blessed, as we feel blessed today…In Jesus' name we honor praise worship Amen."

"Thank you angels." Megan smiled up as if she could see them.

Everyone awed at her, but William and I looked at each other in a knowing look. I knew the angels saw to everything and silently thanked them.

After breakfast we cleaned off the table and left the dishes for later, we just put them on to soak and all went into the parlor.

"There's lots of presents for you and Joey under that tree."

"Mean like surprises in your coat Pa?" William realized that they probably didn't know what presents were.

"Yes… surprises!" Everyone smiled humbly.

The entire family had accepted them as if they were born into the family as our own. One by one the presents were passed out. Joey had never had a big Christmas, though he remembered small ones with his real Ma and Pa. Carla and Cole got Joey real boots and a hat.

Aunt Marie bought him storybooks. Mike got him a fishing pole. Who would have guessed? Hannah had got him three new outfits she made herself… mother got him a man's pocket watch. He was so surprised that everyone bought him something.

"Your present from us is outside." William smiled. He raced to the door and Mike came around the corner with a brown painted pony, saddle and all.

"Ma… Pa… For me?" His eyes were so big! He ran to us and kissed each one and smiled.

"I love you, thank you you're the best Ma and Pa a boy could ever want!" He said boy! William and I laughed. Mike called Joey outside, he put his coat on. Joey rushed to get to Uncle Mike.

Megan was still on her first present.

"Papa... I can't." She pouted looking at William. He smiled lovingly and kissed her cheek.

"This is from Gamma." I smiled and laughed as mother turned red. She opened the small box and it had a tiny pearl bracelet in it.

"Pretty Gamma!" I put it on her wrist.

"This ones from Uncle Cole and Aunt Carla..." William smiled as he helped her with it.

"Uncle Cole and Aunt Carla, I have two baby's! I'll be busy like Mama." She spoke softly but clearly.

"This ones from Aunt Marie..." I gave her the big box. William helped to open it.

"Aunt Marie! A bed! For my babies!" She giggled and looked at William. He smiled nodding.

"This is from Uncle Mike." I looked at William. He helped her open it up.

"A fishing pole! Like Joey's, but my size." We all laughed out.

"You can thank Uncle Mike when he comes in with Joey." I rolled my eyes and laughed.

"This one is from Aunt Hannah." William smiled at Hannah.

"Oh! Oh! Dresses... and a tea set! Thank you Aunt Hannah."

"And this ones from Mama and Papa." William helped her unwrap it and he gave her the small box. Her eyes got wide. I showed her how it opened. My heart stopped and I smiled tenderly at William.

"Read Mama!" Megan held it out for me to read. I held the locket and it said, Papa and Mama Love Megan With all our hearts... Forever

"Oh Papa... Mama!" She turned for William to put it on.

She hugged and kissed both of us. William held her close and whispered in her ear.

"When we go home, there will be lots more for you and Joey." William hugged her.

"You mean at the shack?" Megan looked at me then William. Cole laughed out, as did Carla.

"Yes... my love... at the shack." He laughed and plopped a big kiss on her cheek.

We spent the rest of our time laughing at the children and watching them play. Joey named his horse Patches. William and I loved that name for as a family we were like a patchwork quilt made of many different people from all different places put together, safe warm and covered with love.

All too soon William and I gathered the best presents we could ever have gotten and said our goodbyes. Mother cried as Carla, Hannah and of course Aunt Marie. Even Cole looked water eyed as he shook Joey's hand.

"See you in a few days, and don't you worry, I'll take care of Patches for you. Besides you have Jack to take care of now, he needs you to play with him and get him use to the shack." Cole gave Megan a hug too and Uncle Mike.

"We'll be back!" William waved as we started on our way.

We went through town and saw Mr. Lawrence waving us down. William looked at me and I looked at him. William went pale. The carriage stopped, Mr. Lawrence opened the door.

"Going home?" He smiled.

"Yes. Thank you for all you work, Lawrence." William shook his hand.

"Well I figured you'd want this today, before you go home." Mr. Lawrence took out an envelope.

"What is this?" William looked confused.

"Open it!" Mr. Lawrence smiled. William opened the letter and smiled.

"Thank you, Mr. Lawrence... Thank you so much for caring so much, to do this on this day."

"Merry Christmas!" He waved to the children and we're back on our way home! Home!

"Well now, what was that? Can you tell us Papa?" I smiled a tender smile knowing it was good news.

"Well...this letter is very important." He began.

"Really? Is it about your work?" Joey smiled laying his hand on William's leg.

"No." He smiled at me tenderly.

"Is it about us?" Joey bit his bottom lip.

"Yes." He chuckled.

"Read, Papa" Megan put her arms around his neck.

"Read it?" She nodded.

"I think... I'll let Mama read it." To my surprise he handed it to me.

"Me?" I looked at him and he was still smiling.

"Read it, Mama." Megan smiled her dimples showing.

"Alright..." I held my breath as I opened it.

Lord Andrews,   *December*
24, 2572

It has recently come to my attention that two children have been in your charge. The only family to claim them was proven unfit. The other members in the family declined to take the children.

As per request of the children's physician Doc Richards, he has recommended that there is no better home for these two children Joseph Nathan McKinney age nine born, May the twenty first, two thousand five hundred and sixty three in the day of our Lord…and Megan Kay McKinney age four, born December ninth, two thousand five hundred and sixty eight in the day of our Lord.

To here by adopt for the duration of their natural lives on this day, December twenty forth, two thousand seventy two in the day of our Lord, Permanent and binding…

The said children's names will now and forever be, Joseph Nathan Andrews and Megan Kay Andrews.

Respectively,
Judd Walsh
Hickory Hill, Magistrate

"William, does this mean what I think it means?" I looked at him not believing what I just read.

"Yes." He said softly.

"What does that all mean, Papa?" Joey frowned a little.

"That you are now our true son! And Megan is our true daughter forever and no one can take you away… Ever.!" He smiled at Joey and Megan.

"Yippee!!! Megan, they are our real Ma and Pa… forever!" Megan and Joey hugged both of us.

"Your name is now, Joey Andrews and your name is, Megan Andrews forever and ever!"

"Really and truly you're our Pa and you're our Ma?"

"Yep!" William smiled and hugged Joey again.

The ride home went by so fast for we were all talking about what that would really mean, but William shied away from discussing the shack. William promised to take them telling them they would soon need more clothes. Joey said he needed more work clothes. William and I laughed.

Soon we were turning down the driveway.

"This is your drive way? You got a gate?" The children looked out the window.

"It's pretty big!" Joey's eyes were wide.

"Wait till you see the shack!" William winked at me.

We rode watching their faces as they saw deer jumping through the woods they were so excited.

Then we were at the second gate with guards standing holding them open and bowed as we passed.

"What are they doing? Stealing your gates?"

"No son, they work for me." William laughed.

Then as we were about to turn the last corner, William spoke to them.

"Cover your eyes for the biggest surprise you'll ever have."

"Go on do it, I promise you will be so surprised... I was!" I laughed and William winked.

"Got them covered?" William asked checking their hands.

"Yep!" Joey was so excited.

"Now don't open them until I tell you too, alright?"

"Alright, you hear that Megan?"

"Yes." Megan's tiny fingers covered her eyes.

"The carriage will stop and we will all get out, then at the count of three, you can open your eyes alright?"

"Alright, Pa." Joey was so excited he laughed.

"Yes, Papa!" Megan smiled wide showing her dimples.

"Alright were are about to stop... Now don't peek!" William warned with a low tone. The children nodded.

William opened the door and the children reached for his hand blindly.

"Here you go, Joey, come here my, Megan." He picked her up and helped me out standing behind Joey with his arm wrapped around me. He motioned to Jules to Shhh holding his finger on his lips.

"Alright now children... ready?" William leaned down a little.

"Now on the count of three... One... two... two and a half..."

"Come on, Pa!" Joey jumped.

"Three!" We watched Joey's face go blank. His mouth opened as wide as could be. His eyes went up and up and up and then he looked left and left and left...then right and right and right.

"HOLY COW!" Was all he could say.

"COW!" Megan was looking wide eyed like Joey.

"This... is the... shack?" He could hardly speak.

"Yep!" William and I laughed.

"Pa...you're rich!" Joey still was looking all over.

"Yep! And so are you now son."

"I am? Megan too?" He turned and looked up at William.

"Yep!" He rubbed the top of Joey's head.

"HOLY COW!" Joey shook his head.

"That's just what I said when your Pa brought me here." I laughed.

"I bet you did, Mama." Joey laughed out.

"Do you like it, Megan?" William spoke softly to her. She hugged his neck and nodded.

"Who is that?" Joey pointed to Jules.

"Well, I need to make a formal introduction! Jules, this is Lord Joseph Andrews and Lady Megan Andrews. This is Jules my dear friend and butler."

"Butler? HOLY COW!" Joey held out his hand and shook it.

"Milord." He bowed to Joey.

"Hey... I'm no lord!"

"I'm afraid you are now, Joey." William laughed.

"HOLY COW! Jules... Sir? Can you call me Joey or I won't know who you're talking to."

"As you wish, Milord... I mean, Joey Sir."

"No just plain Joey." He laughed.

"Very well as you wish... Joey." Jules wanted to laugh.

"Good to have you home, Sir."

"Good to be home, Jules... let's get these two frozen children in the shack."

"Shack! Ha!" Joey laughed.

We took the children into the house and Joey could not believe his eyes. Megan hung onto William's neck.

"Rebecca! William!" Betty came running.

"What do we have here?"

"Betty, this is Joey and Megan Andrews our children." I laughed at Betty's face.

"Joey, Megan say hello to Betty..."

"Well hello children." She nodded and winked at William.

"Are you, Pa's, Mother?"

"Yes in a way."

"Oh I get it... can I call you..." Megan cut him off.

"Gamma?" She smiled and held out her arms to Betty. Betty eyes welled in tears.

"My heavens! They are precious." through her tears.

"We'll, tell you all, the long story later, right now I hope there is a tree with a pile of presents under it."

"Oh there is Milord, to be sure! I think there all for two of the most loved children in the world."

"Let's go!" William took Joey's hand and led them to the dining room.

"Pa… this is… can I slide on the floor in my socks?" Joey had a devilish grin on his face as William did.

"I'll bet you doing it." William and Joey plopped on to the floor and took their shoes off. They both started on one end and slid across half of the dining room.

"Heavens!" I laughed and Megan did as well.

"Hey, Megan, come on!" She squirmed out of Betty's arms and kicked her shoes off and ran to her William.

"Rebecca… How…"

"Betty… it's a long story, very long story!" I laughed.

"They're perfect and I see my William loves them so. If I didn't know better, you'd think they were his own!" William scooped little Megan up and he slid with her in his socks. None of them even noticed the tree.

"Betty, call everyone in here." Betty ran out of the dining room.

Soon the entire staff watched William, Joey and Megan and were laughing. William finally looked toward me realizing the entire staff was watching him. He was winded and walked to us with Joey and carried Megan.

"Hello every one and Merry Christmas! I want you all to meet our children, Joey and Megan Andrews."

"Hello, glad to meet you." Joey smiled up at me then William.

"I know it will take time to learn all of them, but they will help you find who you want."

"Pa, do they all live here and work for you?"

"Yep!" William laughed as did everyone.

"HOLY COW!" Joey laughed.

We gathered around the tree and one of the servants brought in hot cocoa.

William and Megan sat on the floor and passed out gifts to everyone and the children as well. I was shocked that William had arranged presents for them.

After we opened all the gifts William played piano and we all sang, it was the best Christmas I could have ever asked for!

Rebecca

~ Chapter 23 ~

We saw Joey yawn and Megan too and decided to show them to their rooms.

"Where shall they sleep?" I looked at William concerned.

"I thought we would sleep in the second floor rooms our first room. Joey and Megan can sleep in your old room and we can sleep in mine that way they can cut through the getaway to our room if they need us." William smiled.

"I'm going to get lost for sure!" Joey looked around with his mouth open wide

"Megan too…" She hid in William's neck peeking out every now and then.

"No, I think you and Megan will have this place down in a couple of days. But it took me a week!"

"There is only one room you're not to go in without me or your mama."

"Which one is that?" We reached my old room.

"I'll show you tomorrow, but for now, I will take you or your Ma… deal?" William looked tenderly at Joey.

"Deal!" They shook hands and William opened the door.

"This is our room?" Joey looked around and ran to the huge bed.

"Yep!"

"William, I heard you were home… WHO…"

"Ah Jon Luke… Nick… Victor… these are our children. I'll explain later." William laughed.

"Joey, Megan, these are your Uncles, Lord Jon Luke Baptiest." He stepped forwards and bowed.

"This is, Lord Nick Baptiest." He stepped forwards and bowed.

"And this is, Lord Victor York." He stepped forwards and bowed.

454

"These men are my most trusted friends. If you ever need me or need help, you may call on them any time. This is Joey and Megan Andrews, our son and daughter."

"Hello men!" Joey said so serious. They laughed.

"I guess you two were really busy!" Nick laughed.

"You could say that… Uncle." William laughed.

"We'll leave you… we just wanted to wish you and Rebecca a Merry Christmas"

"To you as well, say how's Daniel De Spain?"

"Fine Sir and Logan McInnis, he's not doing as well."

"We'll visit him soon." William looked at me concerned.

"Well Merry Christmas to all of you." Nick and Victor slightly bowed.

"And to you as well…" They turned to leave shaking their heads in disbelief.

We showed the children the secret passage and they were content. They took a bath and Betty put their things away, soon we were tucking them into bed.

"I hope you don't mind sharing your room with each other, we'll have you your own rooms soon. We'll be right in the next room if you need us for any reason." William and I kissed their cheeks and they hugged and kissed us.

"Thank you Pa and Ma. We love you." Joey and Megan smiled.

"And we do you too, with all our hearts. But for now we must get some rest. Tomorrow you two must get to know this place, a big day indeed!" They both nodded and we turned the lamp low but not off and we left the doors connecting the rooms open.

"Rebecca… Come." He led me back down stairs and back into the dining room.

"I have something for you." William reached into the tree high and pulled out a small box."

"William!" I never dreamed he had something for me. It was enough with the children!

"Open it my love." I slowly opened the box and there was a locket.

"Oh… William!" Tears filled my heart and eyes.

"Open the locket." I opened it and it read:

Papa Loves Mama
With All His Heart Until Time Is No More

"Oh, William!"

"You like it?" William put it around my neck.

"I love it and you." I kissed him tenderly and then pulled away.

"I have something for you too."

"How... you do?" His eyes went wide. I went behind the tree and pulled out a box from under the tree skirt.

"I didn't see this."

"Of course not, I had Betty put it here after we were through."

"Ah... sneaky!" I handed it to him.

"Well open it!" I held my breath.

"Well it's light, strangely light." He furrowed his eyebrows as he opened the small box.

"Well, what in the world would I do with these?" He held up two tiny booties.

"Oh... I don't know." I wanted to laugh.

"Well, I..." He stopped with his mouth still opened wide and was not breathing.

Then he looked down at me and then back at the booties he was still holding in the air.

"Re... becca... are you... are we?" I nodded.

"You're... You're... We're... A baby?" I nodded again. Tears streamed down our cheeks.

"A baby? A BABY?"

"Yes, William, a baby!" I laughed crying tears of joy.

"Rebecca?" His eyes were wide and his mouth hung open.

I nodded again as tears fell down my cheeks.

"We're... I'm... you're?" Tears streamed down his cheeks.

"Yes... William!" I looked into his eyes and felt his heart being filled.

"We're... having a... baby?" He stood frozen holding the booties still in the air. I nodded again.

"I'm... going to be a... father?" He hoarsely spoke and then looked at the booties and then me.

"Please... say the words." He cried. He bit his bottom lips showing his dimple, his tears unceasing.

"William, you're going to be a father, again. We're having a baby!" My arms wrapped around his still frozen body.

"A baby... A BABY!" He scooped me into his arms and swung me into circles and crushed his lips on mine and then pulled away, tears streaming down his cheeks.

456

"A baby!" I cried.

"I love you, Rebecca!" He suddenly looked from the thunder of clapping.

"What?" He turned around to find the entire staff standing by the archway. He gently sat me on my feet.

"They all knew?" His eyes were so full of joy.

"No, just Betty, she knitted the booties. I sent a wire to Betty, as soon as I could after the doc released me and told Betty to knit me some booties and when we returned, after the presents were opened, to tell the staff to come back and I had her watch for my signal."

"Which was?" He was in shock.

"You silly! When you held up the booties!" I laughed as tears fell down my cheeks. He ran to Betty and hugged her swinging her around in circles.

"I'm having a baby!" He laughed as the entire staff laughed as well.

"I know my boy... I know!" She hugged him. Then he kissed everyone and Jules laughed.

"It's about time, William, about time!" Jules winked and then winked at me.

"I can't wait to tell Joey and Megan! God in heaven! Thank you for making my life complete!" William kissed me deeply in front of the staff and they all clapped.

That night, after we went to bed, William got up and went to the window and looked out. Then he took a knee and bowed his head. I watched him pray and thank God for his life and family. He cried and wept for joy and thanks. I was never so proud of him as I was right now.

William is everything Robert wanted for me and I'd like to believe that Robert chose William to be on the path that very day. Robert believed that everything happened for a reason and there was no such thing as luck. That time was God's time not ours and that we all have a purpose in this life and a destiny.

William waited for God to send him a wife and all the things that have happened with Robert and I, there is no doubt that God was in this from the beginning, there was no reason not to believe.

William came to bed after what seemed an hour and he pulled me to him whispering he loved me more than his own breath. I knew now what that kind of love was now, for I too loved William the same. And now, I was complete...

~ Chapter 24 ~

The next morning we told the children, they were so excited. They said we would be a true family and William couldn't be any happier. He was retired and could now work his estate. William had a son and daughter with another on the way. Though it was his first one, he would not treat it any different than Joey or Megan. No one on God's green Earth was going to tell him any different!

We left for Oak Grove two days before Carla and Cole's wedding. On the way, we stopped to check in on Bethany and Daniel. She was doing a good job for the Doc, and he was well pleased with her hard work. However, Lord McInnis was still down with the fever and was spouting curses and yelling at Bethany. Bethany said for us not to worry, that she could handle him. Though, she didn't care much for him. Bethany is a strong woman, stronger than I thought she was when we first met her. William told her if she needed anything, she mocked his words with him. 'I'm only a moment away'. She laughed and said she would write as soon as she got Daniel home.

Cole and Carla's wedding was simply beautiful. I think it was the first time in my life I saw my brother Cole cry. Mike rolled his eyes and blamed 'us' women rubbing off on him. Cole warned Mike that he was next in line to marry. Mike said he would be going fishing more often, typical Mike!

The day after the wedding, we all gathered at mother's house and William announced the coming of our next child. Everyone was so happy for us. I rubbed elbows with Carla like the old wives tale and she laughed. I told her about the bench in the park as well and that some things just couldn't be explained. Everything happens in its own time. In God's time not ours.

It was all about time and nothing happens by chance. Robert being the way he was and then passing away and William with his waiting on God to send him a bride, Joey and Megan and even their Uncle and Aunt turning out to be unfit with Megan almost dying. William and I knew from the very beginning that we were meant to be together and when we saw the children, we knew that they were going to be ours. We thank God every day for his blessings and there is one thing I do know, in a man's heart is strength and honor, but it's his soul that makes him who he is.

~ Epilog ~

Early one morning on September 10th, I gave birth to a healthy baby girl. We named her Annabelle Marie Andrews after his mother and my mother's middle name. We were so happy with our little girl. Though in secret, I wanted to give William a son for his first child, but in that as well, God had his reasons.

William had brought Joey and Megan in to the bedroom to see their new baby sister and they all sat next to me in the bed. Joey and Megan sat on the other side of Anna and me, so happy with their little sister. I was so full of joy looking at my family I always dreamed about.

I leaned close to William as we watched Joey and Megan marvel over Anna.

"As soon as I'm ready, I'd like to try again, I want another." I whispered softly in his ear.

"And another and another..." He whispered back his eyes tender and so full of love. He was so proud and his life was complete. He had two daughters and loved them both. Though we agreed we would like to try till we have another son, but then the thought occurred to me,

"William... what if they're all girls?" I must have had a blank look on my face for he laughed and took our daughter and kissed her gently holding her in his arms looking so tiny against his immense chest. He took her tiny hand in his as he turned to me kissing me tenderly whispering...

"I have a son but... we just may end up with our own territory after all!" It was an old, old joke, he laughed as he kissed me tenderly.

Megan and Joey giggled. We looked in their little faces and then at each other, Megan smiled. "Papa loves Mama!" She giggled hiding her mouth with her tiny fingers. William bit his bottom lip and smiled showing that dimple and bopped her nose with his finger and nodded, he looked into my eyes with a look only I knew.

"That he does... that he does..."

Rebecca

∞

Just for you, a sneak peak of Bethany…
Love to all and God bless,
Tamalyn

~ Bethany ~

"Wench! Bring me some water!" Colonel McInnis roared.

My hand went to my forehead, rubbing it for all it was worth. Taking a deep breath to compose myself, I went to get Colonel McGinnis's water. The very thought of pouring it right on top of his hot, demanding, utterly intolerant...'Person,' was extremely tempting! I blew out an enormous, frustrated breath.

"I warned you about him, Bethany, he's quite vocal, one would say!" Daniel laughed as he read the newspaper.

"Daniel, he still is very ill with the fever..." I scolded giving him a warning glance. However, I had a feeling that this attitude was very much a part of Colonel McInnis's true character.

"We'll just see about that!" Daniel laughed softly shaking the paper to straighten it.

Colonel McInnis's steal gray eyes burned into mine as I took the cool glass of water to him. His eyes looked so angry and so full of contempt, which, I had to remind myself that he did have a fever! I prayed he wasn't truly like this and doubted anyone would be able to take such a tongue lashing all the time!

The Colonel lay quietly for the moment just glaring at me. I pursed my lips as I handed him the glass of water, holding my temper close.

"Good Morning, Colonel McInnis." I smiled my best as he took the glass of water from my hand, almost was spilling it as he drank it down all at once.

"Colonel, I could help you..." I reached for the glass and his hand caught my wrist in a painful vice.

"NO! I don't need, nor do I want your help!" He roared out, feeling his growl vibrate right through me.

"But, Colonel McInnis...I'm here to help!" With a yank, he pulled me to his face, feeling the heat of his breath on my cheek as my heart pound in my throat.

"I said...I don't NEED, nor WANT your help! Do I make myself CLEAR?" He growled through clenched teeth and then tossed my wrist away from him, as if he held disdain for me.

"Alright, Colonel McInnis..." I bit my tongue in spite wanting to give him a piece of my mind!

"What's going on in here?" Doctor Wilson hurried in the room.

"He's full of it today, Doc. No rest for the wicked!" Daniel teased laughing.

"Daniel!" I narrowed my eyes at him. Daniel smirked and continued to read his paper.

"I'll give him something to calm him down. I need to check on him any way...Bethany?" Doc nodded, and I automatically assisted him with whatever he needed. I pulled the curtain around Colonel McInnis's bed.

"Colonel McInnis, I'm Doctor Wilson and this is my assistant, Ms. Bethany De Spain. How do you feel this morning?" The Doc took his stethoscope out, placed it on the Colonel's chest and listened.

The Colonel's cold eyes glared at me as if I was the devil himself. I looked away not being able to stand his glares any longer and straightened the tray of gauze and tape.

"Fine..." The Colonel spoke in a deep gravely hoarse sounding tone.

"Are you having pain?" The Doc rolled back the sheet and lifted the bandages, infection!

"Yesss..." He growled through clenched teeth, furrowing. His brow, with such deep trenches, that had it not been for those piercing gray eyes and dark thick eyebrows, one would not even see them. How could anyone be so angry?

"I need to have my assistant take you're temperature." Doc motioned toward me as I nodded. Doc gave me a heartfelt smile. Doc knew the Colonel was giving me more than just a hard time.

After shaking the thermometer down and inserting it into the Colonel's mouth, I avoiding looking directly into his eyes as Doc gave him the shot. When the doc poured disinfectant over the wound on his leg, the Colonel's breath caught. He gritted his teeth and growled under his breath, grabbing the sheets in his enormous hands. It was hard not to look up at the Colonel while I assisted Doc in the changing of bandages, but I tried to focus on the thermometer as I took it out of his mouth. I noticed a slight curl appearing at the corners of the Colonel's lips and gave in glancing at him. He didn't appear angry any longer. It had to have been the fever making him to act irrational.

"Still got a fever, Logan..." The Doc nodded as he cleaned his wound on his chest and his face. They were healing much better than his inflamed leg. I could tell by the look on Doc's face, as he checked his leg wound, he was truly worried about it.

"There, now you should feel better soon...and, Logan?" Doc looked over his glasses at the Colonel.

"I want you to give Bethany here, a break. She's only trying to help you."

"I'm…sorry." The Colonel whispered hoarsely.

I smiled slightly, but again, avoided looking into his eyes. They were the strangest eyes I had ever seen! They were so green sometimes and then a blue green. Very strange!

"Eat you're breakfast and then try to rest." Doc turned to me and smiled warmly with his eyes saying, 'be patient' and I nodded.

Doc was truly a caring man, taking time with each patient and spending longer visits with Daniel. They had deep conversations about the Great War and the Union for hours. Some of it was interesting, but most was awful and too unbelievable to hear about.

I followed Doc as he made his way to Daniel.

"So, Daniel, how do you feel this morning?" The Doc smiled well pleased at Daniel's recovery.

"Much better, though it still burns." Daniel was not one to complain about anything, so his wound must have truly been bothering him.

"Where?" I asked, wanting to relieve the pain.

"In my back…I think it's from me being on my backside for so long." Daniel tried to cover up his discomfort by smiling.

"Can you lean forward son?" Doc gently assisted him.

"Ah, I see what it is! Bethany, get me one of those pillows on the other bed and we'll have you fixed up in no time. I think in a couple of days, we'll have you up and walking." Doc always sounded positive, but I had my doubts that Daniel would be out of that bed in a week let alone a couple days. Perhaps he was giving him hope. I brought the Doc a pillow and he placed it behind Daniel's back. Daniel sat up a little higher and he let out a huge sigh of relief.

"Yes...much better! Thank you Doc." His face instantly relaxed, as he blew out a relieved breath.

"You're welcome and you're sister has been a great help to me. I'll hate to lose her when you're well. She has been a Godsend to me, Daniel, and you should be very proud of her." He smiled patting Daniel's leg.

After Doc was through with all his patients, he took his leave for his rounds in town. I went about my morning chores, mopping the floors, wiping beds with disinfectants and checking on the men before preparing lunch for them. Colonel McInnis didn't eat much of his breakfast, so I decided to ask him if there was anything special he might want.

4

"Colonel McInnis, is there anything you would like for lunch?" I tried to smile, but his face was full of anger again.

"NO!" He turned his head away. Proud or not, the man didn't have to treat me this way.

"But there must be something?" I spoke as nicely as I could, but he shot me a hateful glare and without warning and then, threw his plate across the room!

"I said NO!" His actions startled me.

"Bethany...it's the fever...don't take it personally." Daniel whispered softly. Sympathy softened his eyes.

"I know you're right, but he's just so unpredictable!" I shook my knowing that saying anything, was useless.

After cleaning up the mess, preparing lunch was next on my agenda. I decided to make vegetable soup, corn bread and for dessert, a chocolate cake. I happily busied myself for the next hour. When lunch was ready, I realized that the Colonel's actions had not only gone all over the floor, but my smock and dress as well. I needed to change and freshened up before going back down to the battle field!

Looking in the mirror, I thought about mother. I did look a lot like her. My hair hung to the small of my back in a braid and my hair was redder more than auburn, but dark. I was taller than mother, but still not like Susan, my best friend. She was about three inches taller than I and I was considered average in height, but small framed. My eyes are just like mothers, greenish brown and nice almond shape with dark long lashes and nicely shaped brows. Perhaps that's why some people say I take after mother.

I have my father's high cheekbones and skin color with a natural light tan. My lips were defiantly from mother, not to full, but nicely shaped, I thought. Mother insisted that I learned just how to 'pout' them perfectly when I was young. I laughed thinking about mother referring to pouting, as an art!

My best feature, I thought, were my eyes. However, father always loved my nose. I smiled thinking how father would always kiss it before he left for work in the morning. It's rather ordinary straight, but father liked it. Susan loved the shape of my face, which is squarer, rather than long, saying that my defined jaw line and elegant neckline was perfect for any collar or necklace. I wasn't beautiful like Susan, just average I thought. Daniel said, I would always need an escort knowing what other men think and say. He claims I'm a full time job with him having to deflect

5

men away from me. Maybe he's to blame for me never marrying? He keeps them all away!

I shook my head and picked up my oatmeal-covered dress and looked in the mirror one last time, reminding myself that the Colonel didn't know what he was doing. The Colonel truly is a very handsome man as far as I could tell. His hair appeared to be thick and shiny black, though I thought it too long. His face is chiseled yet, rugged with a strong square jaw that flexed muscles when he ate or gritted his teeth. High cheekbones give way to steel gray eyes that held such fierceness, that with a mere glance they could intimidate anyone!

On occasion, he would look at me with stillness and peace in them and then, they were eyes one could drown in. Nice almond shaped eyes amid the thick long black eyelashes that any woman would envy. His strong, straight nose accents perfect full lips, which, on the rare occasion are breathtaking when he smiled. By the length of the bed and how he reached from top to bottom, I knew he is a tall man. His form is very muscular and so immense he appeared to fill the width of the bed. I recalled noticing the leg with the injury looked slightly different from the other now.

His right leg was not as well defined as his left leg anymore. It was sad for something like this to happen to such an obviously healthy man. Yet, he should be thankful that he did not lose it! Doc seems to think that his restrictions in walking would be the hardest for him to accept and I had no doubt Doc was right about that!

I recalled his hands gripping the sheets as Doc cleaned his leg. His hands are so large and strong! I also recalled his inescapable grip as he captured my wrist. There was one thing obvious about this Colonel Logan McInnis, he was no doubt a warrior and fought many battles. His golden skin was scared in various places and I had wondered how he'd survived this long! I also recalled that he still wore his wedding ring, which always implied that he never intended to marry again.

Colonel McInnis is a handsome man, but so overwhelmingly infuriating, contemptible and downright odious at times. Yes, William Andrews was right about the Colonel, he was a hand full!

Doc said he had two small children which made me wonder if he was good to them. Did he act like this with them? I could only hope not! He was definitely not like my brother or Lord William Andrews. William was the sweetest man I have ever known. When I had heard that he had married, I was heartbroken admitting that I had held out in hopes, that

6

one day would have asked for my hand. I guess he thought of me as more as a little sister.

When I meet his new wife Rebecca, I was strangely relieved. She truly was perfect for him and he adored her very much, seeing it when William looked at Rebecca. His eye's held that truth. I will always cherish what he whispered as he and Rebecca, left yesterday..."You'll always be in my heart my Beth. One day, you shall meet the prince of your dreams." I believe he truly, felt my sadness.

I wiped a tear, cleaned up the dishes and took their lunch down to the small kitchen in the back of the office. Doc thought it was a wise idea to have a kitchen down stairs so his nurse wouldn't have to run the steps for warming meals.

I checked in on the men finding them all resting. I couldn't help myself but to go to Colonel McInnis finding him troubled again. I stood next to his bed brushing a lock of hair away from his face. I froze as a soft rumble escaped his lips and feared that I had awakened him, but he remained quiet, which was a blessing all in its self.

"You smell wonderful, my Lady." He mumbled.

I felt his forehead and it was so hot. Remembering what Rebecca had done for Daniel, I took a washcloth cooled it in the water and wiped his forehead, chest and arms.

"Mmm..." He mumbled again.

"My...leg...hot..." He hoarsely whispered with his eyes still closed. I pulled the curtain closed then carefully pulled back the sheet keeping him respectively covered.

A patient responding to my help was very rewarding. It made me feel as if I was truly making a difference. So far, with all the injuries I have seen none had bothered me. If they had, the idea of becoming a nurse would never enter my thoughts. I rinsed the cloth, wrung it out and carefully wiped his injured leg.

"Mmm..." He groaned, breathing in deeply.

I said nothing and continued to cool his leg down, proceeding to do the same to his other leg. My eyes took him in as he lay almost totally unclad and even though a long slash running from just above his heart diagonally to his other side, just under his ribs, his body was truly magnificent. I thought, yes, he was splendid despite the scars. Strangely, the scars he bears seemed to define this man.

As I continued to wipe his perfect leg left leg, I knew the only thing I could do right now for the Colonel, was to pray that his injuries wouldn't make his right leg dwindle too much, as Doc thought it may.

"Mmm..." He rumbled again.

Suddenly, his leg moved! I grabbed the sheet trying to keep the Colonel covered, but it was useless! My heart thundered in my ears as I closed my eyes trying not to look, but now, that was impossible! I quickly pulled the sheet back over him and glanced up at his face. My eyes widened seeing a slight grin slide to one side of his lips! He was awake! Oh Lord, help me! I licked my dry lips and nervously straightened the sheet out. I turned to pull the curtain back and heard him mumble.

"What was that, Colonel McInnis?" I froze looking over my shoulder trying to sound calm.

I can only hope that you're sitting there thinking, "I didn't want this book to end!" If you are, and enjoyed Rebecca, won't you please take a moment to leave a review at your favorite retailer? It matters to me and other readers! So please…SHARE the journey!!!

Thank you!

Tamalyn E Scott

∞

Connect with me
tamalynsbooks@hotmail.com

Follow me on Facebook
https://www.facebook.com/TamalynScottAuthor

Follow me on Twitter
https://twitter.com/TamalynE

Tamalyn is a writer, an artist and loves all genres of music. She has been writing wonderful stories for years! Finally, after raising three kids and the nest was empty, it was time to share these magical journeys with friends, family and anyone who wants to get lost in an amazing journey.

Currently Tamalyn lives in Florida and married her very own knight and is finally living...

Happily Ever After...

Tamalyn's first novel, **Gracey** is available on Amazon, in all formats.

∞